S0-AAL-403

TRAPP'S PEACE

by the same author

A FLOCK OF SHIPS
A PLAGUE OF SAILORS
THE DAWN ATTACK
A WEB OF SALVAGE
TRAPP'S WAR
A SHIP IS DYING
AN ACT OF WAR
THE JUDAS SHIP

TRAPP'S PEACE

Brian Callison

E. P. Dutton

New York

First American edition published 1980 by E. P. Dutton, a Division of Elsevier-Dutton Publishing Co., Inc., New York.

Copyright © 1979 by Brian Callison

All rights reserved. Printed in the U.S.A.

No part of this publication may be reproduced or transmitted in any form or by any means, electronic or mechanical, including photocopy, recording or any information storage and retrieval system now known or to be invented, without permission in writing from the publisher, except by a reviewer who wishes to quote brief passages in connection with a review written for inclusion in a magazine, newspaper or broadcast.

For information contact: E. P. Dutton, 2 Park Avenue, New York, N.Y. 10016

Library of Congress Catalog Card Number: 79-57373

ISBN: 0-525-22230-8

10 9 8 7 6 5 4 3 2 1

Chapter One

Having your throat slit – actually laid wide open from ear to ear – isn't the sort of thing a chap could anticipate might happen to him in the middle of the English Channel in the middle of the night.

Not even when he's an Asiatic gentleman; and shouldn't really be there in the first place . . . !

But come to that, huddling in the lee of an antiquated fishing boat wheelhouse wearing nothing more than your threadbare lounge suit and floral tie to protect yourself against the razor whip of a December gale; desperately clutching the little suitcase containing all your pathetic personal treasures while praying to Allah or Mahomet or Dear Jesus at the same time – on top of trying convulsively not to be seasick as well as home sick and fear sick . . . well, you'd never really expected any of *those* mini-nightmares either, had you?

Of course you wouldn't have realized, when you left home, that there just isn't any established protocol for people like yourself. Or care. Not even one grain of concern.

Not when you happen to be a prospective illegal immigrant into the United Kingdom, anyway. Merely another retching package carried on the Blackbird Run . . .

But then your previously so-helpful benefactors – those shadowy philanthropists who'd bumped into you by sheer chance after you'd found yourself hopelessly marooned in Amsterdam or Brussels or Dieppe – and had offered to try to arrange your passage for the last leg; 'Sorry, Rafiq, pal, but it's gonna cost yer a bit more, mind? Like about a hundred times over the legal Channel ferry fare . . .'; well *they* must have carelessly omitted to mention the fear bit. And the appalling discomfort. And the casual indifference to your basic needs.

They hadn't mentioned the other part either. But in all fairness that was probably because even *they* hadn't imagined that a thing as dreadful as that could happen . . . IS HAPPENING, for pity's sake! When on one particular night in the English Channel you suddenly find your hair brutally seized; your head yanked back until your throat arches like a tight-stretched brown balloon . . . your protruding eyes briefly register one last incredulous glimpse of a hollow-ground butcher's knife slashing under . . . and *in* . . . and AC*ROSSSSS* . . . !

Well, obviously a chap would never have contemplated a thing such as *that* happening to him, would he?

Certainly not after having paid such a high fare to that nice Captain Trapp. For a place on his Blackbird Run . . .

Trapp slouched heavily on the grime-sticky ledge, squashed his already battered nose against the wheelhouse window in order to see farther than the foredeck through the scratched and filthy glass, then peered ferociously at the white-crested rollers bearing down from the west.

'Ayrabs!' he muttered petulantly, ignoring with lofty contempt a thundering sea which reared higher than the prudently extinguished masthead light. 'What the hell do *Ayrabs* want to get theirselves smuggled inter Britain for, then?'

Behind him Gorbals Wullie, balancing easily on the balls of his feet in time with the rearing, plunging motion of the seventy-foot vessel, casually allowed three spokes of wheel to meet the oncoming mountain.

'Teeth?' he postulated after deep deliberation. 'They c'n get free teeth an' that off've the Nashnul Health. Yous can get everythin' free off've the British Nashnul Health; even them wigs the poofy lads wear.'

But Trapp, treating his executive officer's dissertation on the attractions offered by a welfare-oriented United Kingdom with much the same disdain afforded to large waves, merely continued to speculate on his current passenger list while, at the same time, trying uneasily to decipher the tiny warning bell ringing somewhere deep down in his subconscious.

6

Mind you, that twinge indicating the possible presence of danger had served him well on many previous occasions; for Captain Edward Trapp was nothing if not a natural refugee from trouble . . . a born Survivor. But then, with his background he'd simply had to have something extra going for him. Anyone who'd managed to survive for as long as Trapp — despite a lifetime of mayhem, gut-wrenching adventure and sheer bloody-minded pursuit of profit at any cost — well, anyone who still managed to cling so tenaciously to this mortal coil *and* stay as black-hearted and selfish a bastard as Trapp had . . . then they'd have had to have a built-in early-warning system, too.

Just like the one which unsettled the captain right then.

'We got seven of 'em this trip,' he brooded irritably. 'There's them three Paki's what couldn't spare a kilo of fat between 'em. But they're bound to be OK — your Pakistanis, Bangle Deshis, Calcutta Hindoos are all daft as brushes; put up wi' anythin' . . . but Ayrabs? What the 'ell do four *Ayrabs* want in the Land've Hope an' Glory?'

'*Teeth*, like I telt ye!' Gorbals Wullie stressed doggedly. 'Yous c'n get a braw pair o' choppers off've the Nashnul Hea . . .'

'Shut up!' his captain snapped abruptly, head cocked to one side.

Wullie eased the wheel and shrugged huffily. 'Och, but you never could stand tae lose an argymint . . .'

'I heard somethin', stupid,' Trapp growled. 'Di'n't you hear somethin'? A sort of scream, like. From aft?'

The scrawny seaman, still aggrieved, turned his head as a token gesture, then shrugged again. 'Only yon wind oot there. Jeeze but it's blowin' hard enough tae skin the paint right off've this worm-rotten bucket . . . if you'd ever put ony paint *on* the bloody boat in the first place!' he added spitefully.

And that was what really did it. That was the trigger to a temporary lapse which promised to puncture rather more of Trapp than his dignity and position as a shipowner.

'PAINT!' he exploded, almost at a loss for words at the

enormity, the crass extravagance of the suggestion. 'Paint costs money, remember? Apart from which I'm not goin' to have 'er tarted up to look like some millionaire's fancy floatin' gin palace. Not f'r no one . . .'

'Christ but you gotter be jokin',' Wullie sniggered recklessly, eyeing the ravages of sixty years of neglect evincing themselves in the cracked glass and started planking and peeling, rotted frames which formed the command centre and navigation space of the motor fishing vessel *Last Hope*.

But Trapp was well and truly diverted now, because if there had ever been one factor which had constantly threatened his prospects for continued survival – one flaw in the captain's bloody-minded resolve to remain the world's oldest operational pirate – then it was in his Achilles' heel of greed.

In his eternal quest for a profit. By hook or by crook – though usually by the latter. That singular need which encapsulated Edward Trapp's sole motivation, creed, and all-consuming obsession in life.

Which was why, now fully launched on his favourite subject, he swung from the window, directed a pugnacious jaw towards the cretinous ferret shape of Gorbals Wullie, and snarled heavily, '*Paint* 'er, f'r cryin' out lou . . . ! But then you always *wus* bloody useless in the complex fields've commerce though, wasn't you? Got about as much financial acumen as a bankrupt Delhi dung-wallah, 'aven't you . . . ? In fac' the only way you ever earned an honest livin' was ter con some pie-eyed bastard up an alley an' *boot* 'is wallet outa him, wasn't it then . . . ?'

Whereupon the storm surrounding them howled unnoticed. While the creaking hull of the anything-but-good ship *Last Hope* spiralled and spluttered painfully towards the English side of the English Channel with a steadily decreasing complement.

And Trapp completely ignored that warning bell which somehow involved Arabs, never even hearing the next bubbling half-scream from six feet away on the other side of the bulkhead as a third abruptly disillusioned voyager from Pakistan felt his windpipe being severed with one expert stroke.

Which wasn't at all what he'd expected.

Not on Captain Trapp's Blackbird Run.

Perhaps that had always been Trapp's failing – apart from his basic avarice, anyway. That somehow his bloody-minded prejudice against doing the legal thing had invariably thwarted the fulfilment of every project he'd ever devised.

Even from the start; many wars and many, many years before while he'd still been a starry-eyed boy wearing his first uniform as a midshipman of His Majesty's Royal Navy. He'd promised then to do his duty to fight for King and Country with all the pride a little lad could feel . . . until the enemy sank his very first ship, and left him as the sole survivor from a complement of four hundred men.

It had been then that his gift of living to fight another day had initially revealed itself . . . except that the young Edward Trapp never did get to do his duty for the King after all. For it had been the enemy who'd found the life-raft he'd shared with a small section of a dead shipmate for nineteen horrific, lonely days; whereupon they had patched up his physical wounds, were unable to do anything about the mental scars he'd suffered – and finally locked him away in a prisoner-of-war camp until that particular war ended two years later.

By then Trapp had already become a permanent casualty of battle; a hardened, embittered self-seeker who'd learned that survival in his particular barbed-wire corner of hell was based on greed and animal cunning, reinforced by the ability to do unto others twice as much aggro as they could do unto you – an' a bit sooner.

He'd grown to detest waste with a fierce and undiminishing passion. He hated war as a folly in which men died for a futile ideal, and without ever being given the opportunity to make a profit. He developed a withering contempt for his own country and a total indifference to the problems of all others.

But he'd found one belief; one priceless, earth-conquering philosophy . . . That his destiny, no matter what he did or to

9

whom it was done, would undoubtedly be – to survive.

And so he'd embarked on a lifetime of unabashed skull-duggery in which he quickly developed the most twisted, inconsistent set of principles any international pariah could muster. For instance, the self-styled *Captain* Edward Trapp would tenderly assist a disease-ravaged Chinese beggar-woman across a bedlam Shanghai street – yet calmly watch the hand being chopped from a Sudanese thief's wrist with a deprecating, 'It's not what you done that makes you a stupid bastard, Ali Baba. It's gettin' caught that proves you always was!'

He'd fled Macao after a somewhat fraught disagreement with a local Fu Manchu, but hadn't even bothered to warn his current Chinese lady-friend about the gathering wrath of the Tongs. Her dismembered corpse, intimately conjoined with bits and pieces of a few more of Trapp's unsuspecting acquaintances, was discovered on the lawn of the British consulate the next morning . . . Yet the very same Trapp had once spent three days of parched agonies in the desert, scrambling for his life ahead of a posse of homicidally-inclined Tuaregs, after he'd kicked their sheik on a voyage to the Pit for raping a snot-nosed, ten-a-penny Arab urchin.

He had always survived. Through all those years of pimping and conning, and chasing a fast buck by sailing in decrepit, inevitably-to-be coffin ships for some poor bloody sailorman or other. Only they never went down with Trapp aboard. No. He'd always done a pierhead jump; usually as they sailed on their last voyage.

Gradually, as he became a more and more successful drop-out, there had been the development of his business career. Only that had proved even more confusing to any casual observer, being guided by what Trapp primly described as his 'Principles'. 'A gentleman what's engaged in internashnul commerce's gotter 'ave *Principles*!'

Which he undoubtedly had. In his own inimitable, screwed-up sort of way.

For instance, there was the manner in which Trapp first became A Shipowner.

Certainly they'd offended his sense of chivalry from the very beginning, those three Egyptian speculators, by casting un-warranted aspersions regarding the possibility of his stealing the cargo should they offer him command of their gun-running vessel *Charon*. Eventually, and in the absence of a more suitable crook, they were forced to, but Trapp was so deeply wounded by their unjustifiable cynicism that he determined to fulfil his contract with impeccable correctness, delivering every last weapon and round of ammunition to the appointed rendezvous . . .

. . . and stole the *Charon* instead.

But by then she didn't have any owners anyway – not seeing Trapp had delivered them to a waiting patrol of trigger-happy Legionnaires at the same time. As he explained so self-righteously later, 'I done what they paid me for, di'n't I? An' there wasn't nothin' in the contract about the ship, was there then . . . ?'

Then there was the time when Trapp, rapidly approaching the peak of his piratical success not only as master and owner of the *Charon* – probably the oldest, most appalling heap of barely-floating rust outside a breaker's yard – but also as leader of as black a band of cut-throats and thieves as ever graced the inside of the world's prisons, including, incidentally, one Gorbals Wullie frae Glasgae an' Barlinnie Jail . . . when Trapp got involved, in a purely business sense naturally, with the Spanish Civil War. When he accepted a contract to run guns and ammunition into that strike-torn country for a very hand-some price.

Which, strictly according to his principles, he did; risking being either garrotted as a capitalist warmonger by the Reds or, alternatively, bayoneted as a suspected Bolshevik by Franco's mob. But the point is that he did carry out his com-mitment with religious zeal.

The only snag was that, frustrated by the waste of unprofit-able stowage space still left after he'd loaded his first shipment, he then went ahead and negotiated a second contract with the *other* side to do precisely the same thing for them.

The fact that all that money was paid to Trapp without altering one jot the balance of power either way just didn't seem to worry him. But like he said – 'A contract's a contract, ain't it? An' there never was no clause innit ter say my services was excloosive, *was* there . . . ?'

And so came the Second World War.

Even that didn't bother Trapp at first. He simply declared a sort of unilateral neutrality for himself and his cretinous crew, and carried on smuggling and blockade-running precisely as before.

Until he was finally brought face to face with unavoidable reality. And the Royal Navy leaned on him a little, while, characteristically, he even visualized the chance of profit in *that*. Eventually Lieutenant-Commander Trapp, RNR, took Gorbals Wullie – together with the most ill-assorted crew of military misfits the world has ever shuddered at the thought of – on an unsteady, violently unconventional course to war. Because, naturally, it was a special, very different kind of war.

It had been Trapp's War.

But that's another story . . . !*

Yet strangely enough, despite all the mayhem and double-dealing in Trapp's turbulent life, he never really became a dislikeable man. A bigoted, ill-tempered, foul-mouthed intolerant crook – well . . . yes.

But not a dislikeable man.

While later had followed the fringe benefits offered by all the little terror wars: Korea, Borneo, Cyprus and Aden, Vietnam, Ethiopia, even Yom Kippur . . . only he never quite managed to live up to his early intentions. Oh, he was still the eternal survivor; that much had to be admitted. But somehow, after the proper war, he never quite succeeded in his quest for that Promised Land where profit was for the taking and his decks were laid with coin.

So he never did conquer the earth.

Now it was today. And all he had in the world was an argumentatively loyal henchman called Gorbals Wullie, and a tired and virtually unseaworthy old boat called, perhaps a little cynically, the *Last Hope*.

---

* Dutton 1976

Plus an undying, fervent optimism that one day – one day very soon – he really would find that pot of gold.

Somewhere . . .

In some credulous bugger's pocket.

. . . and then the wheelhouse door slid open, allowing a shrieking, buffeting slab of gale to enter followed by the even chillier aspect of a Czechoslovakian Model 61 sub-machinegun with a blued-steel folding stock on the end of it. And one of Trapp's carelessly forgotten Arabs on the end of that.

'. . . so I'm tellin' you, yer daft Scotch egg, that paint's *not* one o' the fripperies I'm plannin' ter throw money away on . . . Jesus CHRIST!' ended a disbelieving Trapp.

Whereupon Gorbals Wullie, moving with the reflex agility of someone well practised in the art of getting out from under while the weight dropped on the next bloke, disappeared through the opposite door in a mercurial blur with only the comment, 'Och, Jeeze, but we bin HI-jacked . . . !' left hanging in the air to prove that the *Last Hope* hadn't steered all that way on auto-pilot alone.

But admittedly Wullie's loyalty did tend to flood and ebb at times – usually the latter, when the heat came on.

Trapp, meanwhile, with the automatic response born of a lifetime in hazard, began to reach for the ancient elephant gun clipped conveniently to the deckhead above him until another dark-skinned man slipped in through the open door, placed the muzzle of an ominously large and destructive Luger at the base of Trapp's spine, and said persuasively, 'Leave it, Captain . . . please.'

So Trapp froze. Instantly. But that was something else he'd learned from a lifetime of surviving – that a pistol in the hand is worth two cannons out of reach.

. . . just as Gorbals Wullie reappeared again, this time going astern very, very cautiously indeed; eyes fixed hypnotically on the butcher's knife held unwaveringly against his middle region.

And without blinking even once, muttered resentfully, 'This is anither fine mess yous has got me intae, Captin!'

13

'Oh, shut up!' Trapp snarled nervously, yet still mindful of his property. 'An' get back on the wheel afore she broaches-to an' dammiges somethin'.'

The man with the automatic barked in guttural Arabic and the knife withdrew a little reluctantly from Wullie. But not all that far. Then the *Last Hope* slid into a corkscrew roll while Trapp watched warily for the first sign of instability among his visitors, only there wasn't any. They were very good indeed.

So instead he spent his rising fury on the scrawny figure of his first lieutenant, currently attempting to ease past the knife-point to reach the wheel without committing involuntary hara-kiri during the next beam sea.

'Hurry UP!' he roared. 'Another like that'll cost me a mint f'r repairs . . .' Then the nightmare prospect of actually having to spend money got just too much for him and he rounded spitefully on the man behind him, ignoring the gun altogether.

'An' YOU . . .' he spluttered, virtually beside himself with rage. 'You c'n just' get off've my ship right now, savee? You an' your oppos. 'Cause you got as much chance as a snowball in hell of me landin' you in Britain after this . . . and the contract's cancelled, see? Without no bloody refund!'

But the man facing him only smiled. It was almost a friendly smile. Almost. 'But we do not propose to go to Britain, Captain.'

Then a mocking twinkle showed in the dark eyes. 'Anyway, *effendi* – whatever makes you imagine a poor Arab could afford to live there?'

'Ahh,' Trapp said cleverly. 'I knew you wus Ayrabs. I even said you wus bloody Ayrabs the minnit I set eyes on you . . . an' Ayrabs is trouble; especially you educated ones. So which are you then – Al Fatah, Black September, them PLOs . . . ?'

'None, Captain.' The leader shrugged. 'I regret to say we seem to be simply common or garden criminals . . .'

From behind the wheel Gorbals Wullie appended a professional amendment. 'So it's no' a hi-jack, Captin – it's a heist.'

'Shut UP!' Trapp retorted with childish predictability. 'And anyway, seein' this ain't no jumbo jet – an' while she's worth a good few dollars on the open market I wouldn't exactly claim she's as valuable as the QE Two – jus' what in Saint Elmo's fire d'you want 'er for?'

'We don't,' the Arab assured him. 'It's you we want, Captain Trapp.'

'Come ter that,' Trapp continued introspectively, 'I'd've sold her to you f'r less than you paid that shifty git what fixed your Blackbird passage up in Brusse . . . *What* did you say?'

'I said it is you we want, Captain. So permit me to introduce myself. My name is . . . ah . . . Fadel. That should be quite adequate for now.'

A heavy sea shook the *Last Hope* angrily, but this time Trapp didn't even glance up at the gun as the warning bell inside him began to clang with positive hysteria. Gorbals Wullie on the other hand, hopefully relieved by the assumption that, seeing they wanted Trapp, then presumably *he* wasn't person- ally involved, offered ingratiatingly, 'Aye? Then it's no' a heist either. It's a kidnapping, Capt . . .'

'*Shut up!*' Trapp bellowed in escalating apprehension. 'An' whaddyou mean – it's *me* you want . . . ?'

Then an even more unsettling doubt struck him and he broke off sharply, staring round. For he'd suddenly remembered he'd had seven immigrants on the after deck when they sailed; but now there were only four in the wheelhouse.

'Them Pakis,' he specified uneasily. 'They started off down aft with you. Didn't . . . they . . . then . . . ?'

Which was the moment when he ground to a halt altogether as his eyes and Wullie's pivoted simultaneously to fix on the butcher's knife. Even in the dim glow from the compass it was possible to detect the sticky red film which covered it.

'Och, Jeeeeze,' Wullie whispered, the cobwebbed recesses of his mind slowly deducing that, even though he didn't actually appear to be a kidnap victim himself, he was still more than likely to be involved. In a very personal sense indeed.

Trapp swallowed. 'But why that way, mister? Guns is quicker. An' cleaner . . . and kinder, come to that.'

The man with the Luger – the one called Fadel – shrugged, holding his watch into the light from the binnacle as if time held considerable importance. 'They are also noisy. While you have a reputation for being a resourceful and violent person . . .'

He smiled fleetingly, only there wasn't any humour in it at all. '. . . and after all; you say we are only troublesome Arabs, Captain. So why criticize us for being cut-throats and . . . ah . . . traditionalists, shall we say?'

'I also got a reputation f'r carryin' out my contracts,' Trapp ground bitterly. 'I had a contract with them poor bastards to deliver 'em ashore. In good condition.'

'I cancelled it.' Fadel gestured with finality. 'No more questions. It is time.'

Immediately the Arab with the machinegun moved forward, nestling the muzzle into Trapp's midriff. Even under the frantic motion of the *Last Hope* the barrel remained as steady as if it were gyro-stabilized.

And so did Edward Trapp.

Apart from his eyes. For after his initial disconcertion Trapp was again the total survivor; the quintessence of durability. In his characteristic way he was even strengthened by that surge of animal cunning which always peaked as his back came hard against the wall. He was ageless and matchless, and lethal as a cornered rattlesnake.

Trapp. With a burning fuse . . .

But until the opportunity presented itself he would simply watch while wrestling furiously with the riddle of why Fadel and his Arabian bully-boys should wish to abduct *him* – a hostage whom nobody would ransom, and without a country which would wish to negotiate his release. And why, in *God's* name, should they deliberately do this in such a coldly horrific way?

For he was not the sort to forget those three little brown men – his cargo and his responsibility – who'd risked everything for the new life awaiting them at the end of their particular rainbows; yet had drowned so gruesomely in their own blood instead.

Whereupon Edward Trapp grew more and more angry. And more and more dangerous . . .

*

He looked on impassively while the leader, Fadel, produced a small walkie-talkie and spoke briefly, commandingly, into it.

All Trapp could detect was an answering crackle of guttural Arabic which meant nothing to him at all because he, even after a lifetime as a world wanderer, had never bothered to learn more than a few coarse phrases of any foreign tongue. More pertinently, those scant VHF transmissions wouldn't convey any information to the many listeners surrounding the English Channel.

Which suited Trapp anyway. An investigation by either the French or UK authorities would merely have transferred him from a Middle Eastern frying-pan into a very long-term European fire. There were many curious immigration officers anxious to have a little chat about his Blackbird connections, and an even greater number of frustrated detectives on both sides of the Channel searching for answers to certain questions raised with monotonous regularity since around 1929. And all involving a certain Captain Edward Trapp . . .

He even maintained his grim self-control when Fadel calmly reduced the clanking engine revolutions to 'Slow' without so much as a by-your-leave to him, Trapp, master before God aboard his own ship – or boat, really; but Trapp always had been a bit inclined to gild his own lilies.

Trapp watched as the *Last Hope* maintained bare steerage way, while the great black waves swept down on them from out of the darkness with the wind clawing mournfully at the tattered, rotting strands of rigging, and sometimes a sea, larger or more deceitful than the rest, tumbled inboard over the scarred bulwarks to atomize spitefully against the decrepit wheelhouse.

All that time he assessed the faces of the men around him; studied them in minute detail. Darkly saturnine in the binnacle glow these were the emotionless, uncompromising faces of men doing a professional task, without the slightest guilt or regret for what had occurred on the after deck.

Apart from Gorbals Wullie, of course; now struggling to keep the skyrocketing bows turned into the sea. For Wullie's pinched features were shiny with the sweat of fear, and sickly white with the realization that – if it was only Trapp they had come for – then he was quite likely to be as expendable as . . . well . . . as three little immigrants.

Before Trapp caught Wullie's eye, then glanced meaningfully up at the deckhead – and at the ancient elephant gun which the hijackers had contemptuously ignored while a look passed between them which made Wullie sweat even more because Gorbals Wullie knew better than anybody else – or anybody else alive, at least – just how big a chance Trapp was prepared to take to preserve his freedom.

And, more practically, his property.

So Trapp waited. And watched. And remembered.

Until they saw the ship . . .

Chapter Two

It came into sight twenty minutes later; a distant mast-head light at first, barely visible through the rain and the black overcast of the Channel night. Then, briefly between wave crests, they began to make out the red and green sidelights as it headed towards them until finally the bulk of the vessel could be detected against the gloom.

To Trapp at that time it was simply another ship on a closing course, so he watched with mounting unease until he could even glimpse the foam flinging in wide phosphorescent gouts from under the looming bow.

'Starb'd the wheel,' he snapped finally. 'We better give way or she'll be into us.'

The man, Fadel, merely said, 'Stay on course, Captain. She knows we are here. They will have us on radar and are expecting us.'

'Expectin'?' Trapp growled. Then swore explosively as the sub-machinegun barrel ground warningly into his ribs.

'I said no more questions,' the leader murmured, eyes fixed on the approaching vessel. 'Now you will please switch on your own navigation lights. Soon they will lose us in their radar clutter.'

'Bugger off!' Trapp snarled uncompromisingly.

Fadel didn't get angry or offended or anything else. He simply shrugged calmly, turned to face Gorbals Wullie, then motioned with the Luger. Immediately the two Arabs standing behind the scrag-end helmsman moved as one, pinioning his arms before he could even emit a startled yelp. One half-blink of a blind man's eye later and the undernourished figure was arched backwards across the wheel, hair entangled savagely in one practised hand while the red glint of the knife slashed horizontally inwards and towards . . .

'WAIT!' Trapp bellowed, suddenly terrified for Wullie.

The knife halted within a millisecond of death, almost touching the furiously convulsing Adam's apple. 'Mary Mother o' God!' Wullie choked hysterically. '*Dae* it, Captin! Put they bluidy LIGHTS ON . . . !'

Trapp closed his eyes momentarily, to stop anyone detecting the frustration in them. Because he knew he'd lost the best chance he was ever going to get of turning the tables; that one brief moment in which all attention had been focused on the long overdue – in Trapp's usually jaundiced opinion – task of cutting Gorbals Wullie's throat.

Only now he'd blown it. Because he'd suddenly found to his consternation that he wasn't quite such a self-centred and flint-hard bucko as he'd prided himself on being.

An' there weren't all that many sailormen around who'd work as cheap as Gorbals Wullie either . . .

'The lights, Captain?' Fadel suggested pointedly.

'Ohhhh shit!' Trapp snarled. Then snapped the switch.

'Flash them three times to identify ourselves. The ship will stop and you will take this boat alongside. They will make a lee for us and have a pilot ladder rigged . . . do you understand?'

'Then what?'

'Just do it! Or should I still use your friend as an incentive . . . ?'

'Aw Jeeeeze,' Wullie spluttered, still transfixed across the wheel. Trapp glowered briefly at the poised knife, then sniffed.

'Let 'im go, then! How's 'e supposed to steer, all spread out like a paralytic bloody starfish?'

Fadel nodded and the two heavies abruptly released the little Glaswegian. Wullie's knees gave way and he slid to the deck before tentatively hauling himself vertical again and grasping the wheel.

Trapp eyed Wullie's usually permanently-glued-on-the-back-of-his-head cloth cap lying where it had fallen, and gestured.

'Put yer cap on again.'

Wullie blinked nervously, still leaning as far away from the knife-point as stability would allow.

'Whit?'

'Yer CAP, stupid – put it back on yer 'ead!' Trapp urged meaningfully. 'I'm not 'avin' my chief officer improperly dressed now, am I? Not at the very moment we . . . go . . . along*side*, like?'

'You're awfy posh all of a sudden,' Wullie muttered blankly.

'Christ!' Trapp reflected savagely to himself, 'the only way that half-witted Scotch moron's ever gonna get the message is if I shove it up 'im wi' a ten-foot boat 'ook!'

But Wullie's vacant stare showed a glimmer of animal cunning. He looked down at the cap – then surreptitiously up at the elephant gun – and said cleverly, 'Och, jus' look at *that*, then. Ah've forgotten tae put ma bonnet on . . .'

Whereupon he bent down, crammed the cap on the back of his lank skull, and adjusted the peak with exaggerated sartorial care.

In fact with very great care indeed . . .

And so they waited for the ship to reach them.

Only, this time, neither Trapp nor Gorbals Wullie seemed quite so frustrated.

Almost co-operative, somehow. And not at all dangerous.

The ship lay stopped some three cables from them, now clearly visible in silhouette and minutely scrutinized by a still-baffled Edward Trapp.

A smallish general-cargo freighter of around six thousand tons gross she was maybe ten or twelve years old. Conventional centrecastle surmounted by a squat, unimaginative funnel; single lifeboat either side and well supplemented by life-raft canisters; a high but rather ugly sheer towards the bows . . . no indication of her nationality yet, an' no bloody wonder, Trapp brooded irritably.

He decided he didn't like the anonymous vessel. Come to that, he didn't reckon he was goin' to go much on the crew she carried either.

A sudden glow bathed her forward well deck as a shaded cargo cluster was switched on. They were close enough to discern a group leaning over the starboard bulwarks, rigging a skeletal rope ladder. Fadel waited until the ladder had unrolled against the hull, then gestured imperatively with the Luger.

'It is sheltered there. You will go alongside now.'

'I *do* know which way the wind's blowin',' Trapp retorted reasonably. 'An' you might tell Chatty 'ere to put 'is gun up. I don't concentrate so good connected to a trigger 'appy sod like 'im.'

Fadel hesitated, then nodded. The sub-machinegun muzzle eased away from the captain's ribs and he exhaled gratefully. 'No tricks, either of you,' the Arab leader warned grimly. Trapp raised a shocked eyebrow.

'Who – *us?*' he protested, then turned and placed one huge, calloused hand on the throttle lever. 'Special sea dutymen close up f'r goin' alongside . . . that's you, Wullie lad!'

He eased the throttle forward and *Last Hope* came round, butting doggedly into the sea with the spray, snatched by the wind, once again hissing angrily across her decks.

'We could have had the windscreen wiper goin',' Trapp offered conversationally. 'If we 'ad a windscreen wiper.'

Closing fast, the high sides of the freighter looming overhead now; near enough to detect lighter patches of rust showing beneath the main engine discharge and freeing ports. But no ensign was visible, nor legible name on the bow, while her port of registry was well out of sight under her counter.

Closer still.

And closer . . .

A wave took the *Last Hope* through a forty-degree roll but she was steadying finally, coming under the lee of the bigger vessel.

'Slow down!' Fadel snapped abruptly, betraying his first hint of nervousness beneath the cool professionalism.

'Sweat, you callous bastard!' Trapp grinned savagely to himself; then he hauled the throttle lever back while the *Last Hope* coasted steadily onwards and at an oblique angle to the steel wall.

'Engine stopped,' he called mockingly. 'But I gotter keep a

bit've way on 'er so's she'll swing stern-to when we goes along-side an' . . .'

'No talking, I said,' Fadel almost snarled while, beside him, the mute with the sub-machinegun brought the barrel down warningly.

Trapp gave a philosophical shrug and faced forward again, watching critically as the gap between the two vessels narrowed fast while the reflected incandescence from the cargo cluster caused a million tiny wavelets to sparkle fleetingly around them . . . and showed as a well-polished gleam lining the twin barrels of that monstrous elephant gun still clipped above Trapp's head.

Thirty feet . . . twenty-five . . . twenty-two . . .

Twenty.

He turned, still casually gripping the throttle. Gorbals Wullie caught his eye and dropped a querying glance to the wheel, then jerked his head imperceptibly to port. Trapp simply smiled, but it was a fleeting, immensely evil smile.

Fifteen feet and still coasting.

The heads lining the bulwarks above them were out of sight now, masked by the wheelhouse deckhead . . . the *Last Hope* penduluming on the sullen swell with the idling splutter of her engine only faintly perceptible above the closing rumble of the freighter's machinery space.

Ten feet.

'You gotter work a boat hard,' informed Trapp doggedly. 'So's she c'n feel the action of the prop against the rudde . . .'

But then he stopped. Dead. As his eyes, casually glancing outboard through the grime-dulled starboard windows, widened in slowly dawning disbelief. Until . . .

'Di'n't I SAY you wus trouble?' he blurted in outraged fury. 'By God, but you di'n't tell me you 'ad a British frigate waitin' for us as well . . .'

And then he slammed the throttle lever hard forward, roared 'HARD A PORT *NOW* . . . !' – and lunged for the deckhead while four disconcerted and momentarily confused Arabs swivelled to starboard as one man.

The *Last Hope*, already approaching its target at a broad angle, surged crazily ahead under fully-restored engine power and, at the same time, listed hugely as the sweat-shiny Gorbals Wullie spun the wheel in an apprehension-goaded blur . . .

. . . before snatching off his bonnet with what seemed curiously misplaced formality under the circumstances. And the manner in which he did it; that appeared a little unconventional too – grabbing it from the after end of his head so's the cloth peak hung free in his grime-engrained fist while maintaining the swing; arc-ing viciously in a fluttering parabola towards the astonished face of the man holding the knife.

Five feet . . . four . . . three . . .

The sub-machinegun barrel lurching back now as the Arab mute realized there simply *wasn't* any frigate out there, or any other diversion other than in Trapp's mind . . . but Trapp's great mahogany paw also dragging the elephant gun down from its clip and snatching for the twin triggers all at the same time . . . Gorbals Wullie's voice screeching, 'Yous bastids! Yous poofy hi-jackin' BASTIDS . . . !' in a fear-pitched hysteria of desperation . . .

Bedlam! And steel. A terrifying, careering steel horizon blanking everything . . .

The *Last Hope* struck the freighter virtually end-on with sixty-odd tons of accelerating inertia. Almost immediately her rotted, ageing frames began to telescope concertina fashion in a continuous splintering rumble while every already cracked pane of glass in the wheelhouse exploded outwards in sparkling fragments.

'CHRIST!' Trapp bellowed maniacally above the increasingly expensive cacophony. 'She weren't meant to do *that*, dammit . . .' Then fired as his back came against the wheelhouse ledge; the only stable body – apart from an equally prepared and grimly clinging Wullie – in a rapidly disintegrating world.

The muzzle flash from the ancient weapon was almost as destructive in itself, igniting the flaked and tinder-dry paint whorls peeling from the deckhead in a rippling, spreading pool of flame while, at the same time, the Arab holding the sub-machinegun disappeared backwards through the wheelhouse door, literally taking off from a cordite-ringed spew of blood and fragmented flesh.

'Christ!' Trapp blurted again, shaken to the core by the chain reaction of devastation his subtle ploy had triggered – while the *Last Hope* continued to condense into a cloud of dry-rot dust; the foremast collapsing across the rearing, splintering bows; the galloping flamelets flickering and flashing delightedly as the coachroof itself began to burn.

And then Wullie's swinging bonnet ever so lightly stroked the cheek of the dumbfounded Arab with the knife – before miraculously opening a hideous gash from his right eye to the tip of his jaw.

But Gorbals Wullie always had been a master craftsman – indeed a positive maestro – in the braw Glasgae traditions of hand-tae-hand combat born of many deliriously happy hours as an apprentice yobbo in pub brawls, fitba' riots an' punch-ups doon at the Mocambo Ballroom.

Which was also why Gorbals Wullie never went anywhere, not even to bed, without his beloved bonnet. And the line of skilfully concealed razor blades which just happened to be sewn into the peak . . .

Pirouetting like a ballet dancer the reassured Scotsman swung to face his second guard; vengefully this time, swaying on half-crouched legs with the cap dangling warily like the sling of a ferrety David facing his Goliath.

'Fancy yer chances, dae ye, Abdul?' he grinned, yellow teeth bared in the mandatory hard-man snarl. 'C'mon then, ye big poofter, 'cause ah'm goin' tae cut ye wide open an' sti . . . !'

So Abdul *did* come on. And kicked him so hard between the half-parted legs that Wullie didn't even have the breath to scream in agony. But it had never really occurred to Gorbals Wullie that maybe they had a Mocambo Ballroom in the Casbah too . . .

. . . while Trapp started to yell a warning as both of Wullie's tormentors, one still gripping that gruesomely dappled knife while spraying blood from his mutilated features, closed in on the convulsed seaman until he – Trapp – sensed rather than saw the danger at his own feet and swung back to catch the rising glint of a Luger coming to meet him.

One stark image lit by the dancing flames of the man called Fadel, still on his knees 'where the impact had catapulted him; and the murderous glare in eyes which, until then, had merely showed a cynical contempt . . .

. . . and the nine-millimetre hole in the barrel which was nearly on him f'r . . .

Trapp snatched the second trigger in reflex, unthinking panic.

The monstrous cannon roared again. It pulverized Fadel's right arm and shoulder while igniting clothing, dust, age-old scraps of gum wrappings and discarded junk, and most of the starboard corner of the wheelhouse itself.

But the biggest snag was that, since Trapp had been unwittingly aiming downwards at the time, the cannon-ball-sized charge also blew a jagged two-foot cavity through the deck, kept right on travelling into the accommodation space abruptly revealed below, shredded Trapp's only shore-going suit and a well-thumbed copy of *How To Make A Million Overnight* . . .

. . . and finally blasted a second hole clean through the *Last Hope*'s already long-suffering hull.

Which, in its turn, immediately caused the English Channel to enter – searching in frothing, gurgling excitement for the rest of that same English Channel currently flooding aft from the shattered bow compartments.

Whereupon Trapp, by now appalled at the devastation his intended minor diversion had caused, choked a third faintly bemused 'Christ!'; then slammed the Mocambo-trained Arab vindictively across the back of his skull with the butt of the elephant gun.

Wullie, meanwhile, lying all drawn up and retching on his back on the deck, had opened his eyes eventually to observe his final assailant – pain-crazed and unmistakably homicidal – half-way through a knife-waving dive on top of him.

Wullie, terrified out of what little wits he had, simply screwed his eyes tight shut again; screeched, 'Aw, dinnae . . . ! Aw, Captin, HELP me . . . !'; and kicked out convulsively in a jerky, unco-ordinated bicycling action during which one boot sole caught the flying knife-man square in the pit of his stomach . . . caused him to describe an immaculate parabola with Wullie's leg acting as a fulcrum . . . and then disappear clean through the gaping starboard window-frame on the end of a long, fading wail of disillusionment.

And, all of a sudden, everything seemed so quiet, and so very peaceful again.

Except for the frantic clamour of the *Last Hope*'s engine, still driving her against the steel side of the mystery freighter with bulldog tenacity. And the splintering sounds of still more rotten timbers compressing and crumbling. And the disconcerting crackle of little flames as they took an ever-firmer hold of Trapp's command.

'Five hundred,' Trapp muttered numbly. 'Five 'undred quid this queen o' the seas cost me. Five . . . 'undred . . . *quid!*'

Wullie rolled over and clawed to his knees, hanging on to the deserted wheel. 'See him?' he stammered with gleeful pride. 'Did ye no' see me sort him oot, then. Bang, bang! The karate chop, eh?'

Absently Trapp pulled the throttle back to neutral. Fuel cost money. The *Last Hope* stopped trying to wear a hole in the freighter and just sat sinking instead.

'Ah'm a . . . a tiger,' Gorbals Wullie announced modestly, almost reverently. 'Ah'm no' feared o' nuthin', and that's a fact.'

'Five hundred bloody quid,' Trapp whispered; fast slipping into shock as the full financial horror of the night dawned upon him.

'Here,' the Tiger said, suddenly nervous again. 'Should we no' be makin' oor getaway?'

Trapp looked around him at the carnage and the flames; and at the splintered foredeck already nearly awash. Then he turned and glared at his first lieutenant with an expression which would have withered a great white shark, far less a tiger, and snarled, 'Don't be so *bloody* silly.'

Before sticking his head through the eviscerated forward window and craning his neck upwards to meet a silent, awestruck row of dark faces lining the rails above.

'Kidnappin',' Trapp bellowed dangerously, ignoring with supreme contempt the battery of machineguns, rifles and various other small arms pointing down at him. 'Throat cuttin' ... Arson, hijack, murder ... breach o' CONTRACT ...'

Furiously he beat at his sleeve which began to smoulder just as water came in through the wheelhouse door. 'I dunno why; an' I dunno who wants me so bad but ...'

He hesitated briefly as a thought struck him. A typically Trapp thought.

'... but ONE o' you bastards up there owes me a thousand quid. F'r replacement. At nett cost.'

Chapter Three

'Fifteen hundred,' Trapp muttered doggedly a few minutes later. 'Fifteen hundred quid them boys o' yours has cost me, mister . . .'

Then his voice trailed off and he found himself suffering a chill even worse than he had felt when the sub-machinegun had first eased ominously through his wheelhouse door.

Yet that was strange, really. Because the man facing him across the cabin of that still-anonymous freighter seemed at first sight to be a most good-humoured sort of chap; especially in view of the somewhat churlish reception Trapp had given to his emissaries a short while before.

Perhaps it was the extended and welcoming hand of the man which triggered the alarm bell in Trapp's subconscious once again; the way the beautifully manicured nails gleamed so pinkly under the lights. Or maybe the almost imperceptible trace of perfume was causing it, hanging like a sick-sweet mockery of the earlier stench of fear and violence which went down with the *Last Hope*.

And then Trapp suddenly did understand what was so unsettling about the suave, quite charming Middle Eastern gentleman before him – it was the expression in his host's eyes. Or rather, the lack of expression, for the pupils which scrutinized him so keenly were bleak as the eyes of a dead creature. Colourless eyes. Chipped ice eyes. Eyes without the slightest warmth of human emotion.

'My dear Captain, how are you?' the Ice Man said. 'I'm Zarafiq . . . Mister Zarafiq.'

'Well, I'm bloody aggravated!' Trapp retorted, the pain of financial injury overcoming his uncharacteristic lack of poise. 'An' if you're head sheik of this bucket, then it's you that owes me fifteen hun . . . two thousand quid. F'r damages an' destruc-

29

tion of plant what was only on hire, so to speak.'

Mister Zarafiq held up an immaculate hand. 'I am desolate, dear Captain. Utterly desolate that employees of mine should have been so . . . so ill-advised in their manner of approaching you.'

'Yeah? Well, they're still approachin' Wullie,' Trapp said pointedly. 'Two at a time, down on your foredeck. They're kickin' the shit outa him!'

Mister Zarafiq registered horror and disillusionment. Except through his eyes, of course. 'Your first officer?'

He turned to one of the two seamen-gunmen standing impassively behind Trapp and snapped an order in Arabic. The man withdrew silently while Zarafiq shook a doleful head. 'One finds it so difficult to depend on hired help nowadays when we live in a world of violence. The molestation of your companion will cease immediately.'

'Mind you, it don't ackshully bother Wullie,' Trapp hastened to assure him. 'He's a tiger, y'see. Not frightened of nothin', he reckons . . . Not like them little Pakistani passengers I had. Before your employees decided they wus excess cargo?'

Mister Zarafiq had obviously plumbed the uttermost depths of distress. 'Ah, those poor unfortunate people,' he murmured dolefully. 'Innocent victims of man's inhumanity to man . . .'

'What you mean is that it's all come as a big surprise to you, naturally,' Trapp broke in dryly. 'An' that you di'n't know about the throat cuttin' an' murder an' that. Or that your boys was goin' to cost me two thou . . . two and a half thousand quid.'

'One finds such difficulty in controlling even one's own destiny,' reflected Mister Zarafiq helplessly. 'Therefore can one ever hope to be able to pre-ordain the path of life for others, Captain?'

'Cut the poor bastard's throat an' you've had a pretty good try at it,' Trapp argued reasonably. 'Come to that, you've managed a bit've rearranging my future right now. What with sinking a good three thousand pounds worth've boat, and a profitable business venture, right from under me.'

'Have a cigarette, my dear chap,' offered the distraught host.

'Or a Martini. A pleasantly chilled beer, perhaps? And do please excuse my not partaking of anything stronger than a small lemonade. Merely another cross we devout Moslems are called upon to bear.'

'An' that's the end of that conversation,' Trapp reflected savagely. 'Epitaph f'r three pathetic little victims; a hollow platitude, a crocodile tear . . . an' a glass of lemonade to wash away the taste of vomit.'

But he didn't say anything more. Because that was the moment when – apart from being a bigger liar and even more parsimonious than Edward Trapp himself – he realized precisely how dangerous and how ruthless a man Mister Zarafiq could be.

For there was a small wooden tray on Mister Zarafiq's desk; full of trivia such as elastic bands and paper clips and things. But there were other items also lying casually in that tray; items which shocked and disgusted even the world-wise and cynical Trapp.

Three rings. Three ordinary, rather worn gold finger-rings. Yet they proved beyond any doubt that at least one of Mister Zarafiq's allegedly unreliable employees was rather more conscientious and well trained than Mister Zarafiq apparently wished Trapp to believe. Whether it had been Fadel or the other injured man plucked from the burning wheelhouse before the *Last Hope* finally sank didn't matter; what *was* pertinent was the fact that one of them had dutifully brought those rings aboard as a prize for his chief, the Ice Man.

Trapp knew he'd seen them once before, if only briefly. For Trapp had a photographic eye for gold. Only once before, but not very long ago . . . on the fingers of three brown men as they struggled to climb aboard his Blackbird boat on the far side of the English Channel . . .

. . . but then Mister Zarafiq sipped his drink, tapped his cigarette languidly against the side of the exquisite bronze ashtray before him, and said conversationally, 'Would you like to earn twenty-five thousand pounds, my dear chap?'

'Thirty,' Trapp growled automatically; still eyeing the rings with a growing and terrible anger.

Then he blinked, and forgot about the rings. Temporarily. 'Pardon?'

Mister Zarafiq smiled; a jolly, amused smile. 'Twenty-five thousand pounds sterling, Captain Trapp. I would be so grateful if you would accept it . . .

' . . . to take sole command of this ship. For a period not to exceed four months from tonight.'

Trapp sat down abruptly. He couldn't help it. Money had a strange effect on his locomotory system when it was discussed in large quantities, and twenty-five thousand pounds was liable to trigger a condition of near-paralysis.

His mind was spinning, too. Emotions and reactions tumbled headlong in a conglomeration of avarice, gleeful disbelief, apprehension and – over-riding all else – wary and justifiable cynicism. For Trapp had already learned not to trust the personable Mister Zarafiq. He wouldn't have trusted anyone, for that matter, who had polished nails and went about causing other people's throats to be slit and fellow businessmen's investments to founder; but Mister Zarafiq was even lower than that, because Mister Zarafiq had proved himself a big-time operator yet with the desiccated morality and the seedy, greedy rapacity of a gutter degenerate.

So what return would the same man, who so casually expropriated the pitiful legacies of three murdered souls, demand for the vast sum of twenty-five thousand pounds?

'I don't kill people delib'rately,' Trapp managed to caution eventually. 'Or traffic in drugs an' that. Mind you, for thirty grand it bears a bit've thinkin' about, certainly.'

'Twenty-five,' Mister Zarafiq corrected in a very emphatic manner. 'Please, my dear fellow, are we not decent, civilized men? Would we ever consider offering violence and . . . and misery to our brother human beings purely for personal gain?'

'Not f'r a measly twenty-seven an' a half thousand quid, we wouldn't,' Trapp confirmed, with precisely the correct mixture of outraged virtue and hypocritical togetherness.

'Twenty-*five* thousand, Captain.' Mister Zarafiq began to

look a little annoyed and the finger-nails fluttered petulantly.

'Twenty-six?' probed Trapp tentatively.

Mister Zarafiq gestured resignedly to the Arab seaman still waiting impassively by the door. The man stepped across and hit Trapp behind the ear with the foresight of his gun. Trapp went over with a roar of black rage and agony while Zarafiq took another appreciative sip of delicately chilled lemonade.

'Twenty-five thousands pounds it will be, then. I am so glad you agree – negotiating terms can be such a protracted and unpleasant task unless one or other of the parties concerned is prepared to make concessions, don't you think?'

The conceding party blinked at the carpet through a haze of blood and an almost irresistible desire to launch himself across the desk there and then and the hell with the consequences. But he didn't. A levelled sub-machinegun suggested he shouldn't for one thing, and Trapp was nothing if not a pragmatist. But there was something else which held him back – apart from a fervent desire to earn twenty-six . . . no, twenty-five thousand pounds an' that was f'r sure – and that was an implacable resolution that he would square the account at some time in the not-too-far-distant future with this smoothly lethal Ice Man.

But not now. Not right away. Not until the books of Trapp International Enterprises were revealing a very satisfying profit.

With which resolve he hauled himself erect; couldn't quite conceal the look in his eyes which should, in itself, have made Mister Zarafiq a very unsettled man; so covered up by forcing a wry, sporting loser's grin.

'With your approach to negotiations, mister, you should've been a diplomat . . . what's the job?'

While he didn't miss the flicker of . . . something in the Ice Man's expression. Wasn't it when he used the term 'diplomat'? But the suave manner was back again, above the glass of lemonade.

'This ship is currently en route for Port Said, Captain. Once she arrives she will load a cargo of used construction equipment . . . bulldozers, tractors, earth-moving trucks, small tools . . . all originally purchased from the Egyptian Government after the completion of the Aswan Dam project.'

'Bound for?'

'Málaga. Spain.'

'And that's the voyage you want me to make with her?'

'Ostensibly . . . yes.'

Trapp raised a knowing eyebrow. 'Which means you have somethin' a bit different in mind?'

'Twenty-five thousand pounds is a great deal of money. I am sure you have already anticipated that your rather restricted period of employment as master of the *Kamaran* will be expected to take a somewhat . . . ah . . . unconventional course, so to speak?'

'So that's 'er name. Genuine, is it?'

Mister Zarafiq looked hurt. 'But of course, my dear chap. Highest Bureau Veritas classification; insured with Lloyds; registered in the port of Massawa . . .'

'Then how unconventional *is* your sort of unconventional, mister?'

Zarafiq held his glass to the light and studied it intently. 'Merely that I should not consider it desirable that you complete your passage to Málaga.'

Trapp frowned. 'Coffin ship, you mean. Scuttle 'er, then claim on insurance . . . ?'

Then he hesitated suspiciously. '. . . except that would only make sense with a clapped-out rust bucket; over-valued an' with a falsely manifested cargo of junk. Yet this *Kamaran* o' yours ain't no beauty, but she's still worth plenty – and accordin' to you she really will be loadin' a genuine cargo before she sails.'

The Ice Man seemed pleased. 'A most astute observation. Which is why the authorities should have no cause to probe for ulterior motives behind the loss of such a well-found ship. Simply another mystery of the sea; inexplicable, but all too common even today.'

Trapp wriggled uneasily; this was a proposal which mortally offended his sense of ethical commercial practice. 'But there ain't no profit in it either, f'r cryin' out loud! An' anyway, you know as well as I do that you could've found a dozen skippers

34

in Port Said alone who'd sink 'er f'r the price of a case of booze – an' with most of 'em it'd be a genuine mistake any'ow.'

Zarafiq eyed his guest appraisingly; thoughtfully. Then he placed his glass on the desk and sat back. 'I think it is time for explanations, Captain. Regarding the *Kamaran*, my interest in her and, perhaps of more immediate concern to yourself, my reasons for wishing to hire your somewhat . . . ah . . . esoteric services.'

Trapp scratched his head absently and his hand came away smeared with blood. He said bleakly, 'It's always a good time, the present.'

'Firstly, you must understand that I am neither the owner of the *Kamaran* nor her cargo-to-be; that I am simply a business consultant appointed, rather like yourself, to manipulate the affairs of my current task-masters. What you might call a . . . a . . .'

'A fixer?' Trapp suggested artlessly.

'. . . an investment efficiency counsellor,' Mister Zarafiq corrected tightly.

'Ah!' said Trapp. With a very cynical leer.

'The world shipping market is, as you are perhaps aware, currently suffering its most serious economic depression since the Second World War . . .'

'Yeah, I do know,' Trapp confirmed pointedly. 'Some bastard keeps sinkin' them. An' you can't get more depressed than when your boat's lyin' thirty fathoms under the English Channel, can yer?'

'. . . and consequently vessels such as this are becoming more and more unprofitable to maintain in service.'

'It's you Ayrabs at fault, mind,' Trapp supplemented reprovingly. 'Steadily shovin' up the price of bunker fuel . . .'

This time he *did* halt abruptly; for it wasn't only the glare in Zarafiq's eyes which suggested Trapp was pushing vindictiveness just a little too far – no. There was a definite tightening of the Ice Man's expression when he'd sardonically mentioned 'bunker fuel'. But why . . . why should a throw-away observation like that cause any reaction at all?

'This also means,' Zarafiq continued stiffly, 'that while the

Kamaran has an insured value of some one and a half million pounds, her saleable worth on the open shipping market could be less than one-third of that figure.'

Whereupon Edward Trapp fell strangely thoughtful, and it hadn't only been the warning in his opponent's bleak gaze. Because Trapp had suddenly begun to understand how, with a little imagination, a one-million-pounds-plus capital investment could be re-circulated from a cost-hungry white elephant. And he also had the feeling that there was more to come; that Mister Zarafiq's counselling was very efficient indeed.

And he wasn't disappointed.

'Furthermore,' the Arab progressed with a rather more benign tone, now that he could see Trapp was a true appreciator of commercial genius, 'the cargo you will load belongs to the self-same group of business gentleman – though naturally this common ownership has been well camouflaged by the use of several subsidiary holding companies. And that cargo in question has an immediate resaleable value of . . . oh, shall we say a further one million pounds?'

'You c'n say that kind've figure as often as you like,' Trapp murmured expansively. Just the mention of money – that volume of money – was as balm to his wounds; a soporific to his simmering resentment.

Until he remembered the three gold finger-rings. And the shattered *Last Hope*, now gone for ever . . . and the fact that he'd already discovered he couldn't trust a single word the Ice Man so convincingly uttered.

'Except it's a bit academic – the value of the cargo,' he added searchingly. 'Seein' you don't figure on ever makin' a profit from that; not unless fish have a need f'r bulldozers.'

Mister Zarafiq smiled. It was a clever, self-congratulatory sort of smile with the slightest hint of patronage. 'But, my dear chap, you really do have such little faith in my capacity for intrigue. Surely you have noticed the great effort I have made to engage your own . . . ah . . . somewhat specialized services?'

'It had struck me.'

Then Trapp allowed conceit to override cynicism. 'Mind you, I gotter admit I have a lot of expertise. Which partic'lar accomplishment did you 'ave in mind?'

'Your intimate knowledge of the North African coast. I can think of no other man with a greater capacity for avoidance of curious authority.'

'You mean 'cause I keep out've the way of gunboats to stay in business.'

'You are too modest. You are the man who actually contrived to run circles around the might of the German Navy *and* wage a most successful war at the same time, some years ago. You are, in fact, a maestro in the arts of clandestine deception, Captain Trapp. I salute you.'

'An' you don't know the half of it, yer connivin', parsimonious fairy,' Trapp promised viciously to himself. Outwardly he merely offered a modest acknowledgement of his due, and a deprecatory shrug.

'Even as the top man in me field, I still can't help you cash in on a scuttled cargo – apart from claimin' one million quid's worth of insurance money for what you've lost anyway . . . can I?'

'You can. Because, sir, that cargo will not *be* on board when this ship goes to the bottom of the Mediterranean. In fact it has already been sold – by my principals, of course – to a most reprehensible syndicate of plant distributors based in the State of Gahman . . .'

'Ahhhhh!' breathed Trapp in unreserved admiration; finally appreciating how it was that Mister Zarafiq proposed to turn commercial adversity into a fiscal *tour de force*.

Even as the smooth and perfumed voice continued, '. . . your skills will be utilized to the full, Captain. In order to off-load that cargo in total secrecy at a pre-arranged rendezvous on the Gahman coast before you return to your original course line for Málaga . . .'

'. . . an' then scuttle 'er?'

'You have hit the eye of the bull, my friend. The *Kamaran* will go down empty and commercially worthless – yet still insured for a total of nearly three million pounds sterling.'

*

It was a pity that Mister Zarafiq had actually put it into words – three million pounds.

I mean . . . well . . . three million pounds. An' in sterling, at that.

It was probably that phrase more than any other which generated a vision within the mind of Edward Trapp; a barely-germinated seed – a seed as golden as if inspired by the touch of Midas himself – which promised to flourish into a money tree more prolific than any he had chanced upon since the gloriously piratical hey-day of World War II . . .

. . . for Trapp had already conceived of the first glimmerings of how he could not only obtain his revenge on the abominable Ice Man, but also show a profit. All it required was a little more patience, and a little more co-operation.

He never even heard the warning bell this time; the one that clanged in a positive hysteria of reproof as soon as he made that rash decision. But avarice had yet another psychosomatic manifestation in the body of Edward Trapp . . .

. . . for not only did it make him deaf – it also made him bloody stupid.

Chapter Four

And that was how Mister Zarafiq became a potentially endangered species; Gorbals Wullie became a temporary tiger; and how Edward Trapp unexpectedly became both master-designate of the motor vessel *Kamaran*, and a conflicting battle-ground for caution versus greed.

And – of much more importance to me – how I became involved yet again with Trapp; and virtually press-ganged into that lunatic voyage of mayhem and bloody skullduggery . . .

Oh, not that I had been ensnared at the start, Lord, no. When that initial and typically macabre encounter in the English Channel was taking place I was still a long way away – homeward bound from Yokohama to Liverpool as master of my own ship; and Edward Trapp merely a thirty-year-old memory which never quite faded; a spectre who still insisted on swashbuckling and grumbling and penny-pinching and glowering from the nocturnal recesses of my nightmares on those nights before I finally slammed awake to stare blindly up at the deckhead above my berth, and remember.

Trapp. And Trapp's War.

It had been *my* bloody war too, f'r that matter . . .

But that was all in the past, thank God. Even the violent meeting between my phantom pirate and the Ice Man Zarafiq had taken place some time before – it was over a month later that I berthed my own ship stern-to in Port Said harbour and made my way by taxi to Red Sweetwater . . .

Actually its title – the Red Sweetwater Nightclub – was a bit of a misnomer. For a start it wasn't so much a nightclub as a degenerate hovel, while the only red in evidence was in the colour of the enticing lamp hanging above the door and the customers' blood spattered across the foyer, a legacy of the previous evening's jollifications.

In fact it was more . . . well . . . blue, really. By virtue of the subject matter of the films they showed continuously above the bar, and the live acts they offered either on the postage-stamp stage or – for a quite exorbitant surcharge – upstairs to those clients whose needs for gratification inclined more towards the physical than the purely voyeuristic.

And then there was the blue haze, of course, which substituted for oxygen; and the blue-veined breasts of the grossly writhing belly dancers. All intermixed with the blue-demin silhouettes of the multi-national seamen and resident bums and drop-outs who gaily contracted each other's anti-social diseases via the Red Sweetwater girls with drunken abandon.

There was even a sort of matching, mottled-blue tinge to the features of an Egyptian queer who was being discreetly garrotted with his own tie in a dark corner just as I entered, though nobody seemed all that concerned. Certainly the two French matelots he'd solicited were carrying out the act with minimal inconvenience to the adjacent tables; every care being taken to ensure that his convulsive kicks didn't reach anyone.

It was that sort of place, like I've said . . .

. . . which seemed to make it so very unnecessary. The consternation and unpleasantness that were caused. Just because I shot a couple of policemen.

I'd been at the bar for about half an hour before the man I was to meet came in. He levered his heavy torso on to the stool beside me without a word and wheezed asthmatically while I hoisted in the final moments of a cinematographic epic starring three ladies, two Japanese male contortionists, two desert mules, an Afghan wolfhound and a basketful of eels.

Well, I think they were Japanese. Though they could've been Philippinos, or even Chi . . .

'Getta fuckin' move on then,' the Fat Man grumbled anxiously.

'I'd like to,' I retorted, thinking about the film again. Then

I remembered, with a shock of apprehension, the real reason for my being there and hooked my foot around the duffle bag beside me, sliding it towards him, concealed by the overhang of the bar counter. It was heavy, and it had already travelled all the way from Hong Kong hidden behind a false panel in my cabin.

It may have been my over-stimulated imagination but I could have sworn the whole place quietened as I did so. As if shadowy, anonymous watchers knew what was happening; could sense a very hot item was being passed.

Fat Man tried unsuccessfully to toe the merchandise from me; unsuccessful partly because his legs were too short to do more than wave fruitlessly in the air below the high stool, and partly because I kept my foot on the bag.

'The money,' I hissed, getting even more nervy. 'You've got to give me the *money* first, stupid!'

But what the hell. We were both amateurs at the game; even if I did pride myself on looking a bit like Humphrey Bogart, while Fat Man could have doubled as a grosser version of Sydney Greenstreet.

Clumsily he produced a newspaper-wrapped bundle which might have been anything if it hadn't been for the wad of green US dollar bills advertising themselves to the world through one tattered corner. By then my nerves were beginning to twang like the wire on a runaway windlass, because it certainly wasn't only imagination telling me we were attracting even more attention than the sweating, grinding torsos just commencing a new act on stage.

'Go on – TAKE it then,' my fellow conspirator urged with a note of stertorous hysteria while, at the same time, staring fixedly at the bottles behind the bar and pretending he didn't even know I was there.

I took a deep breath. This was it. This was the moment I'd been dreading ever since they gave me that bloody duffle bag and those rather enigmatic instructions back in Hong Kong . . .

Dimly I was aware of two virtually simultaneous movements, one on either side of me. The first was of a figure – several figures in fact – jerking erect in the deepest, darkest corner of the room. And of a voice, a chillingly reminiscent voice, blurting incredulously, 'Number One! Stap me blind in me seaboots if it ain't the brassbounder hisself . . .'

The other diversion was from the door. A more violent diversion. Uniforms. Shrill protests from the Egyptian bouncers; the *crack* of a nightstick against someone's skull . . . more shrill Arabic and the scuffle of bodies being thrust aside. A tidal wave of peaked caps and white belts and khaki drill advancing towards me . . .

. . . I deliberately placed my hand on the bundle of dollar bills.

Just as a spotlamp snapped on; freezing me in the act; illuminating my guilt for every befuddled eye blinking through the blue haze of Red Sweetwater.

And a second voice – a well-spoken but faintly accented voice – snapped in unmistakable triumph, 'You are under arrest, Captain Miller. Please stay exactly as you are.'

This time there was no reciprocal movement from the group at the rear; it was almost as if they'd never been. As though the very glimpse of police uniforms had caused them to dissolve once again, and with professional adroitness.

I stared blindly into the glare of accusation. There was the faintest glimmer of a gold-braided cap above it, but nothing else. Even the background clamour had evaporated under the frustrated heavy breathing of the interrupted floor-show participants, allied with the asthmatic nervousness of the fat man beside me.

I said shakily, 'So who the hell are you, then? An' what's the charge, mister?'

'Colonel of Police Rahman al Sidqi, Prohibited Drugs Division. I think you are already aware of the charge, Captain.'

Fat Man squealed, 'Awwwww *shit*!' and pulled out a gun. He couldn't even do that right though, and fell off the stool in a frantically waving pudge of arms and legs. There was a ·38-calibre explosion from beside al Sidqi – suggesting my fellow Briton wasn't the only bloke to get trigger-happy in the Red Sweetwater affair – and Fat Man slammed back against the bar with an expression of shock on his multi-chinned features . . .

... and then all hell let loose.

Someone directed a very French expression of disapproval and a metal chair towards the nearest policeman. Next to him a knife, with a German seaman on one end of it and an Egyptian constable on the other – the pointed one – flashed in the glare of the spotlamp. A lithe and ebony-shining girl darted in a nude, rising scream through a suddenly very ugly mob of anti-establishment visitors to Port Said.

And another voice – another equally familiar nightmare from my past – began screeching vindictively, 'Kill the bastids! Scunner they poofy wog polis bastids . . . Ah'm a tiger, a reg'lar tiger, lads, an' ah'm tellin' yous tae kill them poofy fuzzes, so ah am . . .'

Fat Man gave up trying to support himself against the bar and began to slide to the floor. I snatched the gun out of his nerveless fingers just as most of the Colonel's Prohibited Drugs Division disappeared under a welter of pummelling hostility . . . but then, nobody likes the Egyptian police; not even the bloody Egyptians.

The colonel was still on his feet, though. As well as the adjacent gleam of sergeant's stripes and the ·38 police special below them; both moving determinedly towards me.

'Look OUT, MILLERRRRR.' Another disembodied warning from the secret shadows.

I glimpsed another trooper closing in on my starboard side, followed by another with a swinging baton and a glare of black rage . . .

. . . I fired convulsively. Twice.

Dimly I became aware of someone going out through a window in a clamour of shattering glass. Simultaneously the trooper with the night stick was being pulled down by a brace of compatriot villains with old scores to settle. They were delightedly stamping on his face as more policemen charged through the entrance doors. And more; an' bloody more.

I still didn't move; simply staring disconcertedly at the bodies of Colonel al Sidqi and his sergeant lying in contorted submission under the smoking barrel of Fat Man's revolver. My revolver now.

While, equally ominously, the majesty of the Law was beginning to win.

The German knife sailor screaming in agony as three Egyptian batons homed in on him as one, shattering both his arms. A Frenchman on his knees, spitting blood, teeth and Gallic epithets, while another squad of khaki-clad constabulary kicked him into a grovelling, pleading hideosity.

And even more reinforcements. Sirens . . . Blue again – blue flashing emergency strobes outside in the street; playing through the open doors and across the intently struggling mob . . . I spun round with the fear acrid in my throat . . .

. . . to meet the cavernous barrel of a twelve-bore riot gun levelled straight at my head. I seemed to be one involuntary scream away from having my brains sprayed all over the Nightclub Red Sweetwater . . .

Just before the lights went out. Almost as though someone had pulled the Red Sweetwater's main power switch.

And a disembodied hand yanked me – and the duffle bag – clear across the bar and through a shrieking hysteria of milling belly dancers. And through a rear exit, into the night.

We must have run for a good twenty minutes – myself and my two shadowy pilots – before we finally ground to a rasping, lung-tortured halt.

I didn't have a clue where we were; it was still as dark as the innards of the Cheops Pyramid. Port Said's side streets do tend to cloak all nocturnal movement with a discretion born out of centuries of clandestine depravity. Only the occasional reed lantern of a middle watch silversmith or basket weaver or ox butcher had flashed briefly across the galloping figures of my escorts as we passed, like fairway buoys against the hulls of some outward-bound flotilla.

It didn't matter though. I'd already guessed, with cold certainty, at the identities of my puffing Samaritans. Those long-ago familiar voices raised above the opening stages of the battle of Red Sweetwater had established beyond any shred of doubt that the dead really could be resurrected; that nightmares really

44

could become fact.

I still felt the shock of it, all the same. Whatever I'd been led to expect when I'd originally agreed to perform that crazy charade back there, it certainly hadn't been anything quite as outlandish as this.

When the bulkier of the two figures stepped forward so that the glow from a nearby brazier fell across his ageless, craggy features; and smiled an all-too-well-remembered leer of virtuous reproval.

And said, 'Evenin', mister. So who's been a naughty boy, then?'

He looked just the same as ever, did Trapp. As if thirty intervening years of maritime villainy had glanced off him like breakers under the bows of an unsinkable ship.

It also proved I had been right all the time; that all those sleepless nights had well and truly justified my uncertainty about whether he and Gorbals Wullie really had been dragged down along with all the rest of that insanitary, buccaneering crew of homicidal tramps, in the whirlpooling wreckage of His Majesty's Warship *Charon*; indisputably the most unorthodox and appalling mistake ever to fly the White Ensign of the Royal Navy.

Oh, not that the Royal Navy had agreed with me at the time, mind you. After all, Trapp did help them win the battle of the Mediterranean, even though his motives had been rather more pecuniary than patriotic. They'd even awarded him a medal for it – or they'd given me the medal in actual fact, which had been the only nice part of the war as far as I'd been concerned, seeing it was posthumous, and simply accepted on his behalf.

Except that it hadn't been, had it? Because he bloody well hadn't been, had he . . . if you see what I mean.

'You're dead,' I accused pleadingly; hopefully. 'You died thirty years ago, Trapp. You an' that little Scotch ferret beside you.'

The ferret stepped forward, too. And he really did look like a ferret; a ferret with a three-day growth and a greasy cloth cap.

'Ah'm no' dead,' Gorbals Wullie announced reassuringly. 'Ah'm a tiger, Mister Miller, sir.'

''Is brain's dead,' Trapp admitted. Then he thought a bit and supplemented, 'Well, not dead, ackshully. More still-born really, seein' how it never worked in the first place.'

But he'd always been a stickler for accuracy, had Edward Trapp. I began to feel I was smothering as all my old apprehensions flooded back with the realization that not only was Trapp still alive, but that he hadn't changed one iota. Two ambulances went clanging past the end of the alley, heading towards the Red Sweetwater, and it occurred to me then to flag one down, climb aboard, and claim immunity as a latent casualty of war.

Because, you see, I was different. Quite special in a screwed-up sort of way. Oh, admittedly there were a great many men with thirty-year-old ghosts inside their heads; victims of battle stress – Trapp himself was one, come to that. But in those instances their mental scars had been inflicted largely by enemy action, whereas I had suffered my twitches and traumas from a much more exclusive source . . . from my supposed allies.

In my case all those bombs and bullets and *Kriegsmarine* torpedoes hadn't terrorized me any more or less than the next British seaman. No, it had been all the times between attacks that had caused my psychological wounds; my aggravations had been generated not so much through battling with Hitler's navy as against my bloody own. Against a certain Lieutenant Commander Edward Trapp, RNR, and the sadistic ill-fortune that had made him my commanding officer . . .

I got a grip on myself. 'I suppose I ought to thank you for getting me out of there,' I muttered grudgingly. 'I guess that's a favour I owe you.'

'Two favours, Number One,' Trapp corrected firmly. 'It wus me an' Wullie here what pulled you out've the water an' left you on that bit o' hatch cover after the old *Charon* went down, remember?'

I remembered. I'd often wondered about it later. Though maybe he was wrong when he called it a favour; they hadn't been particularly good or successful times for me since.

'Don't call me "Number One",' I snapped, feeling the old

irritation coming back as easily as if we'd never parted. 'I'm a shipmaster in my own right, Trapp. I've been one for twenty years, dammit.'

'Not now, you're not,' he pointed out slyly. 'Every fuzz in the United Ayrab Republic'll be lookin' for you over the sights o' a gun. You go anywhere near your old ship an' you're good f'r thirty years hard inna wog jail . . . Number One.'

'Aye, but yous is in the shit an' that's a fact, Mister Miller, sir,' Gorbals Wullie confirmed somewhat unnecessarily. 'Yous is a marked man . . . whit's in the bag then?'

I blinked. His abrupt change of tack had caught me off balance, then I saw what he was holding up so curiously – it was my duffle bag. I grabbed it and snarled, 'Mind your own bloody business, sailor!'

'Heroin?' Trapp speculated with the slightest infliction of genuine disapproval; but I was forced to admit he'd always had his principles. I grimly refused to answer.

'Opium, then . . . Maryjooanna?'

'It's nothing, Trapp.'

'It wus enough to start a riot, mister. An' to kill a couple o' policemen for. An' who was your fat mate before they shot him too, eh?'

'I'd never seen him before in my life,' I retorted truthfully.

'That don't quite answer the question,' countered Trapp astutely, then swung as a police jeep with the regulation-issue flashing blue lamp careered across the alleyway exit and vanished. When he turned back to face me he seemed to have forgotten all about the bag.

'Now I *am* a shipmaster,' he volunteered with an immensely superior smirk.

'How d'you know?' I challenged spitefully. 'You haven't seen it for a couple of hours. The kind of rust bucket you sail in, it could have sunk at its berth by now.'

He didn't seem to mind a bit; he simply grinned and looked quite pleased, as though he hadn't had a good insult since . . . well, since *I* last sailed with him.

'Bureau Veritas classification, mister. Six an' a half thousand tons gross o' shiny paint an' sweet-runnin' machinery . . .

47

Name's the *Kamaran.* I'm sailin' soon as I've finished loading. For Málaga.'

'That's in Spain, ye ken,' Wullie supplemented helpfully once again. Trapp cuffed him across the starboard ear with a growl.

' 'E knows that, limpet brain. Mister Miller's a captain too, remember?'

Then he corrected himself with a sideways glance at me. '. . . or he was a cap'n. Until he signed hisself off articles by startin' that gunfight back at the Sweetwater corral.'

I hefted the bag and turned away. Trapp said doubtfully, 'Where d'you think you're goin'?'

'On the run,' I answered tightly. 'The Egyptian authorities are likely to be offensive enough without your bloody help.'

'Ye've nae chance, ah'm tellin' ye. Ye're doomed, Mister Miller; doomed never tae get oot o' this land o' the pyramids an' the sphincters . . .'

'Shut up!' Trapp snarled almost absently. But he'd been saying that to Gorbals Wullie for over thirty years and it wasn't so much an order as a habit. He rubbed the side of his nose and fixed me with the honest, open gaze of a spider inviting a fly to lunch.

'Mind you, there is one way you jus' might get out o' here, me bucko . . .'

'Inna box,' Wullie persisted. 'Deid, an' inna wooden box stowed down the freezer hold.'

'. . . I'm still signin'-on crew for the *Kamaran* . . .' Trapp continued undeflected.

'No.' I forestalled him. 'No way, Trapp. And that's my final word.'

'. . . there's still a berth open f'r a chief officer . . . ?'

I began walking towards the end of the alleyway, and the bright lights and the searching police cars – and the apparent promise of thirty years in an Egyptian labour camp. Even that prospect had more attraction than sailing again with Edward Trapp. It wouldn't be quite so inevitably lethal, for a start; and I wouldn't have as many arguments with the guards.

There was another reason, too, why I didn't dare accept right away. I couldn't afford to let him see what really was in my bag.

'I got half a dozen seamen's discharge books what only needs a photygraph ter make 'em genuine. A bit o' hair dye an' a week's growth o' beard an' you could call in at the local police station an' they wouldn't know you.'

The hypocrisy in his voice was positively honeyed. Edward Trapp had always been a man to extract the last advantage from any situation . . . until he came up against someone as bloody-minded and stubborn as himself.

And then he admitted he had.

'Awwwww, SOD YOU!' he yelled at the top of his voice. 'Keep yer bloody duffle bag, mister. From now on I coul'n't care bloody less what's innit . . .'

I stopped walking, and smiled a secret smile.

It was the first time I'd ever won a game of bluff with Captain Edward Trapp.

We sneaked aboard the *Kamaran* an hour later. It wasn't particularly difficult; pretty well every policeman and every spare floodlight in the Nile Delta had already been positioned round my previous ship on the other side of the basin.

I remember standing there on that strangely inhospitable deck, and blinking across at my old command with a feeling of empty sadness. I knew that whatever happened from now on, I would never take that particular ship to sea again. I'd really sunk to the bottom of the ocean-going barrel now, even though there had been a little more to my meeting with Trapp than pure coincidence . . .

. . . but anyway – that was how I became chief officer of an already doomed vessel called the *Kamaran*.

And how, despite already having fought Trapp's War, I was now miserably preparing myself to fight Trapp's Peace.

Oh, there was one more task I had to complete, even before I could examine the admittedly rather pleasant cabin I'd now taken over . . . It only took a few minutes of thought to discover a suitable place. Quickly I removed a pile of old newspapers lying in the bottom of the wardrobe, and unscrewed the false plywood base. Yes, there was just enough room.

Then I opened the duffle bag – the one which had generated so much discomfort among the clients and visitors to Red Sweetwater; and which had been so grudgingly abandoned by a covetous Trapp – and removed the only object which it contained.

It fitted very neatly into the hiding place I'd found. Once the newspapers were piled roughly on top it would never attract a second glance.

That small short-wave radio transmitter. The one the Royal Navy had issued me with, way back in Hong Kong.

Chapter Five

I skulked aboard the *Kamaran*, virtually living in my cabin, for six whole days until the cargo loading was virtually complete. By the end of it I was hairy enough to have passed myself off as a yeti, never mind the Australian-born Bert Cooper that Trapp's forged seaman's discharge papers said I was.

At least I hoped the book was forged. Because if it wasn't, then the mind boggled at why the real Bert Cooper hadn't any further need for it. I didn't risk asking Trapp – there were rare but carefully selected occasions when he could be unsettlingly honest.

On the seventh day I ventured on deck. To meet what could be loosely described as 'The Crew' . . .

It was as if I'd never left Red Sweetwater. Nearly every pugilistic, hard-bitten face which scowled moronically back at me from the muster line was already vaguely familiar. The last time I'd seen them was when they, and half the Egyptian riot squad, had been kickin' the sawdust out've each other back at the brothel.

'Lovely boys,' Trapp offered approvingly, even proudly, with a proprietary sweep of one great paw. 'Salt o' the earth, them. Every one with a record long as yer arm . . . part o' the contract, see. That I wus allowed to hand-pick the best blokes f'r the job.'

I swung on him immediately. 'Contract? Job . . . ? I understood this was to be a straightforward voyage, Trapp . . .'

He developed a sudden coughing fit to change the subject, and hurriedly yanked the nearest man out of the line like a horse trader displaying his wares.

'Er, this is Choker Bligh, your bosun. Say 'allo to Mister Mille . . . Mister Cooper, Choker, lad.'

The bosun spat on the deck between my feet and growled, 'Fuck you, mate! An' don't try givin' *me* no soddin' orders.'

Trapp urged me aside before I could lash out. 'He likes you,' he assured me solemnly. 'I c'n tell that right away. An' anyway, Choker's even more obligin' when he's drunk – an' 'e's drunk most've the time . . .'

The next for introductions looked like a puddle of oil wearing an Egyptian fez.

'Maabud somethin' or other. Chief engineer.'

The puddle of oil grovelled horizontally, leaving greasy splotches wherever he'd made contact with the deck. Trapp eventually kicked him and growled, 'Gerrup, mister. Mind you, he don't 'ave much personality, but a lotta experience. Fourteen years as chief engineer on the *Cairo Flyer* f'r a start.'

'That's a funny name for a ship,' I muttered bemusedly.

'That's because it wus a railway engine,' Trapp retorted with devastating logic. 'And the lumpy lookin' guy with the scar an' the hare lip next to 'im – he's yer second mate. Name o' Spew . . . Dan'l Spew.'

I stared. Somehow, somewhere, I had to find something that could establish beyond reasonable doubt that Mister Spew had, at least at some time, been a human being.

'Is he qualified – for the job?'

'Outa the top drawer, mate. Two suspected murders; a bagful o' grievous bodily harms; three rapes; couple o' racecourse jobs . . .'

'I meant seagoing-wise,' I snarled desperately. 'As a bridge watchkeeper.'

Trapp nodded violently. 'Christ, yes. He even took a sort o' correspondence course in navigashun once, only 'e di'n't get too far with it.'

I had to ask why. It was something I just knew I had to do.

'Why didn't Mister Spew get very far with his correspondence course, Captain?'

'Because 'e can't read, Mister Mate. Or write, come ter that.'

I began to walk away again; it was getting to be a habit.

Trapp's voice – still as nauseatingly persuasive as ever – floated astern of me, enumerating the other virtues of Second Officer Spew.

' 'E's gotter good pair o' eyes, mind you. Well, *one* of 'em is; the one what didn't get the acid innit . . . an' a lovely nature when you gets ter know 'im . . .'

There was one more thing I had to do before I left the *Kamaran*'s depraved complement and made my gloomy way topsides to view the bridge.

As I passed the truculent Bosun Bligh I nodded in the friendliest possible manner – and then kicked him as hard as I could in those parts which made places like Red Sweetwater his favourite form of recreation. I had to do it hard; I knew I wouldn't get a second chance before he dismantled me rivet by rivet. Then I continued kicking him as he sprawled on the deck until fatigue brought me to a puffing halt.

I waited until he'd stopped retching, then barked grimly, 'Rest assured I have no intention of *trying* to give you orders, sailor. I bloody *will* give you orders . . . an' you shall carry 'em OUT!'

'F**@£*"&****!' Choker Bligh acknowledged, much to Trapp's obvious delight.

'Ye see – he *does* like yer, mister! Di'n't I tell you 'e likes you then . . . ?'

The *Kamaran*'s bridge deck was like the rest of her – functional but unimaginative; a typical product of an almost dying age of mass-produced general cargo ships. Now the tendency was towards specialization and economy; containerization and even larger carrying capacities. The *Kamaran* was too small, required too many men to run and maintain her; but she was still a well-found vessel and the more I thought about it the uneasier I became.

Because there was a mystery in the air on that bridge. It just wasn't Trapp's kind of ship – nothing was Trapp's kind of ship other than the sort which even the breakers' yards wouldn't touch as there's no profit in demolishing rust. So how had he

53

come to command her and, even more unsettlingly, why . . . ?

. . . but perhaps I should explain – about my genuinely disconcerting meeting with a ghost; and about the radio and the subterfuge, and the fat man who got himself so ostentatiously blown away in Red Sweetwater.

The only snag in attempting to do that is that I didn't really understand 'why' myself. I simply did not know the underlying reasons for my being aboard the *Kamaran* in the first place other than as a somewhat confused undercover agent with the task of reporting her daily positions to some obscure Royal Navy station with the call sign of Charlie Tango Wun Fife and . . . well, to wait for orders.

Oh, I was aware of my own motives for having accepted the proposition first raised by those two naval officers back in Hong Kong a few weeks ago; the ones with the Security Department identity cards and the wheedling blarney of the recruiting office. Psychologically they'd selected the perfect time – my already being so disenchanted with the monotony of driving the same slab-sided container ship along the identical maritime taxi route I'd been covering for the past ten years, that I'd have considered any prospect short of suicide as a merciful release.

And I have to admit a lot of my unpreparedness was my own fault. I should have been far more persistent in following up their vague references to 'Britain's closest interests at stake . . .', and 'threat to national security, old boy . . .', but I hadn't been. No more than I really pursued the reasons why they considered *me*, a very ordinary master mariner, as being eminently suited for implanting as a . . . well . . . a spy, I suppose. Aboard some ship called the *Kamaran* carrying certain earthmoving equipment on behalf of a certain Mister Zarafiq; but to a rather more doubtful destination, perhaps.

So I'd gratefully accepted the challenge, content, simply, to trust in God and my Queen and to report back to Charlie Tango. Apart from anything else a little Middle Eastern freighter loaded with bulldozers and picks and shovels was hardly likely to offer a threat even to me, never mind to Britain's national security; it had to be an intriguing cruise, a little bit of spurious excitement to brighten a dull career; a temporary relaxation from the responsibilities of command as an added bonus.

Dammit, but I'd been so taken by the prospect that I hadn't even voiced my doubts regarding the theatrical manner in which they'd proposed to infiltrate me into the world of subterfuge and undercover watch-keeping . . . about the Red Sweetwater ploy which had involved the co-operation of the Egyptian authorities, the appalling acting of a rather portly British Army intelligence major and the – to my mind somewhat over-melodramatic – use of a revolver loaded with blanks. Again, with total naïveté, I'd simply accepted the Navy's assurance that something would happen; that someone would contact me.

And by God but they'd been right about that! The only small point they'd omitted to mention was that the factor guaranteeing *my* particular suitability for infiltration, was to be the resurrection of Edward bloody Trapp. But they'd also known that I wouldn't even have considered the job had I been forewarned of that possibility.

Which, in its turn, made me wonder what else the Royal Navy knew about the *Kamaran* but hadn't told me . . .

. . . but that was the moment when Trapp, flanked by the inevitable Gorbals Wullie, arrived at the top of the bridge ladder. With a feeling of something less than enthusiasm, I took the opportunity of performing the one last task outstanding before I was committed to becoming a fully-integrated and genuine pirate . . .

He noticed the duffle bag I'd brought aboard as soon as his beady eyes rose above deck level. I knew he would; apart from Trapp having a magnetic affinity towards anything he considered might be either valuable or illegal – preferably both – I'd also made a point of casually leaving it where he was bound to trip over it anyway.

You see, I'd already learned that Trapp hadn't changed a bit. The moment was bound to come when, by hook or by crook, he would make an unashamedly devious attempt to discover what really had precipitated the battle of Red Sweetwater – but that was the one thing I couldn't risk him finding out, seeing it wasn't anything like Trapp thought it was, and was now hidden in my cabin tuned to a classified frequency.

I also knew, however, that Edward Trapp had one particular weakness which I could use to my advantage: he simply couldn't resist the opportunity to become the most hypocritical, holier-than-thou preacher there ever was. Or initially anyway – before he went ahead and did precisely whichever villainy had formed in his protagonist's mind in the first place.

'It *is* drugs, i'n't it, mister?' he growled disapprovingly, glance positively probing whatever secrets were held by that innocuous canvas bag.

I pretended complete disinterest. 'You agreed, Trapp. To mind your own business. Now, about the voyage; do we have a full folio of corrected charts and a . . .'

Trapp and Gorbals Wullie moved a little closer to the bag. 'Ah'll put ma money on it bein' drugs, onyway,' the little seaman agreed, eyes beginning to glint like a rat's caught in a spotlamp.

'You 'aven't *got* any money, stupid!' Trapp pointed out contemptuously. 'You spent all yer allowance on that big black wrestler lady up at Sweetwater las' night.'

'. . . and a set of sailing directions?' I persisted.

'Drugs,' Trapp tutted virtuously. 'I'm disappointed in you, mister. Drugs is a wicked thing ter smuggle, an' you bein' such a straight bloke when you wus young.'

'Forget it. Let's concentrate on the passage plan, Trapp.'

'. . . an' f'r money, too.'

'Aye, Captin, the things a man'll stoop tae, jus' f'r money.' Wullie shook his scrofulous head in the sadness of utter disillusionment. By now they were both within an avaricious hair's breadth of diving for the bag and the great unveiling.

'. . . Admiralty Lists of Lights?' I insisted futilely.

'Ohhh the misery; the 'uman suffering what can be caused by them that gets their hands on a bag o' drugs,' Trapp admonished, with tears of near-revulsion at how low a man could sink. 'Oh the wickedness o' it all; the . . . the *profit* in it . . .'

I hesitated, looked suddenly like a lost soul trying desperately to become aware of The Light.

56

'I never thought of it that way,' I muttered uneasily. 'Maybe you're right. Maybe I shouldn't hang on to it just for my own selfish gain.'

'You'll feel a lot better if you gets rid o' the guilt, matey,' Trapp urged, forcing his hand out to take upon himself the cancer which spawned within my duffle bag.

'Gie it *up*, Mister Miller, sir,' Wullie encouraged devoutly. 'Och but the relief ye'll feel once ye dinnae hae the worry of all yon valuable . . . all yon evil hard stuff on yer conscience, an' that's a fact.'

I picked up the bag, and drew a deep and saintly breath of deliverance.

'Thank you, both of you,' I whispered humbly. 'For guiding me back towards the path of righteousness . . .'

. . . and then I dropped the bag clear over the side of the bridge; right down into the inky depths of Port Said harbour. It disappeared for ever, with hardly a splash, but that was probably because of the heavy shackle I'd placed in it a few minutes before.

Trapp did make a few more comments, but I don't think they were particularly constructive. I felt they also tended towards being a little less than congratulatory, considering he'd just successfully rehabilitated a sinner.

Discreetly I retreated from the *Kamaran*'s bridge deck, leaving an inexplicably embittered preacher to kick his fellow gospeller all around the paint-shiny wheelhouse, trying to pretend Gorbals Wullie was me.

I should have known it couldn't last. It was actually a little later that same afternoon when I ran clean out of satisfaction.

I'd ventured back up to the chartroom after Gorbals Wullie had limped petulantly away, and spent a couple of hours laying off our courses for Málaga. Trapp had been there for most of the time, grumbling and muttering and fiddling with irrelevant things, but he hadn't said a word directly to me; only occasionally bellowing ill-tempered invective at Bosun Bligh and the unbelievably grotesque figure of Second Officer Spew as they struggled to supervise the loading of our deck cargo of giant bulldozers.

Then I noticed the Arabs.

Oh, not that the fact that they were Arabs was particularly odd in itself; one does tend to meet rather a lot of them around the Middle East. But these boys were different; they were very hard-looking Arabs indeed.

For a start they weren't working or anything; simply lounging in a huddle at the after end of the boat deck and watching the loading operation. Obviously not part of the stevedoring complement.

Yet they weren't part of the crew either. For one thing they looked clean; for another they didn't wear clothes looking like gear robbed from a mortuary after an air crash into a swamp. Expensive, they were, in lightweight linen and with ominously well-tailored bulges just about where a shoulder holster could be imagined.

There were five of them altogether. A point which caused me considerable unease was the way that one of them – a tall, sardonic-looking Arab with his arm in a sling – seemed to turn quite often and stare bleakly up at the bridge – up at Trapp, in fact – with a look of barely-veiled threat.

He gave the impression of being the man in charge. But of what? I knew one thing for sure – I didn't feel comfortable turning my back on them, not even for the few moments it took to corner a morose and embittered Trapp out on the wing.

Even after he did bring himself to speak to me it was only to go on about the bloody duffle bag, and his imagined loss of revenue.

'Yeah? Well what about all that misery and human suffering you were lecturing me about?' I was forced to counter eventually, before he would drop the subject.

'Wot about all *my* bloody misery an' sufferin', mister? An' Wullie's?'

'Gorbals Wullie hasn't got the mental capacity to worry about tomorrow's breakfast, never mind loss of profits, like you. *He* wasn't suffering over what was in my bag, Trapp.'

' 'E wus after I'd finished beltin' 'im around the ship . . .'

'What about those Arabs on the boat deck?' I finally cut in. 'Who are they, and why are they aboard, huh?'

He shuffled a bit then, and looked shifty. 'They're jus' passengers. Employees of a guy called Zarafiq; sort o' representatives of the owners in a way. Their head sheik is a guy called Fadel – the one with the funny arm.'

I saw the look of . . . was it satisfaction in his eye, but didn't understand it and felt faintly relieved with the rest of the explanation. 'So presumably they're going all the way to Málaga with us, eh?'

He wasn't really listening; just staring down at the oddly sinister group with what had gradually turned to a more worried, almost anxious expression.

'Where's Málaga?' he asked absently.

'In Spain f'r . . . our destination, Trapp. Málaga's the port of discharge for the *Kamaran*'s cargo, according to you.'

'What cargo?' he muttered even more remotely. And that was when I suddenly began to shiver. I'd seen that look of introspective villainy too many times before to have any illusions left.

I grabbed him, swinging him to face me guiltily.

'Trapp,' I snarled vengefully. 'Trapp, you double-dealing, bent-as-an-Irish-corkscrew, parsimonious bastard. The time has come for you an' me to have a long and candid talk . . .'

'. . . so that's all there is to it, mate,' he finished half an hour later. 'All we gotter do is nip in the boats; watch the old *Kamaran* go down by the 'ead; I gets paid the other half o' me contract; Zarafiq's happy . . . an' you're all on a handsome bonus.'

'That's all?' I echoed weakly. 'We only have to offload a whole cargo in a place we aren't even supposed to visit. Then scuttle this ship in the middle of the Mediterranean; and *then* convince the authorities we never went anywhere off our course line in the first bloody place . . .'

'That's all. More or less.'

I glowered at him searchingly. He looked far too innocent

still; much too saintly.

'More or less . . . Trapp. What are you still covering up, Trapp? TRAPP?'

He shuffled again and examined his exploded baseball boots intently. I swung him around and shoved my face hard into his, eyeball to eyeball.

'What . . . are . . . you . . . bloody . . . concealing?'

I was half-way down the bridge ladder when he'd finished explaining *that* part; ostensibly en route for the gangway, the nearest police station, and thirty years' hard labour

'What are you goin' for, mate?' he called anxiously. 'I told yer the truth, di'n't I? Jus' like you wanted.'

I stopped. Only for a minute, mind you. And only then because not even I, with all my knowledge of Edward Trapp, could quite hoist in the enormity of the enterprise his crooked brain had spawned on this particular occasion.

'You have told me, Trapp, that this mysterious Mister Zarafiq has paid you ten thousand pounds . . .'

His eyes flickered a bit guiltily at that and I knew I'd already caught him out, but it didn't matter; I'd no desire to share on a percentage basis anyway.

'. . . to offload the cargo to some secret purchasers, at some equally secret rendezvous in Gahman, before you actually sink the ship. And because, for some inexplicable reason, Zarafiq finds it difficult to trust you, he has placed five professional gunmen aboard to make bloody certain you do what he's paying you to do . . .'

'Yeah, but . . .'

'Shut *up*, Trapp!'

I was aware of my voice cracking in fury, but I didn't care; I just had to get the whole lunatic swindle clear in my own mind before I opted out and back to the dull, honest world of containerships and ordinary people and maybe a few, revitalized nightmares.

'But ten thousand quid isn't good enough for you, is it, Trapp? Because now you tell me that not only have you already taken Zarafiq's advance payment . . . but that you have ALSO sold the cargo to a *second* bunch of crooks – to some of your

60

own villainous mates – which means that now you intend to deliver it to *another* secret rendez-bloody-vous; this one somewhere along the North African coast before Zarafiq's place . . .'

'. . . an' sink the *Kamaran* before I'm due at Zarafiq's illegal destination too, mind,' Trapp argued reasonably. 'I mean, well, when she's scuttled he ain't got no way of knowin' I already got rid of the cargo, has he? So all I'm proposin' is to use his idea, only divert a little more of the boodle into me own pocket.'

'You can't. He'll never believe you, Trapp.'

'Why not? He expects the insurers to believe the *Kamaran* sunk 'erself by accident, don't he? All I'm doin' is the same thing but a bit earlier in the trip.'

I still hesitated on the ladder. The trouble with all Trapp's double-crossing schemes was that they seemed so bloody logical, so convincing. Then I remembered the Arab, Fadel, and that look of promise he'd directed towards Trapp; and the rest of his boys, and the bulges under the shoulder blades, and the cold professionalism.

'And what about Zarafiq's hoods, Trapp? D'you really think they're going to let you get away with it?'

'Aw, they're only Ayrabs,' Trapp dismissed scornfully. 'They don't 'ave the brain o' Gorbals Wullie between 'em. They wouldn't know one bit o' North Africa from Piccadilly Circus, they wouldn't. And when it comes to abandonin' the *Kamaran*, there's always the chance of an accident happenin'; a lifeboat fall partin' maybe, or the ladder they're using's gonna carry away sudden . . .'

He was still following me, accompanied now by an equally ingratiating Gorbals Wullie, even after I'd actually descended the gangway and was walking determinedly along the quay and away from the bloody *Kamaran*.

I'd have gone, too – Royal Navy or no Royal Navy. Clear out of Trapp's life again; only this time for ever and ever.

Well, I would if it hadn't been for the Chinamen, anyway.

The ones who kidnapped us.

Chapter Six

I didn't even notice the smart launch at first. The one moored alongside the wharf ahead of the *Kamaran*'s looming bow.

I didn't particularly register the men grouped irresolutely beside it either, as if they didn't quite know what to do next – until they turned to see Trapp bearing down on them in voluble pursuit of me, and suddenly their not-so-inscrutable expressions cleared as their immediate problem appeared to have resolved itself.

Because the delicate task of kidnapping a shipmaster is made much simpler when that master actually comes ashore from the ship in question, and marches straight into your arms. Which was precisely what Trapp, still escorted by a frantically hobbling Gorbals Wullie, was doing. Presumably that early-warning sense of his had once again been overwhelmed by his anxiety to argue further with me.

He'd nearly come abeam of me by the time we'd steamed abreast of the Chinamen. All they needed to do was to step forward, present the muzzles of two not-particularly-discreetly-held sub-machineguns, and suggest invitingly, 'You all get into fligging boat, chop, chop.'

'Bugger OFF!' Trapp roared absently, sweeping both men aside with a mighty thrust of his paw and carrying on regardless.

Then he stopped; and Gorbals Wullie stopped. And I stopped too, rooted to the spot, as we heard the unmistakable snick of machinegun cocking handles being drawn back to the fire positions.

'Here, they lads has got shooters,' Wullie interpreted unsteadily.

Slowly we pivoted; very slowly indeed.

There were four of them, the first pair with the fire power plus another two – obviously in charge – unarmed and wearing immaculately laundered white tropical rig; shorts, peaked uniform caps and the epaulettes of ship's officers. All watching us warily through Oriental and expressionless black eyes.

'You get in fligging boat . . . Quick time, no noise, hah.'

'Get the polis,' Wullie agitated nervously, probably for the first time in his misbegotten life. Trapp looked bleakly at him, then pointedly at me, and snarled, 'Don't be so *bloody* silly!'

I began to get even more angry than I already was. Scotsmen, Germans, Frenchmen, stateless men, Arabs . . . and now Chinese. Trapp attracted international trouble like a magnet. He was the human counterpart of the bloody U-bend in a lavatory – the part where all the dirt gets stuck. Desperately I stared around, then up at the high bows of the *Kamaran* in search for aid.

Then I breathed a sigh of relief. The troglodyte silhouette of Second Officer Spew lounged above us, gazing down from the rails with detached interest.

Ignoring the machinegun barrel which swung threateningly in line with my chest I began to wave frantically; appealingly.

Mister Spew gestured cheerily back with his one good arm – the one which hadn't been paralysed in a Marseilles brothel brawl, according to Trapp – and then turned conscientiously away to resume his cargo-handling duties.

Mind you, there was no doubt in my mind that he would have noticed the machineguns, and the threat to his captain. If it hadn't been for that eye. The one with the acid innit . . .

'Awwww, get in the fliggin' boat,' Trapp growled.

Resignedly.

I suppose the small ship on the other side of the fairway could have been more fairly described as a yacht, really. At least a yacht in the sense that it didn't appear to have any cargo-carrying capacity; nor would the Kaiser have considered he was letting the side down had he owned it. Apart from which the Westland Gazelle helicopter secured to the snowy-white deck was an accessory far in excess of any standard merchant ship's inventory.

The launch sheered alongside an accommodation ladder diamond-bright with new varnish and holy-stoned treads. Two immaculately turned-out Chinese seamen took our lines without a word as the grumble of the engine cut. Suddenly everything seemed very quiet, and somehow ominous.

The officer with the three gold rings jerked his head. 'You all get . . .'

'I know,' Trapp completed mildly; maybe a little too mildly. '. . . up the fliggin' ladder. Chop, chop.'

I started to say reasonably, 'Look, mister, I don't know what you want me for, but I've just paid myself off back there. I don't have anything more to do with either Trapp or the *Kama* . . .'

Then the foresight of a sub-machinegun raked agonizingly across the small of my back and, after I'd stopped writhing, I chop-chopped in raging but very mute frustration after my rather more diplomatically-acquiescent fellow kidnappees.

Mind you, it *was* my first time to be hi-jacked. Trapp and Gorbals Wullie were beginning to accept it as routine. In fact Trapp was so much at home in the role by then that he even managed to revert to his usual appraisal of other people's assets as we were gun-prodded forward.

'Cost a few bob, did this ship. See that paintwork, mister? Three coats o' best quality marine gloss wi'out no holidays when they wus layin' it on. An' them decks . . . ? Grade "A" sanded Burma teak; none o' yer paper-thin rusty steel. Sixty-'Ong Kong dollars a cube that set the owners back, an' even then they'd've had to fiddle an export licence . . .'

But by that time we'd reached the entrance into the accommodation; and even Edward Trapp became strangely silent as we were urged across the polished brass coaming which led to a macabre and lunatic wonderland.

And to Mister Chang. The most wondrous eccentricity of them all.

*

I didn't believe it. Not at first.

We stood there, the three of us, gazing around in dumb incredulity as our escorts withdrew unnoticed. Oh, admittedly we made a somewhat unconventional trio ourselves – me under my six-day growth and dyed hair; Gorbals Wullie with that grease-stiff Glasgae razor bonnet and his skinny figure encased in a scrofulous, fifteenth-hand Harris tweed suit which defied every effort made by the Arabian sun to parboil him within it ... and Trapp, of course – as sartorially disgusting as ever in baseball boots, a pair of trousers that could have come off a three-month-dead corpse, a yellow-stained and turtle-necked submariner's jersey that I vaguely remembered from the Second World War, all crowned by a verdigris-braided master's cap above which the partly-severed top gently bounced open and shut as he moved, like an opened tin of dog food.

Yet even then we didn't feel too out of place. The interior of that dream vessel's saloon was a fantasy world; a time machine leading to a celluloid past in which good guys and bad guys, and tough guys and sinister guys vied with one another's images to steal the picture. A claustrophobic gallery of hard-eyed, jut-jawed Hollywood heavies gazing bleakly down at us from jumbo-sized frames reminiscent of an electric theatre of half a century ago.

Bogart; Gable; Raft; Flynn; Ameche; Karloff; Edward G. ... ! I rubbed my eyes and stared fixedly ahead but there was no relief; no lessening of the visual impact. I felt myself cocooned, overwhelmed by a nausea of thirty-five millimetre nostalgia.

For that was precisely the effect it had, the pile-carpeted belly of that super-modern ship. Of a giant and lavishly pre-sented movie nightmare; a cinema *grand luxe*; a monument to tasteless decor modelled on all that was ostentatious and brassy and vulgar in the glorious hey-day of the cinematographic screen.

While under those eternally fixed and dead eyes sprawled all the other trappings of that gaudy yet magniloquent era – red-flocked wall coverings; jazzy imitation-crystal chandeliers; cascades of royal purple drapes; coils of chromed tubular handrails and ashtrays and stanchions; green plush tip-up seats and plaster half-nudes thrusting pink-tipped, wire-framed mammaries from arched and hand-painted torsos . . .

'. . . it's beautiful!' Trapp breathed in dewy-eyed veneration, oblivious now to whatever nameless threat hung over his future. 'I 'aven't never *been* aboard a more beautiful ship, I 'aven't.'

'Magic, Captin,' Wullie confirmed. 'All they gangsters; mah boyhood heroes an' that's a fact.'

And finally an organ began to play – a cinema organ, needless to say. And then we met Mister Chang . . .

I stared even harder. I was fully conscious of the fact that my reflexes were letting me down, but I couldn't do anything about it. I just . . . well . . . stared.

The curtains flanking the end of the saloon parted slowly, dramatically, as the organ rose to a crescendo. Then the lights dimmed slowly, and the spotlights came on to bathe the revealed stage in a blue-tinged haze vaguely reminiscent of Red Sweetwater's sordid atmosphere – or the B-movie film set of a Chicago speakeasy, Twenties style.

There were three men before us; two standing and one reclining languidly in a high-backed armchair. The two vertical members of the cast were Chinese, as was the third, but they were dressed entirely in black . . . Chicago hood-type black, with wide shouldered, double-breasted suits, pencil-line moustaches and brim-low fedoras masking only slightly the coldness of their eyes.

'They got Thompson guns,' Wullie stammered nervously. 'Ah've studied them, ah have. Real Tommy guns like a' the mobs used tae rub each other oot wi'. Alla best gangsters like Capone an' Legs Diamond an' that . . .'

'Shut up!' Trapp suggested routinely, not taking his fascinated gaze from the man in the centre; the Man in the White Suit. Because, as seemed bizarrely appropriate in this celluloid environment, White Suit formed the positive image in stark contrast to the negatives flanking him. Where they were black, he was white; even his eyes appeared to have no density at all.

66

Then he spoke. But not in any Oriental dialect.

'You dirty rats,' he hissed. 'You dirty rats hear me good. One false move outa you schmoes an' I get the boys to blast you . . . OK?'

'Cagney,' Trapp whispered ecstatically. 'Pure Cagney, so 'e is.'

'Christ!' I muttered faintly, just before the voice from the stage came again, but altered this time; much more nasal, almost a drawl.

'OK, sweethearts. I gotta proposition for you guys, a real sweet-toothed proposition . . .'

'Bogart now.' Trapp wriggled in pure appreciation. ''Umphrey bloody Bogart to the life, mister.'

'Who's he goin' tae do next?' Wullie twittered, every bit as carried away as Trapp was. 'Who d'you reckon he's goin' tae do next then?'

'You, probably,' I snapped spitefully. 'This could well be your Saint Valentine's day, laddie.'

I gazed tightly around, searching for an exit sign – illuminated, of course – from this crazy ship crewed, apparently, not only by resident lunatics but also a couple of visitors; but there wasn't one. Then I looked around again, taking in the opulent furnishings while remembering the sheer quality of the vessel I was in, the enormous cost of building and running her, and began to wonder just who were the real idiots.

And why we were here at all; and what did the extrovert Oriental in the white suit want of us . . .

'Mad, o' course,' Trapp loftily pronounced with a complete disdain for discretion. It was as if he'd been reading my mind, with the exclusion of his own part in the lunacy. 'All Chineemen is, mind you, but that one in partic'lar's as nutty as a heatstruck stoker.'

But the man in the chair didn't seem to hear. In fact when his voice came again it was even more of a contrast; this time it was soft, with the impeccable accent of an English public school.

'Rather good, what. Oh, permit me to introduce myself . . . my name is Chang. Mister Chang.'

''Ow d'you do,' Trapp retorted, not at all put out by the abrupt change of tack. 'I'm Trapp – Cap'n Trapp. An' this here's my chief officer, Mister . . . er . . . Cooper.'

'No, I'm not,' I snarled childishly.

'. . . an' the tatty Scotch feller, he's nuthin' special.'

'Can you dae Peter Lorry?' Wullie asked hopefully. 'He wis ma very favourite villain, so he wis.'

Mister Chang smiled tolerantly and 'did' Peter Lorre. Wullie and Trapp began to applaud unrestrainedly while I pinched myself to make certain I was awake, and that this really was happening. Then Mister Chang waved a deprecating hand and rather regretfully rose to his feet.

'Thank you, thank you, gentlemen. Your appreciation is more than gratifying . . . one of my little foibles, you understand? It truly is a pleasure to be able to share, all too infrequently, my passion for the great days of the silver screen with fellow moving-picture afficionados.'

I wondered sardonically whether or not he realized that Trapp and Gorbals Wullie would have shown equal, if not even greater enthusiasm for the type of moving-picture show exhibited above the bar at Red Sweetwater. But then Mister Chang altered course yet again, almost imperceptibly this time, and I sensed the crunch was coming.

'I believe you are doing business with an old acquaintance of mine, Captain Trapp. With a certain Mister . . . ah . . . Zarafiq.'

'Ah, now that would be tellin',' Trapp hedged virtuously. 'I don't discuss my business affairs with no one. It wouldn't be profeshnul ethics . . .'

Mister Chang gestured and one of the men in black stepped forward and took aim at Trapp's head. Trapp never even blinked an eyelid.

'. . . but on the other hand I b'lieve in the free exchange of ideas. In a nutshell, Mister Chang – yeah.'

Chang jerked his head dramatically. 'OK, Bugsy, park the rod. There ain't no need to blow the guy away in dis moment a time . . . Thank you, Captain; your frankness is most refreshing. Perhaps you would also confirm that your intentions

68

regarding the forthcoming voyage of the *Kamaran* are a little less than . . . ah . . . honest? That my associate Zarafiq has, in fact, offered you the sum of twenty-five thousand pounds as an inducement to sink her after, shall we say, diverting her cargo?'

'You said he was only paying you ten thousand, Trapp,' I accused in bitter, if not entirely surprised reproach.

'You said he wis only payin' you five, Captin,' Gorbals Wullie supplemented in a squeal redolent of shattered illusions and faith undermined.

'I wus goin' to bank the rest for you, dammit,' Trapp muttered with only the slightest suggestion of questionable honesty. 'You'd jus' spend it all on food an' clothes an' that otherwise.'

But the look he threw at Mister Chang indicated that Mister Chang, just like Mister Zarafiq, had unwittingly placed his career in dire jeopardy. While, being Trapp, he didn't miss the opportunity of scoring at least one return point when it came to the question of revelations – or of establishing that Mister Chang's intelligence service was not the only efficient vehicle for gathering rumour.

'This yacht – it's called the *Illustrious Dragon*, ain't it? I noticed that much when we come alongside after we wus kidnapped.'

'Kidnapped, Captain Trapp?'

'Invited, Mister Chang. Yeah, well I heard about you too, then. Grockle the Fink wus talkin' about you one day. About you bein' one o' the Honk Kong number-one gangster boys . . .'

'Grockle the Fink is a purveyor of scurrilous rumour, sir,' the man on the stage corrected tightly, warningly. 'I am a businessman. Above moral reproach; an impeccable record in commerce.'

'Oh, aye? So all this wus paid for out o' the change the income tax man left you, I suppose . . .'

'Trapp,' I whispered agitatedly. 'F'r Christ's sake be a bit more diplomatic for once in your life . . . while you've still *got* a bloody life.'

But Trapp's mercurial temperament – like his avarice –

tended to over-ride basic good sense.

'. . . can't stand yellow-men crooks what pretends they're bloody pure white lily ange . . .'

'TRAPP!'

There was a very long pause. I could plainly see the less-than-inscrutable rage in Mister Chang's rubicund features, and the way in which the black suits hopefully fondled their Thompson guns; then gradually the tension faded and Mister Chang picked an invisible thread from his virgin breast before he relaxed, and smiled.

'A proposition, Captain. A business proposition.'

'Oh, please yer bloody self,' Trapp muttered, still childishly piqued at the prospect of being forced into dispensing some more of Zarafiq's advance to Gorbals Wullie. Mind you, according to Trapp's standards, that money was more precious than life itself; the sharing of any part of it held much more horror for him than any threatened forty-five-calibre demise.

In fact, on reflection, Trapp would probably have agreed to sign a contract for his own suicide. As long as there was a profit in it.

'How would you like to earn an additional twenty-five thousand pounds, Captain? Plus, shall we say, a further ten thousand pounds as an advance bonus against your word?'

The silence this time lasted even longer. Only Trapp seemed unimpressed; unaware of the ripple of disbelief which stirred Gorbals Wullie and I.

'Oh aye,' he said placidly. 'And 'ow do I do that, mister?'

Mister Chang wriggled in self-congratulatory anticipation of his own genius.

'By offloading your cargo *before* you arrive at Mister Zarafiq's Gahmanian rendezvous, Captain; for delivery to certain Libyan acquaintances of mine instead . . . and finally scuttling the *Kamaran* as if by accident, in order to convince my dear friend Zarafiq that Allah can prove a most fickle and frustrating master.'

'But that's just what you're planning tae d . . . !' Wullie started to splutter before Trapp's elbow paralysed him from the neck down. Mind you, the upper part of him didn't need any treatment.

'You . . . you can't mean you wants me ter double-cross Mister Zarafiq, surely? An' then pretend the *Kamaran* sunk herself before she ever got near to unloadin' anythin' at all . . .' Trapp confirmed hesitantly.

Mister Chang smiled again. Delightedly. 'A jolly clever wheeze, what?'

'It . . . it's a master-stroke. It's a positiv'ly brilliant conception,' Edward Trapp breathed with the wide-eyed guile of an appreciative cherub. 'I gotter admit, Mister Chang – I couldn't never have thought of an idea as clever as that . . .'

'You know what you've done, don't you?' I snarled a little later. 'I mean, you do *know* what you've gone an' done, don't you, Trapp?'

He leaned phlegmatically over the *Kamaran*'s bridge front and calmly watched Second Officer Spew and Bosun Bligh moving around the foredeck; Spew checking, with what few parts of his anatomy still either existed or worked, that the hatch bars were locked, while the megalithic Bligh glowered and kicked at each lashing securing the deck cargo of bulldozers as though they were personal enemies.

'Wot've I done, then?'

I took a deep breath.

'You have, for starters, agreed to perpetrate one of the most colossal insurance frauds in maritime history. Do you accept that?'

'Which one?'

'ZARAFIQ'S. ZARAFIQ'S BLOODY FIDDLE!'

'All right, all right,' he rejoined huffily. 'No need to get irritable.'

'And you have already told me,' I forced myself to continue in a lower key, 'that you've also sold that cargo to your own gangster pals just down the coast a bit, in Egypt. Right?'

'Well . . .'

'*Right?*'

'Yeah.'

I knew I was gripping the teak rail tightly enough to squeeze the sap out of it but I couldn't help myself. '. . . and now, in addition to all that, you have also committed yourself to delivering the same cargo that you've already sold twice . . . to a THIRD PARTY. To Mister Chang. In Libya.'

' 'E wus very persuasive,' Trapp argued doggedly. 'Thirty-five thousand quid's worth. Plus that mistake I made what gives you an' Wullie a bit extra; though it's wasted on 'im – he can't appreciate nothing properly unless it's stolen out've someone's hip pocket.'

'So who,' I persisted, firing each syllable with laborious clarity, 'do you intend to deliver to? Zarafiq in Gahman? Mister Chang's crowd in Libya? Or your own cut-throat oppos here in bloody Egypt?'

'My own, o' course,' Trapp said with a touch of virtuous asperity. 'I got principles, you know, mister. Apart from which, them partic'lar friends o' mine will use my liver f'r buzzard bait if I screws 'em.'

'Oh,' I retorted sarcastically. 'Oh, I didn't realize you mixed with nasty rough people like that. But, you see, there does appear to be one small difficulty arising from that decision of yours – just one tiny additional snag . . .'

I leaned over the rail and pointed with a shaking finger.

On the port side Fadel, flanked by the rest of Zarafiq's Arabian heavy mob, still clustered with ominous watchfulness; drafted aboard to make absolutely certain that Trapp did deliver the goods to Mister Z.

'You may have convinced Fadel that you've been forced to sign on some pretty odd-ball characters as crew for the moment, Trapp. But has it ever occurred to you what's going to happen to that liver of yours when you do try to divert to your mates; when you finally do have to show your hand and double-cross both Zarafiq and Chang at the same time . . . ?'

Because now, grouped on the starboard side and eyeing Zarafiq's already suspicious crowd with furtive hostility, there also huddled a quintet of Chinese hoodlums; each with the mandatory bulge under his pseudo-nautical seaman's rig, and all looking about as genuine in the shipboard environment of the *Kamaran* as chop suey at a bar mitzvah.

But lethal, nevertheless. Professional killers, every one.

'We're dead, Trapp. Whichever choice open to you is finally taken, the moment you do . . . we're all bloody dead!'

Chapter Seven

Of course it was too late for me to leave Trapp by then. The launch from Chang's *Illustrious Dragon* had kept a threatening watch on our gangway until the moment we finally sailed from Port Said. I'd even considered the prospect of going over the wall and swimming for it before we reached the end of the breakwater. But the launch had still been there astern of us; still watching . . .

. . . and now we'd been at sea for forty-eight hours. Yet still nobody had actually shot at anybody, while hardly anybody else had been slugged, mugged, knifed, heaved over the rails in the black of night, or otherwise generally discomfited.

Not that I felt any easier for the reprieve, mind you. Probably a number of kamikazi pilots had suffered much the same sense of false security, simply because nothing bad had happened to them during the first half of their flight – and even then their prospects must have appeared more hopeful than mine, seeing none of *them* had been tricked into carrying Trapp as observer.

The more I worried, the more my real employers' motives came into question. And how much they really knew about the true destination of the *Kamaran* – whichever that was. Obviously they were aware of Zarafiq and the Arab connection; but had they also known about Chang and his Chinese puzzle? And why, come to that, was the Royal Navy so concerned about what was, no matter how outrageous, simply a civil insurance fraud which didn't even involve a British vessel?

And why, come to that, were they convinced that a boatload of buckets and spades presented any kind of threat to Britain's national security? Even allowing for the fact that Trapp was in charge . . .

I'd called them last night for the first time; a hoarsely

whispered entreaty with my cabin door firmly locked to prevent the imminent assault of an Arab gunman, an Oriental assassin or simply a common-or-garden Trapp-type thug.

'Charlie Tango Wun Fife, this is . . . er . . . Watchdog. Charlie Tango Wun Fife, this is Watchdog . . . Charlie Tango Wun, oh f'r Christ's sake, Charlie Tan . . .'

'This is Charlie Tango Wun Fife!' Charlie Tango Wun Fife had retorted, his disembodied tone displaying a firm hint of static-warped reproval. 'Request you observe correct voice procedure . . .'

I didn't know who Charlie Tango Wun Fife was, but I did describe *what* he was. I also passed on a few random comments regarding service voice procedures before I got down to the real, spy-type nitty gritty of reporting that the reason the *Kamaran* wasn't bound for Málaga, Spain, was because the Mister Zarafiq they already knew about had apparently bribed Trapp to offload somewhere else first. But Trapp wasn't actually heading there either, because a certain Mister Chang/ Bogart/Cagney had paid more for us to take the bloody stuff to his particular reception centre . . . only Trapp wasn't goin' there either, dammit, because he also happened to be under pressure from some other trigger-happy band of Tuaregs to deliver the goods that *they'd* already paid him for . . .

There had been a long silence; and then Charlie Tango Wun Fife had said in a very strained voice, 'Wait one.'

So I'd waited one. Then two. Then three and a nerve-twanging four . . . until Charlie Tango Wun Fife came back across the ether and passed on a reply from what I gathered must have been his admiral.

It meant he had to break with service voice procedures himself, that time. Because I didn't think there were any phrases quite like that in any Royal Naval communications manual.

After stripping away the descriptive passages they ordered me to do nothing yet. Simply to wait. And report.

To be strictly fair to the Royal Navy, it wasn't only them who managed to turn those initial two days of the passage into a

75

nightmare for me. And it certainly wasn't the *Kamaran* herself – she was a good ship; a real seaman's pride even if a little old-fashioned.

No, it was more the fault of Trapp's crew. Because they were utterly bloody useless.

Take the meal times, for example. Despite the fact that such a cosmopolitan gathering should, under normal circumstances, have offered a challenge to any chef worth his salt shaker, the outcome smacked not so much of an international gourmet's convention as a gastronomic obstacle course.

For a start Bosun Bligh had volunteered to do the cooking. Or perhaps 'volunteered' wasn't quite the right expression in that Trapp had initially been forced to persuade the *Kamaran*'s chief petty officer a little – like pounding him continuously with a marlin spike until he agreed to co-operate.

Though to be fair to Trapp, this time it had all been the bosun's fault in the first place; why our original cook had suddenly found himself unable to continue with his culinary duties immediately after lunch on the first day.

As Trapp had remonstrated later, 'Yeah, well I knows Choker Bligh don't exac'ly like tomato soup, mister. But that weren't no real reason ter dip the poor bloody chef's 'ead innit, wus it?'

. . . and then there was the general atmosphere in the saloon; again hardly conducive to the sort of jollity and good fellowship one might reasonably have expected to aid one's gastric juices in their task even if Choker Bligh's productions had been digestible.

There were three tables running fore and aft, the two outboard ones being set for passengers and 'special advisory crew' – meaning Chinese who everybody, including Fadel, now recognized for what they were – ocean-going yobbos. Which left the centre table reserved for what could be loosely described as the ship's 'officers'. But even that arrangement wasn't quite adequate; the way we'd placed all Zarafiq's clique to port and all Chang's gang to starboard in order to separate them. Because it still meant that one half of each mob were required to sit with their backs to their enemies on the other side of the

76

saloon, if you see what I mean.

So the final seating plan agreed on was accomplished by every last hood from both factions perching grimly on the extreme outboard sides; all facing inwards towards each other, and all eating stolidly with one hand holding their forks while the other hand rested warily inside bulging lapels.

And all facing the centre table where I, not at all hungry whatever the quality of food, dined precisely in the middle of any impending cross-fire . . .

I gazed morosely around at my companions on that second day out. Trapp, as master, had taken his rightful place at the head of the officers' trough where, with typical disregard for the finer points of etiquette, he now lounged, baseball-booted feet comfortably propped across the table top and dog-tin cap flat aback on his head, awaiting the latest creation from *la cuisine de M'sieu Bligh*.

At the opposite end squelched Chief Engineer Maabud somethin' or other, dripping a steadily expanding film of oil on the carpet and fiddling nervously with what had been a serviette a few moments before but now looked more like a diesel-soaked ball of cotton waste. Nevertheless I felt grateful our ex-engine-driver chief was up for his meal first – the second engineer picked by Trapp was really dirty, the kind've company that would have made a sewer beetle want to take a shower. I did hope Maabud wouldn't succumb to his usual thing, though, and feel socially over-awed in such élite company, because that meant he'd be back down on the deck grovelling, and then Trapp would have to get up and irritably kick him back into his chair, and that would create even greater tension than there already was . . .

. . . and then there was Mister Spew.

It was very difficult to concentrate on eating when you were facing Mister Spew. I mean . . . well . . . so few parts of our grotesque second officer actually worked, while those bits that did only managed to move in articulated jerks which tended to spray the major part of any forkful in a sporadic arc long before it actually completed its voyage to his mouth. Quite often the game of culinary roulette wasn't ended even then, for

Mister Spew's one good eye appeared to have difficulty in focusing properly, so as often as not whatever particles of sustenance which still remained clinging doggedly to his fork would miss his expectant maw anyway, to be propelled irretrievably over his left shoulder.

I did wonder for a while why he didn't simply scrape his dinner straight from the plate into his mouth. For one thing Spew, like Trapp, was hardly the type to feel hidebound by convention and, for another, such a minor breach of manners wouldn't even have been noticed in the saloon of the good ship *Kamaran*.

But then our reluctant chef stormed through from the galley on a tidal wave of blasphemy, dispensing grudging splodges of something unrecognizable from a grease-dripping plastic bucket . . . and I suddenly realized that maybe Dan'l Spew wasn't quite so bloody daft after all.

Later that night I saw Trapp climbing the bridge ladder towards me, followed by Fadel and a second Arab, and my heart sank. I knew the reprieve was over, and that eventually the shooting was bound to start.

Then the dim light from the binnacle fell across Trapp's features and my heart plummeted even further. He was wearing his clever expression, far too bloody clever by half, and that meant the shooting would probably begin even quicker because when Trapp got clever it meant he was even more intractable than usual. And conceited with it.

'Evenin', mister,' he called cheerfully.

I just glowered back and didn't reply.

He didn't reveal the slightest trace of shame. 'You never been formally introduced, have yer? Well, this is Mister Fadel. Him an' his mate here 'ave come topsides to make sure we screws the insurance company on Zarafiq's behalf . . .'

The tall man with his arm in the sling moved impatiently, dangerously. 'Simply proceed with the course alteration, Captain. You have already been warned not to discuss Mister Zarafiq's business arrangements with your hired hands.'

I half opened my mouth to launch some withering broadside, but then became aware of the other Arab sidling around behind me and decided not to risk aggravating the situation even more. Trapp was perfectly capable of doing that without any help from me.

There was another factor to take into account; one which I'd already questioned, and that was the way in which Fadel continually fingered his injured arm while gazing so bleakly at Trapp. I had the unsettling conviction that they'd already met, long before the *Kamaran* ruined my life, and that the menacing Arab gunman had an old score to settle – intended to settle, dammit, whatever we did in the next few hours.

Not that you'd have guessed from the way Trapp was behaving.

'Bring 'er round to port then, mister,' he ordered imperiously. 'The new course is sou' west a half south.'

'What's that in proper language?' I snapped childishly. 'Most seamen stopped using compass points after the Armada ran aground.'

'Just do it,' Fadel advised flatly. He didn't need to add anything further; I could already sense the temperature dropping several degrees in that darkened wheelhouse, yet there wasn't even a gun in sight. Yet.

'Come port to two two zero,' I muttered tightly.

Gorbals Wullie began to spin the wheel and then stopped. 'Come tae . . . whit wis that?'

'That's the trouble wi' these hired hands,' Trapp couldn't resist observing to no one in particular. 'They don't know bugger all about nuthin'.'

'Come port to . . . oh, to south-west and a bloody half south,' I conceded. Wearily.

Trapp bumbled into the chartroom ten minutes later and grinned. 'They've gone below again, mate. Maybe it weren't such a bad idea, Chang insisting on puttin' his boys aboard as well. Now Fadel an' his bunch don't know whether to watch us or the Chinee mob the closest.'

I put on a surprised expression. 'Oh? But why should Fadel be worried? I though you reckoned you'd been clever enough to convince him those Chinese were just ordinary, happy-go-lucky sailormen – despite the fact that they all eat in the saloon, as well as carry enough armament to start the third world war all on their own, of course.'

'Ahhhh, but Fadel don't think that at all. Because I very craftily let 'im see the Chineemen wus different . . . only he doesn't realize they're a part of another opportunist gang; he still thinks they're my own special boys, bodyguards sort of, which gives us a bit o' extra insurance without payin' no premium.'

'How do you know that? How do you know Fadel doesn't suspect you're intending to double-cross his boss in favour of Chang?'

'Because if 'e did then you, me an' Wullie woulda been floatin' astern wearing cement boots by now,' Trapp retorted, with a certain lack of diplomacy.

'But we wouldnae *float* wi' cement boots, Captin,' Wullie's perplexed voice drifted through from the wheelhouse.

'Shut up an' steer,' Trapp roared cheerfully. 'Anyway, mister, how could Fadel suspect a Chang take-over when I'm not even plannin' one? What's our course again?'

'Sou' west a half south,' I muttered, surrendering without a fight.

He looked at me with sly reproach. 'You mean two two zero degrees, don't yer? Proper seamen 'aven't used compass points since the Armada, mister.'

I closed my eyes, fighting the homicidal urge that threatened to overwhelm me, then opened them again and prodded the chart spitefully. 'That's where we're heading. It's called Africa, Trapp. The Independent State of Gahman to be more specific; sandwiched right in there between the borders of Libya and Egypt . . .'

'I know, I know all that.' Trapp finally wriggled with asperity. 'I'm not completely bloody ignorant. And we're not heading there much longer anyway, 'cause that's where Zarafiq expects us to deliver the cargo, an' where his bully-boy Fadel thinks we're goin' . . . until we gets there an' he discovers we ain't.'

I blinked. There were occasions when Trapp's conversation tended to become a little obscure, but I didn't need to consider his meaning too deeply; it had formed the basis for many sleepless hours over the past few days.

'Before you get us all killed,' I pleaded hopelessly for at least the fifteenth time, 'why don't you try and imagine precisely what Fadel and his gang are going to do to us when they do realize they aren't where you say we are?'

I got a certain gloomy satisfaction out of his confused expression that time, but it soon cleared and he looked all clever again.

'Ahhh, but by that time we'll be ready to offload the gear *there*, mister . . .'

His finger stubbed the chart at a desolate stretch of coastline – Egyptian, this time – between Bir Fuka and El Alamein. 'Which is where my contacts 'ave arranged to take delivery. An' once Yussuf MacKenzie an' his mad Tuaregs climb aboard, Fadel won't be given the chance ter say "Shalom".'

'Yussuf Mac*K*enzie?' I couldn't help blurting out.

' 'Is mother wus a Cairo belly dancer an' his father a Gordon Highlander.'

'Wan o' the cream,' the ever-eavesdropping Gorbals Wullie called from the wheelhouse. 'Braw lads, they Gordons. Bonnie fighters every wan. If they cannae find the enemy they get stuck intae each other, they boys . . .'

'Shut up,' prefixed Trapp before adding primly, 'Alter course to one five two degrees, quartermaster.'

'Eh?' the quartermaster echoed blankly from the other side of the bulkhead.

'Sou' east by a half east,' I translated furiously.

'Well how did ye no' say so, then?'

'Bloody ignorant Scotch savidge,' Trapp muttered.

The compass repeater over the chart table began to chatter as the ship's head altered away from Zarafiq's place of illicit business in Gahman until it steadied on Trapp's own rendezvous. Back in Egypt.

And I began to watch the door very jumpily. I had a feeling other people might notice as well, and get a bit annoyed.

'And what do we do if Fadel discovers the double-cross quicker than you think, Trapp? Like before we're under the protection of your pal MacKenzie?'

Trapp grinned in lofty derision. 'He won't. Them fellers isn't navigators like us, mister. Bloody ignorant Ayrab savidges.'

'Plus the fact that there's Chang to consider. Or had you forgotten that his representatives are aboard to ensure that you divert to his destination – which just happens to be in another country altogether, Trapp. In Libya.'

I ground to a halt as there was a movement at the door behind him but Trapp merely sniggered in outright scorn. 'The Chinees? Them heathens woul'n't know the difference if we wus ter steer 'em past Bucking'am Palace, they wouldn't. Bloody ignorant Oriental savidges.'

'Oh,' I echoed faintly. 'Then perhaps you'd better explain it to them.'

This time two Chinamen slid into the chartroom as Trapp swung anxiously. They were making no attempt to conceal the fact that they both carried guns, and both were eyeing the compass repeater pointedly.

'Quartermaster,' Trapp called without as much as a bat of an eyelid. 'Steer her a bit more accurate, dammit. Yer supposed to be on a course f'r . . . where is it, mister?'

'Libya?' I hazarded tentatively.

'That'll be . . . er . . . two three nine,' Trapp muttered, working desperately with the parallel rule.

I tried unavailingly to convert that to compass points for Wullie's benefit, but I wasn't fast enough.

'Sou' west by west a quarter west,' the foremost Chinaman translated with inscrutable expertise.

Which, apart from being a most remarkable feat for an ignorant Oriental savidge, neatly exploded yet another of Trapp's bigoted convictions. And also kicked the props from under his whole strategy of deceit.

*

Naturally it couldn't last. Trapp's master plan was collapsing in ruins; already he was fighting a losing navigational rearguard action. Every time the Chinese, or one of Fadel's Arabs, visited the bridge to check, the *Kamaran* was forced to alter course for either Zarafiq's Gahmanian destination, or Chang's Libyan rendezvous.

Each time they left the bridge Trapp would bring her back round until we were once again making painful progress towards his own offloading point in Egypt. And as he stared grimly astern at our tortured, corkscrewing wake, his mood got blacker and blacker.

Eventually I went below to my cabin. My only hope was that, if I left him up there, they would shoot him first. At least it would afford me one thrill of satisfaction before it was my turn. I even got a spiteful boost out of calling Charlie Tango Wun Fife for the second time. From now on anything I could do to screw Trapp just had to be a bonus, even if such a snide slice of self-gratification did promise to be posthumous.

Even that turned out to be as disappointing as it was vicarious. Any last-minute hopes I had cherished of the Royal Navy's intervention were dashed after I'd tried to explain to the bottom of my wardrobe that the *Kamaran* had now departed from her original Málaga course line for once and for all, and was now heading for Egypt.

Or Libya. Or the Independent Arab State of Gahman.

But North Africa, without a doubt. Oh, definitely North Africa.

For the moment . . .

Charlie Tango Wun Fife only acknowledged he'd received my pleading transmission with one word. It was a lurid but most unprocedural word, and simply established how uncouth some admirals of her Britannic Majesty's Navy could be.

Then I tried to get some sleep. But I couldn't even do that; there was no way I was going to manage that. Not with the knowledge that it was now past midnight; and that meant Second Officer Spew was keeping the watch.

For when Mister Spew was driving the ship lesser threats such as a bullet in the head held little terror. I discovered that fact the moment I eventually dragged my aching body above the level of the bridge ladder.

Just in time to see the street lamps of a whole bloody city bearing down on me at about twenty-five knots . . .

I'd actually been able to hear the music before I ever reached the bridge. It had appeared to be coming from somewhere over on our starboard side which meant that, as I was climbing the port ladder, all I could do was frown uneasily and wonder how an orchestra could possibly be playing some eighty miles off the North African coast in the middle of the night.

As the most obvious solution to the riddle sank in, so I began to run . . .

There was nobody up there, not on the port wing where I'd left Trapp ill-temperedly glowering astern a few hours earlier. I didn't hesitate to look for him; simply skidded in a frantic arc to make for the wheelhouse . . . and then stopped. Dead.

I could make out the hunched figure of Second Officer Spew lounging casually against the forward window ledge, Cyclopean gaze directed vaguely towards the bows somewhere. I could also see there was only an empty space behind the wheel where the helmsman *should* have been, which meant that we were either running on auto-pilot or, as seemed accepted practice on Trapp's commands, whoever should have been on watch had simply got fed up with steering and gone back to bed. I could also view – quite clearly through the side windows – the ever-advancing source of that noctural rhythm.

It was huge. No, it wasn't; it was bloody monstrous! A great, rearing blaze of light thundering directly towards us like a runaway maritime power station playing rock and roll . . . Rows of twinkling portholes; cascades of gaily sparkling fairy bulbs; even the strolling figures of jolly, fun-seeking voyagers clear as the scars on Mister Spew's face . . .

. . . I lunged for the wheel in terror, screaming, 'She's crossing from starboard to port, Spew. We're the *give-way ship*, f'r God's sake . . . !'

Slowly, almost wearily, the *Kamaran* came round as twenty

thousand tons of rampaging accident roared across our bows like a berserk steamroller. I saw her own bow wave smashing into, rumbling clear across our fo'c'sle as we shied away; felt the whole ship leaning against the pull of the turn; glimpsed the rows of suddenly white faces gazing down at us from the steel cliff which kept on passing and passing, and still bloody passing . . .

. . . and then she was gone. Swallowed by the night as a fast receding glow and a fading reminder of how quickly death can take a sailorman even without the provocation offered by Trapp.

'That ship,' I eventually managed to whisper to the still-immobile and relaxed figure of our second officer. 'That was a twenty-thousand-ton cruise liner you nearly had us in collision with, mister.'

Only then did Second Officer Spew stir, and turn to fix me with his one good eye revealing a certain mystification.

'Yeah, Mister Cooper . . .' said Mister Spew blankly, but with a most earnest desire for enlightenment. '. . . an' what ship wus that, then?'

'Five 'undred million Chineemen in the world,' Trapp muttered petulantly a few minutes later, 'an' I has to get the one who can navigate!'

I didn't argue. There was no way you could argue with Trapp when it came to prejudice. Apart from which I was still having difficulty in speaking at all after Mister Spew's latest demonstration of how to sink yourself without really noticing.

'Which course is yous wantin' me tae steer now?' Gorbals Wullie called huffily from the wheelhouse. It had been my turn this time: to kick him all the way back to his place of duty from where I'd discovered him at the galley coffee pot, with a warning that if he ever left the wheel again without being formally relieved, then I personally would ensure he ate his own insanitary bloody hat – razor blades an' all.

'You got any o' them clever-dick Chineemen through there?' Trapp yelled nastily.

There was a moment of silence, then Wullie's voice came back. 'No! No, there's none o' they up here . . .'

'Then steer f'r Egypt, stupid. To MacKenzie's place like you already been told.'

'But, Captin . . .'

'Shut up!'

Trapp snatched for the log and began to scrawl the latest sequence of course alterations. By now there had been so many it looked like the journal of a wartime convoy steering a zigzag to confuse submarines. I wasn't too happy about the casual way he left it lying around, either.

'You know that log book alone is enough to earn us a throat cutting, don't you?' I growled bitterly. 'Anyone with half an idea of navigation could lay off precisely where we're really heading in two minutes flat.'

'An' you just heard Wullie,' Trapp countered irritably. 'There ain't no Chinees up here jus' now.'

'Fadel can't be all that far away. He'd have to be deaf, dumb and thick as Dan'l Spew not to have noticed when we tried to torpedo that liner back there.'

'Him?' Trapp jeered contemptuously. 'You think I'm bothered about the Ayrabs, mister? I told you before, they woul'n't know the difference between the Mediterranean an' a bucket o' water. They ain't civilized like you an' me, you know; they're jus' ignorant bloody . . .'

'. . . savages, Captain?' Fadel finished from the chartroom doorway.

'Well, I *tried* tae tell ye,' Wullie justified desperately from the other side of the bulkhead. 'And anyway, ye never asked me aboot Arabs, did ye?'

'Writing up your deck log, Captain Trapp?' Fadel asked with dangerous calm.

'Ohhhh shit,' I whispered. With hopeless fatalism.

'Jus' routine seamanship,' Trapp hurriedly dismissed the question, trying too late to shove the dog-eared book in the nearest drawer. 'Of course it's all scientific. Complicated like, unless you've 'ad speshul trainin' . . . wouldn't be of no use to someone like you . . .'

86

Fadel gently took the log from Trapp's hand as his companion placed a large revolver barrel beside Trapp's starboard ear. 'Oh, I don't know,' the Arab leader purred. 'I have dabbled a little in navigational theory myself from time to time.'

'When?' Trapp squeezed out almost pleadingly, while I became aware of a chilling premonition that yet another of Trapp's opinions was about to founder. Punctured, probably; by a ·45 bullet. 'When could an ignor . . . a gentleman such as yerself ever 'ave the chance to do somethin' as clever as navigashun?'

But diplomacy never had been Trapp's strong point. Not any more than humility, or the ability to keep up with a rapidly changing world.

'Could you bring yourself to believe they allowed me to do a little when I was sailing as chief officer aboard P & O passenger liners?' Fadel tendered, reaching for the dividers and the chart. 'In fact I spent some twenty-odd years as a deck officer in British ships before Mister Zarafiq was kind enough to offer me a more lucrative and enterprising position . . .'

'Ohhhh, shit!' I repeated, and began to watch the door longingly for the first indication of the arrival of the reserves in the repellent forms of Gorbals Wullie and Second Officer Spew – as yet noticeable only by their absence.

Fadel didn't take very long, not even two minutes. Yet he was still smiling even as he turned back to face us, and suddenly his curious good humour all made spine-tingling sense.

'Now I really *can* kill you, Captain,' he said, and there was satisfaction in the bleak eyes. 'Mister Zarafiq promised I would be permitted to kill you eventually . . . in return for this.'

I watched his hand move downwards, caressing the crippled arm, and finally understood a little more clearly why he hated Trapp so much. Mind you most people did after they'd met him; if it hadn't been for the imminent curtailment of my own future I could easily have been on Fadel's side even then.

But Trapp quickly regained his own composure. In fact already he looked more outraged than apprehensive, more injured than guilty. 'You mean in the Channel that time?'

The scorn in his voice actually made Fadel blink doubtfully as he carried on, 'Christ, but I di'n't do no more than shoot you up a bit, did I? An' you still got one arm left, 'aven't you? So it's not like you wus as bad off as Spew who don't have hardly nothin' that works, is it . . . Anyway, Fadel, I resent your insinuashun that I'm breaking my word with Mister Z; you ain't got one good reason to suggest I'd do a dishonest thing like that . . .'

I felt my own jaw drop, but it didn't matter. There was such conviction, such indignation in Trapp's outburst that even I was beginning to wonder who was misjudging whom. Suddenly it was Fadel on the defensive, angry and confused all at the same time.

'Your courses,' he snarled back, slamming his hand on the chart. 'They are like the wanderings of a camel from a poisoned water hole. To Gahman at first, yes . . . but then towards Libya. And then suddenly back to Egypt. And then Gahman once more . . . but then Libya again . . . and Gahman and Libya and *Egypt* . . .'

'You tellin' me I ain't able ter navigate . . . ?' Trapp bellowed, the lid of his cap bouncing up and down in peevish indignation. 'You tellin' me I been steering the wrong courses jus' because you reckon twenty years onna P an' O boat qualifies yer to be a *proper* bloody sailorman, Fadel . . . ?'

It was ridiculous, like some lunatic black comedy with each of them screaming epithets at each other while the second Arab stood uncertainly behind Trapp, still holding the gun underneath the violently bobbing headgear but unsure now of whether to shoot an' the hell with his leader's personal ambitions, or let Trapp explode anyway as his apoplexy passed safety point . . . or simply to retire to the wheelhouse to guard Spew and Gorbals Wullie – still apparently remaining discreetly under cover while the two main protagonists in this obscure navigational contretemps devastated each other with technical broadsides.

Then I saw his finger nervously toying with the trigger, and realized he was inclining towards the first and most practical option of all – to blow Trapp's stubborn skull clean off his shoulders – and felt sick with fear and unaccountably sad, all at the same time.

Not that Trapp appeared to bother even then.

'You taken magnetic an' not true courses f'r a start, you dry-land bloody Dervish. An' then you ain't allowed for deviation, 'ave yer? Nor variashun . . . an' wot about compensatin' f'r tides an' leeway an' that . . .'

Fadel's features were as suffused as Trapp's. He waved the brass dividers in a furious spiral. 'You take me for a fool, dung of a *fellahin* donkey? You consider me an apprentice on his first day at sea?'

'APPRENTICE!' Trapp boiled. 'I seen apprentices with more brains than you bein' sent for bucketfuls o' steam, dammit! I seen 'em twice as clever as you yet still daft enough ter go lookin' in the bosun's store f'r green oil f'r the starboard lamp, Aladdin . . .'

'Kill him . . . !' Fadel spat in uncontrollable rage. 'Kill this spawn of a Cairo whore!'

Even as I gathered myself for a crazy, suicidal leap I knew it was too late, that I could never get there in time. Already the second Arab's finger was white on the trigger; the barrel of the gun behind Trapp's ear beginning to cock slightly, pulling upwards under the pressure of the coming death.

. . . until, without any warning, a very odd thing occurred.

When Trapp took all the steam out of the dispute by remarking, mildly and disarmingly, 'Hang on a minnit, lads. Well I never. Well, well, well, I'd never 'ave believed it . . .'

And abruptly the pressure on the trigger had eased unwittingly as the gunman leaned forward frowning, intently surveying the area of the chart where Trapp's grubby finger now indicated.

'Kill him!' Fadel snarled again. 'The pig attempted to divert me once before . . .'

'Oh, don't be so bloody intense,' Trapp reproved him with an even more disconcerting and good-humoured tolerance. Ever so casually he eased the dividers from Fadel's unwary grasp and tapped the chart with the points of them.

'Well, well,' he remarked again. 'Good grief. Well, well, well . . .'

Reversing the dividers he began to drum the table top pensively with the top hinge. Now the slender points were vertical, directed towards the deckhead above. He sniffed thoughtfully, raising his left hand to scratch his head; then he dropped that hand and fiddled a bit more with the dividers, tapping an absent rhythm as he scrutinized the chart minutely.

Then his head got itchy again and he began to raise his other hand, this time the one holding the dividers.

''Ere, you look at this then, Abdul . . .' he encouraged the second Arab in a most friendly and confidential way. Not that the position of the gun behind his ear varied in the slightest; the potential executioner's only reaction being to crane his head slightly farther forward over Trapp's shoulder in a reflex attempt to see better.

And then it happened . . .

I was already diving for Fadel as he began to reach desperately for his own gun. 'Shoot quickly, FOOL . . .' he screamed as both he, and I, and maybe for one split second of horror, the second Arab too realized that Trapp's hand – still holding that shiny and so innocuous tool of the navigator's trade – wasn't going to stop to scratch his head at all . . .

. . . when its lazy, preoccupied rise abruptly accelerated to a vicious flashing arc which only completed its travel when the needle-sharp points entered the gunman's staring eye with hideous precision.

Chapter Eight

It wasn't simply the prospect of our immediate free-for-all which concerned me as I finally hurled myself towards Fadel. No, I'd long ago accepted that, when you associated with Trapp, you invited that sort of headlong rush into disaster as a matter of routine.

Only events never managed to end at that; in straight-forward homicidal chaos. Not when Trapp was involved. Somehow he had the uncanny knack of converting every simple, localized crisis into a full-scale bloody cataclysm which invariably embraced everyone else within pistol shot. He'd done that in the war – started off in a small way until his ideas got bigger and greedier, and eventually finished up taking on half Rommel's Afrika Korps as well as most of the German Navy because there was a chance of greater profit in it . . . but that was my other story; my other nightmare.

This was the present. While Trapp had just poked an Arab in the eye with a brass spear. And that Arab had a lot of very nasty friends . . .

I heard someone roaring in fright, '*Spew . . . WULLIE! F'r God's sake help us . . .*' as my shoulder hit Fadel low behind the knees. And then his Luger went off with an explosion which singed the back of my neck, and the terrified appeal got louder until I recognized my own voice . . .

. . . then my hysteria and Fadel's now unrestrained hatred and Trapp's bawling invective became overwhelmed by a steadily rising shriek as the second Arab skittered in demented circles on the deck, fluttering bloodied hands clawing at the glinting protrusion from his skull like a spitted, grounded butterfly.

'*Spew . . . WULLIEEEEE . . . !*'

The gun went off again, deafening in the confined space,

just before I caught a fleeting image of Trapp staring, purple-faced and outraged, as his already appalling cap sailed through the air with a perfectly rounded and cindered bullet hole clean through the peak of it.

'That does it,' he screamed. 'That bloody does it then. Shootin' people's one thing, but gratituous dammige ter property's another soddin' ball game altergether . . .'

Then I saw his face, and knew that typical and black over-reaction to the irrelevant was merely a front; that Trapp's fury was generated by a passion much deeper, much more complex than a mere Luger round through his hat.

Still no Spew . . . still no Gorbals Wullie! Where the hell were they?

Trapp literally fell upon Fadel, fists and feet flailing in a blur of malevolence. The gun was still there though, still pumping shots automatically under the pressure of the Arab's startled clutch. The clock on the bulkhead disintegrated in a shower of tinkling fragments; the chart reared from the table as a furrow smashed a supersonic course from Sicily across to Mers el Kebir . . . the screeching horror of the skewered gunman rose a further octave when his kneecap blew away in a gory fuzz – and then mercifully and abruptly terminated altogether as the succeeding round took him neatly through the left temple.

The barrel swung wildly and laid itself directly at *me*. I lashed out in undisciplined panic and caught Fadel a glancing blow on his injured arm. He stumbled back in agony under the joint onslaught, stubbed his heel against the inert corpse of his associate, and finally went down like a felled tree.

But Trapp hadn't finished. I could only stare blankly in that following moment as he kicked viciously at Fadel's head then began to stamp brutally, maniacally on his fallen adversary's already mutilated limb. Then Fadel was screaming instead; writhing and retching and screaming . . .

. . . I hauled Trapp away. 'TRAPP! F'r God's *sake*, Trapp, there's no need for more. No need to kill him too . . .'

Trapp glared at me murderously, yet there was a sort of vague contempt there too; I remembered over a quarter of a century ago when I'd watched that same look – the eyes of the other Edward Trapp, bitter and unforgiving – only they'd been directed over the sights of a heavy machinegun then, and laid on a lifeboat full of pleading women and children . . .

'But there is, mister,' he snarled with a cold venom which frightened me far more than any rage or passion. 'I 'ad three little Pakistanis once. On a boat in the English Channel. They wus my responsibility; my contract f'r delivery – yet that bastard cut their throats. Sliced their bloody windpipes jus' because they wus in the way, an' 'cause they 'ad a few gold trinkets . . .'

He booted Fadel, and Fadel screamed again. I picked up Fadel's Luger from the deck and pointed it at him tiredly.

'Do that again, Trapp, and I'll blow your fucking head off.'

A foreign voice shouted from a long way away, somewhere aft on the boat deck. Then another, and the clatter of running feet approaching, but Trapp didn't move for a moment.

Then he kicked Fadel once more; very deliberately. The Arab whimpered, and was sick, and finally retched into unconsciousness. Trapp smiled. It was a reckless, wolfish smile.

'Then you'd better pull that trigger quick, Number One,' he said mockingly, while listening to the fast closing sounds of danger. 'It seems like there's a few more wi' the same idea.'

I handed him the gun and walked through into the darkened wheelhouse without another word. I knew he was right, and that it could only be a matter of seconds before we both died anyway, very violently from either an Arab or a Chinese bullet. Even if the *Kamaran*'s crew did stand with us – and I doubted if any of them would – it still wouldn't save us now. From past experience Trapp had made bloody sure none of them owned any weapon more long range than a marline spike or a cut-throat razor, while all we possessed were the two surplus Arab pistols. Even then the Luger must be nearly empty.

Against a double squad of professional killers; one trio of whom would obliterate us as soon as they discovered their leader was *hors de combat* by the grace of Trapp, and the other group who wouldn't waste a lot of execution time either once they checked the *Kamaran*'s deck log against Mister

Chang's pre-paid course instructions.

There was only one person in the wheelhouse – Gorbals Wullie. I could see his eyes following me like a hypnotized rabbit's from where he crouched behind the wheel. I could also make out the somnolent form of Mister Spew leaning in what appeared to be an excessively casual manner over the far side bridge front, staring down into the sea below, but I ignored him; my time promised to be a bit limited, but by God I was going to use it to full advantage.

Purposefully I started to move towards Wullie, hands outstretched in anticipation. He seemed to shrink even more; wizened, ferrety features an apprehensive white blob in the darkness.

'Ah'm awfy glad tae see yous is all ri . . . er . . . Here, ah've been steerin' a braw course f'r you, Mister Miller, sir . . .'

'Come here, you gutless, dried-up little bastard, you,' I called wheedlingly. 'I'm gonna kill you, thistle head! I'm gonna tear your bloody arms out've their scrofulous sockets an' then I'm gonna beat you to death with 'em, you yellow-livered, spineless Scotch ferret . . .'

'But ah'm a tiger, sir,' Wullie protested weakly. 'You ask the captin – when ah gets ma dander up then ah'm a real tiger at the fisticuffs, honest tae God, sir. An' wi' the boots an' the razor . . . an' the heid an' the bottle an' the brass knucklies, so ah am . . .'

'You're nothing but a bagpipeful of wind. You are a cretinous, useless, conscienceless quitter. You could maybe have jumped Fadel back there; just taken him in the chartroom from behind – for Trapp's sake if not for mine, dammit. You must have heard me calling, only you were too bloody chicken-hearted to help, weren't you? And *that's* why I'm gonna punch the porridge out've you, sailor. Now!'

I drew my fist back enjoyably; there was just enough time left. The only problem seemed to be that Gorbals Wullie, terrified as he obviously was, still managed to produce a sly expression of injured outrage.

'And ah wis wantin' tae get stuck in, sir, ah swear it! Och but ma fists wis fair itchin' tae get tore intae they Arab lads

94

an' save you and the captin, so they were. But ah couldn't, sir; ma sense o' duty an' . . . an' discipline, sir, just forced me tae stay here at ma post, sir. Just fightin' back ma true desires because of ma orders, sir.'

I held my fist in suspension and blinked. 'Orders? Whose orders, dammit?'

'Yours of course, Mister Miller, sir,' the frustrated tiger averred with the martyrdom of a truly misunderstood hero. 'Do ye no' remember what ye said ye'd dae to me if I ever left the wheel again wi'oot a proper relief?'

Then a Chinaman with a gun appeared at the starboard door; and an Arab with a gun appeared at the port door . . . and I gathered it was going to be largely academic as to who actually did kill Gorbals Wullie within the next ten seconds. Immediately after me.

Trapp. Now where the hell was *Trapp*?

Another four Chinamen arrived, and two more Arabs. We finally had a full house of heavies, all hesitating and peering through the unaccustomed darkness to discover where the trouble was, and who to shoot.

Only then did Trapp make his overdue appearance, framed in the light from the chartroom door; but again he'd altered disconcertingly. Now, in stark contrast to his earlier fury, he seemed confused and upset; a shipmaster driven to distraction by the perfidy of man.

'Oh my God . . .' he shouted hysterically. 'Ohhhh *God* but they're hi-jackin' the ship. Stealin' my *cargo*, d'ye hear? It's piracy, lads . . . piracy on the high seas . . .'

I stared at him for yet another moment of incredulity, conscious of a strange disappointment – almost contempt – for the way his courage had finally deserted him. Until I remembered that the theatrical, distraught apparition was Trapp.

I began to dive for the deck, dragging a slower-on-the-uptake Gorbals Wullie in a dumbfounded heap beside me, just as the first Arab fired – straight through the wheelhouse and towards the only conceivable reasons for such an accusation.

Whereupon the startled Chinese instantly replied in kind, motivated by the equally certain assumption that Mister

Chang's investment had finally become the target for that anticipated Middle Eastern counter-heist.

So naturally Zarafiq's men fired again. And then the Chinese. And the sole surviving Arab . . . and the last Chinaman . . .

And suddenly it seemed very quiet. Like being in a tomb, during a rest period.

Gingerly I sat up. Shards of broken glass tinkled to the deck as I felt myself for holes while taking in the details of bullet-riddled door frames blocked by similarly punctured and bloodied corpses, and the gaping glassless windows and the shot-scarred wheel. Behind me Trapp stirred too, lifting his head cautiously from where he'd nose-dived at the commence-ment of inter-gang hostilities; then he absently began kicking Gorbals Wullie out of what promised to be a permanently fear-induced state of catalepsy while, at the same time and to my intense satisfaction, looking uncharacteristically subdued.

'You've done it now,' I said firmly, uncompromisingly. 'Oh, you've gone far too bloody far this time, Trapp.'

There were shifty movements from the doorways as the *Kamaran*'s gallant complement gathered now that the shooting appeared to have ended. More and more of their dissipated faces hung suspended in the darkness until there was a sudden stir in the starboard press of ogling bystanders and Mister Spew shambled casually into the wheelhouse, matter-of-factly sidestepping the splayed Chinese cadavers and surveying the aftermath of Trapp's subtlety.

''Allo, 'allo,' Mister Spew greeted us, his one almost-good eye rotating in its socket like an interested ball-bearing. 'Did somethin' happen then? While I wus out doin' me duty on the bridge wing.'

I stared at him. While I thought I knew the answer I still had to ask. Just to make quite sure.

'Didn't you hear anything?' I managed eventually. 'Weren't you aware of anything occurring through here, less than fifteen feet away from you, that seemed just a tiny bit . . . well . . . odd? A little bit noisy?'

His eyebrows met in a ferocious vee as he creakily lifted his one good arm to scratch the back of his skull while trying painfully to think all the way back to four minutes ago. Then his expression cleared as he managed to remember.

'Ahhhhh, but I wus usin' me eye, then, Mister Cooper,' he pronounced with unshakeable logic. 'To watch f'r ships an' that, jus' like you said. And when I'm usin' me *eye*, then you can't possibly expect . . . well . . .'

'No,' I agreed. Because the worrying thing was that it didn't seem odd any more; almost natural somehow, aboard the *Kamaran*. 'No, Mister Spew, I suppose it would be most unreasonable of me to expect your *ears* to work as well. Not at the same time as you're using your eye . . .'

And then I went below to my cabin. And cried for the first time in thirty bloody years.

Trapp, of course, just had to follow me down some twenty minutes later. By that time I'd regained my composure, yet he still seemed uneasy, positively morbid in fact. That didn't prevent me from being spiteful, though.

'Well?' I snapped. 'How's Fadel since you tried to kick him to death?'

'Very quiet,' retorted Trapp, and sighed.

'It's a wonder,' I growled.

'Not really; not seein' Choker Bligh hit 'im over the head wi' a monkey wrench soon as he came round,' Trapp supplemented absently. Then he caught the expression on my face and added hurriedly, ''E's OK now! Choker's made him nice an' comfy down aft in the paint store. He's a tough desert bird, that Fadel.'

'What about the rest of the Arabs you shot?'

'It wus the Chineemen shot the Ayrabs,' Trapp corrected carefully. 'Or most of 'em, at least. Anyhow they're all dead as Tutankhamun except for Fadel.'

He saw me still eyeing him and added with a brief flash of self-righteous spirit, 'Well all I did wus to suggest the ship was bein' hi-jacked, didn't I? I mean I di'n't ackshully say to shoot at each other, did I? And I can't help it if them yo-yo's all jumped to the wrong conclusion, can I . . . ?'

'And the Chinese,' I persisted wearily. 'All passed away too, I suppose?'

He wriggled uncomfortably and looked meek. Too bloody meek.

'I wus . . . ah . . . goin' to mention them. The Chineemen.'

'The Chinee – the Chinamen?'

'Yeah. The ones what got themselves shot . . . by the Ayrabs.'

I tried to stay calm. By God, but I did try very hard to stay calm.

'What about the Chinamen? Are you trying to tell me something I don't know, Trapp? About Mister Chang's Chinamen?'

'I jus' made a radio-telephone call. To Grockle the Fink back in Hong Kong. Cost a king's ransom, it did; all that talkin' at three, four dollars a minnit . . .'

'The Chinamen. NOW!'

Trapp glowered at me resentfully. 'Well how wus I supposed to know . . . ? That Grockle, he said everybody knows about Chang an 'is boys, but I been outa the social whirl f'r a bit, 'aven't I? So how could I know them Oriental chop sueys had a bit of an arrangement on the side; a bit on top of their respectable, day-ter-day villainy . . . ?'

'WHAT *ABOUT* THE BLOODY CHINAMEN?'

'Well, Grockle says Chang's gotta contract with 'em,' he expanded hastily. 'To provide a sort o' part-time heavy mob f'r special delicate jobs – an' this was one of 'em.'

'Contract? Contract with who?'

'The CIA, o' course!' Trapp, suddenly impatient, stared at me in lofty disgust. 'Christ, but everybody knows *that*, mister . . . that Chang's boys aboard this ship was workin' for the United States Governmint. Before they got themselves shot, anyway – by Ayrabs.'

Trapp got peeved at my reaction eventually; glowering like a misunderstood child. But with him attack invariably afforded the best means of defence.

'All right, so what's Zarafiq up to, then? You tell me that, eh. I mean why's he involved with Chang an' the CIA? And if he is, then how does he hope ter get away wi' it – defraudin' the insurance companies? Jus' you tell me that, mister.'

'It's like declaring war,' I was still muttering dazedly, reflecting on how Trapp had disposed of what might have been five part-time CIA employees with one master stroke. '. . . Like declaring war on the United States of bloody America!'

'And why,' Trapp continued, pursuing his own deliberations with growing irritability, 'why are them CIA's so bloody interested in this ship anyway? And Chang, come to that. I could understand if he wus tryin' to pirate some other fixer's gear, but he ain't – *I'm* supposed to be doin' that for 'im – so if Grockle's right, which 'e always is, what's the real connection between Zarafiq, Chang an' them American secret services?'

It was my turn to shuffle guiltily, because I'd just remembered I wasn't exactly being square with him either; but that only made the riddle even more confusing for me – *I* knew the British Government were more than interested in the *Kamaran*'s future too. But why? Why go to all the trouble of infiltrating me aboard, simply for a cargo of bulldozers and picks and shovels?

'Why go to all this trouble,' Trapp deliberated morosely, telepathically, 'jus' for a cargo of bulldozers an' picks an' bloody shov . . .'

. . . and then we'd suddenly stared at each other for a long, long time. Before we began to run . . .

At three o'clock in the morning I stood beside Trapp on the *Kamaran*'s foredeck, and gazed silently into the now exposed depths of number three hold.

Gorbals Wullie was with us, and so were Second Officer Spew and Choker Bligh and a persistently oil-leaking Chief Engineer Maabud somethin' or other. All every bit as quiet and thoughtful.

And then, still without a word, we shambled in line ahead

formation to scrutinize the contents of number two.

Followed by . . . number one hold. Right forward under the break of the fo'c'sle. We'd opened that up too.

With her engine stopped the *Kamaran* rolled uneasily, rather nervously, under the northerly swell while the cargo clusters at the crosstrees threw eerie, restless shadows which seemed to be reaching out for us; snatching at us with threatening, greedy talons. They gave plenty of light to pick out every detail of the huge and crouching bulldozers lashed along the well deck, yet even then we couldn't see what we'd been looking for. In fact there didn't appear to be another item of earthmoving plant aboard. Not a pick, not a shovel, not a pair of rubber boots. Not in any one of the twenty-odd packing cases we'd broken open so far.

Though there were other things, mind you. Lots of other things to stare at.

Like rows of grease-glittering Soviet Simonov Semi-automatic SKS Carbines; and quite a number of Kalashnikov PKS Heavy Machineguns; and piles of shiny little Czecho-slovakian 7·62mm pistols; and cases and cases of associated ammunition, as well as Polish anti-personnel grenades and East German manufactured land mines . . .

'Oh well,' I muttered eventually, consolingly. 'You may have sold the wrong stuff to your Tuareg pal; and signed your own slow death warrant on behalf of Mister Chang; as well as committing what is already, in the eyes of international law, piracy on the high seas. To say nothing of what amounts to declaring open hostilities against the United States of America . . . but at least Zarafiq can't accuse you of diverting his buckets and spades after this, Trapp. You most definitely aren't guilty of doing a silly, dangerous thing like that.'

He eyed me cautiously.

'No?'

I smiled tolerantly, shaking my head. 'Good Lord, no. Because, you see, all you've actually managed to do, old man, is to . . . well . . . to . . .'

And that was the moment when I began to shout. I couldn't help it, but I began to bawl at the top of my voice right there in the middle of the Mediterranean Sea. Loud enough for even Mister Spew to hear, and stare in one-eyed admiration all at the same time.

'. . . to steal the weapons of a whole fucking army, Trapp. An' that whole fuckin' army's gonna be FUCKIN' *FURIOUS* . . . !'

Chapter Nine

I used the concealed radio as soon as my fury had subsided to a burning resentment, and this time I didn't waste time talking to the hired hand; I demanded to speak directly to whoever the hell was running this goddamned lash-up . . . to Admiral Charlie Tango Wun Fife or whatever he called himself.

There was a tight-lipped silence across the ether, and then a gruff voice snapped, 'Watchdog – this is Charlie Tango Control. Pass your message.'

'News from the front,' I said coldly. 'Would you believe Mister Zarafiq's ploughshares appear to have turned themselves into very embarrassing swords?'

He didn't seem surprised. But then again neither was I that he wasn't – if you see what I mean. Because it simply confirmed what I was already finding out for myself; that there were a few minor omissions in the briefing they'd given me back in Hong Kong.

'Report your present course and speed, Watchdog.'

'I don't know and I don't care,' I retorted. 'I've resigned, Admiral. I'm not playing any more.'

The voice from the bottom of my wardrobe growled ominously, 'Say again, Watchdog?'

'You conned me into signing on with Naval Intelligence. You knew perfectly well that I wouldn't have been an outside runner for this bloody job if I'd suspected Trapp was even remotely involved; far less volunteering to sail as first mate with him aboard a crazy-ship full've pistol-packing Oriental G-Men and drop-outs from Al Fatah or whatever . . . Plus a crew of one-eyed hulks an' weirdos an' ocean-going freaks, currently sailing in ever-decreasing circles 'cause Captain Trapp up there's ungraciously coming to terms with the fact that he doesn't have a clue about what to do next . . .'

'Do?'

I halted for breath as Charlie Tango Control spoke precisely; commandingly. 'Then you must ensure that he continues his voyage. It is imperative that the *Kamaran*'s cargo should reach its original destination.'

'*Which* original destination?' I queried bitterly, forgetting temporarily that I'd already resigned.

'Zarafiq's. The *Kamaran* must reach Gahman at all costs . . . I say again, Watchdog – the *Kamaran* must offload her cargo at Zarafiq's original destination.'

'Oh, no.' I shook my head violently at the invisible admiral. 'We've got the hottest an' most lethal collection of armament aboard since the D-Day landings, yet I still don't know who they're consigned to; nor why the CIA are apparently working directly against the British Government . . . nor why Zarafiq ever trusted Trapp in the first place if his arms are so bloody important. Or why, come to that, your Royal Navy is so damn keen to ensure that communist-manufactured munitions are smuggled into what I always understood was a pro-Western Arab state . . .'

'Your Royal Navy too, Watchdog.' The admiral's tone had an edge to it now. 'I would remind you that you come under the Naval Discipline Act, and that the penalties for disobeying a command are most rigorous. Please remember that.'

'You haven't answered my questions again,' I snarled. 'You keep avoiding my bloody questions, mister . . .'

'This is an open radio transmission,' Charlie Tango Control boomed irately. 'You have already broken every security rule in the book, man. I cannot, and will not, communicate highly classified information by these insecure means . . .'

'SCREW your regulations!' I roared in fury then, remembering where I was, dragged my voice down to a more discreet level of offensiveness. 'An' you can take your orders, Admiral, and stu . . .'

'Just do it, Watchdog. Just make certain that the *Kamaran*'s cargo reaches Gahman or, by God, I'll ensure that you never enter another British port or sail aboard another British ship again. There are no options in this assignment, which you willingly accepted – which means that even if you can't stand the heat, mister, you still stay in the blasted kitchen. Over . . . and out.'

And that was . . . well . . . that. I'd only learned one more thing; that if I didn't do precisely as I was told, then I might as well stay with Trapp and the rest of his maritime nomads until the inevitable occurred and they all either hanged, drowned or argued each other to death. I would be a pariah too. Stateless. A refugee from the Royal Naval Discipline Act.

I kicked the wardrobe a few times, then perversely began to feel better. At least I did have an objective, now; and as a heavily disguised Bert Cooper – who would miraculously disappear on the completion of this trip – had no retribution to fear from either Chang or Tuareg MacKenzie or even the CIA . . . All I had to do was gently to guide an already confused and uncertain Trapp's thinking along the Zarafiq course of righteousness and I would be free . . .

. . . until Trapp stormed in, with his face as black as thunder and a mood to match.

And growled savagely, 'I come to a decision, mister. It'll cost a bob or two in sacrifice, so 'elp me, but it's the only way ter keep us clear of all them vindictive bastids at the same time . . .

'. . . so you get Spew an' Bligh to swing them boats out, chop, chop. An' then come below to give me a hand – I'm settin' charges down there to blow this bucket clean out've the water. In just over an hour from now.'

I tried, but it was hopeless. Attempting to get Trapp to change his mind once it was made up was like asking a pyramid to move over to save steering your camel around it. Apart from which he was probably right on this particular occasion – if you considered his reasoning from an unprejudiced viewpoint, and didn't face the wrath of the Naval Discipline Act the moment the *Kamaran* slid beneath the waves.

I continued the argument right up to the minute when he showed me the first explosive in the cable locker – placed, I gathered, by Zarafiq's technical branch before she sailed from Port Said in preparation for a very expensive insurance bang. There were five more to activate – two in the engine room, two distributed along the shaft tunnel, and one right aft in the tiller flat; enough to scuttle her in seconds even in her originally anticipated and empty condition. Now, with a few thousand tons of cargo still remaining, she'd go down like a portion of Choker Bligh's plum duff.

'Look,' I persisted desperately, 'all you'll do if you sink her now is throw away the balance of the money Zarafiq owes you on completion. Why not deliver to Gahman first and then scuttle like your original contract stipulates?'

I could see his eyes misting at the thought of all that money being sacrificed, but he still shook his head fiercely. ' 'Cause if there's one bastard I hates more than Chang, it's that fairy Zarafiq, mister. An' no way am I goin' ter put a smile on either o' their faces by deliverin' what they must both need pretty bad . . .'

Then he hesitated, and there was a look on his face I hoped I would never see if his thoughts turned to me. 'Apart from which I'm goin' to kill Zarafiq. I made a sort o' promise, once . . . an' I can't part 'is cable if Chang or Taureg MacKenzie catches up wi' me first, see?'

And that was when I knew with a chilling certainty that Mister Zarafiq really was doomed. Which made him just like me.

'But Chang and MacKenzie will still be after you, dammit! Whatever you do they aren't going to get the cargo you promised . . . and the CIA won't be too fond of you either, now they seem to be involved.'

'They won't try an' find me all that hard. Not if they thinks the *Kamaran* wus lost in a genuine accident . . . the Chinees is like that, with a funny sense o' fair play; while the Yanks won't risk no more publicity than necessary. Tuareg MacKenzie won't want no part of a cargo like that anyway – he's jus' a small-time operator when it comes ter arms an' stuff.'

'An accident?' I sneered, fast running out of logic. 'You call it an accident, Trapp. Blowing the bottom out've her with half a ton of plastic explosive.'

'Now you're nit-picking at technicalities – an' anyway, who's to tell 'em?' he asked cleverly.

'Fadel, f'r a start.'   .

'He won't be able to,' Trapp said, looking sad. 'The poor, helpless bastard's got hisself trapped in the paint store with no chance of gettin' to the boats.'

'No, he hasn't.'

'He bloody will have done. By the time the ship sinks.'

I didn't dare to argue any longer. That expression was back in his eyes, and there were times when even I had learned to bend before the vengeance of Trapp. Fadel was as good as dead anyway; as doomed as Mister Zarafiq – I wasn't aware of the precise story, even now, but I did know they'd both contracted their fatal illness some time ago, when the throats of three obscure Pakistanis were cut.

'Just get on with it,' Trapp growled, hauling a handful of pencil-shaped objects out of his pocket. 'These are the detonators they give me an' they're all I got . . . .You own a watch, do you?'

I nodded peevishly; it was sheer luck that, so far, none of the crew had managed to steal it. Trapp began to unscrew the fusing mechanism in the casing with the ease of a man practised in the art of blowing things up.

'Good. Well this is a mechanical thingummyjig – once it's wound up we got exactly one hour afore it triggers that relay there . . . an' that makes the circuit from that battery there. An' then that little gilhicky flashes up the boiler, so ter speak . . .'

'All right, all right,' I muttered. 'What d'you want me to do?'

He clipped the first detonator into its housing and started to connect various wires, tongue sticking out in concentration. 'This'll take a while an' I don't want the bows ter start blowin' up while I'm still riggin' the after end. You wait 'ere; gimme ten minnits' head-start, and then wind up the timers quick as you can. One full turn clockwise, mister . . . then head f'r the boats.'

'No distress call? To make sure we're picked up? Which, incidentally, brings me to the small matter of how you're intending to persuade the authorities that the ship actually sank a long way north of here, seeing she should still be on a course line for Spain instead of Africa?'

'That's precisely why we ain't sending no mayday, mister. Because we sank yesterday, didn't we? So sudden there weren't even time ter get them poor Ayrab an' Chinee passengers off . . . which also accounts for the time it took for that northerly wind to set our boats south – like to this present position.'

'I still think you're making a mist . . .'

'Ten minnits,' he said pointedly. 'Or I'll send Dan'l Spew down to 'elp. An' he's more likely to set the bombs off there an' then, trying to make sure 'e does somethin' right f'r a change, seein' you keep on destroyin' his confidence like you do . . .'

He'd vanished before I could think up a suitable reply.

There was only me left now. Me, and the bomb.

I deliberately delayed a little longer than Trapp's specified ten minutes before I commenced my own task. I didn't want to catch up with him before he'd completed priming the devices. For one thing I knew that if I did – after having clambered awkwardly along the length of the ship's belly via the engine-room and the oil-slippery shaft tunnel – I'd have been more than tempted to have applied one additional clockwise revolution . . . to Trapp's stubborn bloody neck. While for another I'd finally made up my mind to . . .

. . . but then, just as I arrived at the last charge, the lights in the tiller flat went out as someone cut the main generator, forgetting, presumably, that it would tend to cease running anyway when the ship sank. I swore and fumbled for my torch, wishing Trapp might at least have waited for daylight, then gave a final vicious twist to the timing fuse and struggled up the vertical escape ladder to the poop.

It was almost as dark on deck, with the still-rising northerly wind clutching spitefully at my hair. Ahead of me I could see only the black silhouette of the superstructure scribing slow, rolling arcs against the stars while, somewhere, someone was shouting a string of unintelligible orders.

I frowned – Spew and Bligh had had over half an hour to lower the only two boats we carried; enough time to launch every lifeboat on a transatlantic passenger liner – so what the hell was all the noise about? Then I remembered that everybody screamed at everyone else as a matter of routine aboard Trapp's commands and tried unsuccessfully to shrug off the apprehension which touched me.

My unease didn't leave as I slid down the rails of the after well-deck ladder. It was an eerie sensation, being aboard a blacked-out vessel without even the comforting mutter of the main engine below your feet. Lonely somehow, as if I were the only human being left alive on the whole of the Mediterranean Sea despite that anonymous voice bellowing from forward.

But I wasn't. For one thing Fadel must still be aboard too, locked in the paint store and an unwitting candidate for a voyage to the bottom when the *Kamaran* finally did go down . . . I hesitated at the base of the ladder and swung to starboard, searching under the break of the poop towards the compartment where the Arab had been imprisoned.

And then I froze.

For now the steel door of the paint store was wide open – and I didn't need a torch to tell me it would be uninhabited. Who could have released Fadel, and why? Certainly it wouldn't have been Trapp himself, because the vengeance of Trapp was an unrelenting force . . .

I began to run for my port boat station. There was nothing I could do regarding the disappearing Arab other than make damn sure I didn't meet him back there on that dark and threatening after deck, and Choker Bligh must be getting volubly impatient anyway, waiting to push the boat off as soon as I abandoned via the lower-deck boarding ladder.

I also began praying that they'd managed to get the boat's engine running; the prospect of the *Kamaran*'s crew trying to row conjured up visions of an epileptic water beetle attempting a getaway during a particularly unco-ordinated spasm. But even then every cloud had a miniscule silver lining – at least Trapp was the one stuck with Second Officer Spew as deputy commander of the starboard boat while I only had to tolerate Bosun Bligh as my number two. And I could always reason with Choker – as long as I got to the engine starting-handle first . . .

. . . then I'd reached the centrecastle deck, and looked over the side to where the lifeboat should be waiting. And stopped dead once again.

Because it wasn't. Waiting there below me in the water, I mean.

Oh, I admit I was far too hasty; far too quick to over-react by leaning out over the rail and hurling a string of imprecations across the dark sea like I did while all the time expecting Fadel to appear from the shadows and try to kill me. For this was the *Kamaran*.

Suddenly that anonymous shouting rose to a positive crescendo of rage, and I swung my torch upwards instead – beamed towards the boat deck – to discover that they hadn't even managed to swing the bloody boats out yet, never mind launch them and pull away from a ship that was expected to blow itself high as an overdosed junkie in about twenty minutes from now.

'Awwww *shit!*' I remarked to no one in particular.

And began to run for the ladder again.

We did get away eventually . . . after struggling dementedly with rust-bound blocks and paint-seized davits, and wasting a few more precious minutes pulling Choker Bligh's hands from around Gorbals Wullie's throat just because Wullie had suggested pointedly that a proper bosun woulda *seen* they things wis workin' when he knew there was due tae be a disaster . . . and inevitably sacrificing a few more vital seconds in disentangling Mister Spew from where he'd inexplicably managed to get himself trapped in the starboard lifeboat falls – plus a lot more time when, after smiling in amiable appreciation of his release, he promptly forgot he was on a ship at all, and shambled straight off the edge of the boat deck into the water fifty feet below . . .

They were still engaged in pumping our accident-prone second officer's bilges dry when Trapp finally managed to manœuvre his frantically splashing boat alongside mine. We lay together about four cables off the darkened ship, and waited tensely for the *Kamaran* to have her accident.

''Ow long now?' Trapp called moodily.

'Four minutes,' I retorted with satisfaction. At least I could derive a certain bleak pleasure from the financial suffering he was enduring, apart from his natural aversion to sacrificing the only decent ship he'd ever commanded. Trapp was very much a seaman whatever his history, and even a pirate could shed a tear as he watched a prize slide beneath the waves for the last time.

A breaking crest came in under our stern and the boat wallowed into the pursuing trough to the accompaniment of Chief Engineer Maabud somethin' or other being seasick instead of trying to get our motor to fire. Then someone else joined in, and someone else, until we had a jolly chorus.

''Ow long now?'

'Three minutes . . . But more important, what happened to Fadel, Trapp? Who let him out?'

'No one did. He's still in the paint store – ain't he?'

'Not any more. The door was wide open when I passed.'

I could sense the growing anxiety in Trapp's growl. 'Well, 'e wus in there. All battened down an' waitin' to become a diver. I even sent Spew aft ter lock 'im in personally so's . . .'

There was silence. For a moment. Until . . .

'*Spew!*'

The sodden hulk of Mister Spew struggled to a sitting position. He still gurgled a bit, and squelched every time he moved, but some parts of him seemed to be working almost as good as new again. He might have got himself chipped about a little over the years but he was rapidly proving indestructible.

'Aye, Captin?'

'The Ayrab, mister . . . did yer lock 'im up like I said, did yer?'

'O' course I did!' Spew affirmed virtuously. '*And* I made sure 'e wus in there afore I did lock it, Captin. I ain't so daft I woul'n't check on a thing like that . . .'

'See?' Trapp bellowed triumphantly. 'Di'n't I tell yer I only employs the cream, mister? Good reliable boys the lot o' 'em.'

'Ho yus, 'e definitely wus in the paint store,' Mister Spew reiterated after laborious reflection. 'I saw 'im meself – when I give 'im the spare key . . .'

There was another silence; a slightly longer one this time. Before Trapp said in a funny voice, 'Why did yer give 'im the spare key, mister?'

'So's he wouldn't be stuck in there, Captin. When the ship went down.'

That perfectly rational explanation caused the longest silence of all.

''Ow long now?' Trapp muttered. Eventually.

'One minute.'

'Oh well,' Trapp commented philosophically. 'I suppose it won't make that much difference whether the Ayrab's sittin' onnit or innit when she blows. Not after she's converted ter bein' a submarine.'

And so we waited, two tiny boats full of seasick sailors, with the wind snapping the spray across our expectant eyes and the white-crested seas bearing down upon us from the north.

'Now!' Trapp muttered, oddly subdued. 'She'll be goin' any second now . . .'

But she didn't. For the pre-arranged time of the *Kamaran*'s violent death came, and passed. The silent black ship remained on the surface ahead of us, blatantly mocking us with her stability and comfort.

Two minutes went by. Then three. And then four, yet still nobody said a word. Until, five minutes after scuttling time, Trapp exploded instead.

'Them bombs,' he snarled furiously. 'Someone's scuttled me scuttlin' charges, dammit!'

'Well, I certainly set the time fuses like you wanted,' I defended myself truthfully. 'One full turn clockwise for each device.'

'I know yer did . . .' he roared back unthinkingly. Then added awkwardly, 'Yeah, well, I jus' thought I'd better check after you finished forward, di'n't I.'

'Obviously,' I retorted, with just the right amount of injured reproach. 'And thank you for your trust and confiden . . .'

'Christ!' someone squealed and I hurriedly swung to face forward again – neatly in time to see the rest of the *Kamaran*'s lights snap on with twinkling abruptness. Suddenly she was indestructibly alive again, all cheery and warm and illuminating the rows of green-tinged faces staring in astonishment.

'Who done that?' Trapp blurted in outraged perplexity. 'She's supposed ter be all blowed up by now. Who put them bloody lights on?'

'Fadel. It has to be Fadel . . .' I stood up in the boat and roared, 'Ship *oars*! Give way together . . .'

'Belay that!' Trapp began waving his arms in peevish temper. 'I gives the orders here, mister. I says where we go an' when we bloody goes . . .'

'Well, you'd better *give* 'em. We've got less than ten minutes to get back aboard, Trapp – Fadel's a seaman, remember? It won't take him longer than that to restart the main engine and switch her to bridge control . . .'

'Stop panickin',' bawled a near-apoplectic Trapp. 'I won't have a chief officer what panics, d'you hear?'

'. . . and he's cold-blooded enough to run both these boats down before he finally disappears over the bloody horizon.'

'ROW!' Trapp bellowed. 'Row like you wus practisin' to be torpedoes, lads . . .'

And so we rowed; splashing and crab-wise, some even falling backwards off thwarts in a desperate, cursing attempt to regain the lee of the *Kamaran* before Fadel used her to kill us instead.

One hundred metres to go . . . seventy . . . fifty, with the great bulk of the ship now towering above us and the surging foam crashing and whirlpooling between the tips of her mercifully still static propeller. But then a sudden rumble and a cloud of black soot; the steady waterfall of coolant from her discharge . . .

'She's started up! Pull together, f'r God's sake . . .'

In the other boat Trapp began pummelling Gorbals Wullie in frustration. 'Row, stoopid! Don't jus' waggle yer oars like a spare whatsit at an orgy.'

'Stop that or ah'm tellin' ye this is the last time ah'm goin' tae travel tourist class,' Wullie shrieked back hysterically.

I craned forward, eyes frantically searching through the gloom while praying Fadel hadn't had time to haul the abandoned ladder back inboard . . . but no! There it was, just ahead now, with the painted white rungs gleaming softly from the overspill of the alleyway lights.

'Make for the falls,' I urged. 'Try to hook on to the falls, Bosun.'

'Go f'r the falls, lads,' Trapp was roaring simultaneously from the starboard boat. 'Get 'er alongside that ladder an' secure to the falls . . .'

'Way 'nough . . .' I screamed, suddenly visualizing what was about to happen. 'BACKWATEEEEER . . .'

The two boats came together with a splintering crash. Oars snapped like matchsticks, men cannoned into one another in flailing disarray, Mister Spew collapsed gigantically into the Mediterranean for the second time that night, and I became miserably aware of water rushing and gurgling through the shattered planking. Locked inextricably together like Roman war galleys we drifted and bumped along the *Kamaran*'s water-line until we finally came to the ladder.

Trapp clambered heavily on to it, gun in one hand and the expression of a man who'd already seen it all before on his face.

'"E keeps on sinkin' my boats, that Fadel,' he snarled dangerously. 'I'm gettin' fed up to the teeth, the way 'e keeps on sinkin' my bloody boats.'

He began to climb in simmering fury, prodding an un-enthusiastic and volubly protesting Gorbals Wullie ahead of him as the spearhead of the assault group. I watched Choker Bligh step on the ladder holding his sheath knife like a beloved friend, then called after them.

'I suppose I'd better hang on a bit and save Mister Spew first.'

Trapp's response was typically petty-minded.

'Oh, please yer bloody self,' he acknowledged indifferently. 'Even if yer does, the stupid bastard'll jus' fall in again . . .'

Of course they never caught Fadel. It was lucky for all of them the Arab had given priority to restarting the *Kamaran*'s engine and not to selecting a machinegun from her rather excessive stock . . . but there were a great many places for a man to hide, and I didn't think we'd see him again until he was ready. I could only hope that I could persuade Trapp not to cut off his nose to spite his face again and that maybe Fadel would leave us alone. His interests, in that way, coincided with those of mine and the British Government – to allow the *Kamaran* to continue her interrupted voyage to Gahman.

If Trapp could be convinced. And if he didn't solve the problem by suffering an apoplectic stroke when he finally discovered *why* those scuttling charges hadn't gone off in the first place.

So it was with a little less than enthusiasm that I finally ran my captain to earth in the engineroom, engaged in what was, to my mind, a most ill-tempered and ill-advised examination of one of the errant devices.

Choker Bligh was kneeling with matching stupidity beside him while, at a more discreet distance, Gorbals Wullie and our chief engineer hovered like athletes keyed up for the starting pistol. Mind you, in fairness to Bligh, it did strike me later that they were unnecessarily tense – if the bloody thing did go off none of us would need to move a muscle to make it clear through the engineroom skylight forty feet above us.

'So there you are, mister,' Trapp greeted grumpily. 'An' where've you been then?'

'I told you; saving Spew for posterity.'

''Ardly worth the trouble. Where is 'e now?'

'Leaking seawater all over the bridge. He's on watch.'

'But we ain't goin' nowhere. The ship's stopped.'

'That,' I explained with enormous patience, 'is why Mister Spew *has* been put on watch. Once we're under way again I'd suggest we tie him up in his cabin.'

'Well, we won't be ever again – under way, I mean,' Trapp muttered grimly. 'Not once I finds out why these flamin' bombs didn't work, we won't.'

I didn't argue right away because that was the moment when Choker Bligh started prodding the dormant charge with his sheath knife. It didn't seem very scientific to me but I wasn't particularly anxious for them to discover the fault . . . and I certainly didn't want them to overcome it. Especially not while I was still in the engineroom.

Then Trapp turned his attentions to it as well and started to fiddle recklessly with the fuse setting, twisting and poking at it. The chief engineer immediately threw himself prostrate along the oily deck plates and began to pray hysterically while Gorbals Wullie stuck his fingers in his ears and screwed his eyes tight shut. Trapp ignored them.

'You sure you activated these like I told yer, mister?'

'I understood you'd checked them yourself,' I retorted pointedly. 'With one of your typical expressions of faith in your subordinates.'

'Mmmmm . . .' He began to unscrew the detonator housing while Choker Bligh inserted his sheath knife under the magnetic clamp and tried to lever the device away from the side plates.

'You'll break yer knife,' Trapp warned helpfully.

Choker Bligh broke his knife.

'F**@£*"&****!' said the bosun. Predictably.

'Stupid bastid,' commented an already disenchanted Gorbals Wullie. Suicidally.

Eventually we managed to prize Bligh's hands from around Wullie's scrawny throat for the second time, then Trapp went back to unscrewing the detonator. I moved over and said anxiously, 'Look, why can't you just forget the scuttling idea and deliver to Zaraf . . .'

He withdrew the housing and held it up. The pencil-shaped detonator had gone.

'Who's taken me detonator?' he asked blankly.

I swallowed and backed away, conscious, at the same time,

of a rather odd scraping sound which appeared to come from the other side of the hull plates; from outboard the *Kamaran* itself. Right then I was more concerned with the purple flush rapidly spreading upwards from Trapp's collar, though.

'Who's stolen me bloody *detonator*?' he screamed in growing outrage.

'Never mind,' I consoled. 'You said you didn't have any more, so now you don't have to make a difficult decision. Now you *can't* scuttle her you've no need to fight your conscience or anything. Just deliver to Zaraf . . .'

'I'll *kill* 'im!'

He took a running kick at the bomb. Even Choker Bligh was on his way to the deck plates this time as it took off from the *Kamaran*'s side, ricocheted noisily off the auxiliary generator, clanged against the block of the main engine and disappeared into the bilges with a muffled splash.

'I'll kill that bloody clever-dick Ayrab!' he bellowed again.

I removed my hands from the back of my neck and uncurled from the foetal position I'd adopted when he kicked the bomb. I blinked at him – I'd never thought of that.

'Who – Fadel?' I asked tentatively.

'An' who else, mister? Who else woulda wanted to scuttle me scuttlin' charges then?'

There was yet another strange noise from outboard, almost as though something heavy was being dragged along the waterline, but again I ignored it. Fate had dealt me an opportunity I couldn't afford to miss and anyway, now I'd got over my biggest hurdle, I was beginning to enjoy myself in a vindictive sort of way.

'Well, he's won, whatever happens. You can't sink her now, so there's no alternative but to go to Gahman seeing you can't just leave her floating around the Mediterranean.'

'Whit about opening the seacocks?' Wullie suggested helpfully.

I took a deep and patient breath. 'Largely because ships don't *have* seacocks. It probably comes as news to you and Trapp, but most shipowners are rather more keen to design them to stay afloat in the first place . . .'

The bumping sound came again but Trapp was in full fury now. 'I'll set her on fire, dammit!'

'You can't do that either. She'll only burn down to the waterline. *And* give away the fact that you were well off course for Málaga before you torched her.'

'Then I'll arrange a . . . a collision.'

'You wouldn't need to,' I said cheerfully. 'Just leave Spew on the bridge for a couple of hours on his own an' we'll have one . . . but you still got the same problem – wrong time, wrong place.'

'I'm gonna sink this fuckin' ship if I has to fill 'er with buckets o' bloody water!'

'. . . only you're gonna find yourself filled first, schmoe – wit lead,' a familiar voice called unexpectedly from above. 'OK, you dirty rats . . . Freeze!'

'Here, that wis clever,' Gorbals Wullie said admiringly. 'Ah didnae realize you could dae James Cagney good as yon, Captin.'

But Trapp didn't answer. In fact he'd gone very quiet all of a sudden, after swinging to stare bleakly up towards the head of the engineroom ladder.

'I still don't think he can,' I corrected nervously, eyes following Trapp's.

I suddenly understood what the earlier bumps had been, then. They were the sort of sounds one ship makes when coming alongside another. A ship like, say, the *Illustrious Dragon* of Mister Chang.

Choker Bligh had turned as well, to gaze at the previously unnoticed group above with an expression hovering between disbelief, truculence and outright derision. ''Oo called me a dirty rat, then?' he growled ominously. 'Which one o' them pansy, fancy-dress Chineemen called me a rat?'

I was rather more concerned with discovering precisely how they'd managed to get alongside without being detected – then remembered Mister Spew had been up there on watch, and stopped wondering. The bosun began to move forward resentfully.

'Easy, Choker; they're only film actin', so keep yer temper

down,' Trapp warned tightly, warily, but our pugnacious shipmate continued to advance in simmering outrage.

'I *eats* Chineemen f'r breakfast,' he snarled. 'Especially
poncy, makee-believe tough guys o' Chineemen...'

Gorbals Wullie perceptively dived for the deck for the
second time. Maabud somethin' or other didn't need to; he still
hadn't got to his feet following his initial prostration.

'Belay that, Bligh!' I roared, watching the guns. 'They
aren't pretending any longer.'

'F**** and **** and **** you, mate!' the bosun bellowed
back triumphantly, not even hurrying as he advanced step by
step up the ladder in scowling retribution. I met Trapp eyeball
to eyeball as we launched ourselves simultaneously for the lee
of the auxiliary generator.

'You shouldn't've given 'im an order,' Trapp bawled
reprovingly. 'You *knows* 'e gets awkward an' bloody-minded
when you gives 'im an order.'

The racketing snarl of Thompson sub-machinegun fire confirmed he was right. It also told us that the film script had
ended.

That now Mister Chang was playing the part for real.

Chapter Ten

And so the ludicrous finally did give way to murderous reality.

No longer was there the nightmarish feeling of being a bemused stage extra on the set of some particularly bad 'B' movie; for this wasn't the lavish interior of a megalomaniac's ocean-going kinema fantasy any more, this was the engineroom of a mystery ship called the *Kamaran*. And that contorted and rather surprised-looking cadaver at the bottom of the ladder wasn't a prop man's creation – it wasn't even the faintly ironic aftermath of a hoodlums' shoot-out as had taken place on the bridge earlier; it was the bullet-riddled body of one of our own shipmates.

Oh, Chang still wore that ridiculous white suit with the low-brimmed fedora, and was still theatrically flanked by his two crow-black professional killers with their antiquated yet devastatingly lethal Chicago Pianos and their ever-so-chilling menace as they gun-prodded us up the ladders towards the *Kamaran*'s deck; but there was no Cinemascope vista to greet us as we stumbled out over the coaming dragging our fear-paralysed chief engineer between us – merely the grey winter dawn, and the metallic crouch of the bulldozers on either side which belied the true nature of the *Kamaran*'s evil cargo. And the sullen, apprehensive faces of Trapp's spineless and degenerate crew revealing a depth of human inadequacy impossible to portray on any silver screen.

While Mister Chang himself had changed, too. All his eccentric good humour had vanished. From the moment of Choker Bligh's execution he never 'did' Cagney again, not even for the gratification of his greatest fan, Gorbals Wullie. Nor did he render a Bogart or a Raft, or the slightest suspicion of an Edward G. . . . in fact he only gave one impression as we continued making our way to the bridge – of a very angry and vindictive Hong Kong gang boss.

All of which blew yet *another* of Trapp's loftily expounded generalities; that the Chinese sense of fair play differs in the slightest from anyone else's. Or did it? Because it had never really occurred to Trapp that whatever Chang proposed to do to him was more than justified by what he'd been attempting to do to Chang.

But that was different. Or so Edward Trapp would have claimed.

I confirmed the source of that scraping noise I'd heard, as I trudged my way along what promised to be my last walk topside. Outboard of us and secured fore and aft now lay the slimmer, more delicate hull of the streamlined *Illustrious Dragon*.

And I learned how she'd managed to get there undetected when we finally arrived on the bridge to find Mister Spew gazing in singular mystification down the hole in the end of a Chinese gun barrel.

'Where did 'e come from then?' Mister Spew asked huffily as we approached.

Nobody shot him so I ventured a reply, gesturing cautiously towards the fifteen-hundred-odd tons of steel next door.

'How about from there?' I suggested ingeniously. 'He – in fact, all of these Oriental gentlemen – may very well have come from that ship there, Mister Spew. The one you perhaps didn't ʒ . . ah . . . notice. When she actually arrived.'

Mister Spew studied our neighbour with his usual frowning concentration, and then a tiny spark must have jolted his brain into momentary activity, and given him A Thought.

'Ahhhh, well that explains it, don't it?'

Even Mister Chang leaned forward curiously despite his annoyance, waiting for Mister Spew's revelation. 'Tell us, Mister Spew,' I encouraged.

'Yeah, well, I wus ackshully keepin' watch out over the *port* side, wusn't I then, Mister Cooper? But that ship's alongside our *star*board side, ain't it? An' you coul'n't hardly expect a man ter keep watch on . . . on . . .'

'. . . on both sides all at the same time, Mister Spew?'

'Yus, Mister Cooper!'

I turned to face Mister Chang's Tommy guns. And sighed.

Mister Chang didn't want to hear Trapp's ingenious excuses. But Mister Chang was indeed a bitter man, shocked by the perfidy of his fellow business associate – which meant Trapp – and the fact that Trapp had managed to prove himself even more crooked than he, Chang, was. Therefore he, Chang, could see no alternative other than to terminate their business agreement in the most expeditious manner available.

'Cancel me contract?' Trapp ventured hopefully.

'Shoot you,' Mister Chang amended. Emphatically.

'But you can't,' Trapp argued desperately. 'If you still wants this cargo deliverin' to . . . where is it f'r you?'

'Libya.'

'Yeah, there . . . Well, how are you plannin' to sail this ship all that way if you kills off me an' my boys, eh? You ain't got enough seamen to crew two ships, have you? While all said an' done your crowd is only Chinee fellers . . . meanin' no disrespect, o' course,' he added hastily.

'None taken,' Mister Chang smoothly acknowledged. 'But while I appreciate the loyalty of your own chaps, Captain, I feel sure that some of them may well be prepared to consider temporary employment with me rather than join you at the bottom of the sea . . .'

It struck me rather cynically that every last one of Trapp's revolting gang of loyalists would fall over each other's knives to get at his throat if such a gesture offered reprieve; but then the chat became a little more personal as far as I was concerned when Chang continued.

'. . . therefore my intention is merely to execute yourself and your officers, Captain. And pray that my humble Chinese replacements can cope with the task.'

Chief Engineer Maabud somethin' or other issued a demented shriek and fell on the deck again, which was a pity seeing we'd only just managed to prop him up after the last bout of hysteria. Gorbals Wullie, on the other hand, began to ease gingerly past the Tommy gun at the head of the bridge ladder.

'Oh well, ye'll no' be wanting me then. Ah'm not an officer an' that's a fact . . .'

'Oh, yes you are,' Trapp snarled spitefully. 'I made you up ter actin' third mate when Choker Bligh got hisself paid off.'

'Congratulations on your promotion,' Mister Chang offered with dry finality. 'But now, gentlemen, I shall return to the *Illustrious Dragon*. You will appreciate that I prefer not to concern myself with the . . . ah . . . more mundane aspects of my profession.'

He straightened his suit fastidiously while I stared around. There could be no escape this time; three Chinese guns covered us in anticipation of the grand finale. Trapp was still trying, though, irritably gesturing towards the simultaneously elevated and condemned Gorbals Wullie.

'Jus' look at yer. I'll not 'ave my officers lookin' like they wus apprentice cleaners inna Bombay sewer. Put . . . yer . . . cap . . . on . . . straight!'

I read the meaningful look that passed between them and tensed, beginning to hope again. But only for a moment – until Mister Chang waved a hand languidly to one of his companions.

'Please be good enough to remove the third officer's head-gear, Chu Jun-min. You may well discover several razor blades sewn into the peak; a somewhat crude and unsophisticated form of defence originating, I believe, in certain lower echelons of Scottish society.'

'Bloody clever-dick Chinees . . . !' Trapp roared in explosive frustration. Gorbals Wullie simply turned whiter than ever through a combination of fear, unaccustomed skull exposure and nationalistic affront. I stepped forward hurriedly, risking the guns in order to delay Chang's leaving.

'You referred to your "profession", Chang. Which one did you mean then – as a hoodlum, or a heavy for the CIA?'

He hesitated and I was relieved to see him smiling, not angry anymore. 'Your intelligence appears to be very efficient, Mister Cooper. I suppose no harm can come of my telling you – I am acting in a dual role, both for my friends in the United States Government and for myself . . . as an international businessman, I must stress.'

'Then why prevent these arms going to Gahman? It's a pro-Western power, isn't it . . . so why should the US wish to deny them military aid, Chang? Even stuff as illicit as this obviously is.'

Mister Chang's smile held a hint of patronage. 'Because the *Kamaran*'s cargo was not bound for a government destination, my dear fellow. Quite the reverse, in fact, as they were intended for a reprehensibly Marxist-oriented group masquerading as the Gahman Liberation Front. To be utilized in displacing the present administration.'

That little bombshell made both Trapp and I stare at each other in mystification; but if he was taken aback, then I was doubly so, for I knew one more fact which only made the riddle even more obscure – because it raised the question of why the British Government should be so intent on not only frustrating what would appear to be a mutually-beneficial American operation, but also in actively supporting a communist take-over.

Trapp, however, was typically more fascinated with the financial structure of intrigue. 'So where does your profit come in, mister?' he growled sullenly.

This time Chang hugged himself with delight. 'Modesty must forbid me to suggest the word "brilliant", Captain, but I do happen to have contrived a marriage of both my dearest political and commercial interests in this particular matter . . . You see, I have already arranged to transfer, for a most satisfactory sum, the *Kamaran*'s cargo to a splendidly right-wing group of chaps known as The Friends Of Libya – and they intend to employ the arms to bring down Colonel Qaddhafi's deplorably pro-Soviet regime. I do so dislike people such as Qaddhafi; idealists dedicated to eliminating the profit motive.'

'Ah,' said Trapp appreciatively, 'then you an' me do have somethin' in common after all, Mister Chang.'

'Not a great deal,' Chang retorted blandly. 'For you will be dead in a few minutes' time, Captain Trapp. While I shall still be alive and making money.'

I could detect impatience beginning to overcome Chang's desire to emphasize his own star qualities, and racked my brain to further delay the inevitable. 'So Zarafiq's just a communist dogsbody, eh, Chang? Or does he have an ulterior motive, too?'

'Zarafiq?'

I blinked; Chang's expression really did appear to be one of genuine ignorance. 'The bloke who planned this crazy voyage in the first place . . . Trapp's original boss.'

'Partner,' Trapp corrected pompously.

'Shut *up*,' I rejoined, much to Gorbals Wullie's satisfaction.

Chang's frown cleared and he looked aggravatingly knowing. 'Of course, Mister Cooper – Zarafiq. Your discretion at this late hour brings you great credit, though naturally we are all aware of Mister Zarafiq's true identit . . . but no. It is very wrong of me to bore you with such repetitive and time-wasting trivia . . . !'

'But we ain't aware,' Trapp snarled. 'An' I'm in no bloody hurry.'

I elbowed him out of the way in a last attempt to prolong the conversation. 'All right. Then what reason could some other western power have for trying to topple the present Gahmanian government, Chang? Say . . . well, say Britain, f'r instance?'

I saw Trapp's eyes dilate in suddenly aroused suspicion and, to divert him from attempting to kill me before the bloody Chinese, added hurriedly, '. . . hypothetically, of course.'

Mister Chang merely laughed in even greater appreciation of my humour before disappearing from sight below the level of the bridge.

'There! You see how well informed you are, Cooper? Don't we both appreciate what a delicately balanced commodity crude oil can be in the scales of power; what a catalyst it can provide for devious political manœuvrings . . . ?'

'But I'm *not* well informed,' I howled in frustration. 'That's the whole trouble, Chang – I don't know a bloody thing, dammit! Chang . . . ? Come back, Chang!'

But the next time I saw him he had already crossed between

our two ships and was making his leisurely way towards the bridge of the *Illustrious Dragon*; a tiny, dapper figure far below me. And I knew with a sinking heart that, when he finally reached it, I would never have enough time left to discover the reason for my own death. What part Gahman's crude oil industry was apparently to play in it. And even more teasingly – why Mister Chang hadn't recognized the name of Zarafiq at first, yet seemingly knew so much about the man himself . . .

We seemed to stand on that bleak and windswept bridge for a very long time, waiting for Mister Chang to direct the last scene – at least for Trapp and Gorbals Wullie, and Maabud and Spew and myself – of the *Kamaran* epic.

Numbly I stared astern, out over the boat deck where the seedily-dressed bit-part players shuffled uneasily under the watchful eyes of two more Chinese sub-machinegunners, and farther out across the after well deck where the monstrous bulldozers still crouched in metallic contempt for our human fragility.

There was nothing on the horizon. No maritime equivalent of the US Cavalry approaching in the manner so dear to a real Hollywood script. In this story-line such an ending was not to be anticipated anyway. The Yanks weren't coming, not this time. They'd already got what they wanted through the devious manœuvrings of Mister Chang; now our only hope would have lain in the low, grey silhouette of a British frigate speeding to our rescue . . . but that didn't make sense either. None of this outlandish, unmistakably-Trapp confusion did . . .

'What're we waitin' for then?' Mister Spew asked impatiently.

Nobody answered. There didn't seem a lot of point in it, because even Dan'l Spew would understand when it did happen.

Down below us Chang reached the *Illustrious Dragon*'s bridge and looked up, savouring every moment of this, his greatest production. Beside me Trapp tensed; even Gorbals Wullie stuck his jaw forward like a cornered rodent preparing for a last mad leap at his tormentors. Chang raised one arm dramatically, and there was a metallic rattle as cocking handles were yanked back on three machineguns . . .

The roar, when it came, was almost as petrifying as the anticipated crash of gunfire.

And I swung involuntarily – to see a blue haze cloud of exhaust scattering in the wind across the after deck as the biggest bulldozer of all detonated into thunderous life. And then began to move . . .

Actually everyone turned with the shock of it. The gunmen; every seaman huddling along the *Kamaran*'s boat deck; the crew of the exquisite craft alongside us; Mister Chang himself . . .

. . . or nearly everybody, anyway.

Trapp's granite fist took one of the Chicago-piano players square on the side of his head; the crunch of shattering bone echoing sickeningly even above the bulldozer's inexplicable growl. Simultaneously Gorbals Wullie lashed out with one frantic boot, missed the second black-suited Oriental altogether, shrieked, 'Och, Jeeze, help me, Mister Cooper, sirrrr . . .' and flung himself under cover behind the already inert body of our chief engineer – leaving me staring into the swinging barrel of a bloody Thompson gun.

I had no option. I grabbed for it; clung to it like a demented leech, yanking and at the same time twisting frantically to one side as bullets ripped a flail of teak splinters from the grubby deck. 'Gettim!' I screamed. 'Aw gettim f'r Christ's sake . . .'

Hysteria! Bedlam! The engine note of the giant earthmover rising to a crescendo of unleashed power. Maabud and Wullie's terrified howls only fractionally less pleading than my own . . . shouting from the *Illustrious Dragon*'s decks too, now, and the chatter of other small arms opening up. What the hell was happening back there . . . but who the hell cares?

'*Hold* 'im!' Trapp bellowed irresolutely, torn between the priorities of reinforcing my gibbering desperation or going for the third Chinese sailor, currently restricted in his field of fire by his own comrade.

'WHADDYATHINKI'M*TRYIN*'TO DOOOOOO . . . ?' I squealed maniacally.

The boom of the earthmover's exhaust a slamming echo from every bulkhead now; and the tormented clatter of gears engaging at high revs. An explosive snap. Then another . . . an' another, like . . . like steel shearing under stress. Or wire lashings parting. The kind used to secure deck cargo . . .

Trapp's arm suddenly hooked around the neck of my trigger-happy assailant. The black fedora skittered away as muscles bulged, the arm constricting effortlessly; a grubby-jersey-covered tourniquet under compression . . . the Thompson gun ceased firing as bulging eyes stared from a suffused black face . . .

The third sailor stepping back in panic now; going to pull the trigger an' the hell with his mate. I started to dive for him but I knew I didn't have a chance . . . yet there was Spew still standing behind; still surveying the grunting, struggling press of bodies with amiable detachment . . .

'Spew! Do somethin', Spew, f'r . . .'

Further shots – a fusillade of confused gunfire; and more wires snapping . . . the clatter and screech of tracks fighting for grip on the steel after deck. Something incredible was happening back there and I was never going to find out what it was . . .

Until Mister Spew said obligingly, 'Aye, aye, Mister Cooper.'

Before he picked the third Chinese gunman clean off the bridge deck. And dropped him neatly over the side.

Nobody paid the slightest attention to Gorbals Wullie as he cautiously eased himself from under the cringing blob which was our senior engineer officer, took a sly glance around to confirm the heat was off, then bubbled excitedly, 'Here, did yous see me then? Did ah no' sort they poofy Chinese fellers oot, did ah no'? Jeeze, but there's nae disputin' ah'm pure tiger at heart. A reg'lar tiger o' a lad . . .'

Then he too caught sight of what was happening down aft.

And added, '. . . so ah am!' before lapsing into stupefied silence. Just like the rest of us . . .

The starboard bulldozer, yellow paint already scarred by a barrage of futile ricochets, was actually beginning to turn. Accompanied by a final firecracker parting of over-stressed lashings – and with one set of tracks grinding full astern, the other straining under forward throttle – the roaring machine was swinging in great sparking jerks to face outboard and slightly ahead; slamming into the steel bulwarks with a diesel snarl of fury, crushing and battering outrageously at the only structure restraining it from powering clean over the ship's side.

'Christ!' I yelled as I recognized the hunched silhouette of the driver, squeezed as low as possible into the armoured juggernaut's cockpit. 'It's the Arab . . . It's Fadel!'

Abruptly Trapp found his voice too. 'What's 'e doing?' he snarled in rising petulance. Then both he and I saw precisely what Zarafiq's first lieutenant was attempting – and Trapp was diving for the Tommy gun still clutched by the dead hoodlum.

'Leave Fadel alone!' I bawled.

'Don't tell *me*, mister! Tell them bloody Chineese . . .'

Trapp hit the trigger and the yammering racket drowned his words. A thick cloud of cordite smoke blew across the bridge – and the first of the two gunmen guarding the *Kamaran*'s terrified crew jetted across the boat deck in a tumbling cartwheel of arms and legs. Immediately the second Changster stopped firing at Fadel and whirled with the fear of death clamping his finger on the button. A wavering spray of automatic fire splintered davits, doors, ventilators, lockers . . . and suddenly there was an emptiness about the upper decks of the *Kamaran*; merely the tail end of a group of airborne sailormen leaping for cover – and a singularly unhappy Chinaman with an empty magazine.

Trapp fired again. With cold deliberation.

Just as the clamour of the berserk earthmover rose to a new high. There was renewed shouting and a pandemonium of gunfire from outboard; running feet and the *whoop, whoop, whoop* of the *Illustrious Dragon*'s siren . . . the threshing of propellers punctuated by the dull chunk of an urgently wielded axe.

Gorbals Wullie said in an awe-struck stammer, 'Would ye look at that, then.'

I started to run for the wing and leaned far out, staring down and astern all at the same time. Below me, on the bridge of the smaller ship, Mister Chang was doing much the same thing, and in much the same manner – transfixed, with nerveless hands clutching the rails before us . . .

The bulldozer had actually begun to mount the bulwarks now; tilting at a crazy angle, lying over towards me with one steadily revolving track almost straddling the crushed and twisted metal barrier. The other, still skidding and sparking and rattling monstrously, spun as Fadel gunned the engine to full screeching power.

'He's tryin' to get it over,' Trapp's spellbound mutter from beside me. 'That mad bloody Ayrab's actually tryin' to drive it clean off've the ship . . .'

'. . . on to Chang's,' I supplemented in horrified fascination. 'Jesus, but he's intending to drop it square on Chang's after deck.'

It had developed into a macabre race by now; Fadel's resolution against the frantic efforts of the *Illustrious Dragon*'s crew. Already her screws were churning ahead in a panic-initiated error, causing the slim length of her to sheer bar taut on the umbilical cords still securing her alongside the *Kamaran*. Two . . . no, three axe-wielding seamen chopping dementedly at her fore and aft springs; a fourth running pell-mell for the last stern rope restraining her after end . . . Chang screaming orders in staccato Chinese – no need for a script any more, not for this strictly off-the-cuff epic he found himself starring in. And more men tumbling on to her decks with hastily issued weapons, firing unavailingly upwards into the underside of the juggernaut appearing above them.

Then there was a *crack*. And another, with the fuzzed and severed tails of manila whipping clear through the fairleads.

'The Arab's no' goin' tae make it . . .' Wullie shrilled in disappointment. 'Bow rope's away! Backspring's awa . . . och, shit, but that's yon fore spring away an' a' . . .'

Abruptly released, the slender hull began to gather headway, water lashing and curling under the rounded counter. Almost simultaneously Fadel's roaring gargantua rocked, squealed a final rage of sparking tracks, and jolted forward and upwards to mount the sagging bulwarks in grating tumult.

'Her stern rope,' I heard myself howling feverishly. 'Her stern rope's still holding her . . .'

But it wouldn't for long. The Chinese seaman with the axe was racing towards it, already preparing to strike – until there was a shattering racket from beside me . . . and the last hope for Mister Chang kept on going right past the bitts on suddenly spongy legs, cannoned sickeningly into the ensign staff on the *Dragon*'s taffrail, and cartwheeled over her after end.

Trapp looked at me over the sight of the Thompson gun.

'It ain't what a British seaman would do – use an axe,' he said straight-faced, and then he turned and looked down from the wing of our bridge. And smiled. Straight into the shocked and staring gaze of Mister Chang below.

It was a terrible, anticipatory smile . . .

The ahead strain came on the *Illustrious Dragon*'s still-secured stern line and she began, once more, to sheer uncontrollably into the side of the *Kamaran*. High above her the fifty-ton pendulum of Fadel's bright yellow bomb hesitated . . . swivelled a little and dipped its nose, curtseying almost as if in farewell . . .

. . . and then started to fall.

Fadel abandoned his seat with the same cold precision he'd applied to every other act of violence he'd ever committed, and right at the last possible moment.

I saw him haul himself out of his seat, clinging to the machine with one hand as the other dangled uselessly, a permanent legacy of Trapp's vindictiveness. Then calmly, almost contemptuously, he launched himself as the juggernaut tumbled from under.

Only one bullet caught him in mid-air; ironically one of the last despairing rounds fired from Chang's decks before the shooting stopped and the survival game began. Fadel jerked, spun, and smashed appallingly to the scarred and tortured deck – and then I dragged my eyes away to watch the end of the *Illustrious Dragon*.

The plummeting bulldozer struck her port bulwarks and carved a vertical gash from deckline to keel, compacting and rending the thin shell plating like paper. Immediately the sea began to rush . . . no, literally to fall into the cavity created. For a shocked second we found ourselves staring into the shiny depths of her incised engineroom, down upon the transfixed image of a little, gaping man wearing a snowy boiler-suit – and then there was only the thunder of water, and the gouting foam between, and the shrieks of drowning sailors.

The *Illustrious Dragon* began to fall towards us, capsizing faster and faster to port with her foremast arc-ing violently and her ventilators blowing off under the pressure of displacing air. Crewmen clawed maniacally to climb an ever-canting deck as a lethal avalanche of heavy equipment started to tear free under the list. Drums, rafts still in their canisters, lockers, even her immaculate motor launch itself tumbled and bounced down, through and over them. Chang's Gazelle helicopter and several screaming seamen careered seawards in a scythe of bloodied, snapping rotor blades . . .

. . . the *Kamaran* shied away in terror, hung for a dazed moment, then began to roll back to starboard as the weight of her arms cargo overcame her obvious revulsion at the mutilation of a beautiful sister. The *Illustrious Dragon*'s streamlined funnel impacted with our centrecastle rail in a screech of rending metal . . . her foremast crashed agonizingly into the break of our fo'c'sle . . . Mister Chang, now able only to cling in abject terror to the wheelhouse doorframe, turned his bewildered head – saw the slab-steel battering ram of the *Kamaran*'s hull bearing inward and down upon him – and died in a long, smearing shriek of disbelief as I turned away and retched.

She went down on her side, with her lovely flared bows rearing towards the sky and our own scarred freighter rolling drunkenly on a suddenly very silent sea. Only a few flotsam scraps surfaced in the whirlpool of the *Illustrious Dragon*'s going – half a dozen face-down corpses; an inverted motor launch; a magnificently varnished accommodation ladder; a flotilla of swirling, unidentifiable things . . .

. . . and a plaster female nude, bobbing and grimacing up at us like some monstrously gaudy mermaid. Oh, and a picture. Of James Cagney.

Chapter Eleven

As soon as we reached Fadel we realized it was hopeless. Whatever the riddles posed by the *Kamaran*'s cargo – and now even further complicated by the suddenly dead Mister Chang's frustrating part-disclosures – they would never reach solution through the bloodied and pain-taut lips of Zarafiq's henchman.

In fact they were to be compounded. Fadel was still fighting, and defeating us as we gazed grimly into eyes which, even though rabid fanaticism was swiftly giving way to the dull sheen of death, still watched us as vengefully as ever.

'Oil,' I said urgently. 'What did Chang mean about oil, Fadel? And how does the *Kamaran* fit in?'

He smiled. It was the same sort of smile Trapp had directed towards the capsizing *Illustrious Dragon* a few moments before, and it made me feel cold all over.

'The Chinaman was a fool. Like all imperialist gangsters he only believed what he wished to believe, Cooper . . .'

The pain hit him and he arched, feet skittering in his own blood. But the smile was still there, beneath the sweat. I knelt beside him and supported his head.

'Then you are a communist? Chang was right when he said the arms are bound for the Gahman Liberation crowd . . . for the Reds?'

And that was when I discovered he wasn't solving riddles; he was simply posing greater ones.

'Ask yourself, Cooper. Why did we go to such lengths to secure the services of Captain Trapp . . . the industrious and so predictable Captain Trapp?'

I blinked. Even Trapp looked momentarily disconcerted. 'Predictable' was probably at the top of the list of most unlikely adjectives to describe his particular attributes ... so what did Fadel mean? What the hell was he insinuating?

Then Trapp had to go and approach the delicate task of extracting information from a dying man with all his usual subtlety. 'You're gonna be dead as mutton inna minnit, Fadel — so where's me detonators? Jus' tell me where you hid the detonators f'r me scuttlin' charges, then?'

The defiant smile faded. 'Detonators?'

'The ones you took while we wus abandoned. To prevent me from sinkin' this bucket.'

Fadel's contempt didn't diminish, though he was clearly confused too. 'But why should I wish ...'

He writhed again, and suddenly there was blood coming from the side of his mouth. '... you must *sink* the *Kamaran*, fools. My ... our employer relies on your ... your ...'

The Arab's eyes closed while Trapp wiggled in thwarted rage. 'Is he sayin' he didn't neutralize them bombs, mister? An' what does 'e mean — I got to sink the bloody ship, eh ... An' what's Zarafiq relyin' on? Relying on my *what*, dammit?'

'He's going,' I interjected hurriedly, bending with my mouth close to the dying Fadel's ear. 'Who is Zarafiq, Fadel? Who is Mister Zarafiq?'

He opened his eyes again, just for a moment. But there was only one expression left in them now. Only one quite unmistakable expression before more blood spewed from the slack mouth and the light in his eyes faded for ever.

'Zarafiq?' he asked.

As though he'd never, ever heard that name before.

This time I was so furious when I reached my cabin that I literally hurled the bundle of newspapers camouflaging the bottom of my wardrobe in a wide, fluttering snowstorm before lunging for the handset like I intended to strangle it.

'Get him!' I yelled uncaringly when Charlie Tango Wun Fife came on the air. 'Jus' get your boss an' never mind the procedure crap! DO you read me loud an' clear?'

'Control,' the metallic voice of my admiral snapped almost immediately. 'Make your report, Watchdog.'

So I did. Most succinctly. I told him all about the abortive scuttling attempt, and the boarding incident, and the way Fadel had died while killing Mister Chang . . . and the way in which a great many other men had died when the *Illustrious Dragon* had been run over by a rogue bulldozer.

And then I told him quite calmly, without rancour, precisely what he could do with political manœuvring which murdered sailors; and with unethical pressures which allowed professional sadists like him to lean on simple-minded amateurs like me in the name of patriotism; and what he could consequently do with the Naval Discipline Act from this moment on . . .

'. . . because Trapp won't change, Admiral,' I assured him. 'I've known him and his pig-headed, bloody-minded determination for too long. He's going to sink this blasted ship one way or another; and it won't make a blind bit of difference whether you, the Yanks, the Soviets, or the whole lousy lot of you together try an' stop him . . . and you want to know something else, Admiral?'

The tone on the radio was bleak. 'Tell me, Watchdog.'

'I won't either,' I promised. 'In fact those detonators I removed all that time ago – when I was working for you? Under the Naval Discipline Act . . . ? Well, I'm just going to give them right back to Captain Edward Trapp, and tell him to go right ahead and cause the biggest bloody explosion in the whole bloody world . . . Sir!'

There was a long silence. I stayed there with my head stuck in the wardrobe and a reckless if slightly fixed grin of defiance on my face, relishing every second of his obvious discomfiture.

Until he said, rather jovially, 'Splendid, Watchdog . . . Your suggestion approved.'

The grin slowly slipped to one side. 'Say again?' I echoed almost pleadingly.

'I do say again, Watchdog – your orders have been changed. You are now instructed to ensure that the *Kamaran* is scuttled with all possible speed . . .'

The old familiar prickle came back again and I gripped the handset nervously. 'Wait a minute. Suddenly you *do* want this ship sunk. And Fadel inexplicably wanted it sunk . . . and Trapp's determined it's gonna be sunk. So now, Admiral who-ever-you-are, I would greatly appreciate it if you would very kindly inform me why it's *got to be bloody sunk, dammit!*'

. . . so he did. He told me, very clearly and without the slightest hesitation. And when he'd finished I could only stare at the handset and marvel at the depths to which politicians could sink as well as ships . . . and feel deliriously happy. Because at last the heat was off. I would be free the moment the *Kamaran* slid beneath the surface of the Mediterranean Sea.

Oh, it still didn't explain Fadel's last impassioned demand; there was still no apparent reason why he and Zarafiq should wish to frustrate their very own operation. For Fadel un-doubtedly was a communist sympathizer, so why prevent arms finding their way into communist hands? But that didn't matter. Not to me. Not any more.

It only occurred to me after I'd signed off that I'd never cleared up that other niggling area of doubt – who, or what, was the mysterious Mister Zarafiq himself? And why had Chang been so vague when his name had been raised . . . and Fadel himself, come to that, who'd actually worked for the man?

But as I said, it didn't matter any more.

I even smiled a greeting when Trapp came in, which should have worried him for a start. But he was wearing his usual black frown and simply glanced suspiciously at the newspapers still littering the cabin.

'Just clearing out,' I said hurriedly. 'For when we abandon again and scuttle her. Properly this time, because I've found , . . er . . . well, I found the det . . .'

'Don't tell me, because it don't matter,' Trapp growled with implacable resolution. 'I been thinking, an' I've changed my mind, mister. I've gotter contract; an' a contract's a contract...'

His jaw set like a defiant bulldog's. '. ₂ . so we ain't going to

scuttle this ship, after all, see? We're deliverin' as requested.
All the way to Gahman.'

'. . . it's the best way I can get even with Zarafiq, I tell yer,'
Trapp insisted for the fiftieth time as he brought the *Kamaran*'s
head round and pointed her towards Gahman. 'Deliver the stuff
like I wus originally hired to do.'

'But that's the whole point,' I retorted wearily. 'You can't
get even with a bloke by doing precisely what he asks you to
do.'

'But it ain't, dammit! Accordin' to Fadel it's in Zarafiq's real
interests to sink the bloody ship . . . so if I don't, then it screws
'im good an' proper. Right?'

'Fadel was dying . . . rambling. You can't take anything he
said seriously.'

Trapp looked at me in a funny, unsettling way. 'So you're
sayin' Fadel was looking at everythin' upside down, eh, mister?'

'Exactly. Dammit, Trapp, he didn't even let on when I
asked him who Zarafiq was . . . pretended he didn't even know
the name.'

I purposely didn't mention that Chang hadn't recognized it
either. That was another problem.

Trapp's voice was meek. Too meek. 'True. So when 'e pretended to be surprised when I accused him of stealin' me
detonators . . . you claim he wus really admittin' to having
done so. Right?'

After I'd worked out what he meant I stared at him uncomfortably. A warning note was buzzing at the back of my
mind; he'd cornered me, damn his clever eyes – because if I
denied the possibility of Fadel's implication, then I was tacitly
admitting that someone else had disarmed the charges . . . and
somehow I didn't feel this was the most diplomatic moment to
come clean on that score. Until I, in turn, was hit by a flash
of inspiration.

'Of course he was. Which only proves my point, Trapp –
Fadel did prevent you from scuttling the *Kamaran* back there.

And that, without any shadow of doubt, underlines his intention of getting her to Gahman. Which, in its turn, means that the only way you can hit back at Zarafiq is to sink her, here and now.'

'No, it doesn't,' he argued somewhat obscurely. 'It only proves Fadel wanted the stuff to reach Gahman.'

'But he told us to sink her as well!' I yelled, pushed beyond all reasonable endurance. 'Half a bloody hour ago, Trapp. He said we had to sink her . . .'

I broke off in horror. I'd finally done it. I'd finally fallen into the Trapp trap of arguing against myself. His eyes glinted triumphantly, but he didn't dare push his luck too far.

'Mind you,' he added generously, 'just before that he also tried to sink Chang – an' save the *Kamaran*. But that could've been for a different reason altogether.'

'Like what?' I snapped, interested despite myself.

'Like because he is . . . was definit'ly a communist, was Fadel,' he continued perceptively. 'And while there must be some reason why he an' Zarafiq don't want their own Red mates in Gahman to get the goods, maybe Fadel was equally worried by the prospects of Chang offering a mob of rightists the wherewithal to give Soviet-backed Qaddhafi the bullet. Right?'

I didn't answer. For once Trapp might have come up with a logical thought.

'Anyway,' he continued doggedly, 'have you forgotten that other remark Fadel made – about askin' yourself why Zarafiq ever got me ter do this job in the first place? About his emphasizin' me bein' . . . what was it . . . predictable?'

'Hah!' I snorted derisively, but he didn't get annoyed for once.

'Exac'ly. I even admit I tends to blow with the wind at times; change me mind on odd occasions.'

'You, Trapp,' I said sincerely, 'have just made the understatement of the year. Being about as predictable as an oven-roasted hand-grenade.'

He smiled; a little tightly certainly, but he did smile. 'So allowin' f'r me slight fickleness, if you'd been Zarafiq an' you really did want a cargo deliverin' – would you have come half-way round the world just to get me to do it for you?'

I frowned. He'd certainly made his point. Had I been Zarafiq, then the one way I'd have been certain of losing my investment would have been to employ Trapp. Especially if I'd made sure that Trapp became my implacable enemy first – like by kidnapping him, maybe. And sinking his little fishing boat . . . and killing a few passengers who'd been his responsibility.

It didn't help me; my interests were apparently coincidental with the extraordinary plans of Mister Zarafiq, in wishing to see the last of the *Kamaran*. But the argument was over, and Trapp had made up his stubborn bloody mind.

For the next hour or two, anyway.

'So that's why we're takin' Zarafiq's cargo right to where 'e says he wants it, mister,' he grinned cleverly. 'But just in case I'm wrong – not that I ever am, mind – but just in case; then we're goin' to prepare a little insurance policy afore we arrive . . .'

I eyed him anxiously. I'd seen him like this before, and it made me very nervous indeed.

'Insurance?'

'Remember the *Charon*?' Trapp mused wistfully; danger-ously. 'Remember 'ow we used to fight the war with the old *Charon* – Number One?'

Chapter Twelve

According to Trapp arrangements had been made for a local craft to intercept us well offshore, and lead the *Kamaran* into the river where Zarafiq's people would be waiting to off-load her.

It had seemed a sensible proposal at first – a glance at the chart showed it to be one of the most desolate and ill-marked waterways along the whole of the North African coast – and explained, at least in part, why we were apparently instructed to make the entry during daylight hours only. Though that somewhat indiscreet proposal did tend to aggravate my already active unease the more I thought about it, considering the illicit nature of the *Kamaran*'s cargo and the clandestine standing of its Marxist consignees.

But then I began to brood on the words of the dying Fadel; to ask myself again and again why a man such as Trapp *had* been so essential to Zarafiq's plan? Because any crooked shipmaster could have been relied upon to bring the *Kamaran* this far – and theoretically we were to be piloted through the only real navigational hazards of the voyage. Weren't we?

Or did the enigmatic Mister Zarafiq have something a little different in store? Assuming Trapp *did* go strictly against form, and still turn up at that offshore rendezvous . . .

Anyway, it had been a seven-hour run into the meeting point. I'd spent six of them arguing with Trapp; the seventh had been utilized in making . . . well . . . preparations. Actually there had been a further task I'd made up my mind to carry out – like replacing the detonators in the charges and sinking the *Kamaran* anyway. But for obvious reasons that had to be a very private affair, and Trapp hadn't left me alone for long enough to go to the bloody toilet with discretion.

He even followed me down to my cabin, still vociferously

demanding my unconditional approval and totally ignoring the fact that we were about to make our landfall at any moment. Mind you, that act of recklessness did hold out one small glimmer of hope for me; with Dan'l Spew keeping the watch there was a reasonable chance he wouldn't notice anything particular up ahead – and solve all my problems by running full tilt into bloody Africa.

Unfortunately Third Officer Gorbals Wullie was also topside, strutting the bridge like a bumptious mini-vulture, and he'd been told very earthily by his captain precisely what would happen to certain parts of his anatomy if he *didn't* see nuthin' an' report it when there *wus* somethin' ter be see'd. An' reported.

Or something?

'Well, you can't say we ain't ready f'r every possible contingency,' Trapp challenged me complacently, flopping on to my bunk and idly leafing through one of the newspapers still littering my cabin like confetti.

'Chang probably said much the same thing,' I retorted acidly, 'before he got himself torpedoed. By a bulldozer.'

'That weren't my fault,' Trapp defended himself primly.

'Oh, no. Not any more than the Second World War was Hitler's.'

'Yeah, well . . .'

He lapsed into sullen but welcome silence and glowered at the yellowing newsprint while I gloomily inspected the mirror, debating on whether to depart this mortal coil clean-shaven, or just stay a scruffy corpse to match the rest of the *Kamaran*'s crowd. Trapp's contingency plans for entering harbour smacked more of the Fleet's preparations before the Battle of Trafalgar – I'd developed the firm conviction he intended to get us all killed even if the Commies were awaiting our arrival with a brass band and a camel-full of cash.

Suddenly Trapp jerked up and muttered, 'Christ!'

I ignored him pointedly; I simply wasn't in the mood for two-month-old news about how the world was going to hell – especially as I seemed scheduled to get there ahead of it. He wasn't going to be diverted, though. Just stuck the paper between me and the mirror and squinted uncomfortably.

It was an old copy of the *Malta Times* with a photograph of a suavely smiling Arab on the front. The caption read: *Middle East oil price deadlock. Gahman Minister flies to further talks.*

Trapp waggled the paper urgently, persistently. 'Know who he is, do you?'

I sighed and scanned the opening paragraph disinterestedly. 'Sheik Rabah Moinzadeh, millionaire oil minister for the Independent State of Gahman . . .'

'No, he's not,' Trapp blurted, then took a deep breath and added warily, 'He's . . . er . . . well, e's Zarafiq.'

'Your jokes usually manage to kill most of the audience,' I growled irritably. 'Please go away, Trapp. I'm very tired and I'd like to shave.'

'It's *Zarafiq*, I'm telling you,' he insisted. 'The bloke who hired me. Fadel's boss.'

I knew then he wasn't joking. I knew that much by the knot expanding in the pit of my stomach but I still argued, more as a plea than a statement. 'But you told me Zarafiq was just a fixer, dammit. A crooked businessman . . . while this Rabah whatsit's a heavy political animal; a government minister . . .'

Before the final stages of panic set in I desperately absorbed the next few lines. 'Yeah, look . . . pro-Western negotiator representing the Gahman Government at current OPEC talks. Apparently highly unpopular with the rest of the oil-producing countries, too – they're the only big exporters still blocking further price increases in crude . . .'

I suddenly broke off, staring unseeingly at the page. It did confirm one thing – that my admiral really had been telling the truth earlier, regarding why the British Government had such a close interest in the *Kamaran* – it also made Zara . . . Moinzadeh? Aw the *hell* with it . . . Zarafiq's motives even more obscure than before. For why should a government minister, of all implausible people, have any connection at all with a plot to bring his own government down? A millionaire at that – involved with politically-dedicated millionaire-killers? Because

Arab power struggles tended to prove violently fatal to the losers . . .

'Maybe the *Times* has made a mistake?' Trapp offered without a great deal of conviction.

'Negative,' I assured him – this time with a great deal of conviction. 'It's you who's made the mistake, Trapp. You an' your bent-as-a-corkscrew profiteering.'

'There's no call to cast aspersions on me commercial ethics,' he muttered weakly. 'Anyway, what difference does it make? Zarafiq's still Zara-bloody-fiq, whatever 'e calls himself on the side.'

'Difference?' I spluttered. 'Difference, you ask? Well, I'll tell you what difference it makes, shall I? It means, you've finally overstepped your mark. It means, you aren't even the target for petty CIA agents an' Chinese Mafia men any longer. Not now, mister. Because this article means you've bumbled your misbegotten way right into the big international league, Trapp . . . in the firing line between governments and super powers an' even the . . . the Shell bloody Oil Company, dammit!'

'Don't you yell at *me*, mate!' Trapp finally exploded, having run clean out of what was uncharacteristic humility anyway. 'Whatever Zarafiq's . . . Moinzadeh's . . . *Zarafiq's* bloody fancy government title is, he's still just a greedy Ayrab at the end o' the day. 'E's still jus' lookin' for a fast buck . . . an' you remember, mister clever dick – I'm still way ahead of 'im. I'm still dictating the action, savee? I'm the one what's goin' to spring all the surprises. *Right?*'

There was an abrupt knock on the door. Trapp flung it open furiously to reveal Gorbals Wullie standing there, looking decidedly uneasy.

'What d'yer WANT?' Trapp bellowed.

Wullie shuffled. 'Ah've come tae report – there's a ship comin' up on the starboard bow, Captin.'

Trapp swung triumphantly. 'See? Di'n't I tell yer then, mister? Thick as two short planks, that Zarafiq. Sent 'is pilot boat out to meet us like a turkey volunteerin' for Chris'mas . . .'

'Och, is *that* all it is?' Third Officer Wullie breathed with obvious relief. 'I thought that – what wi' all they guns an' missiles an' stuff – ah thought it wis maybe a Gahmanian warship . . .'

It was very ungracious of us, on reflection. The way he was left lying on the deck like that, all bruises and scuff-marks and bitter disillusionment. After we'd trampled straight over him, heading for the bridge . . .

Once again I felt I was reliving a nightmare; slipping irresistibly back into the time-dimmed past, with the restless stirring souls of ghosts over a quarter of a century dead suddenly awakening, and touching me with fearful memory.

Even the silhouette of the fast-approaching warship was much the same; still the evil, predatory shape reminiscent of the German *schnellbooten* or the VAS-boats of the World War Two Italian Fleet . . . And I was still there beside Trapp on a sullenly rolling bridge, watching, and waiting, and becoming more and more frightened as I'd done so many times before during the old *Charon*'s violent passage through the sewer of clandestine warfare.

Not even the location had altered all that much, for this was still the coast of North Africa; only there was no rumble of distant artillery as Rommel's *Afrika Korps* fell back under the assault of a long-dissolved Eighth Army; and there were no scurrying, terrified supply ships to provide an ill-defended prey for the *Charon*'s savage rape.

But there was no pride of country now either, nor patriotism to dull the sickness and the horror of before . . . and then I caught the look in Trapp's eyes, and remembered that there never had been, not for him, and realized that only I had changed. Everything else about me, about the world I existed in, hadn't moved forward one little, faltering step . . .

'You know what to do,' Trapp said calmly. 'Jus' get on wi' it.'

I blinked at him incredulously. 'Get on with what? The game's up, Trapp. That's a warship out there – flying the flag of a sovereign state; not some sophisticated maritime crook like Chang or Fadel. I told you earlier; you've got yourself involved with the national leagues now, Trapp, an' you don't do what you're proposing against a whole country.'

He didn't answer for a minute, just gazed out at the approaching craft with expressionless eyes. She was maybe two miles away and moving on a fast interception course. Through the binoculars she didn't look quite so old-fashioned any more; already I could make out the lines of a quick-firing turret gun on her foredeck and the even more unsettling suggestion of a missile-launcher aft. *Schnellbooten* and VAS-boats suddenly seemed almost friendly by comparison.

'You reckon they'll just smack our wrists and tell us not ter be naughty boys again, do yer?' he said eventually. And very mildly.

'No! We'll be arrested and charged with gun-running. We bloody well deserve to be, dammit! But there are diplomatic pressures . . .'

I think I knew, even as I spoke, that I was compounding a lie. I knew it as I stared aft at the grey, stateless faces nervously lining our scarred boat-deck rails . . . oh sure, maybe there would be diplomatic activity on my behalf – especially as now there could be no prospect of the *Kamaran*'s cargo ever reaching the communist forces, and the British Government would be very pleased with their extra-ordinary agent Miller. But there would be no hope at all for Trapp and Gorbals Wullie and Mister Spew and all those other international losers back there. The Gahmanians would throw them inside and forget them . . . but at least they'd still be alive, and still maybe able to con or bribe or slither a way to freedom. Especially knowing Trapp . . .

One and a half miles off. And still closing relentlessly.

' 'Ow many people do yer reckon knows about this rendez-vous?' Trapp suddenly asked. His voice was still calm, almost conversational.

'Not many. Presumably it wasn't exactly advertised in the local press. Us and Zarafiq, obviously . . . a few of the top communists. Fadel . . .'

I broke off. There were yet another group who were aware of the arrangements – I'd told them myself. But the British weren't likely to have tipped off the Gahmanian authorities; apart from the fact that they assumed Trapp still intended to scuttle the *Kamaran*, they would hardly be anxious to admit they'd been interfering in the internal affairs of a friendly state. Especially when, for most of the time, they'd appeared to be trying to engineer its downfall.

'Well, the Commies woul'n't have blown the gaff,' Trapp pointed out with undeniable logic. 'An' we certainly didn't . . . did we, mister?'

'No,' I said. Hurriedly.

'An' Fadel's dead as a shorted-out battery. So who else could've?'

One mile away. Sailors running to man the forward gun, while the missile-launcher aft was swinging, vectoring with space-age precision. White caps clearly visible on her flying bridge now, closed up to action stations.

'You mean Zarafiq himself . . . Oh, forget wild theories, Trapp. And forget what Fadel hinted; a dying man's raving. I still say you're crazy . . . I mean, why should he go to all this trouble – and then cut his own throat when he's virtually succeeded.'

'I dunno . . .' Trapp said thoughtfully, again scanning the approaching warship through his glasses. And then he handed them to me with a funny, mocking smile.

'. . . maybe you oughter ask him yourself, personally. Before he kills yer.'

'Stop engine.'

Mister Spew shuffled forward and grasped the telegraph, frowning in concentration as he tried to remember which way to swing it. Gorbals Wullie, relegated to the wheel again despite his recent elevation to officer status, looked piqued.

'How do I no' get tae do the technickle things?'

''Cause it's 'ighly scientific, see? An' too complex f'r a junior member o' the wardroom to 'andle.'

'Ah'm a third mate.'

'You're bloody stupid . . .'

I only heard their inconsequential bickering as though in a dream, not even really aware of the throb of the engine dying beneath me as the *Kamaran* coasted slowly to a halt. The figures on the warship bridge filled my binoculars now; all dark-skinned and clad in service whites . . . all except one. The grey-haired man in the tweed overcoat who clutched his hat unsteadily against the forty-knot wind of their approach.

I'd only seen a photograph of him until now. On the front page of the *Malta Times* . . .

'Now do yer believe me, mister . . . about Zarafiq?' Trapp prodded from behind.

Half a mile to go and even the missile-launcher was trained on us now.

'I don't see what difference it makes. She's still a Gahman warship; and I'm still damned if I'm prepared to go along with your sort of action against the flag of a Western power simply to avoid arrest . . .'

Trapp was smiling all the time, only there wasn't any humour in it by now. Just a savage, wolfish mockery – and that terrible hatred.

'If you wus Zarafiq – or maybe I should say if you wus a certain Sheik Rabah Moinzadeh, who just happened to have the authority o' a government minister; maybe even 'ad a few sympathetic mates wearin' admiral's stripes. An' you'd been fixin' – for whatever reason you like to pick – to stab your own government in the back by supplyin' arms to the communists . . . An' you knew there were only a few blokes on a certain ship what could blow the gaff on you – what would you do to them, mister? If you had 'em under a gun? With a good excuse to make yourself a national hero at the same time?'

I began to walk away from him. I only turned back when I'd reached the head of the ladder leading to the boat deck and the life-raft stowages.

'I hope you rot in hell, Trapp!' I said as levelly as I could.

He allowed his smile to broaden to a fully-fledged grin. 'You'll be able ter make sure I do, mister. 'Cause we'll all be there together; all alongside each other . . . only you'll still be wearin' that uniform, won't you?'

I blinked at him uncertainly. 'Uniform?'

'In a manner o' speaking. The one you never took off all them years ago, not even after the old *Charon* was sunk. The one you wus still wearin' when I met up wi' you again at Red Sweetwater, mister. The one you've been wearin' ever since you come aboard the *Kamaran* . . . the Queen's uniform, Lieutenant Miller – the uniform o' the Royal Navee.'

And then he leaned out over the rail, leaving me staring after him like a stranded fish.

And roared, just like he'd done so often before, when so many other men had died. 'Panic party awayyyyy . . . *aban-donnnnn ship!*'

Chapter Thirteen

It was the very first time I'd seen anybody doing anything right since I'd joined the *Kamaran*.

As a panic party they were superb. The moment Trapp gave the order our boat deck became a scene of ultimate hysteria. Life-rafts tumbled haphazardly from every stowage to land in undisciplined chaos on the sea alongside; release lanyards were tugged with undisguised anxiety; great yellow and orange balloons unfurled and inflated with irresistible snorts, shoving and bumping like water-lilies manœuvring at the start of a race . . . apart from the rafts that never actually reached the water – those which blew themselves up while still on deck, scattering seamen and jamming alleyways just because some stupid bastard had yanked the lanyard before he jettisoned the gear . . .

. . . and then the actual abandoning. Men spurred into feats of athleticism by the closing menace of that quick-firing foredeck gun, sliding and gabbling down anything that offered a safe passage off the ship . . . ropes, ladders, snaking white firehoses; kicking and struggling to get there first; shoving each other away from – or over, come to that – the bloody rails in a multi-lingual frenzy of fear. And the triumph which transcended anything we'd been able to produce on the old *Charon* . . . the super-star of the *Kamaran*'s epic evacuation – Maabud whatsit, Chief Engineer, Egyptian State Railways retired.

He was magnificent. Still looking like an ambulatory blob of engine oil, he managed to fight his way right to the head of the queue for leaving. Then he changed his mind about going over the rail at all . . . and someone behind started kicking him and yelling for a knife or a spanner or jus' a fuckin' table leg ter smash 'is effin' 'ead in . . . so Maabud shrieked a descending prayer to Allah, reinforced by a shotgun spray of appeals to the mercy of Jesus, the compassion of Buddha, the infinite clemency of Shinto, Baal, Nekhebt, Xochiquetzal, Amen-ra and – just in case – Beelzebub an' a few assorted demons, all the way down to the Plimsoll line . . . and then changed his mind about the whole bloody idea and tried frantically to shin back *up* the rope again despite the flood-tide of survival-bent bodies pouring across his like lemmings on a suicide trip.

'Lovely boys,' Trapp said, watching with enormous satisfaction. 'If that don't convince them Ayrab matelots we're abandonin' f'r real, then I'm a gorilla's uncle.'

'How did you discover,' I muttered cautiously, lying flat alongside him under cover of the bridge wing, 'that I'm still working for the RN?'

In view of the probable outcome of the impending action it seemed a bit academic whether he was angry or not, but I was glad to register only a comparatively inoffensive conceit in the glance he directed towards me.

'I didn't. Not until I saw the look in yer eyes when I needled yer. But you always wus too honest, wusn't you?'

'But you must have had some cause, some reason for suspicion?'

'Just little things. The Sweetwater set-up – too pat by half, after I'd thought about it a bit. An' then there wus the fact that you kept on changin' your mind about whether I should scuttle this bucket or not – an' apart from meself, there's only one crowd can be so bloody awkward an' erratic.'

'Who?'

'The Royal Navy, mister. When they're tryin' to do the impossible an' steer a course dictated by the British Government.'

For a few moments I felt truly humble; quite ashamed, in fact, and grateful for the manner in which he accepted my admitted disloyalty. 'I'm sorry, Trapp,' I ventured, hardly able to meet his eye. 'If I'd known you were involved from the start, I'd never have agreed to do it.'

He rolled over, looked straight at me – and began to leer again. It was that old, deprecating, utterly infuriating expression he always managed to produce when he thought he'd got me cornered.

'Apology accepted, mate. I always knew there'd come a time when you finally has ter admit I've always been right an' you've always been wrong. That you always does the daft thing like a bull at a gate, while I employs me superior brain an' me natural commercial judgement an' me subtlety . . .'

I sat up so suddenly I nearly forgot there was a ready-use missile-launcher and a hotted-up Oerlikon behind the thin wooden screen. But he'd done it now. He'd gone an' done it again, just like he always bloody would.

'*Subtlety*?' I yelled, without the slightest suspicion of humility left. 'You've got all the subtlety of a rogue Panzer division, Trapp. And I wasn't meaning it as an apology, any-way – I meant I wouldn't have agreed to the Navy's proposal if they'd told me you were involved, for one reason an' f'r one reason only . . . because I'd hoped I'd never ever bloody see you again!'

His ever-blossoming grin was as wide as the gulf between us. Yet it still couldn't quite mask the relief which seemed so incongruous under the circumstances.

Until he chortled, 'Lord, but you 'ad me worried for a minnit then. I could've sworn you wasn't never goin' to give me a good argymint ever again, the way you looked so bloody repentant . . . Now shut up an' keep yer head down, jus' like you done in the war – Number One.'

Twenty minutes later. Twenty everlasting minutes láter, and that grey interceptor was still hovering a frustratingly cautious distance off our starboard quarter.

It had been very quiet on board since the crew had gone. Oh, there was still the faint vibration of the slowly-turning main engine as it idled on *stand-by*, and the sigh of wind-strummed halyards above the bridge and the sporadic clatter of an empty beer can discarded in a scupper, but nothing really to indicate there was any human life left within this tension-fraught circle of sea other than the subdued mutter of frightened men in the life-rafts bobbing alongside, and the more distant growl of the Gahman Navy craft's exhausts . . . and the thunder of my own heart-beats as the waiting continued.

Surreptitiously I glanced across at Trapp; yeah, he still looked the same as he'd done all those years before, with flint-hard eyes peering through the hastily formed slot in the bridge wing and that grim piratical determination a carbon copy of our previous war.

Our tactics were identical, too. Disconcert our enemy; lead him to believe the target was abandoned, the crew demoralized – which shouldn't be too difficult, not with Trapp's current band of shambolic anti-heroes – until he dropped his guard, came that little, unsuspecting shade too close, and then . . .

Only it wasn't as simple as that. Not this time. Because there was one major difference – for the *Charon*, despite her mouldering decrepitude, had still sailed to battle as a highly specialized coffin. She had been a proper Q-ship, with con-cealed armament and drop-down side plates and even a basic fire-control system operated from her bridge. She'd worn her apparent nervousness as a shield, and her false colours had been a major weapon in the strategy of surprise.

But this was the *Kamaran*; and she carried no surprise. The Gahman Navy knew precisely what she was, while Zarafiq knew Trapp's history perhaps a little too well to allow him to live long enough to strike . . . apart from the fact that we had virtually no camouflaged fire positions at instant readiness, and no Bofors gun or 4·7-inch havoc to release at the command of a specialist rating's finger.

We had no specialist ratings, come to that – only Gorbals Wullie crouching on the boat deck with a bravado fuelled more by terror than true Scottish grit; plus three vaguely Greek seamen cowering behind the deckhousing without a weapon between them simply because they'd been too bloody paralysed with fright to abandon ship in the first place – and Second Officer Spew, who was the one man I didn't want on board, and who'd already ambled out of sight a few minutes ago carrying a grey-painted box he'd discovered somewhere, despite my frantically hissed plea to jus' lie down an' go to sleep.

Staunch, bumble-headed, screw-everythin'-up-proper Mister Spew . . .

'They're comin',' Trapp suddenly offered with enormous satisfaction. 'Di'n't I say they'd come closer, then?'

I wriggled over beside him and squinted through the peep-hole. The trickle of water under the uneasily cruising Gah-manian's bow had risen to a distinct flare as she turned towards us. A flash from her bridge betrayed binoculars inspecting – searching – the life-rafts in which most of the occupants now cringed, hidden from view by the automatically-inflated canopies.

'Stay outa sight, boys,' Trapp urged unnecessarily. 'Keep under them awnings like I told yer.'

'Oh, they'll do that all right,' I growled with certainty. 'There's a good thickness of rubberized canvas to give 'em protection from that missile-launcher out there.'

'Now you're bein' pessimistic, mister. He won't use no missile on a few tatty sailormen like them.'

'No?' I challenged, with a flicker of hope.

'No . . . 'e'll use his quick-firer forr'ad. Then small arms to finish off them what's still yellin'.'

The hope died abruptly. And so did the bow wave of the grey mini-warship. Once again she resumed her slow appraisal of the Kamaran's concealed panic party.

'The plan's not going to work,' I groaned in frustration. 'Your idea of using your crew as bait isn't tempting enough, Trapp. He'll pick 'em off at long range . . .'

'Yes, it will, an' no, he won't!' Trapp retorted with a hint of asperity. 'I tell you Zarafiq's got to be sure I'm on the end o' his gunsights before he moves . . . I'm pretty special, you know. I'm the only one c'n really put him in queer street with 'is government pals, remember.'

I stared at him in outrage. Dammit, but he actually looked pleased about it, conceited even. Personally I'd have thought that kind of distinction had all the desirability of being the only case of bubonic plague at a world health conference. But I wasn't Trapp.

'Then how's about you going over there an' giving yourself up so's the rest of us can go home,' I snarled, finally nettled by that self-assured smirk. 'And anyway – just say you are wrong? Say Zarafiq knows how we operated in the war, and doesn't risk coming any closer. Just opens fire from there regardless?'

'Then I'll apologize to the boys,' Trapp growled icily. 'An' save a lot o' money on end-o'-voyage bonuses.'

Which proved, if proof were still needed, that Edward Trapp had not changed one little bit . . .

. . . but then the sinister grey ship began to slide ahead again, much more determinedly than before. While Trapp ever so bleakly yanked back on the cocking handle of the tripod-mounted Soviet Kalashnikov PKS before him, then checked the link-belt ammunition feed.

And I did what might have seemed a rather odd thing to a casual observer. I simply placed my hands flat against the outboard end of the *Kamaran*'s bridge wing, and tensed my muscles. And prepared to meet Mister Zarafiq face to face.

Two hundred metres . . . one seventy . . . If Trapp still cherished any lingering conviction that all Ayrabs wus sloppy, then his chagrin must have matched my trepidation.

They sensed that something was wrong, those Gahmanian Navy officers. The abandonment of the *Kamaran* had been too premature; too unexpected. I could see the white caps bent in anxious consultation with the frail, incongruous figure of the man who'd generated this still-senseless riddle; and while the tactical discussion went on, so the patrol-craft ratings remained closed up to their weapons with undeviating concentration. Something had to happen, and soon.

One sixty . . . one fifty-five . . . one fifty metres but slowing, swinging slightly as the cox'n spun the wheel. Still hesitant, and still as grimly alert.

'Come on,' Trapp growled, betraying his inner tension for the first time. 'Come on, c'mon, c'mon!'

Dejectedly I stole a hurried glance aft along the boat deck to where the second wave of our attack was assembled – and discovered my pessimism fully justified. Twenty per cent of our reserve wasn't there at all, yet – that was Mister Spew – while the trio of stranded Greeks were still trying desperately to blend in with the white-painted deckhousing, and Gorbals Wullie was managing to give a most successful impression of an irresolute ferret clutching a machinegun. Certainly there were five more loaded Czech machine-pistols from number two hold at instant readiness beside him, but it occurred to me they were more for self-protection rather than aggression.

'Told yer,' Trapp grunted abruptly. 'Di'n't I tell you they woul'n't use them missiles?'

I began to hope a little again. The warship was still closing slowly but now they'd secured from the launcher aft . . . only the three Arab ratings didn't just stand down; they immediately seized sub-machineguns and doubled smartly forward to line the near rail.

I think that was the moment when I finally did accept the reality of what Zarafiq was; and that there really were no empty cells awaiting the *Kamaran*'s crew back in Gahman. I think the crew got that impression too, and at much the same time; the unhappy mutters from the rafts below suddenly peaked on a crescendo of terror.

'DO something f'r God's sake,' I snarled, ashen-faced. 'Open fire if you're goin' to, Trapp. Before Zarafiq does.'

'Belay the advice, mister!' he snapped back tautly. 'We only got one chance . . . an' I ain't goin' to take it 'til we sees the whites o' their eyes.'

But his hand was clawlike on the butt of the Kalashnikov, and his finger was trembling against the trigger . . .

The loud-hailer, when it crackled, was almost as startling as a burst of gunfire. And Zarafiq's impeccable diction as enticing as honey.

'Captain Trapp. Please, my dear friend, desist from this rather odd and quite unnecessary behaviour.'

One twenty metres now, and circling to come from astern; just too far aft to vector the gun from where we lay . . .

'Show yourself, Captain. No need for such reticence. My naval associates beside me are most sympathetic to our mutual arrangement.'

The foredeck quick-firer swivelling all the time, though. And not on the rafts, dammit! A much higher elevation, allowing it to train along the line of the *Kamaran*'s main-deck bulwarks.

'They still suspect the ship,' I muttered sickly. 'Zarafiq is aware of how we operated before . . . he intends to take out the rafts and us at the same bloody time, Trapp.'

'The rafts, maybe. But not us yet, mister. Not unless they elevate that weapon a good few degrees,' Trapp calculated dispassionately. 'They're expectin' us somewhere along the centre-castle deck – we still got the drop on 'em from up 'ere . . .'

Ninety metres only, now, and one factor at least in our favour – she was nearing at as slow a speed as any gunner could have prayed for. Coming closer and closer, an unbelievable sitting duck, with the tension aboard her almost as evident as among our own gibbering bait in the rafts – or up here, on the *Kamaran*'s top decks, come to that.

'Might I suggest a ten-thousand-dollar bonus, Captain? What incentive that must be to common sense and . . .'

'Ten grand . . .' Trapp breathed ecstatically. Tearing my eyes away from the interceptor I stared at him uneasily; for the first time a hint of irresolution was evident. Money, to Trapp, was like an arrow in the heel for Achilles.

'Trapp. No, Trapp . . .' I cautioned appealingly.

Just as the growl of turbo-charged engines rose to a new note; to a surge of abruptly unleashed power . . . there was something wrong.

I swung hastily to face astern – and blinked. The water under the patrol craft's counter had suddenly begun to swirl and froth, the bows rising as the flare below her stem surged higher and higher . . .

'They've fooled us, Trapp! They're making a speed run; goin' past to run down the rafts an' take us out at full power.'

'We still 'ave to wait . . .' he roared hopelessly. We both

knew surprise was now the only card we had left.

Until . . .

'Awwww Jeeeeze!' Gorbals Wullie shrieked from the boat deck – and immediately began to fire in a panic-stricken reflex which, with a sub-machinegun at that range, could only act as a heaven-sent early warning to the attackers.

'Damn!' Trapp said.

'Trappppp!' I howled beseechingly.

'Well, go on then!' he bellowed back.

I shoved desperately – and the whole pre-loosened section at the extreme end of the bridge wing collapsed outboard, tumbling down to the sea below. At the time it had promised to be a most inadequate modification to make a battleship out of us; now it seemed utterly futile.

Trapp still snatched at the trigger of the heavy Kalashnikov, though. With a terrible, hopeless rage . . .

Gorbals Wullie may have compromised our deception through his agitated lack of self-control, but he probably saved the lives of a great many men in the rafts at the same time.

The warship was already turning in anticipation, sheering violently away as Trapp was forced to fire his first too-hasty burst. A line of high-velocity water-spouts exploded precisely between the accelerating patrol boat and our own hysterical panic party – only the FPB wasn't there any more. Already they were roaring at a tangent from our own heading with the yellow and blue ensign board flat in the wind and the cox'n bent low over his wheel.

Fifty metres . . . forty . . . still getting closer though as she overtook us. 'I'll kill 'im . . .' Trapp raged from suffused lips. 'I'll bloody *kill* that scrawny little bastaaaard!'

But I didn't know whether he meant Zarafiq or Gorbals Wullie. I didn't care all that much either – because that was the moment when the Kalashnikov jammed.

Simultaneously the quick-firer opened up with a measured rhythm. *Slam – slam – slam* . . . But they were having their troubles too. The gunlayer, locked against his restraining harness by the momentum of their unanticipated turn, was still fighting for stability. Only he was winning . . . a diagonal slash of detonations suddenly climbed the *Kamaran*'s hull, peppered the after end of the centrecastle, converted the boat deck around Gorbals Wullie's carefully selected funk hole to a screeching, whining haze of splintered rails and leaping deck planks and colandered ventilators . . . maybe even bits of Gorbals Wullie.

It didn't matter. It couldn't matter. Not right then . . .

'Gerritfree . . .' I screamed. 'Gethatblockage*freeeeeee* . . .'

Suddenly a small object sailed outwards, apparently from under the bridge deck where we crouched. A rock? A stone? Who the hell was throwing stones?

More explosions from the line of the davits now, coming even closer, f'r God's sake. And faces staring up from the racing craft now drawing abeam of us; white figures clinging against the centrifugal pull but with one more – Zarafiq – performing a funny, disoriented dance as he lost balance and staggered aft on the pocket-book fighting bridge.

The Kalashnikov, though. Why the hell was Trapp's Kalashnikov jammed now? Right when we needed it the mo . . . CHRIST!

Sub-machineguns yammering up at us as well, suddenly. Bullets seemingly flying everywhere. The windows in the after end of the *Kamaran*'s chartroom blowing inwards with a crash of diamond-bright splinters; a line of holes ripping through the woodwork a hand's breadth away from and parallel with my right leg . . . yet still more ridiculous things going on around us – another useless object arc-ing outboard to land with an insignificant plop under the slamming bow of the FPB . . .

'GetyerFOOToff . . .' Trapp stormed abruptly, volcanically. 'GetyerbloodyfootoffthebloodyAMMOBELT . . .'

I squirmed away in horror, releasing the jammed feed, and the Kalashnikov began to judder again – but too late. She was abeam of us now on a thunder of full power; ten seconds more and she'd be past and clear, and ready to return out of range and pick us off at leisure . . .

But she wouldn't need to come back. The quick-firer rounds were suddenly slamming into the top of the wheelhouse, chopping radar scanner and radio aerials, monkey island and standard compass into a smash of wreckage. And aiming even lower, correcting all the time . . . the after end of the bridge itself collapsing on top of us; Trapp bellowing obscenities and protecting himself while trying hopelessly to depress the muzzle of the gun at the same time . . .

I found myself blasted bodily sideways with my addled head poised over a hole which hadn't been there in the deck a moment ago. And Second Officer Dan'l Spew looked up cheerily through that brand-new hole, and said, ''Allo, Mister Cooper! 'Ow's things with you, then?'

Before drawing back his creaky arm to throw the third grenade he'd taken from that grey-painted box he'd been so enamoured with. Which did seem a rather futile gesture on the face of it, as they didn't appear to be detonating anyway.

It was a madness, of course. An exclusively Trapp-created world of dementia. Because I lay there, and watched that killer ship drawing away through the hole in the deck, and realized it could well be the last sight I would ever see . . . yet I still managed to be correct, ever so polite, to Mister Spew.

'Mister Spew,' I called, with the blood trickling relentlessly down my forehead.

'Yus, Mister Cooper?' he acknowledged with wide-eyed attentiveness.

'Don't bother to throw that hand-grenade, Mister Spew,' I urged considerately.

'No, Mister Cooper?' he queried, a little mystified certainly but only too anxious to be helpful.

'No,' I answered in tightly measured tones. 'Not . . . unless . . . you . . . pull . . . the . . . fucking . . . pin out first!'

It was a magnificent throw. It left Mister Spew's grasp as if projected by a strangely articulated ballista, and descended on its target with the accuracy of a Cruise Missile.

It exploded just as it reached the patrol craft's bridge and blew both the Arab captain and his first lieutenant into a ghastly, bloodied fusion. It stripped a large part of the cox'n's spine away and folded him over the wheel, locking it inextricably in the full-starboard-rudder mode. It blasted Mister Zarafiq – already teetering and off balance at the head of the ladder – in a very alive but shrieking and tweed-coat-flailing arc clean across the heads of her remaining crewmen, and finally deposited him in the boil of her wake.

She didn't stop to pick him up. Because there wasn't anyone left up there to stop her.

Still under full power she continued to describe a buffeting, flaring orbit away from the *Kamaran* as Trapp and I dragged ourselves erect and stared dumbly after her. Meanwhile Mister Spew stuck his head up through the cavity in the deck, and fixed us with an anthropoid and querying gaze.

'I suppose,' Mister Spew uttered, fatalistically but with the nearest hint he could ever get to of aggressiveness, 'I suppose I'm goin' ter get into trouble again, am I?'

Trapp found his voice eventually, and characteristically. 'Them grenades you wasted with not pullin' the pin. You realize 'ow much they're worth apiece, mister? How much them commies shoreside is goin' to dock off've me fee?'

But there was no real bite to it, merely a shadow of his usual nit-picking disparagement. And then, just as I turned with fatalistic apprehension to search for the corpse of the late Gorbals Wullie in the shambles of the strafed boat deck, Trapp added wildly, 'Ohhhhh, hell!'

And I swung back disconcerted to catch sight of him galloping for the engine telegraph, still rearing crookedly above the debris of the wheelhouse.

I frowned, took one look out to sea where the Gahmanian craft had taken off on her crazy, uncontrolled departure – and then I too was running. This time for the bridge wing overlooking the rafts.

I didn't even hesitate when I saw the tiny figure splashing dementedly at the spot where Mister Zarafiq had performed his grenade-assisted dive. I just flung myself full length, stuck my head out over the end of the bridge, and waved frantically to the pallid, pleading faces gazing up at me.

'Paddle!' I roared. 'She's comin' back – so jus' shut up. An' paddle . . .'

Even then we might have avoided her if Trapp hadn't put the engine ahead like that. But he did, and we didn't, which was typical of the whole bloody voyage anyway.

By the time the rogue warship had come round on a reciprocal course to head straight for us she must have been doing forty knots; probably with an unwitting Arab engineer rating, blind and still below in her engineroom, trying to make her go even faster in what he would have assumed was a tactical withdrawal, not a suicidal return to the fray.

The floundering howls of Sheik Rabah Moinzadeh alias Zarafiq were once again submerged in the wake of the homing runaway as she slammed past him for a second time on her five-thousand-horsepower circuit. Her forward gun was deserted now, its crew racing hopelessly aft and away from where the *Kamaran* must now be rising before them like a high-speed steel cliff. Only one seaman still had the presence of mind to clamber through the wreckage of her bridge to wrestle vainly with her locked wheel and throttles.

She was still swinging, though. Still veering to pass close under – but possibly clear – of our looming bows . . .

I had the ridiculous impression that the life-rafts were also doing forty knots on a blur of paddles – the other way! But that was only because I was still dazed, and the *Kamaran* had begun to slide through the water too, leaving them behind.

I saw what was going to happen. I was even shouting, 'Astern, Trapp! Come astern, man . . .' when the warship finally hit.

She only caught our stem a glancing blow, but it was enough to capsize her instantly. Her after end slammed round in a spraying, crazy arc under the momentum of her swing, and she continued to skip and roll appallingly across an ejected carpet of smashed and dying crewmen . . . while the *Kamaran* herself veered to port – almost chasing the cavorting, disintegrating hulk – but then I sensed, rather than saw, the contraction in the water ahead, and the white flash which seemed to freeze the very sea itself . . . and I was scrabbling for what little cover remained behind the bridge front when submerging electronics short-circuited and the Gahmanian missiles started to explode.

They seemed to last for a long time, those underwater detonations, with the *Kamaran* wincing and bucking in pain as blow after submarine blow struck her deep under her belly. For our party floating astern in the rafts it must have presented a nightmare of concussion, transmitted up through the thin floors of the fragile craft, while for Mister Zarafiq – totally unprotected from the pressures below the surface – it could only have offered a torment to satisfy even the vengeful ambition of Trapp.

Finally it was over.

Stiffly I uncurled yet again, uncovered my head, and looked cautiously around – and then gaped; conscious of an embarrassment I'd never have believed possible.

For Trapp was crying. A suddenly old and very tired man. Just crying . . .

He was simply standing there, gazing aft to where Gorbals Wullie had been before the action began, only now there were only twisted rails and the black pocks of violence, and three shaken Greek seamen trying to extricate themselves from the mess. A Thompson sub-machinegun lay there too, right on the edge of a torn crater where the deck slipped away to the sea, but there was no one left beside it.

Pulling myself to my feet I wiped the blood from my eyes and staggered over to Trapp, but he didn't seem even to be aware of me, didn't make any attempt to conceal the grief which shook his bowed shoulders. Tentatively I put out a hand and touched him gently, helplessly, as Mister Spew joined us from below.

'Like losin' a pet dog,' Mister Spew intoned sonorously. ''E wus just like a dog, wus Wullie. A little Pekingese puppy wiv a flat face. An' a big mouth . . .'

'A Scottie dog,' Trapp snuffled. ''E wus a Scottie dog what I loved like . . . like . . .'

'Er . . . like a dog?' suggested Mister Spew somewhat confusingly.

'But ah'm no' a dog – ah'm more like a tiger!' the voice of Gorbals Wullie interjected with a curiously unspiritual excitement. 'Here, did yous no' see me throw they Arabs intae total confusion, did ye? Man, but wis I no' a real snap-shot wi' the Tommy gun, wis ah?'

We turned slowly, speechlessly. The apparition before us looked far too insanitary and solid for a ghost.

'Where the 'ell did you come from?' the bereaved pet fancier finally demanded with a somewhat less than joyous expression of welcome.

'The port side,' offered the reincarnated and suddenly uncertain Fido. 'But ah'm tryin' tae tell you how ah scunnered they navy lads . . .'

'An' what—' further demanded Trapp in a tone which caused even Mister Spew to move discreetly out of range— 'wus you doing on the port side, when they wus attackin' us from the starboard side?'

'I wis . . . er . . . well, me bein' third officer, Captin, I wis doin' my duty an' . . . well . . . makin' sure no cowardly sailors wis hidin' round there . . .'

Trapp kicked him all the way to the bottom of the ladder. And then glared down, and took a deep breath, and bawled volcanically, 'Third officer? I seen better third officers what coul'n't tie a granny knot! I seen third officers what had been drownded in a flooded compartment f'r a week, an' still wi' more brains than you. Third officer, you says? I seen camel drivers in the middle o' the Kalahari Desert what 'as more idea o' seamanship than you, stupid! So it's an ordinary seaman you are again from now on, yer sneaky Scotch egg. An ordin'ry seaman—an' about the ordinariest bloody seaman I ever did set eyes on, at that . . .'

I tiptoed discreetly into the wheelhouse and began to turn the *Kamaran* on a reciprocal which would take us back to the rafts, and whatever was left of Mister Zarafiq.

I didn't think I'd ever seen Trapp so happy; so blissfully happy and relieved . . .

Chapter Fourteen

Most of the panic party had to be assisted up the ladder from the rafts. Some, through shock and fright, had to be man-handled up the ship's side on the end of a safety line. Others weren't even in a condition to do that . . .

Mister Zarafiq, for instance, was all smashed up inside; the force of those submarine explosions must have split his intestines like a rabbit's under a hammer. Yet he was still alive, still semiconscious when I brought him to the *Kamaran* and slipped a bowline under his limp arms for them to haul him to the deck.

I followed up the pilot ladder, rung by painful rung, with the inert form of the moaning Arab rising jerkily beside me. Oh, I tried to cushion him as much as I could but Trapp wasn't very gentle, and Mister Zarafiq learned, perhaps for the first time, just what it was like to be on the receiving end of someone else's callousness.

Yet even when we'd nearly reached the top the Arab's torment wasn't over. For Trapp simply stopped hauling, secured the line, leaned out over the bulwark – and smiled.

It would have been better – more hopeful for Zarafiq – if his rescuer had struck him.

''Allo, Mister Z,' Trapp said, ever so friendly. 'Feelin' a bit crook, are yer?'

Zarafiq merely dangled there, dripping water from his expensive tweed coat and black blood from his slack mouth, and whimpering softly.

'For God's sake, Trapp,' I called urgently.

But Trapp just continued to smile as if he hadn't heard me. Or didn't intend to.

'You'll appreciate, what wi' you being a business man too, that when an extra service is called for on a contract, then

164

there's gotter be an extra charge to cover it – agreed, Mister Z? Oh, I do hope you don't mind me callin' you Mister Zarafiq, Sheik. Seein' it was your idea in the first place?'

'Trapp!' I appealed again, staring anxiously up at the group of faces now watching sullenly from the rail. But apart from Gorbals Wullie and Mister Spew, heaving grimly on a second recovery line farther along, nobody moved; nobody raised a hint of protest.

'So as there never was no clause agreed which gave you yourself a berth aboard the *Kamaran*,' Trapp continued remorselessly, 'then I'm quite within me contractual rights to ask a little more before I do. Let's say four questions, Mister Z . . . four easy-to-answer little questions, eh?'

'Please, Captain . . .' Zarafiq whispered.

Trapp just kept right on smiling.

'The first is simple . . . like where's the rest o' me money? The balance outstanding on completion of contract?'

'Trapp!'

Zarafiq's lips moved imperceptibly. 'On shore. The group who are expecting the cargo. I could not tell them it would be . . . unnecessary?'

'Unnecessary, Mister Zarafiq? Are you suggestin' this cargo wasn't meant to reach Gahman, then? Which brings me to me second question – why did you go to so much trouble to hire me as master of this ship? What's the special quality I 'ave that made me so attractive, mister?'

Zarafiq's eyes opened and he gazed pleadingly up at Trapp. 'Please, for pity's sake, Captain. No more questions until . . .'

Trapp looked terribly disappointed. He brought his hand up from behind the bulwark and there was a knife in it. He laid the knife regretfully on the rope securing Mister Zarafiq . . .

'You are a dishonest man . . .' Zarafiq screamed in terror, 'but with one reliable attribute – you can be depended upon to cheat your employer . . .'

I could hear the sharp intake of breath along the rail. The ship rolled uneasily, fretfully, and we swung away from the hull, suspended over thirty feet of nothing. Zarafiq moaned like an animal in pain as we slammed back into the steel side.

'It don't quite answer the question,' Trapp said, not at all offended or anything. 'I asked you why you needed me; a bloke you seemed certain would swindle you out o' this very valuable cargo?'

'Let him up, Trapp,' I snarled, my own arms beginning to ache with the strain of clinging to the ladder. 'Let him up, you sadistic bastard.'

'I'll let 'im down inna minnit,' Trapp promised coldly. 'If 'e don't answer *jaldi.*'

'I was in a most embarrassing position,' Zarafiq sobbed. 'While I am a minister in a pro-Western administration I have also become . . . politically affiliated to the communist cause.'

'You mean you been takin' money from the Reds as well,' Trapp translated. It was a language he understood intimately. 'Go on, mister – where does the *Kamaran* figure in this?'

'My . . . my Marxist associates let it be known they were prepared to offer a great deal of money to anyone who could provide adequate arms to ensure a successful *coup d'état* in Gahman. I was foolish enough to suggest that I, and certain Egyptian colleagues, would be able to fulfil such a need . . .'

Zarafiq swung away from the side again and spun helplessly, a great and wicked spider enmeshed in his own web, which fed on corruption and grew bloated on the corpses of people who died in wars of his making. This time when I caught the appeal in his agonized eyes I stayed silent; I even turned away in contempt.

'Go on,' Trapp encouraged, toying almost absently with the knife.

'But . . . but there were penalties. I realized that, having accepted payment from the Communist Liberation Front, I would have to be seen making the most strenuous efforts to ensure that the *Kamaran*'s cargo avoided . . . ah . . . interception. By those anxious to prevent its delivery; fools such as Chang, motivated only by greed . . .'

'Tut, tut!' commiserated Trapp, shocked to his very core by the perfidy of persons less honourable than he and Mister Zarafiq. 'An' then there's the capitalists, ain't there? Like the Yanks an' the British – only interested in stoppin' blokes like you from makin' a few bob because that could upset their friendly strategic bases around the Med . . . only there's one thing puzzles me a bit about that, Mister Z . . .'

I saw him looking pointedly at me with a challenging grin on his lips as he continued, '. . . f'r a time Mister Cooper here 'ad the distinct impression the British wanted the arms to get through. Or they did originally. Now why ever should a true-blue country like the Brits be anxious to see a pro-Western crowd like the Gahmanians outa favour?'

I turned to listen again. I already knew, but I still needed to hear it again, just so's I could believe my admiral for once.

'Oil prices,' the racked man gasped. 'My government had adopted a policy forced upon them by the Americans – of holding them down; of stabilization. But politics can create strange bedfellows . . . North Sea oil has now made the United Kingdom one of the world's largest producers – and any potential exporter would be most anxious to see hawks, even communist-controlled hawks such as Libya, compelling OPEC to raise the price of crude . . . please, I beg of you, Captain?'

'Then why did the British change their mind, Zarafiq,' Trapp continued to press as though Zarafiq hadn't even been hurt. 'Why do they suddenly want ter stop this cargo just as much as the Yanks?'

'Because we – my government – have also changed our minds. We have now agreed to raise the price of oil, meaning there is no longer any advantage to the British in aiding a Marxist take-over in Gahman.'

'Very interestin' – but you haven't explained the need f'r my services even now,' Trapp growled doggedly, toying with the knife a little more ostentatiously than before. 'Go on, Mister Z. We're all listenin' avidly.'

'I am a government minister – and a very rich one. I have no illusions regarding what would happen to me should the proletariat topple my party, Captain. Justice would have to be seen to be done, even to those who assisted discreetly . . . just as it was essential for me to be seen to employ a top-class captain by my communist friends.'

'Ahhhh,' breathed Trapp with enormous satisfaction.

'Because they woul'n't realize you'd made bloody certain I *would* divert the cargo by makin' me a bit disenchanted from the start. You're a very sneaky Ayrab, Mister Zarafiq . . .'

'Let him up, now,' I snarled, sickened by the barbarity of it all. But Trapp shook his head; still looked as implacable as ever.

'Four questions, I said, mister. He's got two correct so far. Zarafiq. Do yer hear me, Zarafiq?'

The dangling man seemed smaller now, shrivelled in his private torment. 'Pleeeease, Captain! We made a bargain . . . ?'

'And I won't cheat yer, Mister Z. Not this time I won't. Two more questions f'r you to answer like I said – but you got to answer them in full, mind. You got to get a hundred per cent f'r each one.'

'Hurry! Please hurry.'

'Number three,' Trapp announced levelly, only the smile had gone suddenly. 'Them three Pakistanis on the old *Last Hope* . . . did you order Fadel ter cut their throats, Zarafiq? Did you 'ave them gutted deliberately, mister?'

A wave larger than the rest struck the side of the *Kamaran*. Zarafiq pendulumed away again, and back with an excruciating scream. He shook his head pleadingly, as if disbelieving such previously unimagined horrors.

'Did you?'

'Yes! Yesssss! They were nothing. I knew – I intended their deaths to anger you; to ensure you would deceive me . . .'

The look in Trapp's eyes was terrible to see. I watched the knife hypnotically – everyone watched that knife and the way it trembled in Trapp's grasp. Even Gorbals Wullie and Dan'l Spew had turned by now, leaving their own burden suspended, just like Mister Zarafiq, high above the waiting sea.

Yet when Trapp spoke again his voice was still very quiet.

'Last question, Zarafiq. All you got to do is give me the solution to one small problem. It's a difficulty you've sort o' created yourself anyway – so it shoul'n't be too hard to answer, should it now?'

'Hurry . . .' the agony that was Zarafiq choked. 'For mercy's sake, what is it you wish me to tell you?'

Trapp simply pointed along the hull a short distance; towards the recovery line still grasped by Wullie and Spew.

A . . . a Thing swayed gently on the end of it. A pathetic, ghastly Thing which twirled and bobbed and still dripped a steady stream of engine oil and seawater to the empty life-raft below.

There was a charred hole drilled right through the face of it; a hole roughly the diameter of a quick-firer round from, say, a Gahman Navy patrol boat. But it was still just possible to recognize that the Thing wasn't simply a Thing after all – that it was actually the pitiful, incredibly forlorn corpse of Maabud whatsit, lately chief engineer of the *Kamaran*.

'You can come aboard, Zarafiq,' Trapp said with incontestable sincerity, 'just as soon as you've explained to me how to make that harmless little man run about on deck again. An' feel the wind on 'is face. An' laugh an' be happy, or cry an' be frightened . . .'

Mister Zarafiq was screaming even before Trapp cut the rope. He continued to shriek all the way down to the sea, after I'd lunged for him, but missed.

But ethics were ethics, even in the game of treachery chosen by Zarafiq himself. And in defence of Trapp – he really had kept to his part of the contract.

Mister Zarafiq had actually been the one who'd failed to fulfil the conditions of the penalty clause . . .

Chapter Fifteen

The shore was less than twelve miles off by the time I'd recovered from my nausea and climbed heavily to the shattered bridge. I wouldn't even have gone up then – but I still had a job to do.

I knew it was hopeless the moment he turned and saw me standing there.

'No,' Trapp growled emphatically. 'I ain't goin' to sink her, mister. Not f'r you, not f'r nobody! There's still a lot o' contract payment outstandin' and I'm planning to deliver – and collect.'

'Dammit but you're still British,' I exploded savagely. 'This is the Mediterranean, Trapp, and God knows the Soviets have a big enough hold in North Africa already. You deliver those arms and they'll have a damn sight tighter one.'

'Yeah? Then how come even you wus originally so keen to see the arms delivered, when I wasn't? Well I'll tell yer, Miller – because it all comes down to money in the end. Even the British Governmint wus prepared to see the Reds in power when there was a chance it'd shove the price of oil up an' up . . . an' anyway, I ain't been proper British f'r a long time. I ain't even been back there f'r years – apart from on the Black-bird run, at least.'

I swallowed. I wished he hadn't said that, especially not in view of the conversation I'd had a few minutes ago with a certain British admiral. I made one last, rather self-conscious attempt to wave the Union Flag.

'So I can't even appeal to your patriotism. You've actually sunk that low, Trapp?'

He made an unnecessarily coarse gesture which tended to confirm the word he used at the same time. I took a deep breath and played my last card.

'Then I'm . . . ordering you to scuttle this ship, Trapp. Or at least turn her round and hand her over to a Western power.'

He stared at me. I stared back at him. It was like watching a pressure cooker with a jammed safety valve.

And then he blew off. Gently at first; ominously gently as the heat built up.

'Orderin' me, mister? Did you say you wus . . . ordering me?'

I sneaked an appealing glance towards the wrecked wheelhouse. Gorbals Wullie and Mister Spew stood listening – yes, even Spew was receiving Trapp loud and clear this time – and the only previous occasion I'd ever seen two individuals preparing for such instantaneous flight was when that bloody scuttling charge had been liable to go off in the engineroom.

The one I wished so desperately could go off now. Immediately.

'*Orderin' me, mister . . . ?*'

'By the authority vested in me under Queen's Regulations and the Naval Discipline Act,' I heard myself mutter – then I thought *Oh, the HELL with it!* and finished off recklessly, 'I've got a radio transmitter on board, Trapp. I've been using it to talk to an admiral – an' he says you'll bloody well do what you're told because . . . er . . . because . . .'

I ran out of courage then. It had never happened to me before in an argument with Trapp; but I'd never had to tell him anything like I was supposed to tell him now, either. I hadn't seen quite that look on his face before, come to that. Or not since the moment when he'd cut Mister Zarafiq's umbilical cord, anyway . . .

'Because? Because what?'

'Because you're . . . still an officer in the Royal Navy,' I choked weakly. 'Because after the war you never turned up to demobilize, Trapp. You've always been posted as "Missing, believed killed". And that means you've never actually been . . . well . . . written off the books, so to speak. An' that means you're still a full Commander, RN. And that means you gotter carry out orders or they'll bloody well hang you!'

'Awwwww Jeeeeze . . .' whispered a pop-eyed Gorbals

Wullie, in the most apprehensive croak I'd ever heard. 'They gone an' done it tae him again. *F'r the second time . . .*'

He didn't say anything at all. Not at first.

He simply stamped off the bridge, demolished my cabin piece by piece until he found the radio in the wardrobe, had a few words of confirmation with a presumably equally-apoplectic Admiral Charlie Tango Control . . . and then gave the Royal Navy his answer.

It wasn't too difficult to hazard a guess at what his answer had been – there were still bits of radio valves and things embedded in the toe of his boot when he returned to the *Kamaran*'s bridge.

I watched him anxiously; worried in case he would be successful in avoiding a heart attack. I now had less than an hour in which to sink the *Kamaran*, and very little prospect otherwise of doing so.

And then, suddenly, I had no prospects at all.

'Mister Spew.'

Very ordinary seaman Gorbals Wullie let out a pent-up shriek of tension and tried to hide behind the wheel. Mister Spew bumbled uncertainly over and gave Trapp a one-eyed stare of ferocious determination.

'Yus, Captin?'

Trapp indicated me with an icy jerk of his chin. 'Ask this officer where he's hid me detonators, Mister Spew. The detonators f'r me scuttlin' charges.'

'Why . . . er . . . . why don't yer ask 'im yerself, Captin?' Mister Spew frowned.

'Because I ain't speakin' to 'im. That's why.'

'The captin wants ter know where's the detonators f'r the captin's scuttlin' charges, Mister Cooper.' Mister Spew asked lugubriously.

'Get stuffed,' I muttered morosely. 'Mister Spew.'

'Smash 'is fuckin' 'ead in,' Trapp commanded, staring pointedly into the middle distance.

I watched Mister Spew's one good arm rise obligingly, if a little unwillingly. It looked rather like a steam hammer operated by King Kong's big brother.

'. . . under the emergency wheel in the tiller flat,' I snarled urgently.

'Go and get 'em, Mister Spew,' Trapp said with deep satisfaction. Or was it disappointment?

Then he condescended to fix me with a crafty, only-too-familiar leer of triumph. 'Oh, an' Mister Spew?'

Spew hesitated at the head of the ladder. 'Yus, Captin?'

'We knows what ter do with them detonators, don't we, Mister Spew? We knows precisely what to do wi' them detonators, don't we?'

'Ho yus, Captin,' affirmed Mister Spew as he shuffled below, leaving an unsettlingly Cyclopean and conspiratorial wink hanging above the ladder. 'We knows all about what ter do wiv them detonators.'

'You bastard,' I spat after he'd gone. 'They're your last chance to stay decent, Trapp. Once Spew ditches them you've really joined the outcasts – the international league of sewer rats.'

'I ain't speakin' to you, mister,' Trapp said complacently. 'But if I wus – then I'd say it's still better than joinin' the Royal Navy. Especially f'r the third time . . .'

I opened my mouth to retort, then closed it again with a snap. For a long moment I couldn't take my eyes away from a point just over his shoulder; a point where the water met the sky in a misty, seaward forming of the horizon.

And then I began to grin. For the first time this voyage it really was my turn to grin.

Trapp glowered at me suspiciously.

'What're you grinnin' for?' he demanded, changeably ill-tempered again. 'I won't 'ave my chief officers grinnin' like Cheshire cats when they're on the bridge, d'ye hear?'

'You can't ask me that,' I reminded him recklessly. 'You aren't even speaking to me, so how can you ask me anyth . . .'

'I'll speak when I wants, how I wants, an' ter who I wants,

mister!' Trapp roared. Only there wasn't any real fire to it; just a trace of uncertainty.

'And I'm not your chief officer any more either,' I persisted spitefully. 'As far as I know I'm not your anything any more, Trapp. But if I was – then I'd be your First Lieutenant . . . Commander.'

'Don't say that. Don't bloody call me that . . . I already told both you an' your admiral – I ain't in no Royal Navy no longer an' that's final.'

'Final?'

'Final!'

'But what about the Naval Discipline Act?'

'F**** and **** and **** the Naval bloody Discipline Act!'

I took one further, intensely satisfying glance over his shoulder and sighed.

'Well, I suppose you'd better repeat that to them, sir. Seein' they've sent a *Leander* class frigate all this way, just to enforce it.'

Of course I shouldn't have been so complacent. I should have known Trapp better than to assume he intended to be diverted from his long-awaited pot of gold by anything so irrelevant as a fighting frigate of the Royal Navy.

Even as he saw it, while the disbelief was still turning to sour resentment, he was on his way through to the skeletal wreckage of the chartroom and grabbing for the dividers.

Suddenly uneasy, I waited in the wheelhouse beside a white-faced and trembling – in other words normal – Gorbals Wullie, who could only mutter over and over again, 'Jeeeeze, och Jeeze butta friggit . . . Aw Jeeze a friggit, Captin . . .'

'Shut up an' steer f'r the coast,' Trapp bellowed back without lifting his head. 'An' ring down f'r all the speed we got, stupid!'

'You can't do it, Trapp!' I shouted. 'She can sink us with one salvo from her weapons systems. Give in, man. Pretend you meant to conform with their orders all the time. I swear I'll back you up . . .'

The revolutions under the deck began to build until every loose item in the *Kamaran*'s wheelhouse – and there were plenty of 'em by then – was chattering and shuddering and racketing frenetically. Then Trapp rushed out of the chart-room with a sneer of triumph and waved the tattered chart aggressively.

'See? There's less than a forty-minnit run to the shore, *mister*! And once I takes her inside them shoals there ain't nobody, not even your fancy grey-funnel line, c'n touch me . . . because they ain't going to overhaul the *Kamaran* in forty minutes, are they? From that distance off they'd need ter be an aeryoplane, they would. An' a frigate sure ain't no aeryoplane.'

I shuffled nervously, all my previous glee shattered by the anxiety of what might happen. Either way I was bound to be the loser.

'But they can still fire at us, Trapp. Guns . . . missiles . . . we haven't a chance.'

The contempt on his face was only matched by the derision. 'Fire at us? They won't fire at us, mister. They won't fire on a vessel flyin' the flag o' a foreign power – and in someone else's territorial waters, laddie? 'Ave you forgot that's the Royal Navy out there, then? The fair-play, lose-wi'-a-stiff-upper-lip gentleman's navy, mister . . .'

There was a distant flash from the horizon, and then a scream like a giant ripping a canvas hatch-cover clean across. Trapp's mouth stayed open for as long as it took for me and Gorbals Wullie to hit the deck.

The shell, when it exploded, lifted half a ton of Medi-terranean Sea above the bridge, then dropped it all inboard as a torrent of cordite-tainted spray. The remaining sections of the wheelhouse deckhead collapsed around Trapp to the accom-paniment of not entirely unfamiliar howls of terror from the after accommodation.

Nobody moved as Mister Spew crawled the last few steps

of the ladder on his hands and knees and stared round blankly, trying hard to think. Then his face cleared as he remembered why he'd come, and he scowled earnestly up at Trapp.

'I come ter tell you, Captin. I don't suppose no one else 'as noticed yet, but there's a *warship* over there on the port quarter . . .'

'Let me guess the bloody rest . . ,' Trapp screamed back in fury. 'Like now you're gonna tell me she could fire at us any soddin' minnit.'

'Bless me if you isn't pure magic, Captin,' Mister Spew said, the star of worship bright in his solitary eye. ''Owever can you guess at the thoughts what's still in me 'ead . . . ?'

Of course she never did catch us – the frigate. As soon as Trapp called their bluff, kept right on running inshore despite that warning shot, the grey and impossibly distant *Leander* hauled off to starboard and simply watched in frustration while Trapp conned the *Kamaran* into the narrowing reaches of the late Mister Zarafiq's secret rendezvous.

He was cocky about it, too. No sooner had we entered than he ambled right out on the wing of the bridge and stuck two fingers in the air towards the White Ensign which had tried unavailingly to claim him – the most unlikely of all unlikely naval officers – for the third time in his misbegotten career.

Then he grinned at me. It was a sardonic, totally unrepentant grin but I couldn't hate him for it any more. Not now. Because I was seeing the old Trapp again; Trapp the Buccaneer, Trapp the Survivor, Trapp the ever-ebullient. And suddenly I knew I loved him very much . . . on occasions.

He pointed ahead, up the river to where the communist trucks were already waiting like patient crocodiles along the bank.

'It's inevitable, mister,' he called with irrepressible conceit. 'I makes a few dollars, loses a few dollars – but I don't ever, never lose the war . . .'

Which was a rather ironic claim to make, really.

Seeing that was the moment when the *Kamaran* started to blow up!

Her bows went first, chopped clean off by the force of the blast. Then a second explosion, deep inside her. And a third . . .

I felt Trapp cannon violently into me, followed by Second Officer Spew, and suddenly the whole bloody heap of us were displaced for a second time as a screeching Gorbals Wullie burrowed underneath the pile like a refuge-seeking mole in a cloth cap. I didn't have time to tell him it wasn't the best place to be – seeing the explosions were coming from below at the time.

'What the hell . . . ?' spluttered Trapp as a fourth detonation followed.

And then a fifth . . . The *Kamaran* began to fall over sideways while water was already rushing and gurgling excitedly up the bridge. A gaily-coloured life-raft – one of the ones originally inflated on the deck as the panic party abandoned – came bobbing past and I grappled automatically for the painter.

'It's those charges,' I said faintly, disbelievingly. 'Your scuttling charges, Trapp. F'r some inexplicable reason every bloody one of them must have gone off together.'

Mister Spew clambered into the life-raft and sat there beaming at us, bouncing gently up and down in the displacing water. He did look pleased; positively delighted, in fact.

'This time,' he announced proudly, but with the slightest suspicion of appeal. 'Now this time you *gotter* admit I done everythin' proper, Captin. Five outa five. That's . . . er . . . near enough to about ninety per cent.'

Trapp stared at him. And I stared at him. Even Gorbals Wullie crawled tentatively out from under. And stared at him.

'What did you do right, Mister Spew?' I asked eventually. And for the very last time.

'Them detonators, Mister Cooper.' He smiled happily. 'I knew exac'ly what ter do wiv 'em, jus' like the captin said I would . . . Because I ain't so daft, really – I 'aven't never forgotten how upset 'e wus that last time. When them bombs didn't go off . . .'

The ebbing current drifted us steadily out to sea, the flagship of an aimless little flotilla of rubbish from the *Kamaran*. Most of her unhappy crew were riding the river with us, all clinging grimly to hope and odd bits of ship.

Trapp still hadn't said a word, simply slouched in the bottom of the orange raft in inconsolable gloom and staring astern at the hulk of the only decent vessel he'd ever commanded, now lying capsized and nearly submerged on the bed of that desolate creek.

Already the communist trucks had gone; stolen hurriedly away in search of another Mister Zarafiq; another revolution . . . but most emphatically not another Trapp.

He only spoke once in all the time it took us to cross over the bar and return to the Mediterranean in our ragamuffin convoy. It was a brief response to Gorbals Wullie – a truly-Trapp-type flash of petulance – when the wizened little Scot looked back at what might have been, then offered loyally, 'Never mind, Captin. We still got half o' Mister Z's advance. We'll hae a braw time back at the Red Sweetwater wan o' these days, eh?'

'No *we* won't, stupid!' Trapp had snarled in momentary animation. 'You still ain't got nuthin', ordinary seaman! 'Cause your half wus in the second half . . . the half we di'n't get, see?'

'He's gettin' better,' Wullie announced joyfully. 'Did ah no' tell ye he'd get better, then?'

We drifted a little farther in strained silence. I watched the frigate coming towards us and felt happy – yet strangely sad, all at the same time. But I wasn't alone in my satisfaction; not when I glanced over and saw the look on Mister Spew's anthropoid but amiable features.

He smiled wistfully, proudly as his one good eye caught mine.

178

'Five out o' five, Mister Cooper,' he said. 'I ain't never got five out o' five for nothin'. Not ever before . . .'

Trapp only stirred at the last minute. When the frigate had lost way and her boats were already slipping from the falls to come and salvage us.

Suddenly he sat up and frowned. Before an all-too-familiar expression of inspired guile wiped the last traces of gloom from the ageless features.

'That business about me bein' a Royal Navy commander, mister. You sure it still holds good – that there ain't no one c'n change it?'

'The admiral told me so himself. They posthumously promoted you to full rank the last time you were killed,' I assured him. But I thought I was only cheering him up at the time; not being bloody stupid.

'An' that frigate there. What rank o' officer would be in complete charge, then?'

I shrugged. 'A lieutenant-commander, probably. Certainly no higher than a full commander like you. Why?'

'So that would make me the . . . ah . . . senior officer then. 'Cause I been a full commander since jus' after nineteen forty-two – an' there ain't hardly no one left in the Royal Navy that was innit in forty-two.'

An uneasy feeling gripped my stomach but I forced it to go away. No. No, not even Trapp could conceive of anything quite so . . . so Machiavellian as that. Could he?

'While that, in its turn, means the captain o' that frigate has ter obey all my orders, don't it? Or else I could 'ave 'im charged, couldn't I, mister . . . under the Naval Discipline Act, no less.'

I stared at him. Gorbals Wullie was staring at him, too, with a mixture of trepidation and suppressed delight. But Trapp wasn't looking at us any more – now he only had eyes for that beautiful, shiny, expensive and lethal warship out there. Already they were proprietary eyes; cunning, oh so characteristically avaricious eyes . . .

'Trapp,' I begged. 'Please, Trapp, don't even think about it.'

But he was a long way away by then. A whole inventive and outrageously double-dealing world away.

'A commercial-minded bloke could do such a lot with a frigate,' he breathed dreamily; determinedly.

'No, Trapp! Pleeeeease . . .'

'Oh, what a lot 'e could do. What business opportunities 'e could take advantage of . . .' mused the indestructible Captain Edward Trapp, the very last of the ocean pirates.

'. . . with a whole frigate. An' guns. And even *missiles* of 'is very own . . .'

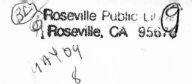
Roseville Public L
Roseville, CA 956

MAY 04
8

ROSEVILLE PUBLIC LIBRARY

S0-AZO-743

φ
                    c.2
W ROD
Roderus, Frank.
The ordeal of Hogue Bynell

OCLC: 8387406   z# 805150

1982

SEP

The Ordeal
of Hogue Bynell

The Ordeal
of Hogue Bynell

FRANK RODERUS

DOUBLEDAY & COMPANY, INC.

GARDEN CITY, NEW YORK

1982

Roseville Public Library
Roseville, California

All the characters in this book
are fictitious, and any resemblance
to actual persons, living or dead,
is purely coincidental.

Library of Congress Cataloging in Publication Data

Roderus, Frank.
The ordeal of Hogue Bynell.

I. Title.
PS3568.O346O7   1982   813'.54
ISBN 0-385-18029-2
Library of Congress Catalog Card Number 82–45303

First Edition

Copyright © 1982 by Frank Roderus
All rights reserved
Printed in the United States of America

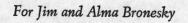

For Jim and Alma Bronesky

c.2
col

The Ordeal
of Hogue Bynell

CHAPTER 1

He heard them coming when they still were some rods distant, heard the clop of shod hoofs and the rattle of bit chains and the faint sounds of good-natured cussing and joking. Hogue Bynell heard them, and his mouth turned down at the corners in a sour grimace. He did not bother to look to see who it was this time—some of them stopped by every month or two weeks in spite of all the time that had passed—but reached instead for the bottle that sat on his desk. He took the bottle, protectively twisted the cork to make sure it was well seated and shoved the nearly full jug into a bottom drawer. He did not feel all that hospitable.

He heard the clatter of iron on rock as the ponies crossed the ballast stone of the roadbed, and a moment later they were beside the shack, tying their animals to the hitch rail there.

The railroad had not installed the rail. It was nonstandard equipment for a relay station out in the middle of the big nothing that stretched from the easternmost escarpments of the Rocky Mountains very nearly the entire distance to Kansas City. Nothing, that is, unless you fancied grass and the livestock that eat it. For a stockman the country was as close to heaven as he ever might expect to get; to an eastern eye it would be a bleak land indeed. Hogue Bynell did not find it at all bleak.

The hitching rail where the cowhands were tying their horses had been erected by a group of Y Knot hands—the brand was stamped:

Y9

and required a special iron to burn; it was also about as close as a man could come to being secure from overburns—one Saturday evening when they got tired of passing freights spooking ground-hitched horses.

Hogue shook his head. That had been . . . nearly a year ago now. It seemed incredible that so much time could have passed already. That he had been here so long already. Absolutely incredible.

He heard the clump of bootheels on the platform that lay between his shack and the tracks a few yards distant. A high-pitched ting and tinkle of spur rowels accompanied the footsteps, and the men reached the open door.

They came in without invitation—it would have occurred to none of them that one might be required—and two unshaven faces split apart into hairy grins. The third man, whom Hogue did not know, hung back by the doorjamb with a carefully blank expression, intent on the business of loading a pipe until he saw what their reception might be in this alien environment. Cowhands and railroad men rarely found ground for common meeting.

"Hog! How the hell are you?"

"You ain't changed since the last time we was here, Hog." There was a snort and a loud ring of laughter. "Nope. Ain't shaved and ain't bathed neither. You haven't changed a bit."

"Afternoon, Jimmy, Goodnight," Hogue greeted. Jimmy Lewis was the first who had spoken. Goodnight Licken was the second. Hogue might have heard the man's real first name once, but if so he had forgotten it; Licken had used to work for Mr. Charles Goodnight, down in Texas, and when he first came North talked so much about the legendary cowman that Goodnight had become a nickname that he still wore. Hogue shifted his chin more or less toward the man who still stood in the doorway. "Who's dumb enough to ride beside you two?" It was as close to a polite request for an introduction as Hogue Bynell was likely to get.

"Pete Morris, that there's the Hog," Jimmy said. Which was as close to a formal introduction as he was likely to give.

"Watch out for him," Goodnight added. "He can whip more men, drink more likker, love more women an' eat more chuck than any other three men you ever seen. He don't look like much, but underneath that gentlemanly exterior he's pure hell."

The compliment, and from Goodnight Licken it *was* a compliment, was delivered in a tone of pure friendship, but Hogue Bynell scowled in response. The boys would accept the scowl as a form of modest denial. In fact it was intended to hide the pain that Licken's words had caused. It had been a long, long time since Hogue Bynell had fought with a man or made love to a woman or even cared that much about the food that was required to stoke his body. As for the liquor, well, he still had that. If nothing else he did still have that.

"Sit down if you're so ignorant you can't think of anything better to do," he said.

The boys, this time with the newcomer stepping away from the door and joining them, unstacked some discarded spike kegs that Hogue kept in a corner of the shack for occasional use as chairs. They sat on the upended kegs near the standard-issue potbelly stove by habit, although at this warm time of year the cast-iron stove was covered with a layer of protective grease. There was a bucket of dirt on the floor beside the stove where they could spit, and the iron door was open to receive spent matches and other burnable bits and pieces of trash. In a few more months the summer's accumulation of crud would be done away with in the first fire of the coming fall. The new man, Morris, as lanky and unkempt as the others, lighted his pipe and made use of the opening to dispose of his match.

"You boys ought to be ashamed of yourselves," Hogue ventured, "taking a man's pay and laying off on him like this." He swiveled his chair around and thought wistfully about the bottle hidden in his desk drawer. If he brought it out, he knew, it would only encourage his guests to stay all the longer. He wished they would go away.

"Huh!" Goodnight said with a loud snort. "You're one to talk. Set there behind that hunk o' wood all the day long. Laze around. An' draw pay for it too."

"I can't argue," Hogue said. "It's a fact." He tried to keep the bitterness out of his voice, tried to make it sound light and easy. He was not sure if he had managed that or not.

He must have done all right, he decided. The others were chuckling happily.

Damn fools, he thought. Didn't know when they were well off. Didn't appreciate what they had. Just being able to go out there and snatch their cinches tight and set off at a lope for the camp and a good meal. That should be enough to satisfy any man. It would have satisfied Hogue Bynell well enough. They didn't know when they were well off.

Goodnight pulled a folder of papers from his vest pocket and began to build himself a smoke. Predictably enough,

Jimmy borrowed the makings from him. In a few minutes all three were sitting with their legs crossed and smoke curling around their ears. As content, Hogue thought, as if they had good sense.

They began to talk. About inconsequential things. About the weather and the state of this water hole or that. About a haying crew being sent to Sandy Bottom Run. About that same old brindle cow—you remember her, Hog, the one with the lop ears an' the crookedy left horn—that was gaunted and looked too poor to be worth shooting but which hadn't missed calving once in eleven years now and was the talk of the countryside because of it.

They did not realize it, but each reminiscence, each reference to a remembered watering spot or to that old cow—she had caught Hogue afoot once, when he had stepped off his horse to free a calf mired in thick, gooey mud, and bowled him over with a hooking horn that could have speared him but instead only sent him flying, with bruises to nurse for the next week or so—brought a fresh stab of misery into Hogue's gut.

He remembered the places and the things they were discussing. All too well he remembered them.

Jimmy and Goodnight and the new man chattered on, and Hogue Bynell sat listening in silence, wishing they would go away but unwilling—he did not know himself why it should be so—to send them away.

Hogue sat silently with his ears tuned unwillingly to the conversation that filled the crude, trackside shack, and for a few minutes there he felt a vague sense of embarrassment at what these men were seeing across the standard-issue railroad desk.

Loss of interest in food had caused the fat and even much of the muscle to slough away from what had been a huge and powerful body. He must look shrunken to them now, he thought. His shoulders had thinned and had developed a slope that never used to be there, and his jowls sagged, where once he had been quite moonfaced. His dark brown hair was overly long (he had been whacking at it with shears from time to time but knew he did a poor job of barbering) and had not been brushed in the months since he had last been to town. His eyes remained the deep blue that Jimmy and Goodnight might remember from before, but they no longer had the sparkle and the clarity of robust good health, and the whites were dulled by alcohol and disinterest.

If he stood—which he did not want to do, no matter how long they chose to stay—he would be the same six-foot-three as before. But that would be about all that was unchanged. His weight. . . . He could not really guess what it would be now. He had been something over two-forty in the past. Now. . . . He had no idea and did not particularly want to know.

Hogue sighed. The boys were chattering on, directing their talk to him but not really expecting him to participate. They probably thought they were doing him a favor. He did not think so. Tonight, as always when they came to visit, he would have nightmares again. And that bottle in his desk drawer—he wondered if they knew about it—would be empty before he even began his futile attempts to sleep.

Still, he could not hate them or even dislike them. They had no way of knowing. He sat and listened to the things they had seen and the things they had done in the past few weeks. The wrecks and the blow-ups, which horses had unseated which riders at which morning rope-outs, who had gotten a heavy serving ladle thrown at him when he incurred the cook's wrath . . . and how he had managed to accomplish that easy-to-do feat but had been unfortunate enough to be caught at it.

Tales like those had once been part and parcel of everyday life for Hogue. Now they were so many knives thrown straight to the pit of his stomach.

The visit dragged on for—not hours; Hogue checked the bulky pocket watch the railroad had issued to him—for nearly an hour, although it seemed like more, until Jimmy and Goodnight and Morris rose together as if some signal had been passed between them.

"Reckon we been here long enough to ruin your afternoon nap," Goodnight said. "That's what we really came for, y' know." He chuckled. "Can't let you get away with more'n we can."

There was some good-natured cussing and more than a few lewd jokes, and the three were gone.

"We'll tell you about some of the things that ol' boy done in his time with the Y Knot." Hogue heard Jimmy's voice, pitched low but not quite low enough, as they snugged their cinches and mounted on the far side of the flimsy wall that was Hogue Bynell's protection from summer heat and bitter winter winds alike.

Hogue winced.

He could remember those stories all too well himself.

When they were gone, when the ponies had been mounted and their hoofs had once again rattled across the ballast of the roadbed, Hogue sighed and reached into the drawer for his bottle.

The clickety-tick of an incoming message interrupted him, and almost without conscious thought he reached for his message pad and a pencil. The letters flowed from the telegraph machine onto the paper with hardly any need for a translation stop inside Hogue's brain—it had not always been like that; he used to have to work at it, but now it was so automatic he scarcely had to think about a relationship between what he was hearing and what he was writing—and the routine train order was ready for posting.

Hogue tore the order from the pad and rolled it into a pickup pouch.

As automatically as he had accepted and receipted for the train order, Hogue reached for his crutches and clumped his way out onto the platform to rig the pouch for a flying pickup by the midday eastbound.

He stood with a crutch under each arm, a tall, gaunt figure of what once had been a huge and powerful man. But now he was only large and—he suspected—pathetic to see. The right leg of his sturdy broadcloth trousers had been cut off and neatly pinned beneath the stump that ended ten inches below his right hip.

The doctors had told him that he would come to accept the loss of the leg as normal, that he would adjust to it to the point that he would scarcely miss the lost limb.

The doctors had been wrong.

CHAPTER 2

It had been a good life while it lasted. The dreams of open country and a free life had begun in the sweat and grime of a Missouri farm and become realized in South Texas and along the long trails that led from Texas across the Indian Nations to the raucous railheads of Kansas.

Hogue Bynell had become a hand. He thought of himself as a top hand, and sometimes he had even drawn pay on that elite basis.

He took to the life of a cowhand with the enthusiasm of a young lover in the midst of his first affair. The grinding monotony of long hours and foul weather and unrelenting labor of the trail drovers could not begin to blunt his eagerness.

He learned to wear his hat brims wider and his boots tighter than any city dweller would deem remotely acceptable, and when he went into a town—any town, because they all came to look alike to him—he wore his gloves with their fancily embroidered attached gauntlets tucked under his belt as a badge of office, a clear statement to any who cared to look that this man was a cowhand and therefore was not to be trifled with.

He learned that money was for blowouts and good times, that as long as a man owned a saddle, a pair of spurs and a good name he was a free man. And in the big-grass country a good name had nothing to do with morality, geniality or any of the other, "normal" yardsticks used to measure character inside town limits. On the big grass a good name came from knowledge of cows and horses and a willingness to do the work. Beyond that, character was a personal and private matter, of interest only to the individual and to those he might choose to annoy.

Hogue Bynell liked the way of life. Given the choice, he would have continued in it indefinitely. He had not been given that choice.

He had come to the Y Knot outfit, which ranged from Cheyenne Wells south to the dry lands below the Arkansas and from east of Pueblo very nearly to the Kansas border, some five years before. He had to do considerable thinking to reach that figure. He tended to remember the years by seasons and shippings and droughts, rather than by any numerical designations.

The Y Knot crew had been a good one, the work neither easier nor more difficult than it would have been anywhere else. The only thing that really distinguished it was that there was no brush to buck here and the roping was easier. Hogue had taken a look around at a country where a man could ride for days and see nothing but grass and beef and an occasional rock, and he had declared himself at home. He sold his chaps, unnecessary in country where there were no thorns to be fended away from the legs, to a wide-eyed kid signing on for his first job, and Hogue settled in to stay. Or so he thought.

In addition to grass, grazing livestock and rocks there was one other feature common to the open plains.

Dry washes and jagged arroyos crossed the nearly flat land here and there, running water at only the rarest of times, sandy nearly always. They did not carry nearly enough water for their presence to be marked by tree lines or the growth of brush along their banks.

On a dreary afternoon in March with the ground still greasy with melting subsoil ice, Hogue had dabbed his rope onto a feisty, crossbred steer that had broken a horn and needed doctoring. It was something Hogue had done in the past more times than he could remember even if he had had a reason to try to count them all. It was part of the everyday work, and he thought not a thing of it.

The steer had resisted the rope, as was a steer's God-given right if not exactly a steer's natural duty, and Hogue's horse had gone about the business of teaching the cantankerous bovine who was the boss and who the bossee.

As a student of the Texas cowmen, Hogue Bynell was a tie-fast roper just as naturally as a California or Oregon buckeroo was a dally man. The free end of Hogue's rope was tied hard and fast to his saddle horn on the day the rope was cut from the bale to be stretched and rubbed, and it was not removed from the horn until the day it was replaced. That was the way Hogue and a thousand others like him had been taught to do it and that was the way he would continue to do it for as long as he could hold a coil of hemp in his hands, plain and simple. There was no other way to work.

This time, though, the steer put up a fight that would not have shamed a Mexican black bull, of which Hogue had roped at least his share in the past. It was an effort that was exceptional for a crossbred northern steer but nothing Hogue had not handled many times before. If anything the challenge was an unexpected pleasure.

The fight went awry when the tight-pulled hemp of

Hogue's rope scraped across the already painfully sensitive stub of the steer's broken horn. A gout of fresh blood sprayed from the new damage, splattering the steer's near shoulder with bright red blotches and sending the half ton of frightened animal into a frenzy of motion.

Hogue's horse slipped on the poor footing caused by the melting ice in the soil and very nearly fell. Hogue, securely locked in the saddle, thought the whole fight delightful. He automatically shifted his weight with the movements of the horse beneath him and laughed out loud.

The horse righted itself and backed away from a sudden charge of the steer, scrambling to the rear to regain tension on the rope, as he had been taught in the hard school of cow work.

But behind the horse was the sharp-cut bank of one of those countless, nameless dry washes, unnoticed in the midst of the fight that had been going on, and the horse's back legs reached the edge before Hogue could spot the danger and spur the animal ahead.

Again the greasy footing displayed its treachery, and when the horse, a solid, heavy-bodied sorrel, tried to scramble out of danger, its feet slipped over the edge, and horse and man plunged backward for half a dozen feet to the pea gravel and hard sand of the wash bottom.

Hogue tried to jump clear, but the toe of his boot hung up for a fraction of a second in the stirrup—tapaderos were no longer in fashion, he reflected time and time again afterward, or the accident likely could not have occurred—and he was able to throw himself only partially clear of the falling body.

Horse and man landed together, and Hogue was able to distinctly hear the crack of a bone snapping in two. It sounded very much like a half-dried limb being broken into firewood-size pieces. At the time, Hogue was hoping it was one of his own bones that he heard break, rather than the horse's. His bones would knit—they had had to often enough before—and the sorrel was one of the best circle horses he had ever had in his string.

He got his wish. The bone was his.

The horse rolled, came to its feet and shook itself like a dog before it trotted a few steps away and stood with its reins dangling, waiting for instructions from the man who was its master. The rope that had been tied to the injured steer was dangling also. The immense pressures applied by the sudden fall had broken the three-eighths hank of fibers, and the steer was long gone.

Hogue knew that he was hurt, but he was not particularly alarmed. He had been hurt before. The pain was somewhat more extreme this time than before, but a man could not ask for everything. He had not done anything really stupid, like breaking his neck. It was only a leg. Again.

Experience told him there was no point in trying to straighten it alone. He set his teeth against the pain, deliberately decided against looking under his jeans to see the damage that had been done, and began crawling toward the waiting horse.

He made it to the sorrel and pulled himself hand over hand up the stirrup leathers to the saddle.

Getting his injured right leg over the cantle was a bit of a problem, but eventually he managed it. He did some fancy cursing along the way, and if there had been anyone around to hear and record his words he might well have found a niche in local history for the broad range and choice selections of his invective. As it was, his talents went unrecognized.

He made a mental note of where the steer had last been seen. Someone else would have to come out and finish the job or the wound might fester and $32 worth of beef on the hoof be lost to the owners of the Y Knot. Then he rode slowly back to the camp they were using for this early-spring working.

The cook cut his jeans off him—which Hogue deeply resented; the trousers had cost $2 at the next-to-the-nearest store they could reach or $2.15 at the nearest—and announced that the break would heal in time but that they would have to coat the injury with hot pine tar to avoid putrefaction. The jagged end of a broken bone had come through the skin.

Hogue did not look forward to the burn of the tar, but he was not particularly worried. This was not the humid Gulf Coast, where wounds festered easily. This was the dry, high plains, and here man and animal were mostly free of that problem. Here a wound healed quick and clean.

The cook attended to his duties, and the boys, including Goodnight and Jimmy, ribbed him for his carelessness and stupidity, and Hogue began making plans about what kind of hell he could raise from a horizontal position the next time the supply wagon rolled into town. There were several selections to choose from in that planning, and Hogue ultimately decided to reject none of them. It surely would take long enough for the leg to heal that he would be able to try them all. If his money held out.

The wagon would not be going to town again for another

ten days or so, so he had plenty of time to anticipate the various pleasures he planned.

By the third day of Hogue's enforced indolence, the cook and the camp boss were beginning to look worried about something.

By the fifth day, Hogue was beginning to work his nostrils and wonder what the ugly smell was that was bothering him.

On the sixth day, the cook tried to undo the too-obvious damage with a Y Knot branding iron heated beyond the dull gray that marks a properly fired iron to the cherry red that is used for cauterization.

On the seventh day, the camp boss admitted that he had made a mistake and dispatched Hogue in the camp wagon on a jolting trip to town.

There a doctor who claimed extensive wartime experience with just such cases shook his head in response to all of Hogue's protests, gave the injured cowboy a bottle of bonded rye to suck on and prepared his knives and saws for use.

The gangrene had already gone too far, the doctor said stubbornly. The leg came off or its owner died, and Hogue was not going to be given the choice. When Hogue demurred, someone shoved a nasty-smelling fold of gauze under his nose, and that was the end of the argument.

When Hogue came to again, there was only an expanse of flat-lying sheet where his right leg should have been and another bottle of rye on the bedstand to help him ease the pain.

That had been just over two years ago now. It had been that long since Hogue Bynell sat on a horse or held a rope in his hand. Or thought of himself as a man.

In the meantime he had had to find work. He had given it a great deal of thought before he arrived at his decision.

He could have clerked in a store or done some sort of menial make-work, but the thought of being in a town where people would see him and point at his back all day every day was intolerable.

Being a sheepherder would have been all right. They practically never had to look at another human or be looked at by one. But a one-legged man could not chase woolies any more than he could work cows, even if damned sheepherders only did wear one spur. So that was out.

Finally he decided on the railroad. A telegraph operator could do his work sitting down, and the railroads were always looking for fools who would be willing to endure the lonely isolation of a relay station. Hogue even had one in mind, out on the big grass where there was nothing but a shack and a set of shipping pens that was used twice a year.

Hogue Bynell was not a stupid man. He was capable of learning, once he set his mind to it.

He set his mind to the problem of learning to interpret clicks and clacks and make them come out as letters, and when he was satisfied with his own proficiency he crutched his way into the trainmaster's office in Pueblo and told the bossman he was ready to go to work.

The bossman was impressed, not so much by Hogue's proficiency, which was undeniable, as by the fact that this one-legged stranger made no mention of either pay or relief time in his request for a job that no one else wanted. Relay Station 12 was a problem post and always had been.

Hogue spent a month, without pay, learning the line's peculiar way of doing things and then became the line's lowest-paid telegraph relay operator.

He had been there ever since.

He intended to remain exactly there for as long as he had the strength to fist a key and enough hearing to read the dots and dashes.

A man cannot ask for everything. Hogue Bynell asked for nothing. Except possibly to be left alone.

That would be quite enough right there.

CHAPTER 3

The actual work at the relay station was not enough to keep a man busy, which probably caused no end of complaint for the sharp-penciled accountants who had to justify the pay that Hogue Bynell and other operators like him drew from the line, however little that might have been.

The MK&C was neither the busiest nor the most prosperous of lines. But it made do.

The route ran from an eastern terminus at Kansas City, Missouri, through central Kansas, into Colorado north of the Arkansas River Valley to a western terminus at Pueblo. The country served was mostly grass, the freight mostly beef on the hoof. The eastern third of the line also hauled grain and served farm communities with their freight needs, but there was relatively little traffic on the western two thirds of the line.

Four regularly scheduled freights, each with a single passenger car attached but sparsely occupied, passed Relay Station 12 daily. Specials would shuttle back and forth perhaps three times weekly for one reason or another.

Bynell's job was to receive and relay train orders from the trainmaster in Pueblo to the engineers on the steam-driven, coal-fired locomotives. The appearance of a special anywhere on the line would require one train or another to shunt onto a siding until the other was safely by on the single set of through tracks. Railroads tend to frown on collisions, and freights are not noted for any quick-stop abilities. It was Hogue's job and that of the other operators like him to ensure that no accidents occurred.

In the year and a half since Hogue had taken over his post on the big grass there had been no accidents on his stretch of the line, nor were there any near misses.

The work was essentially mechanical and untrying, and the trainmaster—who had a reputation of being mechanical and without humor—had come to accept the Relay 12 operator as one of the machines under the master's care. Perhaps more reliable than most pieces of mechanized equipment but a machine nonetheless.

Once each week a work train routinely stopped at Relay 12 to deliver groceries, clothing, liquor or whatever else Hogue had submitted on his weekly shopping list. The actual buying was done in Pueblo by an office boy, and the amount spent each week was carefully tabulated and deducted from Bynell's pay. A relay operator was given a roof and a bed out of the generosity of the line. Anything beyond that was his own responsibility.

Hogue's primary expense was for liquor—locally bottled bar whiskey. He did not feel he could afford bonded liquor although in fact he never had any idea of how much money he might have riding on the company books; he had drawn cash from the line on only three occasions, when he chose to take relief time in town, and each of those times he had regretted leaving the station. His food bill was very small. As he neither went anywhere nor had anyone around who would have to smell him on a regular basis, he required practically nothing in the way of soap and clothing.

Having little to do during his waking hours except to stay awake and listen for the clatter of the telegraph key, Hogue spent most of his time carving lumps of coal into cunningly crafted horses, steer heads, saddles, jackrabbits or anything else that came to mind. He sculptured from memory but was becoming more than barely proficient at the exercise. There being no market that he knew of for such homemade time wasters, he burned the pieces in his little cooking stove on those few occasions when he got around to eating.

A few of the crewmen from the regular work trains knew about his pastime, and once one of them had asked him to carve a "horsie" for his daughter to play with. The brakeman offered to supply Hogue with wood for the carving and to pay him a dime for his efforts. The request was not repeated. Hogue threw an almost empty bottle at the man and just missed his head. At it was, the brakeman went home that night reeking of spilt whiskey and caught the Holy Ned from his churchgoing wife.

As far as Hogue was concerned, he was employed by the railroad but was not necessarily part of it.

The train crews were an inescapable part of his existence on a once-per-week basis, but they were neither friends nor co-workers. They were simply there. They delivered what he had to have and they took away his list for the next week's delivery, and that was that. They were as useful to him as a dependable horse once had been. He had felt more attachment for the horses.

As far as Hogue was concerned, he was *not* a railroad man, he was simply an employee of the line. Hogue Bynell was and intended to remain a cowhand. Down on his luck and out of his proper employment, but a cowhand regardless. The railroad merely served to avoid starvation.

Once each month, the work train also delivered to him a letter.

None of those letters had been answered since the last time Hogue requested a few days of relief and rode the work train back into Pueblo, which was nearly five months now, but the letters addressed to him care of the MK&C continued to arrive, all in the same spidery handwriting. The crewmen on the work train might have wondered about the letters, but none of them ever asked the Relay 12 operator about them, even though the penmanship was unmistakably feminine.

The lady's name was Mabel Cutcheon. *Mrs.* Mabel Cutcheon. Widow of Jonathan C. Cutcheon, of Pueblo, who had run a dry-goods store catering to cowhands and cattlemen until a piece of gristle lodged in his throat had cut him short in the middle of his forty-eighth year.

That had been sometime before Hogue's accident, and the widow had taken immediate aim on the big, sometimes rowdy but always polite cowhand who dealt at Cutcheon's Emporium whenever he was in town.

There had been a time back then when Hogue was almost tempted to allow the widow to succeed in her goal of taking Mr. Bynell to an altar. The lady was not unattractive for her age, was warmhearted and certainly did not have to be paid for the time she spent with him. That was a unique experience for a cowboy who had left home at an early age and who had never before associated with any woman with whom a female choir singer would be seen talking on the street.

The accident had eliminated that temptation. There were

some things that a man simply did not do, and accepting charity from a woman was in that category. It seemed perfectly obvious to Bynell that any continued expressions of interest in him would fall in the same charitable ranking as the adoption of a Mexican brat or the taking in of a stray cur. A one-legged man is not a whole man is not a man, and that was that.

Hogue had some vestiges of pride left, although rather few, he thought, and that one he chose to cling to. As far as he was concerned, the widow Cutcheon was no longer within reach, her protestations to the contrary notwithstanding.

He accepted a few dinners from her after the accident but nothing more than that. When the pressures built within him, until he learned to submerge his baser inclinations in light but regular applications of cheap whiskey, taken internally, he resumed his old habit of seeking out the soiled doves who wore red clothing and rather little of it.

For a time, he had been willing to continue his relationship with the widow on a level of friendship, but his last visit to her home had brought him closer than he wanted to be to temptations that he did not want to acknowledge. He did not want that to happen again and so no longer answered her letters with the long, dull instruments he used to prepare day after day in the isolation of Relay Station 12.

Hogue felt himself much more satisfied with life now than he had been then. He was very nearly entirely disconnected from the world beyond the station walls, and he liked it that way.

If the Y Knot hands would quit coming by to visit, he would like it even better.

And one of these times—soon, he thought—he would get

rid of the small metal box in his desk that held more than a year's accumulation of letters, all of which were signed, "Affectionat'ly y'rs, Mabel."

One of these times.

Until then, Hogue Bynell was doing just fine, thank you. Just fine.

CHAPTER 4

The visitors showed up two days after the Y Knot cowboys had stopped by for their every-so-often chat. Hogue heard them coming when they were still some distance away. He might be a cripple, but there was nothing wrong with his hearing.

When he heard them, he assumed they were more boys from the Y Knot. No one else ever rode here except during the spring and fall shipping seasons, when large crews of hands would be there to crowd the beeves onto specially laid-on trains of cattle cars. But this was not the time of year for that, and anyway he would have received train orders if any-one were shipping off season. So it could not be that.

As always he heard the approach of the horses, but this time they also came from the wrong direction to be from any of the Y Knot camps that Hogue could remember. They came up behind the shack and did not have to cross the tracks to reach the hitching rail.

Odd, he thought. He made a sour face. Two sets of visitors in less than a week were three times as many people as he wanted to see.

They tied their horses at the rail, and a moment later he could hear their boots on the wooden platform. There was no sound of spurs ringing with their steps, which was also odd. Hogue had never heard of a ranch that supplied its men with horses so tame they could be used without loud cussing and hard spurring. It was for sure the Y Knot never laid out the cash for over-gentle animals like that.

When the men reached the doorway, Hogue saw that both of them were total strangers.

Well, they could go as easily as they had come. His jug was hidden in his desk drawer and his crutches were down out of sight along the wall, and the hell with the pair of them.

"This isn't a regular station," he said curtly. "The trains don't stop here and I don't sell no tickets." He ducked his head and pretended to be reading a train-order copy that had already been posted and picked up.

After a moment, he realized that the two men were not leaving, as he had expected, and wanted, them to. He looked up again.

Both continued to stand in the doorway, looking at him. He did not like that. He did not like them. He was no freak in any traveling show to be gawked at by passersby.

The one on the left was of medium height and a hefty build, much as Hogue had used to be, except considerably shorter. The one on the right was the same height give or take an inch and much leaner. Both were bearded and had wide-brimmed hats pulled low over their eyes.

Both were dressed like cowhands. Trousers pegged into their boot tops, vests worn over their flannel shirts, neckerchiefs knotted around their throats and hanging loose. No gloves or gauntlets, but that did not mean anything. Gloves were out of fashion these days and bandannas were in. Sometimes Hogue thought that cowhands were as fashion-conscious as schoolgirls were reputed to be. He felt vaguely disloyal when he had such thoughts, but once in a while they popped into mind in spite of that.

Still, there was something about these two that made Hogue doubt that they were engaged in the husbanding of cattle anyway. Maybe just that they were a bit too clean. A hand cannot work without gathering a layer of horse sweat and horsehair, dried manure and dried dust and dried blood. It simply was not possible, given the work that had to be done.

These two were carrying enough dust on their clothes, but the other ingredients were missing.

Besides, they did not look to him as though they knew or cared all that much about beeves. It was nothing he could put a name to, just an impression.

And he did not care enough about either man to bother examining his impression. He just wanted them to go away and leave him alone.

"I said—"

"We heard you." It was the stocky one, on the left, who had spoken.

Both of them came on through the doorway to stand inside.

Hogue scowled at him. He had become rather good at scowling in the past few years, although he had not had much practice at it before then. They ignored him and looked around the shack.

There was little enough there to require study, Hogue knew.

The front portion of the tiny shack was occupied by the desk and by a broad shelf of instruments and wires. Beneath the shelf were some storage cabinets and the lever to throw the never-used signal flag. Hogue did not even know why they had bothered to install the thing, since no passengers ever entrained here, but it was standard equipment and therefore had to be part of any station that was built.

The back part of the shack held the potbelly stove in the center and beyond it, away from the desk, the smaller cooking stove and the piled spike kegs that sometimes served as chairs. Closer, between the desk and the back wall, there was a rope-sprung bunk. Some pegs over the bunk and a small trunk shoved under it were all the wardrobe Hogue required.

There were no pictures or fancy doodads on the walls. No paint, either, for that matter. Looking at it fresh, which he had not done in more than a year, Hogue would have had to admit that as a home the relay shack was not much. Still, it was all he needed. He certainly did not care what impression it left on visitors.

"We're passing through," the stocky one said. "Thought we'd stay the night here under a roof an' get an early start tomorrow."

"It's early to be stopping," Hogue objected. It was only midafternoon.

The stocky man shrugged. "Our horses are tired. They need the rest."

Hogue gave him a shrug in return. "It's a free country. You can camp where you like."

The stocky man smiled. The expression looked like it did not fit his face. "We'd sure appreciate the loan of your roof. It's been a long time."

Hogue grunted. He was not about to commit herself to an invitation he did not want to give.

"I'm Charles Porter. Everybody calls me Chuck. My saddle

partner here is Alonzo Trapp. You can call him Al. Everybody does."

Hogue managed to restrain himself from uttering expressions of great joy at the acquaintance.

"And what do they call you?" Chuck seemed to be an almighty insistent sort, Hogue thought. But he answered the
man.

"Mighty pleased to meet you, Mr. Hogue. Mighty
pleased."

Hogue corrected him. Chuck smiled apologetically. That
did not look natural on his face either. "Sorry 'bout that,
Hogue. We wouldn't want to give you offense."

Now they were on a first-name basis all around, it seemed.
Hogue was less than thrilled.

The clickety-tap of the electromagnetic receiver gave him
a diversion that he welcomed. He turned away from the odd
pair and began to copy the message, even though the signal
was meant for Relay Station 10, off to the east.

Hogue had never seen Relay 10, or any of the others for
that matter.

For some reason—possibly to impress potential investors—
the relay stations all carried even numbers. There was no Station 11 between Relay 10 and Relay 12. Hogue had met the
operator of Relay 10 when the man passed through for relief
time on the work train. The fellow was thin and mousy and
nervous and in spite of his isolation did not drink. He also
had two good legs and could have been doing something better with his life than sitting in some shack with nothing but
the wind and blowing cinders for company. Hogue did not
like him.

He copied the message verbatim and made a show of filing

it away, although actually he would get around to burning it eventually. When he looked up again, Chuck and Al were still there, but now they had helped themselves to seats on a pair of his kegs.

"I don't have food enough to feed you," Hogue lied. The truth was that he had more than he needed. And if any grub-line riders ever came through he would probably break down and feed them. He had been in that situation a time or two himself in the past. But these two did not look as though they were grub-line riders, and neither looked underfed.

"That's all right," Chuck said. "We have aplenty of our own. Don't want to put you out any. We just want to rest our horses and borry your roof for a while. That's all."

Hogue grunted again. He could not think of much he might say that would dissuade them. The damned men seemed perversely intent on hanging around where they were not wanted. "Suit yourself," he growled.

They did. Chuck and Al—Hogue had already forgotten their last names—sat as content as a pair of dead clams and whispered to each other, dirtying Hogue's plank flooring with their cigarette ashes while Hogue pretended to concentrate on papers on his desk.

He copied a few more messages meant for other stations, took down a flimsy for the 5:12 eastbound ordering the engineer to off-track at Antelope Siding until a westbound special freight cleared, and rolled the train order into its pouch. He laid the filled pouch on the edge of his desk and deliberately procrastinated for a while. He had plenty of time before he had to hang the pouch on the hook for the flying pickup.

There had been a good many westbound specials lately, he reflected. Probably because of the mining activity up in the mountains. The Denver and Rio Grande had been carrying freight up there for some time, but generally connections with it were made from the east by way of the Union Pacific and Julesburg. Now there was some new little outfit open: the Florence and Victor or some such name. And there was a good bit more traffic on the MK&C to connect with it. If Hogue cared anything about the railroad he would probably find that gratifying, but he did not.

Still, thinking about it gave him another distraction from the unwelcome presence in the shack.

The two men were ignoring him as completely as he was ignoring them, though. That was something to be pleased about. Not much, but something.

An hour ground slowly by, and Hogue began to look at his watch more and more often. Before long he would have no choice.

And eventually he did not. The 5:12 would be along within two minutes of 5:12, plus or minus. The trainmaster would see to that or there would be absolute hell to pay along the line. No one got off schedule on Henry Bertram's track. *No* one.

And it was already approaching five o'clock. The order had to be posted. There was no choice about it.

If Hogue had been feeling irritation before, it had nothing to compare with the mingled frustration and anger he was beginning to feel now.

But there was absolutely no help for it. He had to post the order on the hook. And he had to walk out onto the platform to do that. *Crutch* out there. Like some damned gimp. Which he was, he reminded himself bitterly.

If he had to do it, he would do it. He bent and picked up

his crutches and came nimbly to his full height on the powerful limb that his one good leg had become. He did not himself realize how much change there had been in that previously seldom used left leg—a cowhand rarely thinks in terms of walking or running and cares very little about legs except in terms of reaching a saddle—but for some time now Hogue had been able to hop around the inside of the shack without benefit of the crutches without really being aware that he did it as easily as he did.

Now he was conscious mainly of an acute embarrassment as these unwelcome strangers would be treated to the spectacle of Hogue Bynell, Telegrapher and Chief Cripple.

Bastards, he muttered to himself.

He swung himself forward on the crutches with the ease of long habit and forced himself to not look at his guests. He did not have to look, in any case. He *knew* they were staring at him.

He went out onto the platform and crossed it to trackside, using his goad pole to place the courier pouch onto the hook, where the engineer of the passing train could snag it, and raised the signal flag on its standard to alert the train before it reached the shack. Backing up and making another pass was not easily done with something as ponderous as a railroad train, and woe unto the poor operator or crewman who blew a pickup.

Hogue turned to make his way back inside. Damn them, he told himself. Damn them to hell and back two times. He would buy their round-trip tickets himself if he could.

Both of them, moonfaced Chuck and silent Al, had come to the door to gawk at the cripple while he did his work. They were standing there right now.

If he thought he was man enough to whip them, Hogue thought, he would take a swing at them right now. But with what. A crutch? That would be ludicrous. Instead he gave them an icy glare and swung past them with as much dignity as he could muster.

Hogue went back to his desk and buried himself in work that did not exist. He hoped the two would go away. He just hoped they would go away soon.

CHAPTER 5

Hogue did not need an alarm clock. The eastbound 4:43 took care of that for him. It was odd, really, that that was the only train he ever heard passing. Day or night, the others could rumble past a few feet away from his bunk and he would never hear them. But the 4:43—or the opening ticks of his receiver—would bring him bolt upright from a sound sleep.

As always, Hogue sat up and reached in the semidarkness for his shirt and trousers. Damned annoying, this not being able to put his pants on without the bedside or a chair to sit on, but it was one of the things he had gotten used to. He had learned to keep everything he needed close at hand so he did not have to go awandering in the dark. It had taken him a few nasty tumbles before that became a firm habit.

Leaving his crutches where they were, he hopped first to the can of dirt beside the stove and tried to get rid of some of the previous night's lingering foul taste by spitting. It never worked, but he tried it every morning.

When that failed he hopped to his desk and took a short pull at his bottle. That did help. He felt almost human again.

Hogue shook his shoulders to throw off a morning chill and picked up his crutches. He needed to make his usual morning trek around to the outhouse. For a man on crutches that short jaunt could become quite an adventure on wintry mornings, but he would not have to worry about that for some months to come.

He reached the door and stopped in puzzlement.

Those two men, Chuck and Al—he had to think for a moment to recall their names—were gone.

He had become quite blunt with them the night before, they insisting that they wanted to sleep inside the relay station with a roof over their heads and he insisting just as firmly that they were not going to.

Finally they had made a camp of sorts across the tracks with their horses—exceptionally fine animals, Hogue had seen—tethered to picket pins so they could graze during the night.

Now the site was empty except for a black, barren circle where they had built a fire shortly after nightfall.

Odd behavior, Hogue thought. The two had been so set on staying, so determined that their horses—which Hogue had thought looked to be in fine shape—should be rested.

And now it seemed they had pulled out during the night sometime.

They had not even come inside to get a drink from the water barrel. There was no well or spring at the relay station, so drinking water was hauled by the work train along with other consumables. Hogue knew good and well he could have slept through their breaking camp fifty or sixty yards away. But he would *not* have slept through some stranger's presence inside the shack itself. No way.

So they had picked up and left without even coming in for that. He would not have expected, or wanted, a farewell from the odd pair, but a drink of water . . . that was something else.

He shook his head and looked more closely at the scorched earth where their fire had been.

It was not of enough interest that he would want to bother navigating his crutches through the loose rock ballast under the ties, but from where he stood he could see no hint of smoke or any rise of heat shimmer from coals that should have remained where the fire had been.

That meant the men probably had not stayed long enough to refuel the fire. They must have left shortly after Hogue turned in for the night.

Not that he really cared what they had done. Just as long as they were gone. That was quite enough. Still shaking his head, he continued along the platform and around back on the often used path to the backhouse.

Hogue was carving another lump of coal. Eventually the jagged piece of soft black rock—or whatever the stuff really was, he did not know for sure—would become the head and neck of a pronghorn antelope. Hogue had plenty of life models to work from; all he had to do was walk to the door and nearly as often as not there would be a white-rumped antelope or several within his view. At the moment, the piece resembled only a curiously shaped lump of coal as he began to mold the slightly outcurving line of the neck leading to the throat. Detailing, including small incisions made with the point of his pocketknife to provide hair on the animal's smooth hide, would come later. Right now he was concentrating on a rough shape for the piece.

It was pleasant enough work, and he had nothing else that he needed to do. The early westbound had already roared by, a minute and a half late and making up time. There had been no order on the hook to be picked up, and the engineer had not stopped for coffee and a chat.

The work train always came in the morning hours, but that would not be until. . . . Hogue could not remember if it was two days or three until it was due again. He sometimes lost track of the days of the week, although month, date, and year had to be included on all of his paperwork. That he had to keep up with, the days of the week he did not. The work train came on Fridays.

Another eventless day loomed. Hogue welcomed it. He yawned and began to undercut what would become the powerful jaw line of an adult pronghorn buck.

Damn!

He could hear horses. Again. They were distant, but he was sure of it. A ridden horse has a completely different pattern of beats on the earth from a loose animal. These seemed to be moving at a road jog.

The place seemed to be becoming more popular than the Pueblo terminus the past few days.

Hogue felt angry enough to spit. As it was, he slammed his knife onto the desk top and threw the so-carefully started pronghorn carving into the corner beyond his little cooking stove. The partially worked carving hit the wall and shattered.

The ridden horses moved closer. With any luck, they would ride on by.

They did not.

They came up behind the shack, and Hogue could hear several men tying up at the hitch rail.

Whoever they were, he did not want to see them, but apparently he had no choice. They were crossing the platform.

Then they reached the doorway, and he *really* did not want to see them.

There were three this time. Chuck and Al and a wizened little fellow who was dwarfed by the other two even though neither Chuck nor Al was particularly tall.

The newcomer had a stubble of beard that was obviously sloppy rather than deliberate, and the color of the facial hair was much more white than dark. Streaks of dirty gray ran through the hair on his head, too, along with a liberal accumulation of grease. The man's clothes looked several sizes too large for him, and his boots looked as if they would have been rejected by a besotted Indian.

Even I am not as much of a slob as that, Hogue thought critically.

Not that Hogue was apt to like the man in any event, but this guy was a down-and-out'er of the first water. Hogue wondered if he was a hobo who had gotten drunk and fallen off the rails. Maybe Chuck and Al had picked him up somewhere along the tracks and brought him back here for the railroad to adopt. Maybe that was it.

Well, Hogue Bynell did not need a pet. He was doing just fine without drifters and bums, thank you, and he would tell them exactly that.

He opened his mouth to speak, or perhaps to snarl, but closed it again without a sound.

There was something new about Chuck and Al, too. And he did not particularly like it.

This morning, both men were wearing guns. And while that in itself was not particularly startling in this country, both of them were wearing their iron low with fancy thongs tying the holsters to their thighs.

That was a trick Hogue had seen just twice before in all the years and all the cow towns and trails he had seen, and neither time had the wearer been anything but pure mean.

An honest cowhand wears his gun, if he wants to wear one, which he probably does not to begin with, any old dangling place he can put it or it winds up shifting into.

The big-time gunfighters, and Hogue had seen a couple of those, too, wore their guns in cross-draw or shoulder rigs under their coats. They at least pretended to be gentlemen about an ugly business.

But this tie-down business. That was more likely for creeps who thought they were something special. And that kind of idiot Hogue Bynell or any other halfway sensible human person ought to avoid.

Hogue noticed too that gun-toting Chuck and gun-toting Al were not smiling this morning or making any pretense at being friendly.

Both of them, in fact, looked downright serious.

Hogue wondered if they would go quietly away again if he ignored them. Somehow he did not really think they would.

CHAPTER 6

"You weren't all that friendly last night," Chuck said. "We think you owe us a small favor. Sorta to make up for that, if you know what I mean." He was not smiling when he said it. None of them were.

Hogue grunted a noncommittal response. He was reasonably sure he was not going to like whatever this favor turned out to be.

"What it is," Chuck went blandly on, "we'd like you to deliver a message for us on that pickup hook of yours. To the early-afternoon westbound. That's all we want. You do that an' then we go quietly away. Very simple. Nobody bothers nobody else. We get what we want and we ride off down the tracks like we'd never been here. Okay?"

Hogue grunted again. He had a feeling he already knew what the answer would be, more or less, but he asked the question anyway. "What kind of message?"

Chuck grinned. "A siding stop, that's all."

"An unscheduled siding stop, right?"

Chuck shrugged. "You could say that we're making the new schedule. Temporarily."

"And I suppose you know somewhat more than I do about the freight that westbound might be carrying."

There was that grin again. "We got no way of knowing

what it is you know about it, but in case you've figured it out, yeah, there's a payroll on that train."

"And you figure you could use it better than the boys it's intended for," Hogue said.

"Don't worry about it," Chuck said. "The railroad's insured for the loss. An' anyway they could afford it even if they wasn't. It's no skin off your nose."

Al spoke for the first time. As far as Hogue could remember, it was the first time the man had said anything at all directly to him although he had done some low-voiced yammering at his partner the day before. Hogue disliked Chuck in much the same way he disliked nearly everyone he met these days, but that was nothing compared with the way he felt about Al.

"It'll be plenty skin off you if you don't do what we say," Al said.

The three of them moved on inside the shack and began helping themselves to seats on the spike kegs he had not yet gotten around to replacing in the corner where he usually stored them. The newcomer had to fetch a third one off the pile and seemed to be having difficulty handling it. Whoever he was he still looked like a bum as far as Hogue was concerned. Certainly he got no points for the quality of the company he kept.

"Why not hang out your own message," Hogue asked, "and leave me out of it?" It seemed a reasonable enough question.

"We'd kinda like things to be real normal around here until that train goes through," Chuck said. "And we'd like the message to be normal too. You know. The right form. The handwriting they're used to seeing outta this station. All that. It wouldn't hardly do to tip them that anything's different today. Wouldn't do at all." He crossed his legs and leaned back with his hands hooked around an upraised knee, a perfect picture of a relaxed human being in a state of idle contentment.

"Just to be sure about that," he went on, "we brought along our friend J. Kenneth Harlinton here." He smiled slightly at the incongruity of referring to such an obvious tramp by such a formal name. "J. Kenneth used to be a telegrapher for the Yew Ess Gov'ment. It's a fact. It's a fact. Back during the Big Wah, that was. Pronounced 'war' if you're a Yankee. Which J. Kenneth was. I wasn't, myself, but I don't hold it against him any more.

"Anyway, J. Kenneth is just gonna sit here and kinda listen to what comes in over that noisy contraption you got in the corner there, and he's gonna listen to anything you send *back* over that thing, an' if you try to tip anybody to what we're doing, well . . . you get the idea."

"If you don't," Al added, "you soon enough will." He stroked the scratched wooden grips of his revolver and looked like he would positively enjoy an excuse to use the thing.

There are sons of bitches, Hogue reflected, and there are sons of bitches. Among them, he thought, Al seemed to be a prince of sons of bitches.

"Like you said," Hogue muttered, "it's no skin off my nose."

"*That's* the right attitude," Chuck said encouragingly. "No fuss, no trouble and we go away soon. We won't be back to bother you again."

Hogue sighed. In a way they were right, actually. The railroad probably was well insured against thefts. Certainly

ought to be if it wasn't. And it was not like there was anything at stake here except a few dollars. Well, perhaps more
than a few dollars. Quite a few dollars or it would not be
worth all this effort to stage a robbery. That was logical.
There was a good bit of mining going on in the mountains
nowadays, and miners have to be paid. Without the mines
and the miners there would be no need for the railroads to
serve them, so without them Hogue would not be here to
begin with. And while Hogue might be willing to take his
pay on a company account kept in some dim office in Pueblo,
it was pretty well known anywhere in this part of the country
that miners are a contrary lot. Cowhands—which Hogue no
longer was, exactly, but whose attitudes he still carried—
thought of underground miners as slightly worse than daft at
their best and somewhere the far side of insane as a general
rule. Unlike normal people, i.e. cowhands, who would take
their pay in any hard coin including silver (although not in
any form of paper, which *everyone* found suspect), hard-rock
miners insisted on being paid in the same yellow metal they
were hauling out of the ground. They would take their pay
only in gold coin. And therefore the coins had to be hauled in
from somewhere else. The stuff was mined out here, but it
had to be refined and minted elsewhere, which meant mining
payrolls had to be transported into the mountains just as the
crudely smelted gold had to be hauled out of them.

The result of those assorted facts and prejudices was that
there were payrolls of closely guarded gold coins being
shipped into the high country from time to time. And this
crowd Hogue was now having to deal with, or to ignore as
best he could, seemed to think there was such a shipment on
the 1:20 westbound.

Hogue sat silently thinking what a dandy trick it would be on Chuck and Al and friends if there was nothing on that train but bolts of cloth and kegs of nails and such mundane articles of freight as that.

A dandy trick, he conceded, but hardly his problem.

His problem as he saw it was to get these bothersome people off his back just as quickly as possible with a bare minimum of trouble.

If that meant the train would be robbed, well, that was the MK&C's problem.

It really was not like they were asking him to cause any real damage. A few minutes of delay on some siding between here and the Pueblo terminus would cause no harm. There were no eastbound trains the westbound would run afoul of even if it was delayed an hour. So it was not like they were telling him to cause a wreck.

And a mild concern about the likelihood of a head-on collision was about as far as Hogue Bynell was willing to become interested in this nonsense between the railroad and a pack of would-be train robbers.

After all, it was not as though Hogue himself was some sort of railroader who actually cared about the railroad line. He performed as was expected from his end of things, and they did the same from theirs. There was no affection involved on either side. It was expected of him that he would not allow any collisions to take place. But no one had said anything about him having to take any guff off a bunch of armed robbers.

So it really was not his worry, he reasoned.

He would write their fake train order and they would ride away and that would be the end of that. In the meantime all they had to do was let him alone and everything would be just fine.

Perhaps he should have known it would not be quite that easy.

CHAPTER 7

Chuck and Al were sitting side by side on a pair of kegs muttering to each other, and J. Kenneth Whateverhisnamewas was sitting beside them but somehow managing to keep himself apart from them, among them but not really *with* them. A different breed of carp altogether, Hogue thought.

Not that he cared. About any of them. He reminded himself of that sternly, several times, and believed it. An obvious rummy like J. Kenneth Whozits—he could not remember the last name—was of no possible interest to him. The fact that J. Kenneth was a former telegrapher gave them no more of a meeting ground than if the man had once been a circus acrobat. Hogue Bynell was employed as a telegrapher for the sake of expedience, pure and simple. If he could no longer work as a cowhand it did not necessarily follow that he no longer was, or would have preferred to be, a cowhand. That he was and expected to remain. The railroad and the clattering wires meant nothing to him. Nothing at all.

He closed his eyes and tried to shut out the presence of the other three men.

They would wait here for a short time. They would do what they had come to do. And they would leave. Now or later, they were of no real interest to him.

Deliberately Hogue let his thoughts wander. That was a

dangerous thing at times and something he usually tried to avoid, but now he welcomed the distraction.

Once, back when he had been a whole man, he had been considered—had been, actually—a lusty man, whether with beef or bottle or bed. Those times were past now, submerged in the embarrassment and the shame he felt when he was among strangers, but there were times when he could not help but remember the way things had been.

Now he welcomed the reverie of some of those times, deliberately dwelling on thoughts he might otherwise have avoided, thinking about the times when he and Goodnight and Jimmy and others in the brawling Y Knot crew would head for town and for the blowouts that invariably accompanied any break from the dull, difficult routine of ranch work.

He remembered this fight and that saloon and some bawd and before long his forehead showed a slick sheen of new sweat, and Hogue knew that if he did not force his thoughts away from such things in very short order he would very soon have to request some time away from the relay station and make another unwelcome trip into Pueblo just to satisfy the demands that a man's body will impose on him no matter how much he may despise the weaknesses of his own flesh.

Hogue wiped the back of his forearm across his head and, without thinking, for the moment almost entirely forgetting the presence of the others, reached into his bottom desk drawer for the bottle he always kept there.

The bottle was uncorked and raised halfway to his lips when he realized his mistake and paused with the container poised in midair while he glanced quickly toward the would-be robbers.

If he had hoped the object in his hand would not be noticed, he was disappointed. All three of his unwelcome guests had stopped whatever they might have been doing a moment before and now sat looking at him and at the bottle of cheap whiskey. Hogue cussed himself rather thoroughly as he saw Al's eyes widen and the dawning spread of a smile on the lean, bearded face of the fellow. It was too late entirely to shove the bottle back into the drawer and pretend that it did not exist.

Still, he tried. He jammed the cork back into the slender neck of the bottle and without haste replaced the jug in the drawer. Maybe—

"Don't be so quick to hide that purty thing," Al said with a grin. "It wouldn't be friendly of you t' not offer a man a drink"—Al gave him a smile that contained all the charm and friendliness not of the Hindu flutist but of the snake the flutist might be trying to impress—"crip," he added.

Hogue gave Al a stony stare in return. Al had not found a virgin when it came to name calling; Hogue had been called a cripple before. And a great deal worse.

"I'm not your friend," Hogue said softly, "and so far you haven't given me all that much reason to think of you as a man." The desk drawer remained closed.

Al began to chuckle. He stood and dropped a half-smoked cigarette onto the plank floor, stepping over the butt and allowing it to smolder where it was while he glided with a probably deliberate show of casual grace across the floor to Hogue's desk.

"I really do think," Al said, "that you oughta change your mind and try to be sociable here."

Hogue swiveled his chair to face the door and tried to ignore the lanky gunman who was standing over him. His anger— he had to keep swallowing it back, had to keep reminding himself that Hogue Bynell no longer had the right to anger and defiance and pride. Whole men might have that right. Hogue Bynell did not. It was a difficult thing to remember at times. A taste of bile rose in his throat, but he swallowed that back too. He tried to ignore the man and at the same time to not seem to be cringing from him. He might have managed either of those separately, but the combination was proving difficult to handle.

Al laughed. He did not sound particularly upset. "Oh well," he said, "if you won't offer, I reckon we'll have to help ourselves."

Al placed a steadying hand on Hogue's right shoulder and leaned heavily onto the one-legged man as he bent over and pulled the desk drawer open. He got the bottle and put all of his weight onto Hogue's shoulder as he straightened up into a standing position again. "Thanks. I really didn't think you'd mind." He laughed again and carried the bottle back to the keg, where he took a long drink himself before offering the bottle to the others. Neither Chuck nor J. Kenneth joined him.

Hogue had some fleeting thoughts about kicking himself, then thought bitterly that that was a hell of a poor idea for a one-legged man. Use his lone leg to kick himself with and he would fall flat on his face. Or in the other direction. For a brief moment he idly wondered just which way a one-legged man *would* fall if he tried to kick himself where he needed it the most.

Chuck, in the meantime, seemed to have acquired a look of vague distaste. Or perhaps it was unease. He glanced sideways toward his partner, who was now taking his third or fourth long pull at the bottle. The container had been a quarter full; now there was little left. Al was knocking it back more heavily than a sensible man normally would.

"Join me," Al said in a too-loud voice. But he did not offer the bottle to his partners again.

Within a few minutes the jug was empty. Al tossed the dead soldier into the open door of the potbelly stove with a clatter of breaking glass, and Hogue began to cuss some more. He would have to clean the stove out before he could light it the first time he wanted to use it this year. The labor was no less than he deserved, he quickly decided. He should have known better than to show a whiskey bottle to a robber.

Al leaned back and rubbed his fingertips up and down his belly. He belched once and grinned. "Lousy stuff," he declared, "but it sure beats creek water."

Chuck grunted something in return. J. Kenneth was ignoring both of them.

They were not, Hogue decided, a particularly close or brotherly crew of train robbers.

"You know," Al speculated, "I'll just bet you that where there's one thing of interest, say a jug or a gun or even a pile of cash money, why, there might be something else that ain't been shared and maybe oughtn't to be overlooked." He grinned. "Just to make sure we all stay friends here while we're waiting. You know." He got up again and began to prowl around the tiny interior of the relay shack.

CHAPTER 8

Hogue stared stonily forward, toward the doorway and the blank side wall of the shack. Behind him he could hear Al rummaging untidily through the few things that Hogue owned. If things had been different. . . . Hogue shook his head. Things were not different. He was what he was, as little as that happened to be now, and he could not change it. He just had to wait it out. They would be gone soon enough, and—

The back of his head exploded into a sheet of unexpected pain, and Hogue's upper body jammed suddenly forward into the hard edge of the desk.

"You were holding out on me. Sonuvabitchin' cripple, you were holding out on me." There was more triumph than anger in Al's voice.

Hogue knew what he would see, but he turned to look anyway. Al had found the bottles—four of them there were —in the wooden crate Hogue kept under his bed.

"If I'd tried to hide them I would have done a lot better job than that," Hogue said mildly. His head hurt and there was an ache of pain remaining in his chest, but he tried to let neither show. He wondered what Al had hit him with. Surely not with a fist. Still, he did not feel any blood running down the back of his neck. And he would not give the outlaw the satisfaction of seeing Hogue reach back there in search of blood.

Al was laughing again, a higher-pitched sound than before. The laughter did not sound altogether rational to Hogue. The man seemed awfully pleased with his discovery.

Al uncorked one of the fresh bottles, took a long pull at the opening and renewed his search among Hogue's personal belongings. Hogue turned away. He did not particularly want to watch the performance, and there was nothing he could do to stop it.

"I think you made a bad mistake," Chuck observed. He was speaking to Hogue, but his eyes were on Al.

"He's your partner," Hogue said, half accusing and half hopeful.

"My partner, your problem," Chuck agreed.

J. Kenneth was still ignoring all of them.

Chuck began to roll a cigarette. He and Al both smoked entirely too much, as far as Hogue was concerned. He cared only because of what the two of them were managing to do to his floor. The place might be a dump, but it did not have to be a pigsty as well. And after all, Hogue had to live in it, while they would be able to walk away anytime they wished, on two sound legs apiece.

Hogue tried to build a good hatred for them, for all three of them, but he had barely begun when the telegraph receiver opened with a clatter that must have sounded like just so much aberrant noise to the uninitiated. To Hogue it was the call sign opening his key and identifying the incoming message as being for Relay 12.

By habit, Chuck and Al and their intrusion were forgotten, and his attention was on the rattle of the electromagnetic receiver, his hand already reaching for a fresh pencil and an always present message pad.

He began to write, his fingers quickly catching up with the letters that had already been sent and then smoothly following the flow of sound, translating clicks and clacks into written letters that formed words he did not bother to read while the message was being sent. It was entirely possible for a good operator to take down messages flawlessly by the hour without ever once himself reading what he was writing on his pad. Hogue's instructor had been able to take down incoming copy without an error while maintaining a perfectly normal conversation completely apart from anything contained in the messages. And the instructor claimed to know a man—Hogue had never met him and was not sure if he believed it—who could take down a message with one hand and send another, quite separate message with the other hand. Hogue had been totally skeptical about that when he was still learning how to read the noisy wire; now he was not so sure, although he still did have some doubts.

When the message was complete, Hogue automatically threw the brass switch to turn his sending key on and tapped out a quick receipt for the message.

It was routine stuff, Hogue saw when he read it. A pickup order for two empty cattle cars that had been on a siding east of Relay 12. There was probably a great urgency involved, Hogue thought dryly. The cars had been on the siding for two and a half months to his own certain knowledge. The order was to be put on the hook for the regular afternoon eastbound, which would come through sometime after Chuck,

Al and company had finished their business here and gone away. Hogue would not mind posting it then. Far from it.

He shoved the pad aside. He could transpose the message onto the proper form and bag it later and—

He stopped in the midst of his line of thought.

They had *told* him that J. Kenneth Whatshisface was an old army telegrapher. But for damn sure nobody had *shown* him that.

Interesting. And after that unnecessary whack on the head, it would not hurt Hogue's feelings even a little bit if he could get away with a message to alert Pueblo and Relay 10 about what was coming.

He folded the slip of paper he had just copied the newly arrived message onto and stuck it into his shirt pocket.

"In case you're wondering," he said to no one in particular, "that was routine traffic. The westbound will be twelve minutes behind the normal schedule. Loose ballast on the road between here and Relay 10, so they're ordered to reduce speed until a work crew gets it fixed."

Chuck nodded his acceptance of Hogue's lie, but J. Kenneth looked at him for the first time in quite a while and cocked his head.

After a moment the wizened little rummy smiled. His teeth and gums looked as though it had been a long time since he had taken any care of them.

"You are entitled, I believe, to the inquiry," he said, "but I must disappoint you." To Chuck he said, "Not that it matters, Charles, but the gentleman received an order for an eastbound engine to pick up several cars from a siding which they identify by a milepost location. I suspect you do not truly care where it is."

The man's voice—Hogue had not really noticed until then how completely quiet J. Kenneth had been—was totally unlike his appearance. Startlingly unlike it. Although he looked like a tramp off the rods, J. Kenneth sounded like a gentleman of some considerable culture and breeding. His voice was low on the tonal scale and very smooth. It sounded quite strange coming from such an unattractive source and no doubt was the reason for the formal references by initial and middle name. With the education and background the man must certainly have, Hogue thought, the reference was a biting and unkind reminder of some sort and certainly was no pleasantry to the man on the receiving end of such a crude form of humor. Hogue wondered briefly how J. Kenneth Whatsit had come to be tied up with a crew like Chuck and, particularly, Al. He decided almost as quickly that either J. Kenneth was one of those who believed that enough money would cure any ill . . . or the man had reached a point where he believed that nothing at all mattered anyway. If he had to take a guess, Hogue would judge it to be the latter.

Not that he cared.

Nor did Chuck seem to particularly care that Hogue had been lying to him. He shrugged once and looked away. Obviously he cared nothing about the railroad's affairs involving any trains other than the one carrying the payroll shipment. Hogue seriously doubted that the man would be so unconcerned if there were any development about that movement, though.

Hogue looked at J. Kenneth and shrugged. He got a tentative smile back in return.

But that answered that. J. Kenneth could read his wire exactly as advertised. So much for any thoughts of mutiny. Hogue yawned.

"What was that again, Mr. High-an'-mighty?" Al asked from behind Hogue's back. Hogue had almost forgotten the man, or more accurately had almost been able to force Al from his thoughts.

Patiently and politely, J. Kenneth repeated what he had told Chuck. Again Hogue was struck by the cultured tone of the man's voice.

"And this one-legged bag of manure lied to you about it, eh?" Al said with a giggle. Hogue wondered how much was left of that newly opened bottle Al had found a few minutes before. Too little, Hogue suspected. He chose to ignore the insult and concentrate instead on the state of the mind that had delivered it.

Al giggled again, and Hogue felt himself involuntarily stiffen. There was something about Al—

The back of his head exploded with pain for the second time, but at least this time he had a hand braced between himself and the cutting front edge of the desk. It was not quite as bad that way. At least the pain was contained in a single place this time.

"Mister," Hogue said calmly, "I been busted up by the meanest horses you ever seen an' prodded by the rankest bovines that ever walked out of Texas. If you think you're gonna make me break down an' bawl from a little ol' thump on the head, you're in for a disappointment, and that's a fact."

Al broke into a fit of loud, rasping laughter. "You sit there and talk mighty feisty, crip, but I don't see you tryin' to do nothing about it." He took a painful hold on Hogue's shoulder and spun his chair around so they were face to face.

"Yeah, you talk pretty feisty, but I don't think you got a white man's guts, crip. If you do, why, come ahead an' try me. I'll hop on one leg and everything. Just to make it square."

Al leaned close and breathed into Hogue's nostrils, glaring at him from scant inches away.

They stayed like that for some time. It seemed like minutes but must only have been seconds on a clock. Still, it was long enough to be uncomfortable. Hogue knew without looking that the other two were watching them, wondering themselves if the one-legged telegrapher would have the guts to accept the challenge and fight the half-drunk outlaw.

Hogue swallowed, hard. He wanted to. He wanted to haul off and bury his right hand wrist-deep in Al's belly. He wanted to, and from where he was sitting he was perfectly positioned to do just that. A few years ago he would have done that and a great deal more.

But that was years ago. And it was now that he had to make his decision: take his licking like a man or back off like a coward.

Hogue blinked. He felt empty inside. And . . . frightened. That was the truth. He had participated in half a hundred barroom brawls with and without friends to side him, and he had never once backed down from any man during all those years with the cow camps.

But that was then.

He blinked again and squinted his eyes shut. When he opened them again he shifted his gaze away from Al's accusing stare down toward the man's open collar. He willed his muscles to go slack, and he waited meekly for whatever Al might choose to do next.

Al laughed again, the outburst sending a fine spray of spittle into Hogue's face. Hogue turned his head away.

Al straightened and stood for a moment over Hogue. Finally he reached out and, lightly, with an insulting gentleness, patted Hogue on the cheek. Al turned to the others and said, "Don't worry none about this ol' cripple. He won't be bothering nobody again. An' *that's* the fact here."

CHAPTER 9

There had been a time. . . .

Hogue remembered one in particular, remembered it well. He had been working on a trail crew for John Blocker, moving a herd from the hill country north of San Antonio on their way to Ellsworth, where the buyers would be waiting with eager pens, ready to scratch off bank drafts in numbers much larger than Hogue or any of the other boys could hope to comprehend.

The herd had been carrying a Z1 road brand slapped on top of a dozen other ranch brands from all the places where the steers had been picked up. Not a very big herd, a little over two thousand head, which was not much by the standards of the time, but the steers had been acting like a bunch of mixed stock instead of like steers. They were spooky and rank and hard to handle. It wore the boys to a nubbin trying to keep them together, and they never did settle enough to begin putting on weight along the trail the way a well-managed herd should do. That was not Blocker's fault; Hogue had worked for the man before and knew that he was a better drover than that. It was just the way things had been working out.

The weather was against them, for one thing. Wet and unusually cold for the time of year. The crew could not sleep well and were tired all the time and argued with one another constantly. They were on edge and that probably contributed to the edginess of the bovines, and altogether it was turning out to be a bad drive. If Blocker had not had a rule about guns and sheath knives being kept locked up in a chest on the bed wagon, there might have been even more trouble than there was, Hogue realized.

Like nearly every other trail boss, Blocker also had a rule that there would be no liquor in camp, but the man was sensible. He was able to see that his crew was close to the point of breaking by the time they were into the Indian Nations, and he was bright enough to try to do something about it.

Hogue chuckled now and then when he thought about the Nations and how far from the truth lay all the popular conceptions of that country.

The penny dreadfuls—and the drovers read them as avidly as did any uninformed Easterner—painted the Nations as a place where a white man's scalp was always in danger. That was a crock of Grade A crap. In all the parts of it Hogue had seen, in all the parts he ever did see, it was a place where civilized Indians and rather uncivil whites ran stores and farms and businesses and where the blanket variety of red men begged and burnt lice and did whatever it was they did to keep themselves from starving. Which as far as Hogue could ever see had not been much.

Liquor was supposed to be outlawed by federal order all through the Nations, but no one has yet figured out a way to keep a man from making a fool of himself when he really wants to, and that was as true in the Nations as it was in Kansas City or Boston or any other place. The only difference was that in Kansas City they called the places saloons and in Boston called them bars and in the Nations called them hog ranches. The quality of their wares might differ one place from another, but the end result was always the same.

Anyway, Hogue remembered, they were passing within a few miles of one of these hog ranches that sat on the bank of a sometimes creek that now was running full due to all the rain they had been having.

John Blocker stopped the herd on a flat of grass that was better than it had any right to be except for that unusual wetness and told the crew they would be able to spend a couple evenings relaxing in the hog wallow, taking turnabout holding the herd while the others partied it up. That struck everybody as a right fine idea.

Hogue was one of five boys who rode what was by then a rather well-defined trail from the camp to the hog ranch for the last trip there. Everyone else had had his time to relax, and the herd would be heading north again in the morning, and that probably had something to do with the attitude of the people who hung around the place. Once this bunch was gone there would be no further opportunity for any of them to benefit from the cash Blocker had advanced to his men for their evenings off.

The place had been no worse than Hogue expected, which meant that it was pretty bad but did offer the several commodities the riled-up drovers had come in search of. The whiskey was vile and the two available women were bone-deep ugly, but, again, that was no worse than was expected. They were there, which was all the cowhands asked.

The corners of Hogue's mouth twitched and he came very close to smiling when he remembered the boys he had been with that night.

Billy Barbero was a kid making his first trail drive, and he had passed out early in the festivities, which probably saved him, at least temporarily, from getting a dose of the social disease that inflicted nearly every trail hand.

Tom Crowley got sick to his stomach a little while later and made the place smell even worse than it had to begin with, which Hogue would not have thought possible if he had not experienced it himself. Tom volunteered to take Billy back to camp with him, which left three from Blocker's crew in the place.

Mort Oliver found a place to curl up in a corner of the dirt floor next, and Bug-Eyed John Sneffels keeled over a little time later. They had seemed to be having a good time; Hogue still was. He laughed at them and called for another drink.

The next time Hogue looked around, some greaseball of a buffalo hunter who probably had not been sober enough to shoot a rifle accurately in the past several years was busily trying to enrich himself by going through the pockets of Hogue's fallen friends. A dumpy squaw with just as much grease in her hair, whom Hogue knew from recently past experience was not half as lively as a man would like, was acting as the buffalo hunter's assistant in that operation.

They probably thought Hogue was too far gone to notice or to care if he did happen to notice, but Hogue Bynell had never been high on the notion of letting a friend down.

Hogue knocked back what was left in his tin cup—after the first few you could not taste it anyway, which was a blessing—let out a croak that was intended to be a lion's roar and began a stumble-footed charge at the offending pair.

Hogue felt himself grinning now toward the unseen doorway of the forgotten railroad shack.

That had been a fight to remember.

He was more than a bit foggy between the ears to begin with. He reached them and launched a powerful right toward the buffalo hunter's jaw, but the punch somehow went astray and connected instead with the squat, brown woman. Which might have turned out to be a blessing, considering all the tales Hogue had heard about what a squaw can do to a man. Anyway, she was out of it as completely as the other Blocker men were, right then and there.

Hogue lost his balance and fell plumb on top of the buffalo hunter and Bug-Eyed John, which did not seem to bother Bugs any but did knock the wind out of the buffalo hunter. Both he and Hogue came to their feet weaving and puny after that.

The hunter, who was very nearly as drunk as Hogue was, made the mistake of trying to work on Hogue's midsection. The theory was all right there, but the application left something to be desired. Hogue's belly was about as hard as it was broad, and all that windmill flailing was taking as much out of the buffalo hunter as it was out of Hogue.

In the meantime Hogue was taking some wild swings of his own, aiming them in the general direction of the buffalo hunter's head and letting fly. The fourth or fifth massive punch connected by some fluke of fortune, and the buffalo hunter went out like a candle in a windstorm.

Hogue stood over the assortment of fallen bodies and wondered if he should join them or if it would be worth the effort to stay on his feet.

The buffalo hunter turned out to have some friends in the place, though, and before Hogue knew what was going on a couple of them had him wrapped up from behind and were turning him around to where they could do some damage.

There were three of them, all more or less drunk but certainly carrying less of a load than Hogue was, and two of them were engaged in the task of pinning Hogue's arms to his sides from behind him. The third planted himself at Hogue's front and let fly.

With the assistance of his two friends, the man landed a beauty, flush on Hogue's jaw. It should have dropped him like a barrow in a slaughterhouse, and no doubt the three thought the fight was over and they could begin picking pockets where their buddy had left off.

Instead, for some reason the impact served to clear Hogue's head of the blurriness the alcohol had brought on. He shook his head and stuck out his jaw and spat out some of the blood that was beginning to collect in his mouth from the impact. He grinned at the man who was standing in front of him, and the fellow's eyes widened.

"All *right*," Hogue told him.

A flexing of massive shoulder muscles and a powerful surge upward with his arms shook off the two who were clinging to him from behind.

It was still three to one, but now it was a great deal more equal than Hogue's opponents had intended.

The one who had been doing the punching tried to take care of it with a boot to the crotch, but Hogue blocked that with his thigh and, willing to accept a good idea when he saw one, planted the pointed toe of his own boot square on the offender's jewels. The man doubled over with a high-pitched squeal and was not heard from again.

"Two to go," Hogue said cheerfully as he turned to face the pair behind him.

They came at him in a rush of flying fists, seemingly so many and so busy that it looked to Hogue like it should have required twice as many men to throw so many punches.

He did not even try to sort out what belonged to whom but ignored the flurry about his ears and stomach, accepting the punishment they gave, aware of it without being particularly concerned about it. He could feel the dull thump of their fists but did not find the repeated impacts to be especially painful.

He laughed out loud and chose the one on his left as a primary target, concentrating on that one and ignoring the other.

A hard left over the heart brought the man's hands down, and Hogue formed his right hand not into a fist but into a knuckle-forward wedge that had the approximate consistency of a sash weight. This he stabbed with considerable force under the man's chin to a point immediately above the Adam's apple.

Which left only one for him to deal with.

That lone gentleman no longer seemed inclined to continue the contest. He looked at his fallen companions and turned very nearly as bug-eyed as Bug-Eyed John Sneffels. Immediately thereafter he turned and tried to run.

"Whoa up there, neighbor," Hogue said happily.

He grabbed the fellow by the nape of his neck and without thinking about the strength that was required picked him bodily off the dirt floor. The man screamed.

There probably was no need for further combat, but Hogue was not thinking about that at the time. He set the man back onto his feet, turned him around, took careful aim at the unresisting figure and laid the man out with a solid right cross that landed flush on the side of the fellow's unprotected jaw.

Hogue stood towering over the now numerous bodies that littered the floor of the filthy hog ranch, feeling strong and pleased and quite content to get back to work chasing those miserable bovines come morning.

He stood over them. . . .

He *stood*. That was the key to the whole thing.

A wave of bitterness swept through Hogue, wiping out the remembered sense of pleasure as if it had never been.

That had been from another time. It might well have been another man.

At least then Hogue had been a man. Now. . . .

He sighed. If he was going to spend the rest of his days hobbling around with one leg beneath his belt—and he damned sure was going to do that—it would be so much easier if he could forget that he had ever had two good legs to hold him upright, the way a man should be.

Someone born with only one leg would have much less of an idea about what he was missing. Hogue's memories would not allow him that slim measure of relief from torment. And the game of "if only" held no relief at all.

Hogue cursed softly to himself and cocked his head. Behind him he could hear Al alternately taking a gurgling swallow from Hogue's bottle and rummaging noisily through Hogue's personal belongings.

And there was not a thing a one-legged man could do to stop him.

Hogue wished that bottle was in his hand instead of Al's. At least *that* he still could do.

CHAPTER 10

"Well, well, what *do* we have here?" Al had given up searching through Hogue's private things around his bunk and was rummaging now through the desk drawers immediately beside the relay operator. It was becoming more and more difficult for Hogue to ignore him.

Al straightened and grinned and held up a small metal box that was held closed by a hasp but had no lock. There had never before been any reason to put a lock on anything in the shack. Hogue would not have thought about such a precaution.

Now Hogue was regretting that. He grunted softly to himself as he turned his head away and willed himself not to look at the grinning Al while the man pawed the box open.

"Now, what kinda goodies do we have here?" Al asked no one in particular. "A little stash of—" He cursed and pulled a handful of now crumpled paper from the box. "No money at all, crip? Nothing but this junk?" He cussed some more. Al sounded disappointed and annoyed at the same time.

With any luck, Hogue thought, the creep would throw the letters away. Burn them if he wished. Hogue should have burned them himself long since and now wished that he had done so. He did not know why he saved them anyway. They were the letters Mabel Cutcheon had sent him. He had no reason to save them.

But he did not want some miserable stranger pawing through them, regardless.

Hogue thought about turning, snatching the wad of papers from Al and tossing it into the stove, setting the letters afire. He thought about it, but he did not make any motion to do it. Instead he kept his eyes averted.

"Bunch o' crap," Al grumbled. He took another drink from Hogue's bottle.

"Is there anything there that we should be interested in?" Chuck asked. "They must be important if they were put away like that."

"It don't look like it."

Hogue could hear Al sorting through the letters. Then the man was still. Reading, Hogue thought. If the bastard could read. There were enough who could not.

Apparently Al was not among the ranks of the unwashed illiterates. Unwashed, yes, but not illiterate. After a few moments he began to chuckle.

"Hey, I ain't believing this," Al said. "This ol' crip has himself a lady friend. Serious. I ain't lying to you." No one challenged the statement, but Al went on as if someone had. "Listen to this, will ya: 'My *dear* Mister Bynell.' That's the way . . . just a minute. . . ." There was the soft rustle of paper before Al said, "Mabel. That's the way she signs it. Not Miss something nor Missus something, but ol' Mabel. Just her first name."

Al reached up and poked Hogue painfully below the ribs. "Are you close to that, crip? You been gettin' some from ol' Mabel? Is that why she signs her name so loose, huh?"

Hogue felt the heat rise in his face, but he remained silent. He sat quiet and helpless, knowing there was nothing he

could do about this or about any of the rest of it. He damn
sure should have burned those letters a long time ago. It was
his own fault that he had not.

"Let's see what the ol' hussy has to say in here," Al mumbled with obvious pleasure.

There was a minute or more of silence while Al read
through the letter in his hand.

"Huh!" Al said with a snort after a time. "She says she's
needin' you to come trim her wicks again." The man laughed
nastily. "Nothin' about dippin' your wick but some about you
trimming hers. You a regular visitor there, crip? Or just when
she can't find nothing better to warm her up? I'll bet that's it.
A one-legged man, there's gotta be lots better around. I'll bet
you just get the crumbs when she can't find nothing else. An'
at that she must be a greasy ol' hawg to give you any time in
there atall. Ain't that the truth, crip? Well, ain't it?" He
poked Hogue in the ribs again. Hogue ignored the pain.
Tried to ignore both kinds of pain the man was causing.

"Well, answer me."

"You already know it all," Hogue said. "I can't tell you
nothing."

Hogue kept his eyes away from Al. In doing so he caught a
brief flicker of expression on J. Kenneth Whatshisname's
gaunt, pinched face. It might have been sympathy. It might
as easily have been disgust. Hogue was not sure. Not that it
mattered. All three of them would be gone soon. Whenever
that was it would not be soon enough.

He looked at Chuck, too. The stocky outlaw seemed content enough for the moment. Perhaps because Al had been
diverted by the letters and was no longer so diligently sucking
at the whiskey bottle. Probably Chuck cared nothing about

what else went on inside the shack as long as it did not inter-
fere with the robbery they planned.

With a sharp bark of laughter Al went back to his letter
reading, and Chuck began to roll another cigarette. J. Kenneth looked as though he was uninterested in the whole
thing.

Hogue tried to assume the same sense of detachment that
J. Kenneth was exhibiting. Hogue had had enough practice
in the last year or so at the art of shutting the world out. It
should have been easy for him by now. Somehow this time it
was not quite as simple as it should have been.

CHAPTER 11

It was not like that at all. Al Trapp's snide suggestiveness could not change a single grain of the real truth, and the real truth was that Mabel Cutcheon was a good woman.

A far better woman, in fact, than Hogue Bynell deserved. He had believed that much *before* the accident. He felt it to be all the more true now.

A hussy, Al had called her, with his dirty mouth and obscene thoughts. Well, Hogue was no halo-bearing saint himself. Often enough he had joined the other boys in wisecrackery and dirty jokes. But he never would have applied any of them to a woman like Mrs. Cutcheon. No one who saw her could ever do that.

Mabel Cutcheon was anything but a trollop, as anyone could plainly see with a single glance.

That kind wore feathers and face paint as if to advertise themselves as being no better than a squaw.

Mrs. Cutcheon wore no makeup at all save an occasional dusting of powder, as was proper for a lady, and her hair was always, at least in public, kept neatly pinned into a bun. Her eyebrows were properly unplucked and her limbs always decorously covered. Hogue doubted that the freckled skin of that vee beneath her throat, where a man's flesh will become wrinkled and leather-hued from exposure by an open collar, had ever seen the light of the sun.

Not that Mabel Cutcheon was prudish. She was not; certainly not in the privacy of her own rooms.

She was a warm and giving person, cheerful and honest and fully human.

She was a lady, plain and simple, and the likes of Al Trapp had no business dragging a good woman's name down to their own crude level.

Hogue fought back a pang of resentment. He was no longer man enough to leap to the lady's defense. He had to keep reminding himself of that.

With a sigh half of impatience and half of annoyance, he forced such thoughts from his mind and tried instead to think of other, better things.

For instance, the time that particular letter referred to. Hogue remembered that well. Better than he really wanted to. He tried nowadays to keep such memories out of mind, for they were not always easy to bear.

That time had been, he thought—no, he was quite sure, actually—the first time he had visited Mrs. Cutcheon's home following the accident. The first time he had gone there on crutches with a pants leg pinned up.

She had visited him, frequently, while he still lay in the doctor's clinic bed, and she had insisted on this outing to her home as soon as he learned to operate his crutches without help. Dinner at the Cutcheon house was to be his first trip away from the clinic—which the doctor liked to dignify by calling it a hospital—by himself.

The distance was nearly five blocks, but Hogue had managed it. At the time, he was still taking his weight on the tender sockets of his armpits and had not yet learned to use his hands and arms to accept the strain, so by the time he reached the familiar doorway he was uncomfortable and in need of rest.

Mabel had had sense enough to allow him to negotiate the front steps on his own, without offering him any assistance, although he had seen the stir of a frilly curtain at her front window and knew she was already aware of his arrival and would be there watching in case he should fall. He had been grateful to her for that measure of understanding, and he thought at first that the dinner would be accomplished with less embarrassment than he had been expecting, and dreading, might happen.

He knocked at the closed and curtained front door, and she had waited a decent interval before answering his knock.

She led him to the small parlor, where he had visited more than a few times in the past, before the accident, and if she moved perhaps a bit more slowly now than she had done before, allowing Hogue to keep pace with her, she at least did not make a show of it, and again Hogue was grateful to her.

They talked for a while, about inconsequential things like the state of business at the dry-goods store she was still operating after the death of her husband, like her difficulties in securing a good clerk to handle her business affairs and in finding reliable suppliers for the many things she needed to maintain in stock.

Hogue really had as little interest in the affairs of a dry-goods store as she probably did in the operation of a beef ranch, but the topics were comfortably neutral and the conversation was more important for its own sake than for its content.

She offered him a glass of wine, which he accepted, and drank one with him. She was, after all, not a prude and held no convictions that would condemn a drink or two for a man nor a sip or two for a lady.

After a decent interval she led him into the tiny niche that served her for a formal dining room, and he took a chair at the head of the table, where her husband had used to sit. That was, Hogue realized, the first time he had been invited to sit in that particular spot. Always before, he had been seated across from Mrs. Cutcheon at the side of the rectangular table. He wondered if the change might have some significance.

The table had already been laid with the best she had to offer. If not elegant by Boston standards, the table settings were certainly far finer than Hogue was used to dining from, either in a cow camp or at the clinic.

A pair of coal-oil lamps with hand-painted decorative shades gave scant but attractive light to the small room, and Mabel did not offer to light any more for their meal.

The food had been ready in advance of his arrival, waiting in her warming oven, and she served it with a minimum of fuss. They ate largely in silence, but Hogue found it to be a comfortable silence and the food to be exceptionally good. He did not think his judgment of the meal had been affected by its comparison with the plain fare he was accustomed to at the clinic, either. Mabel Cutcheon was quite a good cook, as was amply demonstrated by that dinner.

Later she left him in the parlor with a cigar and a glass of raspberry brandy for company while she "rid up" in the kitchen.

Hogue felt very nearly comfortable for the first time since he had awakened to the sight of that ugly, barren, flat expanse of sheet in the bed where his leg should have been.

While Mabel was busy in the kitchen, he tried to repay her kindness with a gesture of thanks.

Practically none of the lamps in the house seemed capable of producing a clear, steady butterfly of light. Why there seemed to be no woman born who could ever properly trim a lampwick Hogue did not know, but that seemed an axiom that no man could ever understand.

At any rate, he took out his pocketknife and whetted it carefully on the counter of his scuffed left boot and, crutching slowly from one table to the next, proceeded to trim and clean every wick in every lamp in the parlor and the vestibule. He was working on the lamps in the dining room when Mabel completed her chores in the kitchen and caught him at his work.

"That is exactly the task Mr. Cutcheon used to undertake. Every Sunday afternoon before nightfall, without fail," she told him. "You have no idea, Mr. Bynell, the things a woman comes to miss when there is no man in the house."

Hogue shrugged. "Is it Sunday?" He had lost track of the days and had no idea.

"No, but. . . ." She stopped there and looked slightly embarrassed. "You've come to know me well enough,"—she hesitated—"Hogue"—the use of his first name alone was quite rare—"that I should be able to tell you . . . I am past the point of missing Mr. Cutcheon now. But I have been missing the visits you used to pay here before. . . ." She repeated firmly, "Before." It was enough. He knew before what.

"Yes, ma'am." Now it was Hogue's turn to be embarrassed. He knew quite well what she was referring to now.

Mabel Cutcheon was a good woman but a human one. She

admitted, delicately, to needs and desires that Hogue had never known ladies had. Before Hogue's accident, she had shared with him moments that a crude type like Al Trapp could never understand and which, somehow, had done nothing to lessen her in Hogue's perception. She remained a good woman in Hogue's view.

Now, delicately, she seemed to be inviting him to continue the relationship they had begun, in spite of his disfigurement. Inviting him, he thought, to that and perhaps to something more.

His seating position at the table, the lighting during the meal, now her reference to the absence of a man in the house. He thought. . . . He had no right to such thoughts. Hogue had clamped down with bitter stubbornness on that. He had no right to think anything about this good woman.

Even so, Mabel Cutcheon had seemed to understand the difficulty he was having.

Abandoning her usually oblique forms of invitation and suggestion, she eventually became quite bold and—Hogue swallowed hard at the memory—offered herself to him as a woman gives to a man.

It had been—he squinted his eyes shut—a miserable experience. The worst of his life. Far worse than the accident itself. Perhaps worse even than that awakening to his new status as a castoff and a cripple.

For the first time in his life, Hogue Bynell had been unable to perform as a man.

And that had sealed him in his bitterness.

On that self-same visit when he had trimmed the wicks of Mabel Cutcheon's lamp and which Al, unknowing, had now made crude reference to.

Oh, there had been nothing in her letter, mailed long afterward, that would in any way refer to what had happened during that visit. There never would be.

Hogue remembered the letter quite well. That one and nearly all of the others. Always their tone was cheerful and circumspect and pleasant and warm and. . . .

And there was nothing that could ever come from them. Which was why Hogue had long since quit responding to any of those letters, which still continued to arrive with monthly regularity.

There was no point in his writing to her. Or to anyone. He was useless to any decent woman, and he knew it. And Al guessed it, more accurately than he would ever know.

Bastard, Hogue thought. If only. . . .

But "if only" gathers no cows. "If only" would not cause the clock to spin any quicker. Hogue was sick of "if only." All he wanted now was to be left alone. That would be quite enough. If only he could have that.

He shut his eyes and tried to shut out the sounds of Al pawing through Mabel Cutcheon's private letters to a man who no longer existed.

CHAPTER 12

There was never enough work at Relay 12 to keep even a one-legged man really busy, but at least the late morning usually gave Hogue something to do with himself. For no reason that he had ever bothered to wonder about, that period was usually when the line sent most of its wire traffic.

This day, the busy period started slightly earlier than usual. There was a special eastbound due at Relay 12 at 10:09. It would cause no interference with the westbound Chuck and Al and company were interested in, but Hogue was ordered to post for it a flimsy telling it to pick up the empty cars on the siding to the east and to rescind the previous train order originally intended for the regular P.M. eastbound.

Routine stuff, but now it irked him. It meant he would once again have to use his crutches in full view of his unwelcome guests.

Hogue looked at his watch: 9:53. My, he was thinking, how time flies when you are having fun. He scrawled the new train order onto a standard form ready for the pickup pouch, but even as he wrote the order and initialed it he was wondering if he should just let this one slide, post the order to the P.M. eastbound as he had first been told. The empties would arrive where they were needed regardless, and he would be saved that much more embarrassment. It would not be a victory over Al, by any stretch of the imagination, but. . . .

He glanced over at J. Kenneth, who was looking alert and interested in his surroundings for the first time in a considerable while.

No, Hogue decided, if he failed to post the order as he was instructed, J. Kenneth would tell the others about it, and then Hogue would have Al to deal with. Probably painfully. They would undoubtedly decide that he was trying to tip the line to a problem at Relay 12 by refusing his orders.

Bastards, he thought.

He rolled the flimsy into a cylinder and snapped a gum rubber band around it and dropped it into one of the pickup pouches that always lay beside his desk. He picked up his crutches and stood.

"Where are you goin' with that?" Chuck demanded. Hogue could feel, without looking, a threatening tension in Al behind him.

"It's a train order," Hogue snapped. "You want things to keep on going normally around here, don't you?"

Chuck looked pointedly at the former telegrapher, J. Kenneth.

The scrawny gentleman-turned-derelict nodded. "I read the order as he received it," J. Kenneth said. "Quite routine."

"You heard what that noise box said maybe," Chuck corrected him, "but you ain't seen what he put on that paper. Read it over. Make sure it's what it should be."

J. Kenneth shrugged. "Whatever you say." He did not wait for Hogue to crutch over to him with the pouch but instead came to Hogue. He unrolled the flimsy, read it, and replaced it in the pouch exactly the way it had been. "He attempted no surprises."

Chuck grunted.

"Can I get on with my work now?"

The stocky outlaw made an impatient gesture toward the platform, which Hogue took to be approval. Bastards, he thought again.

He made his way out onto the platform and stood for a moment looking toward the distant horizon, beyond the browning grass of the rolling plains toward the Picketwire and the flatter, drier country where a man had to fight heat and mesquite as well as cattle and boredom. A *man*, Hogue reminded himself bitterly. That was something he would not have to worry about ever again.

Still, standing outside there, where he could see the grass and the immensity of the sky and the big, beautiful emptiness that he had come to love, in spite of what remained inside the shack behind him he found himself breathing just a bit deeper and feeling just a bit fitter.

If only. . . .

Seven pronghorns were grazing idly on a knoll half a mile south of the station, and Hogue paused to watch them. For that brief period he did not feel bitter about any of it. He came close to smiling when one of the tiny figures, probably a calf (lamb? he did not know which an antelope should be called) bounded high into the air in a playful leap and raced around to the other side of the small herd.

Hogue thought briefly of the carving he had been working on before. He really would have to do another. Maybe even one good enough to keep. He had come to really enjoy the pronghorns in this past year or so. Always before he had thought of them as a source of meat. Now they were something closer to companions.

With a sigh, Hogue reminded himself that the eastbound special would be along in a few minutes. He crutched his way across the platform to the post where his pouches were hung and rigged the train order for pickup.

A wire loop carried the pouch on the hook, and the passing engineer could snag it with a short staff and hook of his own just by reaching out from his cab. There was no need for the trains to slow in their passage. It was an efficient system.

He had no particular desire to return to the company inside the shack, so Hogue leaned against the tall post and waited. Already he could hear the approach of the special from the west.

He looked up at the pouch dangling in the thin, healthful air of the high plains. Above it and mounted to the post was the red-ball flag that was also part of the standard railroad equipment. In all the time Hogue had been at Relay 12 he had never had occasion to flag a train, had never had a passenger come here to board a train. Still, it made no difference at all to the planners of the MK&C if a piece of equipment was going to be needed at any particular station. The standard-issue items were installed regardless, and anything that was not standard was absent unless an operator wanted to buy it out of his own pocket.

Hogue shook his head. The line was implacably set in its own ways, but at least it let him alone. There was that to be said for it.

He looked to his right. The special was closer now; he could hear it quite plainly. It seemed to be making good time.

For a moment, Hogue wondered what would happen if he tried to signal to the crew, tried to warn them somehow from—

He heard footsteps behind him and turned. Al was there, grinning. "Just so's you don't get any ideas," he said. "I'll be in the doorway there watchin' you. Move just a li'l bit wrong and I'll put a slug through your knee." He laughed. "I reckon you know which one."

Hogue turned his head away. Yes, he knew which one. There was only one.

Hogue thought about that for a moment and found himself trying to swallow against a suddenly desert-dry throat. It was bad enough as things were. The thought of losing his remaining leg too would be beyond his ability to bear. Absolutely beyond it, he knew.

That bastard Al had unerringly found the single greatest weakness Hogue Bynell could possibly have now, and Hogue had no doubts at all that the man would not be beyond using that weakness against him. On a whim as easily as by necessity. At least the others, Chuck and J. Kenneth, were interested in the outcome of a particular job. Al seemed to be just plain mean.

Hogue pretended to ignore the threat and turned to watch the rapid approach of the special.

The engineer spotted the hooked pouch waiting for him— there were trackside markers warning him well in advance of every station shack he would pass and alerting him to look ahead for possible orders—and Hogue could see the man lean out of his cab with a staff held casually in his left hand. This was something the engineer did several times daily.

Hogue did not know the man—he knew few enough of

their faces and practically none of their names, even on the work trains that stopped there once a week—but the striped cap and set of his chin were familiar enough. That was one thing about the engineers, Hogue admitted. There were no drunks or misfits or creeps among them. They were the elite of the line and, as far as they were concerned, the elite of all creation. They took their work seriously. Much more so than you would find with a half-wild bunch of crazy cowhands, at least half of whom would be looking for a practical joke to pull at any given moment.

The intensity of the engineers—and of a good many others on the line as well—had been hard for Hogue to accept at first. He was not entirely sure he had accepted it yet. Or that he cared enough to want to.

The railroaders were just damn-sure different from the boys he used to ride with.

Not as good, Hogue amended stubbornly. *Too* serious. A man ought to be able to have some fun in his work. Hogue sighed. He no longer expected to have any fun in anything.

The engineer deftly snatched the pouch with his hook and gave a short nod that might have been meant for Hogue or might have been simple satisfaction at making the pickup. By the time Hogue turned to look at the already receding engine, the engineer was back inside his cab and there was no sign of the pouch that had just been taken aboard.

Hogue stood braced on his crutches and his one good leg and felt the pull of the wind caused by the passage of the short freight a few feet from where he stood on the platform.

Having that much noisy, heavy steel and wood passing practically within inches had been rather frightening the first few times, but Hogue no longer thought about it.

He could hear the loping, protesting roll of the massive wheels over the rails and could smell the lingering scent of coal smoke when the train was gone, but in moments it was as if the special had never gone by.

There was a knoll just to the east of the station, and the tracks curved ever so slightly there, so the special was lost to view in very short order. Hogue did not miss it.

For the first time, though, he thought that perhaps he should have a bench put onto the platform so he could sit out here and watch the pronghorns at play. A bench would have come in particularly handy right now, as he did not really want to go back inside with Al and Chuck and J. Kenneth, but his only alternative would be to stand outside on the platform, where, too soon, his hands and armpits would begin to tire from the need to support himself on the crutches. Standing around on railroad platforms or street corners could no longer be considered a long suit.

He turned and began to make his way back to the relative comfort of his chair.

CHAPTER 13

The telegraph key had begun to clatter before Hogue was well into the shack, and he had to hurry the last few paces—swings, in his case—across the wooden floor. He swung hastily into his chair and let his crutches fall against the wall where the never-used flag lever was. More unnecessary but standard railroad equipment; Hogue had long since removed the bar-iron handle and used it now as a poker for his stove.

He had begun to receive the incoming message in his head before he ever reached his chair, and now his fingers flew as he caught up with the letters being formed one by one by the unseen telegrapher somewhere to the west.

Hogue accepted the message and receipted it from long habit, but this time when he threw the switch to disengage his key and sat back in his chair, he was wearing a deep frown instead of his accustomed scowl. He swiveled the chair to face the wall and sat there for some time in silence.

"You may as well tell them," J. Kenneth prompted after several minutes. "I did read it, you know." The man's tone of voice was not unkind.

Hogue grunted.

"So what was that all about?" Chuck demanded. Hogue turned the chair to face him, continuing to ignore Al. For the moment, though, Hogue did not speak.

"Well?"

"That message. . . ." Hogue's voice trailed off into silence again. He remained undecided what to do about it.

"I *know* that much, dammit. What'd it say? J. Kenneth?"

"Give the gentleman a moment to work it out in his own mind, if you please."

"Well I *don't* please. I'll do the workin' out around here. Now, what'd it say?"

J. Kenneth shrugged and waited for Hogue to speak.

"That was a message from Pueblo," Hogue said. "They're putting on a special this afternoon. Eastbound."

"It wasn't about the payroll train?" Chuck demanded quickly.

Hogue shook his head.

"So what, then? It don't mean anything to us."

J. Kenneth turned his head away and coughed softly into his closed fist.

"What it means," Hogue explained, as much to himself as to the robber, "is that there will be another train on the track this afternoon. Coming toward the one you want."

"So?"

"So I've been told if there's a delay of as much as fourteen minutes on that westbound payroll train, I'm supposed to notify Relay 16 to put the special onto a siding. Otherwise there might be an accident. A head-on, you see."

"There won't be no delay in the payroll train's schedule, will there?" Chuck asked suspiciously.

Hogue shook his head again. "I don't see much chance of it. The trainmaster's pure hell-on-wheels. They run it tight on this section."

"All right, then. We got no problems, right?"

"I didn't say that. Not exactly."

"What the gentleman is trying to get across to you," J. Kenneth injected, "is that a delay on the siding, such as we propose to create for our own, uh, particular purposes, such a delay would likely result in a head-on collision between the payroll train and the eastbound special. *That* is what he is trying to explain, Charles."

For a moment, Chuck looked worried. "Before the payroll train reaches the siding where the boys are waiting, you mean?"

J. Kenneth looked expectantly toward Hogue.

"No," Hogue said. "After it left there. Unless it took you less than fourteen minutes to rob the train, and I don't think that'd be real likely."

Chuck looked relieved. "If that's all, don't worry about it. Once we got the payroll, who cares what happens to the damn train."

Hogue turned his head away. Yeah. You bet. Who cares what happens to the damn train.

In a manner of speaking, Hogue did not either. It was only so much iron and wood. A train had no feelings. A train was not like a horse or a cow or even a pronghorn, that a man should care about it. A train did not feel or sweat or get tired. Not ever. It was just a thing. Or rather, a collection of things.

But there were *men* on that train. Those men were already somewhere to the east and right now were rolling this way. And somewhere to the west, probably making up in the Pueblo yard this minute, there were other men who would be riding the eastbound special later on in the afternoon.

Those men were not the cowhands Hogue used to ride with and who Hogue still cared about in spite of himself.

They were just a bunch of railroaders. Practically no better than foreigners, really.

But they were men, dammit. And they were depending on Hogue Bynell's abilities to keep them safe when they rode the steel rails.

Now here were these miserable sons of bitches telling Hogue Bynell to not worry about it. Go ahead and kill a bunch of railroaders. It wouldn't matter so long as the payroll was safely robbed before then.

Hogue shook his head and turned his chair once more to face the blank, undecorated wall of his tiny relay shack.

It was a stinking position he was in. That was all there was to it. Stinking. He wished that bastard Al had not finished off the bottle from the desk drawer. This was not a great day to stay sober. Hogue sighed and let his chin drop toward his chest while he glowered at the wall. The boards in front of him really should have been mirrors instead, because he felt like glowering at himself.

CHAPTER 14

Hogue was visualizing the siding. Avoiding thinking about the problems ahead, actually. He did not want to think about that.

He could practically see Chuck's and Al's gun-hung, bloody partners waiting there already.

Hogue knew the spot well enough. He and the other boys from the Y Knot had spent enough time there in the past, not waiting to commit a crime but just goofing off. It was a good spot for that. Or for hiding, which in essence was what the boys used to do there. Probably still did.

The siding looped to the north of the main line, a curving parenthesis of steel separated from the main track by only a matter of yards. For miles to east and west alike the land around it was flat, scarcely rolling grassland too sparsely covered to hide a fully grown jackrabbit.

Except for that outcropping just to the north of the siding tracks.

Hogue knew perfectly good and well why the gang of robbers had chosen that particular siding for their work. They chose it for the same reason that Hogue and the Y Knot crew used to go there.

Not seventy-five yards from the siding steel, there was one of those outcroppings of rock that show themselves here and there in the big-grass country. Sometimes red, sometimes gray but for some reason mostly yellow or almost white rock, the outcroppings are a little less usual than a clump of trees on the open grass but not much more so. Some places, they are actually quite common.

Hogue had no idea what caused them. There were those who said the rocks had once been buried and that the land had worn down around them. Others speculated that the land surface had been there first and some underground force had once caused the rocks to push up through the ground like so many jagged spears. Hogue did not know the truth about that. It could have been either way. Certainly most of the outcroppings were jagged enough to have come up after the land was formed. Some of them looked almost like giant spearheads. And all of them were weathered and pitted, some looking not unlike giant hunks of Swiss cheese with wind-gouged holes and pockets marring their flanks. Frequently where you found one formation you found a handful of them, covering several acres.

Once, up in Wyoming, where a bunch of them had gone with a small herd of heifers for delivery to an Englishman putting together a new ranching operation, Hogue had seen the place they called Hell's Half Acre.

That outcropping was like a cave without the roof on it. A pit containing a bunch of extremely jagged spires on its floor. Along the edges of the pit, beneath the drop-off from the flat ground above, they found enough buffalo skulls and bleaching bones to make a fertilizer collector a rich man in a single gather. Someone said the old-time Indians used to drive buffalo off the flat country to fall onto the spears of rock and die down below, back before the white men brought them rifles and ammunition to make that method of killing inefficient.

There were such places all through this country, and the one where the robbers were now waiting was a good one. For hiding in, anyway.

The outcropping covered perhaps a dozen acres, no more, and was clearly defined. The rock formations rose perhaps fifteen feet above the level of the land, and there were a bunch of the formations, each individual rock shaped something like the blade of a spade, and each one standing alone. There were patches of level, grassy ground between them, where a man could ride a horse and wind between the separate blades.

That was what had attracted the Y Knot boys there.

Frequently when they were working that section of the country they would slip into the rocks about noontime to take a bit of rest. Most times of the year you could find a little shade once you got in among the spears, and shade was a rare and valuable thing on the plains.

What was more, this particular outcropping was big enough that you could get all the way inside it. Most of them consisted of a few spires or lumps of rock, but you were on one side of the formation or the other. This one was massive enough that you could ride right inside it.

The attraction of that was that a foreman could ride right past or even circle plumb around it and never see a sign of any of his hands.

A fellow could slip in there and loosen his saddle, let his horse take some time to stand in the shade and blow, and the hand could stretch out on the ground and get a little much-needed sleep before he headed out again to the heat and the dust and the hard work of handling livestock.

Oh, Hogue had done it often enough. He and the other boys. He could not count the noonings they had taken in there. Or the number of afternoons they had lingered past the nooning to talk and smoke and nap when they should have been out earning their wages.

Hogue almost smiled at the memory. The feeling had been very much like the ones he had had when he was a kid and would slip away from the schoolhouse to hunt frogs or manufacture bark whistles or search for a piece of twine that he could pretend was a real catch-rope and use to lasso stray hounds. The feeling had been very much like playing hookey, and the grown cowhands had enjoyed it quite as much as schoolchildren always did.

Now there were a bunch of armed men hiding in those rocks, waiting for Hogue to toll an unsuspecting train into their trap.

The rocks were only a matter of yards away from the siding tracks, and a score of men could hide in them without anyone from the train being the wiser.

If the train crew got a message—*when* the train crew got a message—from Relay 12 ordering a layover, why, they would lay over. There was no freight so valuable and no guard so suspicious that a train order would be questioned, much less disobeyed. Once Hogue hung that flimsy, the train would stop on the siding, and that was that.

The robbers could come boiling out from the rocks and be on them with guns drawn before the crew knew a thing about what was coming. There would seem to be nothing amiss that would give them any warning. The attack would come as a total surprise, which was undoubtedly what Chuck and his friends would want.

It should work to perfection, and the crew would not have a chance to defend themselves.

Which was perhaps just as well. Surrounded like that and with no warning, the crew and whatever guards might be on the train probably would not even try to defend themselves. There probably would be no time for it.

And the robbers would know that. They would have no reason to begin shooting. The whole thing should go off without anyone being hurt.

And that much Hogue could live with. Hell, the railroad carried insurance. Even if they did not, the line could afford the loss of one payroll. It was only money, after all.

But now. . . .

The way things were shaping up now, that robbery would go along just exactly the way it was supposed to. The gang would come out waving their guns, and the crew would see they had no chance, and the robbery would take place without anyone having to be hurt.

But there was no way in hell even the most efficient bunch of train robbers could open a safe and unload a payroll of gold coins and take their leave within fourteen lousy minutes.

No way.

If they were smart—and Hogue had no reason to believe they were anything but; whoever had planned this had done a job of it—if they were smart they probably would take an extra moment to dump the steam pressure in the engine's boiler. That would give them that much longer to make a leisurely escape before the train could be brought back to a head of steam and roll on down to the next relay station to report the loss and get a posse moving out of Pueblo.

And that— Dammit, Hogue thought, that would mean the westbound freight would be somewhere on the track and again would be completely unsuspecting when the eastbound special came rolling toward them out of Pueblo.

Fourteen minutes of leeway, and that was all. Anything more and there was certain to be a head-on.

Hogue groaned aloud.

Sure you can see for a long way out on this flat country. But a railroad engineer does not have to drive his train the same way a teamster has to watch his draft animals. A train is going wherever the rails take it, and the engineer really does not have to pay much attention to what is ahead until the trackside markers tell him there is a station or a signal coming up.

There were not even herds of buffalo around any more for an engineer to have to worry about. A stray cow or two was the most interference an engineer could expect to find on his track, and those were not enough of a bother to be worth trying to stop for. Even if that could be done, which it probably could not; it takes miles of preplanning to bring a fast-moving freight to a full stop. Emergency halts were just not possible. The engineer had to shut down his driver wheels and signal to the brakemen to set their screws. The brakemen had to see the signal—they would not be looking for trouble, any more than the engineer would be—and clamber from car to car tightening wheels a few degrees at a time and then back to start all over again by retightening the first of the cars that were their responsibility.

So even if by some unlikely chance the engineers saw each

other in the distance, why, it would still be next to impossible for them to avoid a collision.

No, Hogue thought, if this robbery went ahead as planned, the odds were the next thing to pure certainty that there was going to be a collision.

And that men were going to die in the cabs of those two opposing engines running against each other on the same slim set of track.

And Hogue Bynell was going to be responsible for that. Because he was the man who would be passing the fake train order to the engineer aboard that westbound freight carrying the payroll.

That engineer, whoever he was, was very probably going to die as a result of Hogue's false order.

Hogue picked his chin up off his chest and set his jaw. He swiveled around to face Chuck Porter.

"I ain't gonna do it," he declared. "I ain't gonna send that train off to a certain head-on collision."

Al Trapp was still behind him, and Hogue felt like cringing in his chair. He tried very hard not to and to keep from showing the fear he was already beginning to feel clutching at his bowels.

"I just ain't gonna do it."

CHAPTER 15

Actually it did not hurt nearly as much as Hogue had anticipated.

The back of his head—that seemed to be a favorite spot for Al to thump on—felt as though it had some cauliflower lumps on it, and certainly the skin had parted here or there. He could feel some blood trickling past his collar and down his back.

But really it was not so bad.

For the most part he felt numb where Al had hit him. Tomorrow and for several tomorrows afterward it would hurt much worse than it did now. Hogue knew that from frequent experience in the past, both in fights and in the knocks a man takes when he sets out to brand a calf or ear down a feisty bronc. A kick in the jaw by the youngest and weakest of calves is worse than the best punch a prize fighter might be able to throw. And Hogue had absorbed his fair share of kicks and gouges, one way or another.

So it really was not all that bad.

He shook his head to clear it. The wetness at the back of his collar was more annoying than the pain.

"You're gonna change your mind, crip," Al said. He sounded quite pleased about the whole thing.

"Nope. Can't do it," Hogue said stubbornly.

"Betcha you're wrong," Al said happily. He paused to take another long pull from the bottle he had been sucking on.

Hogue looked across the small room toward Chuck. The stocky robber was the only one around who might have any effect on Al Trapp's actions, and it was obvious from Chuck's bored expression that he really did not much care what Al might end up doing to the one-legged telegrapher.

J. Kenneth, well, Hogue thought, it did not matter a fig's worth what *he* thought about any of it. For what it was worth, which was nothing, the old rummy looked as though he was distressed by the thought of any physical violence. But both he and Hogue understood that he had no voice in the matter. This would be up to Al and possibly to Chuck if he bothered to take a position on it. Hogue suspected that Chuck might care about the results but not the methods.

"I think," Al said thoughtfully, "I just might start in to bustin' his fingers." The man grinned sloppily. He was beginning to look well on his way toward being drunk. "That's the way he makes his livin'. I reckon that might go a ways toward convincin' him of the error of his ways."

Chuck shrugged. He pulled the makings from his pocket and began to build a smoke.

"I would not if I were you," J. Kenneth said. He said it slowly, as if he were unwilling to enter the discussion.

Chuck looked at him with an expression of mild annoyance, but Al's rapidly darkened features made it look as though he would be as willing to devote his attentions to J. Kenneth as to Hogue.

"We di'nt ask you about it," Al snapped.

"I was merely going to mention," J. Kenneth said, "that

our plan here is for Mr. Bynell to receipt for any wire traffic that comes through. He cannot do that if his fingers are broken." The runty little has-been was not looking Al in the face but had turned his head away.

"That's what you're here for," Chuck said in a bored tone. "Just in case."

"And I have tried to explain to you before," J. Kenneth said softly. "This gentleman and I use the same sequence of dots and dashes to form our letters. But that is as far as the similarity goes. The—how shall I explain this—the *rhythm* of the keying, the pauses, what we refer to as the quality of the fist . . . that is as individual as a man's own signature. If I send a message, the letters and the words will be quite correct. But any reasonably adept operator, and I assure you both, the railroad hires none but the most adept of telegraph operators, any reasonably adept operator would be able to hear a difference between my fist and his. If I am required to use the key there is the possibility, somewhat better than a remote possibility, I might add, that your plan will be detected. At least that a suspicion might occur. If you are willing to take that risk. . . ." He let his voice die and deliberately shrugged. "Naturally I shall transmit whatever messages you ask of me."

Hogue was surprised. And grateful. It was more of a defense than he ever would have expected from a man who had so obviously been defeated by life.

Chuck looked at his colleague in crime with more suspicion than fondness, certainly without any shred of respect in the look he gave the scruffy little man, but after a moment the stocky robber grunted and turned to Al. "Leave the crip's hands alone," he said. "Convince him, mind you, but leave his hands be. Maybe J. Kenneth has somethin' there after all."

A pouty expression not unlike that of a spoiled little girl who has not gotten her way crossed Al Trapp's face. But Hogue noticed that he did not give Chuck any argument.

For a brief moment Hogue thought about giving the bastard a grin just to make him mad. He sighed. There had been times, times not too very long ago, when he would have done just exactly that. And then would have waded into the three of them and maybe would have whipped them too. But those times were long gone now. The moment times like that had ended was cleared defined by a surgeon's saw. Now. . . . Hogue flexed his fingers, acutely aware for the first time of how much his livelihood depended on them now and how suddenly he could be robbed of that life, just as he had once been robbed of another and much beloved way of life. Bastards, he thought. But he kept his mouth shut and his face impassive as he thought it.

He still was determined, though. No matter what, even if it meant that Al would break his hands and turn the nimble, trained fingers into a clump of claws, even so he was not going to give in and do what they asked of him. Not now. Not and cause a head-on. He just could not do that.

While Hogue Bynell might not be much of a man any more, he thought with no small amount of satisfaction, there was still a bit of the old pride left in him. Whatever Al might come up with, Hogue intended to take it.

"Hey, Chuck," Al said. He had brightened somewhat after his bout of pique a moment before.

"Umm?"

"I just had me a thought."

"Yeah?"

"When this here job is done, what would you say to a bit o' fun over in Pueblo?"

Chuck shrugged. "Prob'ly."

"What I was thinkin', Chuck, we got this ol' broad's name on the crip's letters here. It wouldn't be much of a trick to find her. You know. Have us some fun with her. Tell her her cripped-up ol' boyfriend sent us around."

Al cupped Hogue's chin in a harshly squeezing hand and hauled it around so that Hogue was looking into Al's face.

"How does that sound to you, crip? We could have all manner o' fun with that lady friend of yours an' tell her it was you said we was welcome to it. Would you like that, crip?"

Hogue was no more impressed by that threat than Chuck seemed to be.

Shoot, Hogue thought, even a robber can only be so dumb, and even Al could not be *that* stupid. Certainly Chuck was not.

There was law in this part of the country now. A whole lot more than when Hogue had first seen it. Even so, a man could get away with very nearly anything he was strong enough or mean enough to want to get away with.

But there were some things that could get a fellow hanged or maybe flayed alive in the rankest, foulest, roughest sort of jerkwater hole-in-the-wall. And messing with a decent woman was right up at the top of that list. If Al did not know it, Chuck surely would.

If Al or anyone else laid a hand on Mabel Cutcheon or on

any other decent woman, he was a sure candidate for a hanging.

Anywhere in the country a man could pull a robbery, and there would be a posse on his trail. The possemen would have themselves a fine chase, and the whole thing would be as much of a social outing as it was an effort to regain the stolen funds. The men would have themselves a fine old time of it. And if they caught the robbers, that would be fine. If they did not, well, they would still have a good time and count it an effort well spent.

If the robbers happened to kill someone in their robbery, the chase would be more intent and more prolonged. They would give it an extra bit of effort and would be altogether more serious about the affair. But, again, they would not be devastated if they failed.

If, on the other hand, it was a molester of decent women they were after instead of some soul who had gotten into robbery and murder, why, in that case there would be no play at all within the posse. In that case they would be hard and serious and intent as hell.

In that case they likely would not come back until they had left a rope and some cottonwood fruit somewhere behind them.

Nossir, Hogue thought, old Al was not going to frighten him with that kind of threat.

Hogue looked calmly toward Chuck and ignored Al.

"Hey, Chuck."

"Umm?"

"I think I got it this time."

"Yeah?"

"For sure this time."

Chuck grunted.

"You ever visit one o' them hospitals during the war?" Al asked.

"A time or two."

"And we all seen plenty o' boys afterward hobblin' around with empty sleeves an' empty pants legs and such, right?"

The answer to that was too obvious for Chuck to bother making a reply. Everyone had seen those same pitiful sights after the war. The battlefield surgeon's principal technique for curing a shattered limb had been to cut it off. East or West, there were still a great many men who would never be sure if their enemy had been wearing a uniform with a color different from theirs or if they had been harmed the more by the medical people who had been supposed to help them.

"Right," Al answered himself. "An' d'you know what they all complain about when they're begging for drinks? Sure you do. They all of them bitch 'bout their stumps." Al took a drink and smiled. "Them ol' stumps is supposed to hurt something awful. So that there's the thing to work on." He grinned all the broader. "An' if that don't work, why, we can always give the crip here *another* stump to remember us by."

"Just so you don't mess with his hands," Chuck said. "J. Kenneth said don't mess with his hands, right?"

"Right, Chuck. I won't have to touch his hands atall."

Al left Hogue's side and headed toward his friend. He began to poke kindling into the open mouth of the potbelly stove, whistling while he went about the chore.

Hogue wondered for a moment what the man might be up to there after the threats he had just been making.

And then Hogue realized what it was that Al intended.

Hogue began to feel sick at his stomach.

CHAPTER 16

"In that box over there. No, dammit, the one in the corner. Yeah, that's it."

Al sounded positively cheerful as he crumpled some of the second-copy flimsies from Hogue's files and shoved them into the potbelly stove. He laid some split kindling sticks in on top of them and began to cram chunks of wood in on top of it all.

In the meantime Chuck was pawing through the food box Al had pointed out to him.

"There's some bacon here," Chuck said. "How does that sound to you?"

"Anything," Al told him. "My gut feels shriveled up like a raisin. Bacon's fine. See any eggs?"

The question was probably asked as a joke. Except in towns of fairly substantial size, a man could go for months without seeing an actual egg in this part of the country. But Chuck shook his head seriously in response to it.

"There's some tinned stuff," he said.

"Crackers?"

"Yeah."

"Bacon an' crackers will do," Al said. He definitely sounded cheerful now.

Hogue looked around to where Chuck was still rummaging through the box of foods. Hogue paid little attention to food himself, and he had no idea how long the slab of smoked bacon might have been in the box. For all he knew—no, for all he *hoped*—the stuff was rotten and would poison them. It was too faint a possibility to be a hope, really, but what the hell, he could always wish for it.

Hogue glared back toward Al. The fire was beginning to catch now, flame from the wadded paper licking at the dry kindling and fresh tongues of bright yellow flowing around the more solid pieces of chunked wood the line delivered to the station winter and summer for cooking as well as heating purposes.

In a short time, too short a time, those chunks of hard wood would be reduced to coals. Hogue shuddered at the thought of what a sadistic man might be able to think of with a batch of coals at his disposal. And Hogue had no doubt at all that that was exactly what Al Trapp intended.

Meanwhile the creep would cook his dinner over the same coals.

If Hogue had a gun. . . .

But he did not. That was the thing. He had no gun and no knife fit for fighting with, not even the mobility of his own broken body to fend them off with. Even his crutch, the symbol if not exactly the cause of all his problems— even that was too unwieldy to serve as a proper weapon in such close quarters.

Hogue grimaced. Oddly enough, though, his thoughts at the moment were not on what might lie ahead. He was thinking about the lousy stove and the fact that Al had started a fire in it without first cleaning it out. There would be several months of nonburnable junk accumulated in there, and Hogue would have a time cleaning it out after the ashes were cool. Hogue allowed himself to work up an anger about that and deliberately tried to ignore the other thoughts he might have been having about the fire.

J. Kenneth, for his part, shifted his crate away from the growing heat of the fire and stared studiously out the doorway toward the freer, cleaner world beyond.

Bastards, Hogue was thinking. All of them.

Al fed more wood into the now loudly drawing fresh fire while Chuck used Hogue's butcher knife to slice off several thick strips of bacon from the slab. Hogue watched the process and was not particularly surprised to see Chuck wipe the knife blade clean of the rancid grease left by the bacon and then tuck the long butcher knife between his belt and holster. Not that Hogue had really expected the man to be stupid enough to leave the knife where Hogue could grab it, but still. . . .

The four of them sat in an awkward silence while Al continued to feed the flames. The sound of the fire had settled into a dull, constant moan that seemed to fill the small shack.

Hogue looked away and licked his lips with a tongue that had gone as dry as his lips had suddenly become.

He kept thinking now about the coals that were forming inside the belly of the stove. And about the stink of burning hair and flesh that rose every time a hot iron was applied to the flank of a calf.

How many branding fires had Hogue built, and how many irons had he pressed into living flesh? He had no way to remember them all.

Now it was going to be his turn.

CHAPTER 17

There had been that time—oh, he could not even remember for sure now how long ago it had been—'way back before he ever thought about coming to this part of the country. Back in South Texas it had been, and Hogue Bynell had not been more than eighteen or nineteen years old at the time. Back when he was still trying to prove to the grown men he worked with that he was as much of a hand as they were. And that had been a long time ago indeed.

He had been working that fall for Harlan Platt down on the Frio River in that spiny, spikey, double-tough country known as the brasada.

Hogue, young Hogue, had been one of the few who had chosen to come back to Harlan after the trail drive north into Kansas that summer, and he was still rankling because he had had to ride drag and swallow dust for every one of those long miles. Now older hands who had not even gone with Platt on the drive north had been given the choice jobs of cutting the calves from the herd and heeling them with their short, heavy, rawhide reatas and dragging them to the branding fire, where other older, experienced hands were doing the actual branding. A beardless Hogue Bynell and a bunch of wet-behind-the-ears kids from neighboring outfits were assigned the lowly chore of doing the mugging.

Whenever a fresh calf was dragged close enough, it was

Hogue's job to throw it if it was still on its feet or hold it down if it had already fallen and keep it there while one of the older hands slapped the iron to it and another's knife blade flashed to notch the ears and, if it was a bull calf, castrate the bawling little beastie.

A real old timer—Hogue remembered too late and winced at the thought of how he had looked down on the old codger at the time—with a twisted, nearly useless left leg that somebody said was an injury from some long-ago battle with marauding Mexicans, had been hobbling around from fire to fire with a tin bucket of grease in his bony old hand and a cloth swab on the end of a stick. It was his job—any kid old enough to walk could have done it—to swab each fresh burn with the salted grease. Otherwise, late in the season or not, there was the danger of screwworms getting into the burn wounds. In South Texas it seemed as though there was *always* the danger of screwworms. Some years they got so bad there wasn't a ranch in the country that could feed its men rice, because the damned grains reminded everybody so of the screwworm larvae that were eating into the living cattle.

Hogue remembered that and remembered the old man—at least he had seemed old from Hogue's then-young point of view, although he might not have been any more than forty. Briefly Hogue wondered what the old fellow's name had been—he could not remember now—and whether being crippled had bothered him then as much as being one-legged bothered Hogue now.

Probably not, Hogue decided with more than a little bitterness. At least that ancient had had some sort of leg underneath him, even if it was not right. And at least he had been able to do some sort of work at the branding. For Hogue there would not even be that much. Not ever again.

But back then Hogue had been young and tall and stout of limb if not as bull-strong as he would become with his maturity. And his blood had been running hot.

He mugged calves day after day, each and every afternoon as the morning's gather was sorted and roped and dragged to the branding fires, and with every calf Hogue flanked and with every whiff of stinking hair smoke that reached his nostrils, he became angrier.

He resented the look of every older and more experienced mounted man who rode to the fire with a kicking calf at the end of his rope, and finally he had had enough.

Hogue and some downy-cheeked kid who claimed he was from England but who was probably lying about that because he talked like a damnyankee and no damnyankee in Texas at that time would ever admit to being a damnyankee—anyway, the two of them had been trying to flank a yearling heifer that had been missed in the last fall's branding and who now was big enough to be a handful for any two men, let alone one man, Hogue, and a dumb kid who did not yet know enough to wipe himself.

Hogue was having to do nearly all of the work himself, and the more he tugged and lifted and wrestled, the ranker that yearling heifer became.

She bawled and Hogue swore and both of them sweated, and after more than a minute of the standup fight—which had begun to attract some unwelcome attention from the branding crew nearby—the damnfool kid's hands had slipped and the heifer got a hind leg free just about the time Hogue was bending to try a fresh hold on the miserable beast's fore-leg, thinking he would pick her up and fling her down if he had to go down in the muck and manure with her.

As soon as that hind leg was free, the heifer used it. She humped her back and gave a little hitch to the side and let that back foot fly.

If Hogue had been standing just a little bit farther away from the lousy heifer, he would have been gumming his food for the rest of his days, and as it was her hoof caught him a glancing jolt on the chest and some part of the foot found his chin and snapped his jaws shut so hard his teeth hurt for three days after.

It knocked his hat off and bloodied his nose and stood him upright with a flush of quick anger already threatening to make his ears as red as the blood that was beginning to trickle out of his nostrils.

The heifer gave another kick that shook the damnyankee kid loose, and that freed her from the catch-man's heel rope at the same time, and she darted back for the safety of the herd that was being held by more of those older, experienced hands.

Hogue saw the heifer go and did not care a little bit. Not that there was anything a man on foot could have done to stop her anyhow.

He glared at the heifer and then at the kid who was supposed to be helping him and finally at the mounted, laughing men who were sitting their horses in comfort all around.

"All right. All *right!*" he shouted. "You think that's funny? I'll show you funny."

He picked up his hat and dusted it off against his breeches and very deliberately settled the battered old hat back where it belonged. He hitched up his pants and took his belt in a notch tighter against the activity that was about to follow.

He spit on his hands the way he had seen a professional prizefighter do once and balled his work-hardened hands into fists.

And then young Hogue Bynell proceeded to wade into that whole damned crew.

He decked the damnyankee kid with the first swing, which perhaps was not entirely fair, since the kid, who may have been English after all, was nothing like a fair match for Hogue.

Then he turned on the nearest rider and dragged the fellow down to punching level, leaving a mighty startled horse to bolt off with its saddle empty and reins dragging.

From that point it had turned into something of a free-for-all except that no one was choosing up sides. Hogue had already done that for them, and he was all there was on his side of it.

The boys on the roping horses came sailing in after him and the much older fellows working the irons backed away, and some of the hands who were supposed to be holding the gather came to add their licks, and inside of two minutes the herd was spooked and running and half the horses that were under saddle that day had gone off to join the running bovines, and the patch of cleared ground where they had been doing the branding was a mass of dust and flailing arms and hard fists so that a man couldn't see what was up and what was down.

It was a helluva mess, actually.

Hogue grunted to himself.

He wished he could remember that he had come out of that one a winner.

The truth was that he was bunged up and sore and scabbed over in more places than a poorly educated man would be able to count.

And he was out of a job, too. Spent that whole next winter shunting horses from pen to pen at the livestock market in San Antonio, because it was already too late to catch onto a riding job, a real job, anywhere in the country. Especially anywhere that might not have heard about his little fiasco down on the Frio, because there were rather few outfits, he discovered, that had not gotten the word before he showed up with his request for work to do.

Still, by damn, it had been worth it. He had showed them.

And that was the last job he ever took where he was not treated like and paid like a full-grown hand.

Hogue sighed and sat back in the swivel chair the railroad provided for him at his desk. His hand fell involuntarily toward his thigh and he reached down to massage the tender folds of neatly fitted and sewn flesh at his stump.

He had been a *man* back then, Hogue thought, and the smell of burning hair and live meat had been just part of the job that was his to do.

Now . . . he felt cold.

The smell of cooking bacon did not make his mouth water. Not this day. Now it made his stomach turn over with a queasy anticipation.

Hogue Bynell felt a growing terror that made his gut sour and brought the taste of bile to his throat.

Al Trapp was looking at him. And grinning.

CHAPTER 18

"That was a pretty good meal, crip. You should've had you some. Y' might not have much appetite later on." Al grinned again. "Unless, of course, you change your mind an' do what we need done."

Trapp did not sound as if he expected—or wanted—Hogue to change his mind.

"You really should listen to them, Mr. Bynell," J. Kenneth said.

At least, Hogue had noticed, the undersized rummy had not joined the other two in their meal. J. Kenneth had sat in silent disapproval throughout. Hogue looked his way.

"These, uh, gentlemen are quite capable of inflicting whatever pain is required to gain your compliance, Mr. Bynell. Charles will do so as a matter of perceived necessity, Alonzo as a matter of pleasure. In neither instance are you likely to benefit, Mr. Bynell. I truly suggest that you do as they wish, and the three of us will be gone in short order."

Hogue looked at the little telegrapher and set his jaw.

All that remembering, painful and otherwise, had reminded him that, by damn, once upon a time he had been willing to take on anything and anybody and damn the consequences.

He had been whipped that time down in Texas so very long ago. He had been whipped bad. He had known that when he started the fracas, had known he could not fight so many and hope to come out of it with a whole skin.

And that had been over an issue of wounded pride. If the lives of two train crews were not worth more to him than his own sensitive pride once had been, well, there would be something plain wrong with him. Wouldn't there?

Hogue assured himself that there would be something dreadfully wrong indeed if that were so.

He set his jaw and looked J. Kenneth square in the eyes. He shook his head slowly from side to side.

Al Trapp had been watching the exchange. Now the outlaw laughed, and Hogue did not like the sound of Al's laughter.

"You'll do what we want," Al said. He sounded . . . different from before. There was some new quality in the man's voice, and for a moment Hogue had trouble trying to decide what it was.

Finally he got it. Trapp sounded almost . . . *nice*. Almost pleasant. It was as if there were a bond of affection between Al and Hogue now.

Al Trapp had something seriously wrong with him, Hogue decided. Seriously wrong.

But even so, he could not now transmit that train order. Not when it would mean the loss of life. At the very least it would have to mean that. At the very least the engine crews on the trains would be killed. Maybe some brakemen as well.

No, Hogue thought, he could not do that. Not to anyone, not even to trainmen.

But it surely was a lousy position he had been put in here. He looked at J. Kenneth and shrugged. The rummy looked away.

"No need to wait, is there?" Al asked. He was directing the question to Chuck.

The blocky straw boss shook his head. "No, but remember what J. Kenneth said. Don't touch his hands. Do whatever else you got to, but leave his hands be. We might be needing those."

"Whatever you want," Al said cheerfully.

Al tossed his tin plate and the fork he had been eating with into the now empty woodbox with a clatter. He was done with the utensils and obviously did not care about them any further. If anyone cleaned up his mess, it would have to be Hogue.

Hogue glared at the man. It was no consolation at all that the two must have had a terrible meal. The fire Al had built had been roaringly hot when they were cooking on it. Entirely too hot for the purpose of cooking. But now it had died somewhat and there would be a deep bed of cherry-red coals left in the stove. That, after all, had been Al's primary purpose in building the fire. The food had been an afterthought.

Hogue was still hoping the both of them would curl up with the miseries in their bellies from the elderly bacon or from rat poison or from some unseen hand of justice or. . . . Or from anything, really.

Not that he expected it. It would just be nice if it were to happen.

It was just as well that Hogue was not expecting anything like that, because it did not happen.

Al stood and belched with contentment and rubbed his now full stomach and smiled pleasantly at Hogue. "Reckon you should get yourself ready, ol' crip."

Hogue sat where he was, frightened but still determined

that he would *not* write out the falsified train order that they demanded.

Al approached him and reached down to touch Hogue's shoulder. "You wanta lie down on the desk there by yourself or should I plant you there myself?"

Hogue kicked him.

Al might have forgotten that a one-legged man still does have one leg left for kicking purposes, at least when he is sitting down.

Hogue planted his one remaining foot in Al Trapp's crotch.

Al squealed like a knife-stuck hog and jumped back.

Hogue knew at once that the reaction was out of proportion to the small amount of damage he had been able to do. The chair seat was too low and the angle too far off for him to get a square hit on the target. But Al acted initially as if it had been the most devastating blow ever struck.

Unfortunately that response did not last very long. A moment later, Trapp had regained his composure.

Any trace of pleasantness, feigned or real, was gone from the man's face now. He looked as though he was ready to kill Hogue with his bare hands. He took a step forward and then another. Hogue shut his eyes and tried not to cringe away from him.

CHAPTER 19

Hogue Bynell had been pounded on many and many a time before, by horse and cow and human hand, but this was something else indeed.

He hurt as he did not know it was possible to hurt. It was worse by far than the break that had eventually taken his leg, even worse than when the leg was long broken and rotting.

For the past little while—he had no idea how long it had been going on although he thought, rather dispiritedly, that it had not really been nearly as long as it seemed—he had been drifting in and out of consciousness.

He was reasonably certain that he could remember hearing Chuck order Al not to injure his hands or his head, probably to make sure there would be no brain damage that would make him useless to them. And he had an impression that J. Kenneth had been saying something, or maybe yelling something, a time or two as well. He was not sure.

About the only thing he was sure of, certain-sure of, was that he hurt like hell.

And Trapp was not even using anything on him except his bare hands.

All the choice little tricks and twists were still to come. Irons or coals or whatever, none of that had yet been applied.

For that matter, Al had not yet bothered to ask if Hogue was willing to give in and write out the train order.

That would come later, probably, but for the moment Al seemed interested only in extracting a measure of personal revenge for the kick Hogue had launched at the outlaw's cods.

One thing anyway, Hogue thought drunkenly. At least so far the only thing Hogue Bynell was sorry for about that kick was that he had not been on target better than he was.

He rolled his head and looked up at Al—somehow, Hogue was not sure when, he had been picked up and thrown onto his back atop the broad work surface of his desk—and tried to give the man a nasty grin. He did not really know if he had managed the expression but he felt somewhat better for having tried.

Some of it must have gotten through anyway. Al redoubled his efforts, and this time he apparently forgot Chuck's warnings because his blows from a hammered fist began to fall on Hogue's head and face.

In a way, that was quite nice. Almost immediately, the pain Hogue was feeling lessened, and he began to feel himself slide down a long, gray chute toward a sort of warm, soft darkness.

Pain.

Hell, pain was practically an old friend. Certainly it was an acquaintance of very long standing.

Pain could be a part of any day when you rode rank horses and fought wild cattle for your living.

It did not have to come from trying to make a living either. It could come as well from a man's play.

There had been that time—Hogue's thoughts and his recall were totally clear on the subject, and for the time being he was able to escape whatever it was that Al person was doing to him—when Hogue and Goodnight Licken and a Y Knot rider named Coy Forrest asked for some time off and rode all the way over to the mountains on a hunt.

They told the boss man they were going after elk, which made it all right on several counts. One would be that while the three of them were off playing they would not be drawing pay from the outfit. The other was that if they brought back a few packhorses loaded with elk meat it would go toward their winter supplies and the outfit would have another cull or two to sell come spring. So it was all right with the boss.

The truth was that Coy was even crazier than Hogue and Goodnight, and had it in his head that he was going to find a grizzly bear up in those high mountains and was going to dab a rope onto the thing. Hogue and Goodnight were just crazy enough that they wanted to go along and watch, so the three of them cooked up the story for the foreman and took off with the outfit's blessings and a string of Y Knot horses.

That had been a fine ride, Hogue remembered. The high country was already being filled with miners in the spots where discoveries had been made, but there was so *much* country up there that even a loony bunch like those miners were could not fill it and ruin it, no matter how hard they tried.

The three of them had trailed their string up the Arkansas to the place where the river flow filled the bottom of a sheer, rock-walled gorge that must have been a mile high above the level of the river—well, that was an exaggeration maybe, but not much of one—and they had had to turn aside.

They rode north from there, ambling in no particular direction and no particular hurry up one canyon and over another ridge, and from every high place it seemed as if they could see even farther than they had seen from the one before.

The country was different up there. Lots of trees. Lots of rocks. Not much grass although enough to feed a hobbled horse. And mostly the ground ran to up-and-down rather than north-and-south.

It was not really a cattleman's sort of country, but Hogue liked it anyway. He liked being able to top out one of those high, rocky, wind-barren ridges with the few scraggly junipers all twisted and shaggy and being able to see the sawtoothed white of distant mountain ranges that might have been as little as fifty or as much as a hundred miles away. And more waves of peaks in between.

A man's heart gets a peculiar kind of lift when he sits on a horse on a mountaintop with the whole wide world spread out at his feet.

So, yes, Hogue had really enjoyed that trip, and he had an idea that Goodnight and Coy enjoyed it too, although of course they did not discuss any of that. There are some schoolteacherish thoughts that a man likes to keep private.

They were enjoying the trip, but they were not finding any bear or even much in the way of elk. There were enough mule deer to keep them from being hungry but not much else, so they kept going.

A few days out from the river, they climbed into a high mountain valley of decent grass surrounded by mountains, the sort of place the old timers used to call a "park" up in this part of the country, and there they began to pick up signs of more and better game.

In particular there was bear sign. Droppings and clawed

trees and what Coy Forrest claimed quite seriously was a "feel" of bear in the area. Coy claimed to be something of an expert on that subject, although Hogue wondered, if the fellow was so much of an all-fired expert, why he hadn't gotten around to roping a bear before then.

At any rate, neither Hogue nor Goodnight particularly cared, and if Coy wanted to stop, that was all right by them. They made their camp on a broad, grassy meadow beside a thin, cold stream and hung a few bells around the necks of their packhorses before they hobbled the animals and turned them loose. A hobbled horse can cover an amazing amount of territory in a single night's time, and a smart one can manage to hide behind a lone aspen sapling if you do not string a bell on him to make him give himself away.

There seemed to be no roads or mines or even prospectors in the park, and while white men had undoubtedly been through the area a thousand times in the past fifty years, Hogue liked to privately suppose to himself that the three of them were the first humans who had set foot in that area since the last Indian tribe moved out.

Hogue and Goodnight would have been content to lie up along the sides of the creek to soak up some sunshine and sleep through the lazy afternoons and maybe try to snag a few trout, but Coy would not have it that way.

There were bear around, he kept insisting, and big grizzlies at that, and he wanted one of those rascals and would have one or his name was not Coy Forrest.

Neither Hogue nor Goodnight would really have cared if Coy had decided to change his name, but they had come to see the man rope a grizzly and so they would go along with him now.

The thing to do, Coy told them, was for the three of them to split up and go in three separate directions looking for fresh bear sign.

Once they spotted a good place that a really big grizz was using, they would all come back together, and Coy would have his chance to do his roping. Hogue and Goodnight would act as his hazers to run the bear near his rope, and then it would be all over for old Mr. Silvertip.

As far as Hogue was concerned, it was all just a good excuse to ride out and see more country, and that was all right by him whether or not they ever saw a bear. At least up in this park they could count on finding some elk and they would still have jobs when they got back down onto the big grass, where a cow's legs did not have to grow with one side short and the other side long for hillside grazing.

The first day out, neither Hogue nor Goodnight reported seeing the first lick of bear sign, but Coy swore up and down that he had spotted some telltales to the north and east of their camp, so that was the area they would all search the next day.

That might have been believable enough except that Coy also told them that he had roped a yearling elk that very afternoon but had not killed it, as it would not have provided enough meat to be worth the bother. If Hogue had really cared about what they were supposed to be doing on their trip, he might have started to get annoyed with Coy by that time, but he did not and so let it pass unchallenged.

At any rate, the three of them rode out to the northeast the next morning and followed the creek for a few miles before they split up.

Coy gave himself the "beariest"-looking area to search,

which was due east. Goodnight rode north. And Hogue split the line between them, following a bend in the creek toward a huge, dome-shaped rock that he had been admiring ever since they had topped the last rise and gotten it in view.

For some reason, Hogue was quite taken with that dome of slick rock, and he got it in mind that he would like to see the lay of the country from up on top of that thing.

He rode straight for it, ignoring half a dozen herds of mule deer and a small band of cow elk even though he had a borrowed carbine slung under his leg and could have taken home some meat if he had wanted. Instead he wanted to climb up that rock, illogical as that was and in spite of the fact that it was plain from a long ways back that no horse was ever going to make that climb. If he did it, it would have to be afoot.

Hogue reached the base of the dome by late morning and found that, up close, the rock was both a whole lot bigger than he had expected and a whole lot less smoothly formed.

Down around the base, it was jagged enough to make a goat fretful, and some places it looked as if it would take a healthy bird to make it from one handhold to the next.

Still, Hogue had set his mind to it, and he intended to get to the top.

He rode around the base a little, casting back and forth for the most likely-looking spot to begin his crawl, and finally he just said the hell with it. He slipped down out of his saddle, loosened his cinches and tied the horse to a picket pin so he would know for damn sure the animal would be there when he got back. He had no desire at all to walk back to camp and take a hazing from the others when he and his horse came in separately.

Full of determination, Hogue began to climb.

He did all right for the first fifty feet or so, but that was hardly a good start on the job he had set for himself. Then his luck changed.

He was reaching for a handhold far overhead when his slick-soled riding boots slipped and his feet shot out from under him.

Hogue's head bounced off a rock harder than any calf is able to kick and bounced off a second rock even harder.

He slid nearly half the distance he had been able to climb, fell free off a narrow ledge to the next-outward hump of hard rock and slid the rest of the way down to the gravelly soil and sparse grass of the relatively flat land at the bottom of the rock dome.

When he came to, his scalp was laid open across the right side of his head, his left ankle was badly twisted and probably sprained, and he was scraped bloody raw over a large share of his body surface.

To say he was in agony then would have been a masterpiece of understatement. It would have been far enough short of the mark to be considered a lie, much like calling Grant a social tippler on rare occasion.

There was nothing on, in or about Hogue that had not hurt then.

Yet he had been able to grit his teeth and cuss himself for a damn fool, then crawl back to his horse, undo the stubborn knot he had put into the picket rope, tighten his cinches and take himself back to camp in time to be there when the others rode in to report on their day's findings or lack thereof.

That and the few days afterward had been just about all

the pain Hogue thought there could be in a single human body.

Until now.

Now that fall and the healing period afterward seemed about as painful as a mashed thumb, at least in comparison, and Hogue would gladly have gone through it twice again if it would convince Al Trapp to lay off of him now.

He groaned and tried to bite back the sound and could not help thinking about Coy Forrest. Hogue had heard that old Coy broke his neck down in Arizona Territory while he was trying to rope a javelina pig.

Hogue wondered if Coy had ever gotten a chance to put a rope on a bear. Any sort of bear. Hogue kind of hoped that he had, although it sure had not happened on the trip they had taken together that time.

And, no, Hogue Bynell was damned well *not* going to give in to these creeps and write out the train order they wanted. No way.

CHAPTER 20

"Back off, Al."

"What?"

"You've played with him long enough," Chuck said. "We aren't here for that, we're here to do a job. It's time you get down to it."

Trapp looked disappointed. But he did not argue. He stood up—he had been bent over Hogue's supine position atop the hard and now sweat-slick surface of the railroad-issue desk—and turned away.

Hogue lay there with the pain a constant boil deep in his gut and felt a slim measure of pride returning. He had taken Al Trapp's punishment and he had not broken and that was much to be thankful for. And proud of. There had been little enough in recent years that he could point to with any satisfaction. So maybe he was one-legged but not as totally worthless as he had been thinking. Maybe there was still something left of the man he once had been. Maybe. . . .

Trapp was returning to the desk now.

The son of a bitch was carrying, rather gingerly, a small shovel.

Hogue recognized the shovel. It was the little pressed-tin scoop Hogue used from time to time to clean the ashes out of the stove.

The shovel was smoldering. Or, rather, small wisps of

smoke were rising from it. Hogue lifted his head and strained his neck to see, although he did not really *want* to see. He already knew what the shovel contained.

"Strip his breeches off," Al ordered.

Chuck and now even J. Kenneth moved to help.

Hogue felt them fumbling with his belt, felt the buckle being tugged tighter and then quickly falling free, felt strange hands opening the buttons at his fly. He had become almost used to having others handle and dress and clean him when he was in the makeshift hospital that time. Now . . . this was different. Now the feeling was terrifying.

The men stripped his trousers from his hips and left him lying there chilly and exposed in a way that went far beyond the physical sensations he was experiencing.

Hogue gathered what strength he had left after the beating Al had so effectively administered.

He tried to lash out at them. Tried to roll away and flail his arms and fight them off.

He had neither the strength nor the leverage. Chuck held him down on one side and J. Kenneth on the other, and Hogue was powerless to resist them.

For the first time in . . . for the first time ever, really, he regretted the loss of weight and muscle he had undergone since his accident. There had been a time when— That time was long past. He could do nothing to help himself now. It no longer mattered what once was or what might have been, and Hogue understood that but was unable to stop himself from regretting it.

"Bastards," he hissed at them.

They ignored him.

Trapp used a free hand to complete the brief task of pulling Hogue's shortened and sewed-off pants leg from his stump, allowing the trousers to dangle from Hogue's one remaining leg.

Hogue felt a wave of shame flood through him when Al Trapp looked at the bare, exposed, almost flat knob where Hogue's leg so abruptly ended.

The flesh there was acutely tender.

Flaps of living skin and meat had been left below the point where the bone and muscle were severed and forever taken from him.

Those flaps had been folded and snipped and fitted with a seamstress's care and sewn into place.

Until now only the doctor and Hogue himself had seen them.

Now Al Trapp looked at the stump with dispassionate interest, and Hogue felt the sense of shame grow, felt his face heat up and knew that he was reddening with the embarrassment of it.

The embarrassment was worse than the pain of the physical beating had ever become.

Hogue wanted to turn his head away, would have hidden if he could, but his eyes were locked on the contents of the small shovel with a will of their own.

There were coals in the scoop of the tin shovel. Coals from the fire Al and Chuck had cooked their lunch over. The coals glowed a pulsing red heat that demanded Hogue's attention.

"They say it's awful tender down there," Al said cheerfully. "This is your chance, crip. Speak up now an' you'll be just fine. Do what we ask an' we'll put these li'l red apples right back into the firebox over there. It's up t' you, crip. Just do what we ask."

"He'll do it, you know," Chuck said. "And we can get along without you if we must. You won't accomplish anything by making us do this. Give in, man."

Hogue bit his lip and squeezed his eyes shut. He shook his head.

He had his pride—some of it—left to him. He could not give in now. He would not do it.

"Please," J. Kenneth pleaded in a soft voice. "Do as they want. Please, Mr. Bynell."

Hogue shook his head.

His eyes were closed but he could hear Al Trapp's short bark of pleased laughter. He could visualize the wolf-like grin that would be on the sadistic bastard's face even if he could not see it. He did not have to see it to know it was there.

"I can't," Hogue whispered. His voice, he discovered, had become hoarse.

The reasons for his refusal hardly mattered any more. The reasons no longer had much to do with the two trains that would collide if he gave in, nor with the men who would die if the false order was sent.

Now it had become a matter of simple pride to Hogue Bynell.

He had not really known he had anything left of a man's pride.

Now that he had discovered a remnant of manhood inside himself, he wanted to keep it. It was much, much more than he had known he had. He wanted to hold onto it and know it was there.

"Go to hell," Hogue said. He was pleased to hear that this time his voice was firm. "You won't get nothing from me today, boys." He would have given them a manful laugh of defiance too, but he could not manage that.

He lay back and waited.

He had taken pain before. He had endured everything that had been thrown at him. He would endure this too.

He was sure of that.

He heard a movement from the direction where Al Trapp had been standing, heard the scrape of a boot sole on the wooden floor, felt a hand on his thigh above the stump, a firm hold placed there.

It would be coming now, and—

Hogue screamed.

The sound was torn unwillingly from his throat.

Under and through the terrible noise of his scream, Hogue could hear the sizzle of his own scorched and burning flesh. He could smell a sudden odor of braised meat.

"*STOP!!!*"

His body bucked and contorted under the restraining hands of the men who were holding him pinned to the desk top.

"*For God's sake stop.*"

Hogue heard himself begin to whimper.

"*Anything. I'll do anything you say.*"

Hogue Bynell loathed himself. Disgust for his own weakness rolled through him like cold water entering a drowning man's lungs.

"Anything," he whimpered. "I'll do what you want. Just stop."

CHAPTER 21

Hogue sat slumped in his railroad-issue swivel chair, his mind numb and uncaring.

It did not seem to matter at all, now, that he had done what they wanted of him. He had written out their train order in his precise, careful hand, using the correct form and the correct wording and doing it exactly as Chuck and Al and J. Kenneth wished.

That did not seem to matter now and neither did much of anything else.

Hogue sat with his trousers pulled back up where they belonged and his fly more or less buttoned but with his belt unbuckled and dangling from the first and last loops at his waist. That did not matter either. The others had seen his stump, so what could an unbuckled belt matter anyway?

They had also seen Hogue Bynell crumple as completely and as uselessly as a child in the grip of the night terrors.

So how could it matter even that they had seen and had abused his stump?

Next to that, the physical deformity was as nothing.

An hour before, Hogue would have been shocked by that thought. Now it seemed quite perfectly plain.

Now that it was too late, that is. Now the damage had been done.

Hogue felt . . . empty. A rusted bucket with a rotted-out hole in the bottom, of no use to anyone for any purpose.

He had felt bad before. He thought he had discovered how low a man can feel back when he awakened and for the first time saw that flat, level, empty expanse of sheet where his leg had been.

That was almost laughable now, realizing the feelings he had had then and how wrong he had been.

At least then, if he had not been a complete man, he had at the very least been a human being who might still retain some shreds of pride.

Now. . . . There would be none of that now. There could not be anything left to be proud of now.

Oh, he had been so damnably proud and brave and convinced of his own resolve, hadn't he?

You bet, he told himself.

Until that first touch of a coal to his flesh. And then the screaming and the crying and the giving in.

Sure, it was perfectly all right that a pair of unsuspecting trains smash into each other head-on. It would be perfectly all right for half a dozen men to be smashed along with them. So what about a little thing like that? Hogue would not have to be there to see it happen. It would just be a flash of news along the wire when someone discovered it, when one of the trains failed to show up on schedule and someone was sent to investigate. It would just be a rumor by then, just so much talk.

Hogue would never have to look at the blood or listen to the screams of pain or see the globs of gray and red and white splattered amid the wreckage. Maybe some poor bastard of a trainman would have his leg crushed and have it amputated. So what? Hogue would never have to face him about it.

And all that was all right. Obviously. Just so good old Hogue Bynell did not have to stand a little pain. *Jesus!*

Hogue sickened himself.

He sat staring sightlessly toward the floor, uncaring what might be going on around him in the small shack, despising himself as a coward and worse.

And when the key clattered into noisy life beside him, Hogue reached for it without thinking and began to accept the incoming message. Just exactly as he knew they would want him to do. Exactly as they asked of him. So he would not again incur their displeasure. So they would hurt him no more.

That, after all, was the only thing that seemed to have any remote interest or acceptability now.

There simply was nothing else left for him.

CHAPTER 22

"Let me see that." Trapp took a quick step toward him.

Hogue flinched away in a sudden grip of renewed fear, but all Al did was snatch the message form from Hogue's unresisting fingers. Al peered at the form and seemed to be puzzling over it. Hogue realized that the man could read poorly if at all. Not that it mattered. Very little seemed to matter any more.

"It's routine stuff," Hogue mumbled.

Neither Al nor Chuck was willing to accept his statement. They looked to J. Kenneth for confirmation.

"He told you the truth," the little man said. "Let him relay it on if you do not want to raise suspicions."

Trapp glowered at Hogue. "Make sure you send it straight, then. Ol' J. Kenneth will be listenin'."

Hogue did not bother to answer. There was, after all, nothing he could say. He bent to his key, threw the relay switches and began repeating the transmission for the benefit of the next station down the line.

When he was done he noticed, somewhat fearfully, that Trapp had wandered behind him again and was again pawing through his private things. Hogue tried to pay no attention, but in truth he was aware of every motion Al Trapp made behind him. Any movement might signal another blow.

Trapp was prowling through the metal box again, the one where Mabel Cutcheon's letters had been stored.

"You know, crip," Al said cheerfully, "you're really just about worthless, ain't you? No good to this here woman. No good to the railroad. Jus' no good at all. Ain't you?"

"That's right," Hogue agreed dully. "No good at all." He was not now agreeing with Trapp for the sake of expedience. It was, he thought, the simple truth. He was no good at all, not to anyone.

And, he thought to himself, maybe the bastard could not read well, but he could read to some extent. And more's the pity, Hogue thought. He squeezed his eyes shut.

Mabel Cutcheon had been one of the good things that had happened to him in the past, but now that possibility was gone as completely as his leg.

The simple things had been . . . nice . . . back before the accident, after her husband died, when Hogue would come into town on those rare occasions, feeling tired from the hard work of riding and working cattle and fighting bad horses, physically tired but nevertheless feeling strong and fit and capable of very nearly anything.

Then he and the widow lady might have a bite of dinner, much better than anything to be found in a line camp or burnt over a solitary fire made from dried cow chips in those broad, barren, thoroughly delightful stretches where there was no wood to build a fire with but only dried grasses and dung and whatever else a man might be able to scrounge.

They might eat in the widow's kitchen, a pleasant meal much less solitary than those Hogue was used to, or they might once in a great while eat in one of the decent public restaurants of the town, with Hogue standing treat and taking pride in being able to squire a woman out in public like that where everyone would see them and know that this big hulk of a hardworking male was able to find company that he did not have to pay for and that he had the wherewithal to pay for their meals at the inflated prices such restaurants charged, sometimes as much as a dollar a meal although it was very rare indeed when they might choose a place so fancy.

Still, those times had been a source of pleasure for Hogue. He had felt a sense of pride then, a sense of worth.

Now. . . .

Now those days were gone, right along with very nearly everything else Hogue Bynell had known and cared about.

Now there was nothing else left that Hogue could take pride in. Nothing. Not even the tiny spark of satisfaction he might have been able to gain from doing a good job for the railroad.

He squeezed his eyes shut even tighter.

It was odd, he reflected, that he had not even known that he was able to take any pride in his job.

Sitting at a desk with a pair of crutches propped against the wall beside him and fiddling with a damned electromagnetic key was not what he had ever considered to be a man's job. It was not like working cattle or breaking horses or getting a *real* job done no matter what man and predator and Nature might throw against him. It was a far cry from that.

But he had done it well.

He had a reputation, he knew, of never making mistakes. Of keeping his section safe. Of always being there when he was needed.

Funny that that had never meant anything to him.

And now that was ended too.

After this day, Hogue Bynell would have the reputation of an operator whose section had been the scene of disaster.

He would be an operator who had allowed a collision on the line.

Worse, he would be known as an operator who had *caused* a collision.

Oh, the others on the line might not say anything to him about it. There would be the excuse of duress. Al and Chuck and J. Kenneth would be known about.

But Hogue knew good and well that that would not make any real difference to the other relay operators or to the train crews who would pass through in the future.

They would look at Hogue and he would be able to see in their eyes the accusations even if they were never spoken.

Each and every man who passed through Relay 12 in the future would know, absolutely *know* that in Hogue Bynell's place *he* would have done something different. *He* would not have caved in to them. *He* would not have allowed, much less have caused, a wreck on the line.

But not old Hogue. No, not him. He went right ahead and let the head-on happen. But then, what could you expect from a useless damned cripple? The line ought to fire him. For that matter, Hogue thought, maybe the line *would* fire him.

Then where would he be?

What could a one-legged man do to provide for himself? Swamp saloons? Roll over and wait to die? Or just take a shortcut, buy or borrow a pistol and put a welcome slug through his own temple?

That might be the best answer after all, Hogue thought.

Hell, it wasn't like there would be any loss. Not to anyone. Not to the line. Not to Mabel Cutcheon. Certainly not to Hogue Bynell.

That just might be the best answer, Hogue thought.

It might be the best answer possible. Save himself a lot of pain. Save the line the trouble of firing him. Save Mabel Cutcheon the bother of her pity. Undeserved pity at that.

Hogue Bynell was not worth pitying. He knew that. He was not even worth that much.

Jesus!

He wondered if he should look for a way to do it now or if he should wait.

Waiting probably would be better, he decided. If he tried it now, he would have to make a grab for Al's gun or for Chuck's. They would probably think he was up to something and would hurt him again. Certainly they would stop him.

No, he thought, it would be better to wait. He had more than enough money on account with the line to pay for a pistol.

Any old gun would be good enough, he thought. He did not even have to buy a good one. It would only have to fire one time. Any old two-dollar castoff would be good enough for his needs.

In a way, that thought pleased him. Not even good enough to justify the purchase of a good gun. That was justice for you, he thought. Not even good enough to be worth a good gun.

He might have wept except that he knew he was not worth his own damned tears.

Jesus! The unspoken thought was more plea than exclamation.

CHAPTER 23

It had not been such a bad life, Hogue thought.

Oddly, he no longer felt any bitterness or even much in the way of depression. All that was past. All the necessary decisions had been made. Now he felt . . . contented. Reasonably so, at any rate.

And it really had not been such a bad life.

He remembered that first job, so long ago now, that first drive up the long trail from Texas across the Indian Nations to Kansas. It had been exciting, even if he had been going along as a wet-behind-the-ears young un. Appropriately so, he realized now, because that was exactly what he had been back then.

He had lied about his age in order to get the job, but he doubted now that he had fooled anyone, least of all old Mr. I. P. Conroe, who must have been in his mid-fifties at the time but who had seemed immeasurably ancient to a gangly, wild-haired boy fresh off a Missouri farm.

There was a freedom and independence in the cow business and among cowmen that said that all men were at least the equals of all others and that no son of a bitch deserved the title "mister." By rights it should have been IP or Connie or some nickname that Mr. Conroe was called, but the man had had a sort of innate dignity about him that led even the most experienced and the roughest of the hands to call him

Mr. Conroe, although there were probably not a dozen other men on earth who would have gotten that title of respect from any of them in a face-to-face conversation. With Mr. Conroe it had simply seemed the natural and proper thing to do.

Hogue smiled to himself, remembering the old gentleman.

Always neatly attired, wearing suit coat and vest, collar and tie in the midst of the dust and shouting and confusion of the loading pens or out in the middle of the big grass several days' ride from any place that might charitably be termed a civilized location. No matter what, Mr. Conroe was always dressed in a manner fit to greet a lady in, from the brim of his brushed hat to the knee-tall boots with his trouser legs tucked into their high tops and the gleam of wax polish showing under the dust.

He had been quite a man, old Mr. Conroe, and Hogue owed him a great deal for having swallowed a green kid's lies without a hint of disbelief and hired him to do a job in spite of his obvious inexperience.

Hogue sighed.

That first job had not been much: hey-boy for the cook. They had not been three days out of Kerrville when the night-hawk, who was two years older than Hogue, decided he was homesick for his mama and accepted the shame of being a quitter in order to ask for his wages and start his long walk back home.

They had needed another night herder to replace him, and Hogue had boldly asked for the job. Swore he was a rider and the very next thing to a top hand and could handle that or any other job the trail boss might put onto him. This even though the only riding he had ever been able to do in his life was on the broad back of a draft horse going from field to harness shed and back again, that and an occasional brief excursion aboard one of the milk cow's weanling calves, occasions that had rarely lasted long enough for Hogue's father to catch him at it and whale him for disturbing the stock.

That lie had probably been as easily detectable as Hogue's others, but old Mr. Conroe had given his trail boss the wink and a nod and Hogue was given a riding job—of sorts.

For the rest of that trip, Hogue remembered, he had had to pay for his lies, because the men took him at his word.

He could do any and every thing they threw at him? Fine. He could night-herd the remuda of horses *and* help the cook gather wood and water at every meal stop.

At least the men had had the decency to give him fairly gentle horses those first few days, but the gentlest of a trail string was none too gentle, and the Conroe remuda was no exception to the rule. Hogue learned to stay on by falling off, and by the time they reached Ellsworth that summer he was no longer falling off so often and they were no longer bothering to give him a gentled animal once the herd was settled and it was time for the kid from Missouri to leave the fire, bolt a quick meal and take over the responsibility of herding the horses through the long, dark and sometimes scary nights of the open country.

Hogue reflected afterward that he probably did not sleep more than three hours on any given day during the two months it took them to reach the Kansas shipping point, and that small amount of rest had to be grabbed on the run, so to speak, as he bounced and rattled around in the back of the cook's bed trailer hitched behind the wagon.

It was a wonder he had survived it, Hogue thought later,

but in the ignorance of youth he had thought it all quite grand.

Oh, it had been nothing at all like what the wild tales and his limited reading had led him to believe.

There were no stampedes to sound like thunder across the rolling plains. Nothing remotely like that. This was a market herd, after all, and old Mr. Conroe had been too wise a man to mix culled cows in with his beef for such a long trip. The entire herd, several thousand strong, was made up of mature steers, and those steers had already experienced very nearly everything that Nature could show them. They plodded forward day after day in a mile-long thin trickle of slowly moving meat on the hoof, pausing to snatch a mouthful of grass here or to take a drink there. The herders did not so much drive them as control their drift in a desired direction so that at the end of the drive the steers would be heavier and in better condition than when they left Texas.

That kind of herding was hardly exciting. Dusty, hot and boring, yes, but hardly exciting.

Still, Hogue had loved it.

He had heard stories about attacks by wild Indians, too, but he did not understand where those tales might have originated.

Oh, they saw Indians along the route. When they passed through the Nations, which was for a major portion of the trip, every so often a band of blanket-wrapped Indians would come by. But they were not there to fight. They came to beg for food or offer their women for sale or demand a toll in edible beef, and they left behind them no wounds more serious than a louse bite.

Nor were the hands Hogue rode and worked with festooned with revolvers and daggers the way Hogue had been led to believe they must always be.

Old Mr. Conroe was one of those who believed that the causes of temperance and good will were enhanced by the elimination of temptation. Neither firearms nor liquor was allowed on the drive, although Hogue happened to know, due to his association with the cook, that a jug of sour-mash whiskey and a Spencer repeating rifle were kept in the wagon. The whiskey was there in case of need for genuine medicinal purposes, and the rifle was present so that a broken-legged animal might be humanely destroyed if that became necessary. Neither had to be used on that first drive north.

Hogue had heard too about the extremes of weather that might be encountered on the drives, but those he had to wait until later years to experience for himself. On that first drive, he learned that the summer days are hot and that when it rained one became wet. On the other hand, rain settled the dust for the next day or two, so there was a benefit even in that.

They fought no enemies and forded no floods, they merely moved slowly forward for day after day under a sky that seemed too big for half a dozen worlds to contain and across limitless miles of undulating grasslands. And they moved as free men, with no fences to contain them or rules to bind them.

That was the thing. The men were as free as the country, and it was a life that Hogue loved. One that he expected to claim as his own for as long as he lived.

He sighed.

He had almost managed it too.

Almost.

He had managed it for a long, long time. That would just have to be enough.

And, really, it had been a good life.

He thought back on it fondly, and for the first time since he had awakened to that prairie-flat expanse of empty sheet where his leg had been he was content with what had been and accepting of what was to come.

It had not been such a bad life, Hogue thought.

CHAPTER 24

And this was not a time to be feeling sad or unhappy or down on himself, Hogue thought.

As a matter of fact, he did not. Not any more. He felt better than he had in— He could not remember how long now.

There had been such *good* times.

He chuckled softly to himself. He remembered the first time he had ever been chapped. Not the last, it hadn't been, but it was the first.

It was on his second drive north, nighthawking for Dave and Cletus Morgan from Beeville and thinking he was plumb experienced after one completed drive and a winter of mavericking at a dollar a head in the brasada for a group of men who called themselves the McMullen County Stockmen's Association.

Yes, he had been experienced enough, all right.

Experienced enough now to doze for short catnaps in the saddle while his night horse carried him along with the remuda and to let the horse's change of motion wake him if anything happened.

Experienced enough to give the cook's hey-boy hell whenever the kid—he was seven months younger than Hogue and on his very first drive—did something in a way other than Hogue would have done it.

Experienced enough to get his dander up and come back

with some smartass remark whenever one of the regular
hands did or said something that experienced old Hogue
thought was beneath him.

Oh, he had been a real pistol on that trip, Hogue thought
ruefully.

Was a pistol and carried one too. After all, he was tough
and experienced and practically grown-up. If the rusted and
decidedly inexpensive thing did not fire more than one time
in three pops of the cap through its pitted and dirt-clogged
chamber nipples, well, that hardly mattered. The point was
that Hogue was grown-up enough to carry a gun if he felt
like it, and no one was going to tell him different.

Not that anyone tried. The Morgan brothers were looser
with their crews than old Mr. Conroe had been and never
tried to tell their men what to do unless it concerned their
cattle. And even then they expected a man to know what
needed doing and get it done without being told.

The rest of the crew put up with Hogue's overstuffed
breeches and excessively tight hatband for quite a while, actually. They gave him room to run in, and run he did, boss-
ing the hey-boy and swaggering around the fire with his
dollar-fifty cap-and-ball gun on his belt and generally acting
like an idiot.

The end of that period of his life started when smartmouth
Hogue saw the hey-boy, whose name was Jimmy something
—Hogue could no longer remember the rest of it—grab a
kettle of sonuvabitch stew off the fire when the concoction,
which no two cooks ever seemed to make the same way,
started to boil over.

Hogue knew good and well from firsthand experience why
the kid cared if the kettle boiled over. The loss of a little juice

and maybe some floating dried peas would do no harm at all, but if the stuff burnt onto the outside of the cast-iron kettle, it would mean some hard, long scrubbing, which Jimmy would have to do, before the cook would be satisfied with the thing again. So naturally Jimmy wanted to avoid the problem before it occurred.

At any rate, when the mess began to run over the side of the kettle, the kid grabbed for the bail and yanked it aside to cool a bit before it might be set back onto a less hot section of coals.

Naturally enough, the metal bail of a boiling pot is going to be close to the temperature of the kettle itself, and Jimmy did not take time to go fetch a rag from the wagon tongue to protect his hand. Of course if he had waited to get the rag the kettle would have gone on boiling over and the damage would have been done; he would have had some difficult scrubbing to do, which was what he was trying to avoid in the first place.

Hogue knew this as well as Jimmy did, and the season before, he might have done exactly the same thing. This year was different, though, and Hogue did not have to act as any man's hey-boy. So when Jimmy yelped and began blowing on his hand after the kettle was safely off the fire, Hogue set in to laughing and pointing.

"You're about the dumbest kid I ever seen, Jimmy-boy. I swear you are. Listen, you ain't handling any of the food, are you? I mean, you don't actually touch anything that us working men has got to put into our mouths, do you? Because, I swear, I think you're likely too damned dumb to wipe yourself proper. I'm scared you might be gettin' something nasty onto the food, kid. I worry about that. I really do."

Hogue said that and laughed and stamped his right boot ā few times in his mirth and laughed some more at the misery that was showing in Jimmy's eyes. That had been a really good joke on Jimmy, Hogue thought, even though no one else seemed particularly amused by it.

The cook was one of those men who do not much care what anyone else says or does, but some of the regular hands had begun drifting in to the evening fire ready for their supper and were standing around smoking and watching after a full day in the saddle.

One of them—Hogue could no longer remember who it might have been—gave Hogue a sharp glance that should have been a warning and went to the cook's wagon for a pot of grease drippings that was always kept available there for purposes of frying meat or greasing the wagon axles or softening leather or whatever else might be required.

The man carried the pot to the kid and used a wooden spoon to sling a dollop of the salty grease into Jimmy's palm. He gave Hogue another sharp look but did not say anything to him.

Hogue shrugged it off and made sure he was the first one in line when it came time for the meal to be served up. He ate quickly, as had become his habit, primarily because all of the hands ate quickly, and dragged his saddle out of the bed wagon, ready for his night's work.

That saddle was not much to look at and had been available at a bargain price because the tree was cracked, but Hogue was proud of it. He bought it, wrapped the tree with green rawhide and sat it with pride. This year, by damn, it was *his* saddle he was sitting, not some borrowed thing, and therefore it was as fine as any hand-carved, concha-mounted, custom-made article you could buy in San Antonio, and everyone knew that the best saddles anywhere were the ones that were made in San Antonio.

He looped his bridle over his shoulder and carried his gear out to where the remuda was being held inside a rope corral while the men came in to offsaddle their day's choice of mounts and catch out their night horses. The night horses would be kept on picket ropes close to camp while Hogue herded the rest of the remuda anywhere they could find good grass and not be too close to the bunched and rested herd of cattle.

Hogue dropped his saddle onto the ground and took his rope from its keeper beside the horn. He was not much good with a rope. Not yet. That would not come until much practice and a fair number of years had passed. But he was competent enough to catch the horse he wanted, given a small enough area to work in and a good many tries in which to do the catching. He slipped under the stake-held corral rope and carried his rope and bridle into the flimsy enclosure with the waiting horses.

He knew the one he wanted, which was a bald-faced spotted horse that no one else wanted because of the white on its feet and lower legs. Everyone knew that white feet were soft and likely to go lame no matter how carefully a man did his shoeing. Still, Hogue liked the horse because it had a remarkably smooth, indeed lazy way of going that made it easy for the rider to catch a little sleep while he was nighthawking.

The horse did not particularly want to be caught this evening and kept ducking away from Hogue's sloppy loops. Hogue did not yet know enough to build a small loop and throw it straight and fast, nor how to roll a loop under the neck of another horse to forefoot the one he wanted. He kept trying to catch his animal with large loops and a great deal of arm motion, and that simply was not working. After half a dozen tries he became angry with the horse—not himself, certainly—and turned around in disgust to cool off for a moment before he made another try.

It was getting on toward dark now and the light was poor, but even so he could see that some damned rodent, a weasel or a marten or some such fool thing, was nosing around at Hogue's saddle, probably attracted there by the salt of horse sweat or perhaps by the grease that was used to soften and preserve leather as old and worn as that in Hogue's fourth- or fifth-hand saddle.

Whatever had brought the little animal out, Hogue did not want it chewing on any part of that fine saddle. And he was not going to stand for it.

Without thinking, Hogue yanked out the decrepit old hawg-laig from his belt and threw down on the intruder.

There was only one chance in three that the gun would fire anyway, but this time it did.

More than that, the burning powder from that chamber ignited an adjacent chamber's powder charge, and there was one hell of a bang when the gun went off.

The pistol twisted sideways and threw Hogue's arm high. At the same time, the twin charges of explosive powder created a fireball in the dusk that seemed four times as great as the already huge gouts of flame that came from a normal discharge of a cap-and-ball revolver.

Hogue let out a yelp of surprise and let go of the offending weapon, which flew high into the air, as his arm was already moving in that direction.

Noise, flame and flying objects—all together they were just too much for the remuda, which was already more than a little nervous from all the commotion Hogue had been causing in their midst with his unfancy rope work.

The horses dropped their heads and laid their ears back, gave one loud collective snort of alarm and fled.

One strand of hemp rope was not going to stop them. In all probability a four-rail fence would not have stopped them.

The horses snorted and stamped and were gone, leaving Hogue in the center of a fallen rope with his hands empty and a rather foolish expression on his face.

He looked around, but the horses were no longer anywhere in sight.

When he looked back, at least half of the crew were standing there looking at him.

"Go fetch 'em in, boy," one of the men said.

"I don't have—" He had been about to say that he did not have a horse to ride after them. But that was rather obvious already. Hogue shut up and swallowed back the words, hitched his bridle higher onto his shoulder and began walking.

It was well past dawn before he got back to camp.

At least he had been able to recover all of the horses. One of them must have fallen, because it had a large, swollen lump on its near shoulder, but at least he did have all of them back.

At that, though, the day's work had been delayed, and if any of the men had any really hard riding to do that day they might find themselves on horses that would not be as fresh as they should have been. Hogue was in trouble and he knew it.

No one said a word to him, though, when he brought the

remuda back into the rope enclosure, which had been re-erected in his absence. No one spoke to him while he slipped as quietly and as unobtrusively as he could to the fire and helped himself to a tin plate of breakfast. Everyone sat in complete silence while he ate. Or tried to. He finally gave up trying to swallow the sawdust-dry bites of whatever it was he was having and set his plate aside.

"Hog, we got to thank you," one of the men said.

"Yessir?" Hogue was feeling more than a bit subdued and was not inclined toward smart-alec remarks at that moment.

"Yes, we do, Hog. Fact is, we haven't had much to talk about here lately. Just the usual old stuff. Now we're gonna have somethin' new to discuss, other than which steer's got the widest horns."

"What d'you . . . ?"

He grinned. "Why, Hog, ol' son, we're gonna have us a trial. An' *you* are the guest of honor."

Oh, they had had a trial, all right.

One of the crew, the one who had helped Jimmy the hey-boy the evening before, acted as the prosecutor. Everyone else acted as jury. There was no defense counsel because, as a member of the jury cheerfully explained, "Yer guiltier'n hell anyhow, so there ain't no reason fer one."

The prosecutor was able to come up with an impressively long list of Hogue's assorted sins, commenting on this one, acting that one out with a theretofore undisplayed gift of mimicry and mime.

The man had Hogue's swagger and tone of voice down pat, and he used both to great effect.

Before he was done, he had the entire jury, including young Jimmy, in tears with howling laughter.

Before he was done he even had *Hogue* going into fits of laughter. Which probably helped make the experience less painful than it might otherwise have been.

When they were done, which was not until lunchtime, the jury was polled and the men one by one solemnly declared that Hog Bynell was, as the man had said, "guiltier'n hell."

Hogue marched himself willingly to the nearest wheel of the cook wagon, shucked his britches on command and bent himself over the iron rim while one of the men removed his chaps and soaked them in the water barrel. The wet leather was then applied with some vigor to Hogue's backside, including several good swings that were offered by Jimmy the hey-boy.

It hurt, all right, but not really all that much. It might have hurt a great deal worse if the men had not all been laughing when they swung. But by this time the object lesson had turned into an entertainment form much more than a form of punishment, and none of the blows were delivered with malice. Not even those applied by Jimmy. Hogue grinned at them when they were done.

He also accepted the experience as a lesson of sorts. There was a distinct difference between pride and arrogance. The first was considered to be more than acceptable on the trail; the latter would not long be tolerated.

After that, Hogue got along quite well for the remainder of that drive. And for a good many afterward.

Come to think of it, he reflected now, he did not know what had happened to that old pistol. He did not remember ever seeing it again after that chain fire.

He chuckled and thought about how his bottom had smarted when it hit the saddle *that* night. Whew!

CHAPTER 25

There was still a trace of smile on Hogue's lips when he turned his head to see what the noise was that Trapp had just made behind him. The man was sucking at a bottle again. The sight of the hint of smile seemed to infuriate him as soon as he saw it.

"What are you looking at, cripple? Huh? Huh?" Al stepped forward and punctuated each "huh" with a hard blow to the side of Hogue's head.

Hogue shrugged and turned his head away. He ignored the punches, genuinely not caring about them. Any slight amount of pain that Al Trapp might cause him now would be only temporary in any event.

It was odd, Hogue thought, how a man's perspective could change like that. He had tried not to care about pain before; now he really did not care. Al could punch and pummel all he wanted. It would not bother Hogue. Not in the long run.

In a way his decision had freed Hogue. He felt very much at peace and not at all concerned about what Trapp or Chuck or anyone else might do. That was nice, Hogue thought.

Sometime during his chain of thought, Trapp quit hitting him. That was all right too.

Actually, Hogue thought, there was no reason at all why he should not try to do something constructive with his last few hours.

In fact, if some constructive act were to turn out to be his last act, why, that would be rather nice. Yes it would, Hogue decided. Rather nice.

An act like, say, stopping the robbers from halting that train. Not that the money mattered. But Hogue would like to know that the crews of those two trains did not have to die because of Hogue Bynell's worthlessness. That would be a very nice thing to be able to remember. Assuming that memory would be possible. Hogue was very unclear about what was supposed to happen to a person after death. There was uncertainty enough about life without going into all the extra complications posed by thinking about death and what might come afterward. It was not a subject Hogue had given much thought to. In any event it would be nice to know for as long as was possible that he had not killed any trainmen.

The ghost of a smile forgotten but still clinging to his lips, Hogue reached for his crutches and levered himself upright.

"Where the hell do you think . . . ?"

Hogue did not hear Al's question. He stood and with deliberate calm tucked the padded crosspiece of one crutch under his left arm to give him balance. The other he inverted and held with both hands.

"I *asked* you. . . ."

Hogue swung the crutch. He had seen a little boy swing a stick at a hard, white ball once. He did not know the name of the game that was being played, but he had admired the economy of motion and the apparent power that went into the boy's swing. Now he swung his crutch in much the same manner.

Too late, Al realized that something had gone seriously

amiss with their apparently cowed cripple. Trapp jerked an arm up over his face in an effort to fend off the blow.

The slim, heavy double billet of wood whistled through the air in a swift arc that ended when the hickory shaft smashed into the side of Al Trapp's face, splintering his cheekbone and breaking his jaw with a snap that was as loud as the crunch of breaking wood had been. Trapp went down like a poleaxed shoat.

Hogue was unclear about the sequence of events over the next few seconds.

There was the sound of boot steps and a great deal of shouting. He knew that for a fact.

One of the others—Hogue had a vague impression that it was J. Kenneth Harlinton, improbable though that seemed—picked Hogue up and slammed him back against the edge of the big desk, almost breaking Hogue's back in the process.

The other one, it might have been Chuck, was bent over Al Trapp's fallen form.

There was more shouting, some cries of anger and possibly even of fright. Hogue was still carrying what was left of his broken crutch. The fragment of wood was torn away from him.

Hogue expected to be beaten with his own club. He did not particularly care that he would be, but he did expect it. Instead both Chuck and J. Kenneth now were bent over Trapp.

Hogue was surprised to find himself on the floor too now. He did not remember falling after he hit the desk. He pulled the chair closer and began to climb up it until he could swing around and drop into place on the seat. The horsehair-covered cushion on the seat had long since formed itself to

Hogue's body shape. It felt comforting now as well as comfortable.

Trapp was not moving, had not moved since he hit the floor without so much as a bounce. There was a little blood on the floor beside his head. Not much, just more than a trace of it.

Chuck looked up at Hogue dispassionately. "You killed him surer'n hell," he said calmly.

Hogue felt curious rather than frightened now. He fully expected Chuck to retaliate for the death of his partner, either to use his revolver to blow Hogue's brains out or to batter him to death with the piece of crutch that was now lying on the floor between them. Hogue would have preferred the gun but did not really care all that much either way.

"You're sure about that?" he asked.

"I said I was. Broke his head." Chuck prodded the side of his ex-partner's skull. "Feels like mush."

"I don't guess I will apologize," Hogue said.

Chuck grunted. He was looking at Hogue with a cold calculation that it took no great talent to be able to read as impending murder.

"I wouldn't." Hogue had almost forgotten about the little rummy who was kneeling on the floor beside Chuck, but it was J. Kenneth who had spoken. He laid a hand lightly on Chuck's forearm, not to restrain him but to underline his words. "You and Al were never that close, Charles. Certainly not close enough to jeopardize the success of this, um, venture of yours. You still might need Mr. Bynell there."

"He did kill Al."

"Yes, and if necessary you can dispose of him. *After* the westbound has passed through and you know that everything is proceeding as it should." The little man's voice was still mellow and cultured.

Hogue was more than a bit surprised, but it seemed that neither of them regarded the loss of Al Trapp as being extremely serious.

"It's a matter of principle," Chuck said.

"Fine," J. Kenneth agreed. "But do wait until later. You never know what might happen. As witness our friend here. Would you have thought he would be able to kill Alonzo? Certainly I never would have entertained that as a possibility. I doubt that you would either. So do wait, Charles. You might still need him."

Chuck grunted and said, "We already have the paper we needed."

"You do indeed, but I do not have Mr. Bynell's hand on the key. There is yet a few minutes to wait, Charles. Do you want to take the risk? Or face the consequences if you guess wrongly? I think not."

"Where is the damn paper anyhow? We don't want him tearin' it up the way he tore ol' Al's head up."

J. Kenneth patted his breast pocket. "I have it right here."

"Put it in the pouch. Go ahead an' do it now, and do it right. And don't let him"—he jerked a thumb toward Hogue —"near it. You don't need him for that."

"Whatever you say, Charles."

J. Kenneth got to his feet slowly. He moved with the deliberate control of a physically feeble person, and Hogue wondered how the little man could have had enough strength to fling him aside the way J. Kenneth seemed to have done a few minutes before.

"I suggest," J. Kenneth said, "that we take the precaution of removing this second crutch from Mr. Bynell's reach also."

"I'll do it." Chuck left his dead partner's side and picked up the crutch from where it had fallen. He stood and towered over the seated figure before him. Looking Hogue square in the eye, obviously wishing that he was about to strike Hogue's head instead of the unfeeling wood of the desk, Chuck threw the single remaining crutch out the door. "Now try an' go someplace," he said in a voice that contained a threat despite its softness of tone.

Hogue shrugged. Now or later, gun or club, it really did not much matter. He turned his head and looked at the body on the floor between his desk and his bunk. Al looked smaller now than he had when he was alive.

CHAPTER 26

Hogue Bynell had never killed a man before. Not in all those years and all those brawls. Never.

Oh, there had been opportunities enough, he supposed. There had never before been a necessity for it. Perhaps there had not been a necessity to kill now. Certainly there had not been a necessity to kill now, Hogue decided. Hogue was going to die anyway. It hardly mattered whether he did it himself or allowed Al Trapp to do it for him. So there had been no necessity to kill this time either. Now that he thought about it, it was plain enough. A minute or so before, he had not had time to do that kind of thinking or Al Trapp would still be alive.

Instead he was a deflated shell of what had been a man, an empty husk with the ear of corn ripped away and the husk discarded.

Hogue looked at him and shivered.

Always before, fighting had been something he did in fun or, once in a while, in a spurt of hot anger. Never coldly. Never with indifference.

Maybe, he thought, that was the difference between a good old boy and a killer. A good old boy fought, sure, but it was a form of entertainment and a release. A killer must fight coldly. Hogue had always thought of himself as a good old boy, a hand. But that was the way things used to be. Now he did not know.

He thought back, trying to remember the few times in the past when he had seen men who were killers. Or who were said to be killers.

There were few enough of those times. Very few indeed, considering all the places he had been and the things he had done with his life.

Hogue had never personally seen any of those men who were legendary in their reputations as killers. He had heard about them. He had listened to stories about them and songs that were made up about them. But he had never seen any of them. Not in Newton or Ellsworth or Dodge City or Tascosa or Cheyenne. The closest he had ever come to seeing any of those legendary killers had been a few holes in a few walls where someone would point to them and say that So-and-so had put that hole there when he gunned down thus-and-such other fellow. But, hell, no one ever believed that kind of bull, including the man who was telling the story. It was just a way to get a visitor to stand a round of drinks. Everyone knew that, including the man who was being taken for the price of the round.

The closest Hogue had ever come to seeing a real killer, he thought, was once in Fort Griffin when a seedy-looking kid in a shapeless coat and needing a haircut was pointed out to him as Will Young. Hogue had never heard of anybody named Will Young, but the local man said Young was pure hell with a gun and had shot he did not know how many men. Seven or eight at the very least.

Hogue remembered that he had not been impressed much. Young had looked like just another down-at-the-heels yahoo, as far as he could see, the only difference between him and anyone else being that he was all alone at one end of the bar where they had been and was not talking to anyone, including the bartender. Nothing special about him except that he was being ignored by everyone around him and was ignoring them back.

There had been that time, Hogue remembered, and then there was the hanging Hogue had gone to once down in Big Spring.

There had been no question that that fellow had been a murderer. Tried and convicted for it. There had been a dispute over a milk cow, and this man—Hogue could no longer remember his name—had cut down on the offending neighbor and blew a milk-pail-sized hole in the man's liver with a scatter-gun. Wounded a couple of others, too.

The convict never said a word on the scaffold, Hogue remembered. Never seemed to take much interest at all in what was going on around him. All of the excitement that time had been in the crowd, with families coming in from all around the country, bringing the kids and packing baskets of lunch and buying souvenirs from the vendors who had showed up to hawk jewelry and medicines and imitation-silk neckerchiefs with the date embroidered in one corner. The excitement had all been in the crowd, not in the man who was being hanged. The fellow had not even kicked much when he dropped. And the smelly mess that had come afterward, well, that could not be blamed on a man who was already dead.

No, Hogue thought, both of those two examples had seemed darn well aloof from the rest of the world.

Not at all the way Hogue had felt that one time he thought he might have killed someone.

That had been in Canada, in the Panhandle country, in a barroom fight that threatened to get serious when the fellow Hogue was fighting with pulled a knife and took a slash at Hogue's gut.

His name—Hogue had not known it at the time but he had sure found out about it afterward—was Cooper. George Tomlinson Cooper. They called him Tommy or sometimes Coop.

He had pulled the knife and made his cut and did manage to slice some buttons and the front of Hogue's vest, and it turned out to be a fortunate thing that he was wearing a leather vest that did not cut so handily as cloth would have.

Hogue had gotten mad then. Really mad, not like in a normal fight when mad was just an excuse to have the fight, and he had set in to kicking Tommy Cooper. In the cods to drop him and then in the ribs and belly and the side of his head. He had hardly known what he was doing, he was so mad, and some of Cooper's friends had finally pulled him off the unconscious cowboy and held onto Hogue until he got his senses back.

They thought at first that Cooper was dead and then they decided that he was dying, and Hogue could still remember the sick feeling in his own gut when he looked down at Tommy Cooper on that floor and thought that maybe he had killed the man.

Hogue had helped them carry Cooper to a room and sat there while a doctor was brought to bind and bandage him and mix some powders to pour into him, and Hogue had sat in that room helping with the nursemaiding for the better part of three days before they were all satisfied that Cooper would get better. Hogue had paid every penny of the doctor's fee and the room rent and would have signed away his hope for Salvation, too, just to know that Tommy Cooper was going to get well again.

It had been a sick, empty, terrible feeling that time, and relief had been more potent than a jug of Taos whiskey the first time Tommy Cooper opened his eyes and looked like he could know what he was seeing.

That had been some time, Hogue thought.

Now. . . .

He looked around behind him.

There was no doctor who was going to mix a powder and make Al Trapp open his eyes and see again.

The difference was that this time Hogue did not care.

That was odd, he thought.

He really *ought* to care. He had taken a human life. He ought to care about that. At least a little. He did not.

Hogue searched inside himself, wondering about that, trying to examine why he felt so detached from the whole thing. That did not seem right, somehow.

He looked again at Al Trapp's cooling body.

No, he decided, there was nothing that he—

Hogue jerked his swivel chair sharply to the side and began to vomit onto the plank floor of the railroad shack.

CHAPTER 27

Hogue did not want to feel anything, care about anything. It seemed rather obscene to be feeling emotions and caring about having taken a life now that he was as good as a dead man himself. Particularly since it was his own idea that he should be a dead man.

Make Chuck Porter do it for him or do it himself—what should that matter? It should not matter. Somehow Hogue could not quite make himself believe that it did not matter.

And it was funny, he thought, that he was no longer fretting about the reason he had come to that decision.

Useless. Utterly without value. That was the reason for it all. Worthless old one-legged Hogue Bynell. Hogue knew he was worthless. So had Al Trapp. But now Trapp was dead, and it was worthless, useless, valueless old Hogue who had killed him. And Trapp's friends had not even bothered—not yet—to avenge their partner. Hogue still sat in the shack with them, waiting for the westbound to go through and pick up the message pouch so a bunch of other thugs and cretins could help themselves to a payroll. While their buddy Al lay dead on the floor of Relay 12.

Wouldn't that make Trapp angry? Hogue thought. Furious, he agreed with himself. It really would. Just being killed by a worthless cripple would be enough to make him furious. The rest of it would be piling insult onto fatal injury.

Hogue shook his head. Having thoughts like those, he wondered if he might be going crazy in addition to everything else. He wrinkled his nose. The smell of his vomit was sharply sour and unpleasant. He would have gone outside if he could, but one crutch was broken, smashed to splinters against Al Trapp's skull, and the other one had been taken away from him. Hogue was not expected to need crutches ever again, though. Chuck expected to see to that.

Hogue sighed. Off on the other side of the shack, Chuck and J. Kenneth were discussing him, Chuck speculating out loud that they really did not need Hogue any longer, so they really should go ahead and put him out of their way, J. Kenneth advising caution just to be sure. Hogue pulled his railroad-issue watch from his pocket. Had he wound it that morning? He could not remember now. He wound it—carefully, lightly so as to make sure he did not overwind it and jam the sensitive spring mechanism—just to make sure. It was still running, at any rate. There was very little time left before the westbound would come rumbling through, picking up the message pouch on the way past and shaking the small shack with the immense power of its drivers when it roared by without a pause.

There would be a pause soon enough, Hogue knew. There would be a pause at the siding long enough for a bunch of shouting, shooting idiots to come tumbling out of those rocks and grab off the payroll.

That would be nothing to the pause that would take place afterward.

The delay would be more than enough to ensure that the westbound payroll train would run smack into the engine of the eastbound special that would be riding the single set of rails straight for them.

That pause would be a permanent thing for the engine crews on both trains, maybe for their brakemen as well.

How many men? Hogue wondered. How many would die there? Would they bury them there at the accident scene? No, he did not think so.

Someone would come along with sledgehammers and spikes to replace the rails that would be torn up and with hoists and winches to right the rolling stock and lift it back onto the tracks and with wooden boxes to hold the bodies of the men who were dead. A good many wooden boxes, if Hogue was any judge of it. They would take the boxes with them, to wherever the men had been from, and there would be families to gather around and cry and friends to tell lies about how fine each of the dead men had been. Hogue wondered what friends would gather and what lies they would tell over the box that would be hauled away from Relay 12.

None, he thought bitterly.

No, dammit, he told himself sternly. It was a lousy time for lying, even to himself.

There would be the boys from the Y Knot. There would be Mabel Cutcheon. She was a good woman, and they had been something to each other once, might have been even more if he had not been so sensitive about things that she swore bothered him more than they would ever disturb her, and so she would come. Out of a sense of duty if nothing else. And the boys from the Y Knot. They were a good crew. They came around to see him when he was alive, in spite of the way he treated them. If they were friends good enough to stand for Hogue's sourness when he was alive, they would damn sure be good enough friends to come and lie over his coffin when he was dead.

Even some of the men from the line might come. Maybe the crew from the work train or some of the men from the terminus office. Hogue wished briefly that he had made some carvings for those men's children, the way they had wanted him to. It was too late to do anything about it now, of course, but if he had it to do over again he would do it differently.

He thought with more than a twinge of regret that he might have brought some real joy into some of those families back wherever the train crewmen lived. He could carve a fine animal; he probably could carve one hell of a doll if he ever set his mind to it. He just bet that he could have done that. He wondered whose homes he would be sending pine coffins into instead of the carved figures and cute dolls he really should have made but did not.

He wondered briefly what would happen to the pay he still had on account on the company books. He had no idea how much it was, but it should be a fair amount by now. For sure he hardly ever used any of it.

He could leave it to someone, he thought. Mabel Cutcheon or maybe some of the children of the men who would die in the wreck when those two trains collided. That was probably the better idea, he thought, but how do you word a will for the money to go to the issue of someone who is not dead yet? Because probably the wreck would happen after Hogue was already dead. He would not be able to know who or how many or hardly anything at all that a man should know when he sits down to write out his will. He wondered if it would even be possible to word it out, even if he were a lawyer, which of course he was not. He shook his head. There were as many complications to dying, it seemed, as there were to living.

Hogue sighed. It was such a shame there was no longer time for him to make a carving or . . . *something.* He wished he would be able to leave *something* behind. Almost anything. Anything except a memory that he was the one who caused a head-on and took those lives. Because that was sure to happen. That was a lousy legacy for a man to leave behind, even a useless, one-legged man.

But that was damn sure all Hogue Bynell would be leaving behind him. That was a thought more bitter than any of the others Hogue had been having this day. And that was all he would be leaving. No kids, not even a horse and saddle to be delivered over to some chosen friend.

He looked around behind him, toward his bunk. There was certainly nothing of any value over there to be distributed. Nothing that anyone in his right mind would want. The food and liquor would be used up by the next Relay 12 operator. Unless that fellow turned out to be a tall, underweight, one-legged son of a bitch, the clothing would all be burned. The letters would mean nothing to anyone. The carvings had all gone into the firebox. There was nothing else. Nothing at all left from the life he had led. And when he was gone there would not even be memories of it. Except that one last one, everyone remembering that a man named Hogue Bynell had been the one to cause the big wreck that killed however many men it turned out to be and orphaned however many children who would grow up despising his name.

That was some damned legacy, all right, Hogue thought.

He was getting maudlin again. He knew that. He wished he also knew how to stop it.

He looked up. Chuck Porter had his revolver out and was idly toying with it in his hands. *That* would stop it, all right.

Hogue felt a wave of resentment sweep through him.

You have no right to do this to me, he wanted to shout at Charles Porter. *You have no right.*

CHAPTER 28

Hogue glared at Porter, his resentment growing and threatening to overwhelm him.

Chuck saw the expression and before he could realize what he was doing recoiled from it. He jerked and half turned in his chair, as if about to run, before he seemed to realize what he was doing and regained control of himself.

"You damned worthless cripple," he snapped. The revolver in his hand steadied on Hogue's chest, and for a moment Hogue thought Chuck was going to pull the trigger then and there and not wait until the train had passed.

"That's right," Hogue agreed. "Worthless. I must be. I did what you bastards wanted me to. But not so worthless that your buddy ain't lying there dead on the floor."

"I'm not forgetting that either, cripple. When we're done with you, you'll answer for killing Al. Just see if you don't."

Hogue laughed. He was genuinely unafraid of Porter now. Hell, there was nothing left for him to be afraid of. Not any longer. "I can wait," he said lightly.

"Keep acting like you were a minute ago an' you won't have to wait any more," Chuck threatened.

Hogue smiled at him. "Afraid, Chuck? Of a worthless, one-legged man? And you with a gun in your hand? Now, that ought to kinda tickle me. It's a compliment, in a way. I think it does tickle me, in fact. Yeah, I'm sure of it."

"Shut up." Porter looked away from him.

"Whatever you say, Charles. After all, you have the gun."

"Don't you forget it neither."

"I won't. That's a promise."

Hogue was feeling better. In fact he was feeling pretty good. He looked at J. Kenneth and gave the little telegrapher a wink. J. Kenneth looked away from him too. What J. Kenneth was telegraphing now was nervousness.

By damn, Hogue thought, both of these fellows were getting nervous around him now. He had killed Al Trapp, who was supposed to be the mean one of this crowd, and now both of the others were acting like they were half scared of him. More than half, maybe. For sure they were uneasy. Even if Hogue did have only the one leg and a reputation for uselessness.

Or maybe, to give himself the small scrap that was his due, maybe his reputation was not actually for being so useless at that.

He had, after all, been a helluva hand when he still had both his legs.

And since then he had been a better-than-fair telegraph operator.

That was the truth, too. The whole section of the line knew that if Hogue Bynell sent it, it was right. If he posted an order, it was correct and would be obeyed. No matter how strange it might sound, it had to be right, because Hogue Bynell just did not make mistakes. If that was because he was so uninterested in anything outside his lousy little relay shack that he was never distracted from his job, well, so what? The fact remained, he was the most reliable damned operator on the section. That was probably a large part of the reason Porter and J. Kenneth and the dead Al Trapp were here right now. With some other operator, an engineer might well have questioned an order that put a large payroll car onto a siding out in the middle of the big lonesome. But if the order came from Relay 12 it had to be accurate. Right?

Damn straight, Hogue told himself.

And now these miserable outlaws were beginning to be afraid of him.

So maybe ol' Hogue had been doing some underestimating around here, he told himself. If a rough customer like Porter could be afraid of him or a cultured, educated man—and deadbeat rummy or no, J. Kenneth was both of those—could be worried about him, it was just possible that they might have reason to be.

For that matter, Mabel Cutcheon was a fine woman. Not the sort to go silly over nothing at all. That was one of the things that Hogue admired about her. And she had always claimed to find enough to favor about him, before the accident but afterward, too.

And the little bits of nothing that were inside the Relay 12 shack were almighty little for a man to leave behind him. There ought to be more than that to show for a man's life.

Maybe . . . maybe there could be. If he set his mind to it. If he decided to get his back up and *do* something instead of waiting for the end like some sulled-up old cow that has called it quits and lies down to wait to die. Hogue never could understand that before in man or animal, although he had seen it happen in both. Now he had been doing it himself. *Had* been. He did not have to if he did not want to. Not any more he did not.

Hogue looked across the room at Chuck Porter and at the gun in the outlaw's hand. There was a look of quiet speculation in Hogue's gaze.

CHAPTER 29

"I got to go to the backhouse."

"What?"

"I said—"

"I heard that part, dammit," Chuck snapped. "Can't you hold it?"

"I've been holding it. Now I got to go. But I got to have my crutch to do it with." Hogue gave the blocky man a look of mingled disgust and exasperation. "Man, I ain't gonna run off nowhere. An' you got the gun. Your damn pouch is hanging out there on the hook ready for pickup. What am I gonna do, leap up that pole an' snatch it down without you seeing? Come off it. I just gotta go, that's all. Hell, I didn't *plan* it."

Porter looked annoyed. He also looked nervous. About Hogue probably but also almost certainly about the train that was due to arrive within minutes. He glanced at his watch and then at J. Kenneth.

J. Kenneth shrugged and looked away.

"You can hold it a few minutes more."

"I can't, I tell you."

Hogue looked angry. He rose from his chair and tried to hop forward on his one leg, but the leg seemed to buckle for a moment. He had taken quite a beating earlier and could have been none too strong now. He toppled and flailed his arms.

Hogue grabbed at the back of his chair but its casters let it roll aside. He made another desperate grab for the iron-hinged wooden lever that stood beside his desk, but that just moved on its hinge and gave way beneath him.

He fell heavily to the floor and lay in a sprawl near Al Trapp's body. As he lay there, a dark, wet stain spread across the front of his trousers.

Porter and now even J. Kenneth Harlinton broke into loud laughter as a look of acute embarrassment spread across Hogue's face.

Hogue turned his head away. Muttering softly to himself, he began the painfully slow and difficult process of pulling himself back upright and into his chair. He sat staring stonily toward the blank wall of the shack near the doorway.

CHAPTER 30

They could hear the high-pitched, moaning screech of the train whistle.

Porter closed the cover on his watch and tucked it away in a pocket. "Right on the money." He guffawed. "Right on a whole bunch of money, get it?" He and J. Kenneth were both smiling now.

Hogue, pretending to ignore them, was holding his breath.

The train order, written in Hogue's own hand and following the exact style specified by the line, was hanging in its pouch on the hook outside. As soon as the engineer read that order, he was as good as a dead man. If the outlaws did not kill him, and probably they would not, then the eastbound special would. But, either way, he was a dead man and so would be any who were riding in the engine with him.

The train was coming closer now. They could hear the clatter of steel on steel as the wheels hit rail joints and were jolted on their axles, the hard steel of the wheels banging on the hard steel of the rails.

A moment more and they could hear the powerful, muted roar of the driving engine as well.

It would just be so much noise to Porter and to J. Kenneth. To Hogue there was a particular quality in the sound that brought a smile to his lips and a leap of fierce pleasure to his heart.

Hogue swiveled his chair to face Charles Porter. He felt perfectly safe in doing so. He doubted that at this moment either of the other men remembered his existence.

In another few moments they would again be aware of him. But not now.

CHAPTER 31

"Aren't they going rather slowly for a flying pickup?" J. Kenneth asked. There was a hint of beginning alarm in his voice.

"They can't be, they're—Gawda'mighty, they're stopping!!!" Porter stood with his revolver clutched in his hand and stared incredulously out the open door toward the track, a matter of only feet away.

The engine had already passed the platform, but there could be no doubt now that the following cars were moving very slowly indeed or that what speed they did have continued to diminish.

The men inside the shack could hear the sharp, whining squeal of set brakes protesting against their load and now the shouts of brakemen who rode atop the boxcars.

Porter took a step forward, as if to move in wonder for the doorway. Or perhaps to bolt toward it.

His concentration was on what was happening outside the shack, and he may not even have seen the tall, angry form that was leaping across the small room toward him with a curious, hopping motion.

With the agility of long practice, Hogue was bounding across the room, his one leg driving him with a speed that very nearly approached that of a two-legged man.

One rope-hardened hand clamped down on the wrist of

Chuck's gun hand, and the other attached itself firmly to the outlaw's throat.

J. Kenneth threw himself aside in a sudden panic, but for the moment he had been forgotten by friend and foe alike.

Hogue threw himself onto Porter, and his weight carried both of them to the floor, slamming into the still warm side of the stove and dropping down to the planking, where Porter's physical advantage was lessened if not completely eliminated.

Hogue no longer cared about advantages or disadvantages anyway. He had Porter's wrist in one hand and throat in another, and this was very nearly the old sort of rough-and-tumble Hogue had found himself in so many times before. Punch if you can. Claw, scratch, bite and kick; do whatever it takes to win. Hogue did.

Porter had been there too, and he was a powerful man.

The outlaw ignored the grip on his gun hand, ignored for the moment the much more dangerous grasp around his throat and tried to knee Hogue in the crotch.

The maneuver was expected. Hogue blocked the knee with his thigh and found the needed motion was even easier with no leg beneath that thigh to get tangled up in his opponent's legs. He laughed into Charles Porter's ear and followed that by sinking his teeth into the same ear.

The two of them rolled over and over, crashing into the stove again and knocking it askew with a billow of black soot that rained down onto both of them.

Porter was raining punches onto Hogue's neck and shoulders with his free hand. He succeeded in knocking Hogue's hand away from his throat. Hogue shifted the point of his attack and began punching Porter in the belly as, still tangled, they rolled over and over.

A leg of Hogue's bunk collapsed as the two bodies jammed into it, and the side of the bunk fell, catching Hogue painfully across the top of the head.

Blood from a cut flooded Hogue's eyes. He released his bite on Porter's ear long enough to bury his face against the other man's shoulder and wipe the blood out of his eyes with Porter's shirt. Then he levered himself higher against Porter's body and again clamped his teeth into the bleeding ear. Porter screamed and began to pummel Hogue all the harder.

J. Kenneth was backed into a corner now, looking like a cornered and very frightened rabbit.

"Help me, you little bastard," Porter shouted at him. "Grab a club. Anything. *Do* something."

J. Kenneth's eyes darted outside the relay shack toward the track. The train was at a full stop now.

J. Kenneth did something. If not exactly what he had been ordered, he at least did do something. He picked himself up and stretched his legs, making a dash for the open doorway and the freedom of the big-grass country beyond it.

Porter saw him go. He opened his mouth and might have shouted something at his departing partner except that at that moment the growing numbness caused by Hogue's grip on his wrist made him lose his hold on the revolver, and the gun fell to the floor between the two men.

Both grabbed for it, but Hogue was the quicker, if only because Porter had so little sense of feeling left in that hand. Hogue grabbed the gun by the barrel and began trying to bash the butt into Porter's skull.

It was no longer a fight at that point. Porter was no longer interested in doing any damage to Hogue, he was intent on trying to keep Hogue from caving his skull in the way Al

Trapp's had turned to a dead, mush-soft pocket where Hogue had hit him.

The two men were still on the floor locked in that combat when the MK&C engineer and his fireman stalked into the relay station to ask the operator just what in the hell was going on around there.

CHAPTER 32

A pair of brakemen, burly and hardened by their work, by exposure to the elements and by the even harder life they lived when their working hours were over, came stomping into the tiny shack. They dragged a shrunken-looking, terrified J. Kenneth Harlinton between them.

"This would be the other'n?" one of them asked.

Hogue smiled. "It would for a fact, boys. Welcome back, J. Kenneth."

"You will explain to them, I hope, that I did try to help you, that I did make every attempt to—"

"I'll tell 'em you tried to help hold up the train," Hogue said, cutting the little man short. He grinned. "You might find this kinda hard to understand, J. Kenneth. An' ol' Chuck here too. But railroaders get real irritated when somebody tries to cause a head-on. *Real* upset."

Still grinning, he looked Chuck's way, and J. Kenneth followed the motion of Hogue's eyes.

What J. Kenneth saw there was hardly encouraging. Porter had been in a tussle when J. Kenneth left so hurriedly, but the man had not been in bad shape. Now his face looked much like a mask hastily fashioned from ground meat.

"We could use a little information from you, J. Kenneth. You know. Stuff like how many fellas are waiting up there for the train to pull in at the siding. How they're armed.

How they figure to approach the train. Stuff like that. Unless, of course, you want your new pals there to talk to you like these other railroadin' boys have been talkin' to Chuck." Hogue grinned. "It's your choice."

J. Kenneth swallowed very hard. "But what . . . ?"

"What happened? Is that what you're asking?" Hogue laughed and so did a half dozen of the railroad men and baggage-car guards who were crowded into the little shack.

"Well, I'll tell you what happened, J. Kenneth. You know that red-ball flag out on the post? No? Take my word for it, it's there. Never been used before, but it's there. Standard-issue stuff. The railroad puts one on every platform, right along with the hook for the pouch you boys were so bent on hanging out there.

"Like I say, it's never been used before, but it's there. What it is, you see, is a signal to stop the train. For freight or passengers or whatever.

"You boys hung the pouch all right, an' that was picked up with the hook just like you intended. But a little while ago when you and Chuck was laughing so hard about the crip fallin' down and wetting himself, well, that lever I fell down against is what throws the signal.

"Jake here," he hooked a thumb toward the engineer in his floppy, striped cap, "thought it was odd as hell to see a pouch and a red ball too, but rules are rules, and he went by the book. Hooked in the pouch an' stopped the train at the signal."

Hogue was grinning. J. Kenneth was not. Jake was grinning. Charles Porter, at his feet, was unconscious.

"Now, J. Kenneth, if you'd be kind enough to tell us what we want to know. . . ."

J. Kenneth complied, eagerly if not happily, answering

every question the railroad men put to him and offering more tidbits of information that they did not think to ask.

"I'll be riding along with you," Hogue said much later.

"I don't think—" the straw boss of the guard detail began to say, but the engineer cut him off.

"Shut up, Lou. If Bynell says he's going, then he's going. He's earned the right."

"But he only has. . . ."

"One leg? Damn straight he only has one leg. So what? A man don't need any legs to shoot a rifle or to be smart enough to think straight. Hell, he thought straight enough to put the kibosh on this robbery. I'll bet he can shoot straight enough when that door rolls back an' the Walker gang comes face to face with a bunch of Winchesters. Just prop him in a corner with a gun in his hand an' stay out of his way, Lou."

The engineer clamped a firm hand on Hogue's shoulder. "You civilians just wouldn't understand, Lou, but this here's a *railroadin'* man. They don't come no better than that."

The group moved together toward the waiting train. There was still work to be done, but Hogue did not doubt for a moment that it would all get done. A report had already been telegraphed to Pueblo. By now they would have quit making up the eastbound special, and that was probably the same engine they would use to haul a load of deputies and railroad security men out toward the siding. Not that there should be much for the special crew to do by the time they got there. By then the Walker gang should be dead or in irons, whichever way they preferred it.

Afterward, Hogue thought, well, he might take a few days off. He could use some time in town. Spend some of that money he had on the books. And maybe—he smiled to himself—maybe while he was there, after he bought himself a

M33

new crutch and some decent clothes, why maybe he just might drop by and pay a visit to Mrs. Cutcheon after all. It could not hurt. Could not hurt at all.

They reached the end of the platform, and Hogue hopped nimbly down into the gravel bed, using his single crutch for balance but getting along just fine. He liked it that no one felt it necessary to offer him any assistance. And he liked it too, he discovered, that the other men matched their pace to his as a matter of course. Oddly enough, he did not feel in the least embarrassed or upset about that. A week before, he probably would have.

And did you hear? Hogue asked himself. That engineer, Jake, had called him a railroadin' man. Now, any cowboy knows that that is not supposed to be any kind of a compliment. But still. . . . It was kind of nice anyway. Coming from a railroading man, that is. Let a cowhand say that to him and Hogue would punch the son of a buck. But from an engineer, well, it was not all that bad.

Hogue squared his shoulders as they reached the open door of the baggage car, where the safe and payroll were kept. He accepted a boost into the interior of the car and looked for a place he could sit near the door.

"Hand me that Winchester, boys, we got some work to do down the line. And don't none of you civilians get in my way, hear?" He gave the engineer a wink as the door was being slid shut against the outside world.

Hogue hurt like hell. His head was gashed open. He had bruises and pains over most of his body. His stump was still raw and sore from where Al had pressed live coals to it. There was not a muscle in his body that did not ache or pain him one way or another. Hogue Bynell felt just fine.